THE FOLLOWER III

Our Indestructible Hero Continues His Fight for Our Country around the World

John Durbin Husher

Inks and Bindings
888-290-5218
www.inksandbindings.com
orders@inksandbindings.com

Contents

Dedicated to Peg, Jay, Karen, David

Prologue

The Follower, Axel Tressler, continues to use his special powers to overcome major problems faced by this country in all parts of the world. Axel is born with unique energy capabilities believed to be due to a plane crash endured by his mother before the birth of twin boys. Axel is born several days after his brother Adam and mother are rescued from the crash's remains. Later in life he is found to have these unique energy capabilities that are at three increasing levels. His original design of a voice actuated, computer chip that is implanted in his body allows him to call up these energy levels to face the different obstacles his missions require as well as providing him as a walking communication center. Later in life, the U.S. Science Agency (USSA) provided Axel with a special transparent and indestructible body covering made of spider web and titanium nanotubes. This allows him, as the Follower, to be fearless as he seeks to uh this country's enemies around the world; all done in anonymity. These feats are completed without losing his personal identity as a university professor of biology.

The Follower and the Terrorists in Silicon Valley

D r. Kim, chief scientist for the United States Science Agency (USSA), contacted Axel Tressler, alias, The Follower, over the course of several months about some weird findings the agency had uncovered concerning two dead bodies, one found on the East Coast and the other on the West Coast. In both cases, the pathologists had no explanation for the bodies' condition. Their internal organs had been torn up, as if piranha fish had been inside their bodies. Blood vessels were shredded, especially in the lungs and the major vessels leading from the heart. "The medical people," Kim told Axel, "have been mystified."

A couple of months passed before Kim called Axel again. Kim was normally quite calm and detached, but in this case he couldn't contain himself. Axel had never heard him sound so dramatic or excited.

"Axel, we've found another dead body in South San Francisco in the same conditions as the other two I told you about. These cases have been lifted to the highest levels of the top people in the government and the medical community. They even have the DEA involved. Last night the head of DEA called me and asked if our agency could help them. We, through you, have been quite successful in the past in resolving issues for them. So I talked to my superiors here about having you take a position at a west coast company that has been working on nanoparticles. There are two companies, one on each coast, that have nanoparticle programs that have been partially financed through our agency. Because of that, we send technical people to these companies with no problems. We believe these deaths might be connected to these companies. Our scientists have theorized that the damage to the bodies could have been caused by improper use of nanoparticles. With your advanced degree in biology, you have the proper background for this kind of work. You are the perfect person for figuring out if there is something strange going on at this company. Besides your obvious technical background, we might be able to use your physical strength and your unique properties if you find any terrorist activities. What do you think?"

Axel thought for a few seconds and then said, "This sounds quite interesting, but what makes you think they would allow me to go to work for them? They are working on proprietary material."

"It should be no problem. We're putting money into the company, and we'll just tell them we have worked with you before and believe you would bring a lot of talent to the company," said Kim. "We will also tell the CEO, in strict confidence, about the ravaged bodies and that we suspect terrorist activity. Your prime responsibility will be to find out if there are any leaks of the work being done by these companies to terrorists out of the company."

"Don't you think they would want to know where I worked before, and the kind of experience I had that would relate to their work? Why would they want to let a stranger in on their proprietary work?"

"We can get around that," said Kim. "First of all, we would tell them that we'll pay your salary, so they don't have any arguments about costs. Then we can provide them, in confidence, some of the data about your past experiences working with us. We wouldn't tell them about your special physical powers and your special communication skills, but would only rely on your strong capabilities in the field of biology. After that, the load will be on your back. If you go there and provide some help within a short time, they will be excited about you and the rest will be no problem. We believe you are sharp enough that once you see what they have been doing, you will be able to contribute to the operation. Meanwhile, you will be close to the culprit, if there is one there. You have a way of ferreting out problems. This should be right up your alley. Besides, it gives you a fantastic opportunity that very few people get. You get to learn a new technology. A new technology that is far in advance of what you are teaching at the university.

"Even better, you get to carry out an agency mission while staying close to your home. You will get to see Tori every day, unlike other times when you were away from your fiancée for long periods of time. We believe this has a lot of advantages for you and for the agency, and hopefully for the country."

"I have to admit, that all sounds enticing," Axel said. "I will talk to Tori tonight and see if she has any problems with it. I don't think she will, but you can never tell about women. They are pretty smart and very intuitive, and she might see some bumps in this that we don't. While we are at it, tell me what you think about the other company on the East Coast. That company could have the same problem. In fact, even though the deaths were on both coasts, they might have been done by only one company. They just completed the experiment in a different part of the country. What are you going to do about the other company?"

"The other company is in Boston. We thought we would wait to see what you recommend after being at the company in South San Francisco."

"That makes sense," agreed Axel. "What's the company's name?"

"It's fairly easy to remember," Kim said. "Its name is Aortica. I guess they named it after the aorta, since they felt they would be doing a lot with the nanoparticles that related to the aorta."

Axel told Kim that he felt the assignment suited him well. "What you have described is precisely the kind of experience a professional biologist would enjoy, because of the advanced field of work. I don't believe Tori will have any problems with my engaging in this venture, since I will be remaining home, or at least in proximity to home."

Axel told Kim to start processing what he thought he'd need to clear the way for him at Aortica. "I hope you don't have to make up too much of my resume, but if you do, you better let me take a look at it, so I know what I'm supposed to have done. I am confident that whatever you put in there will be something I know or have experienced. At least with my internal communication capability, I can keep in touch with the scientists at the agency. What I don't know, they will, and they can phone it to my internal computer,"

Kim agreed, and said he would be back in touch.

As Axel had suspected, Tori thought the new assignment was good exposure for him. "You can gain some unique experience from this venture," she said. "One of these days you might want to start a company of your own, and all of this experience is going to pay off. Besides, I can see you every night and you can bring me up to speed, and I won't be worrying so much." Axel laughed at that.

As the days passed, he got anxious that he hadn't heard from Kim. He had prepped his substitute to take over his classes at the university, telling him to start coming to his classes immediately, so he could see where each class was in its studies. He was now excited about this new adventure, and it took every bit of his cool not to call Kim and tell him how eager he was to start.

One afternoon, when Axel had just completed his course teaching for the day, he got a fax from Kim that came by way of his school computer. He read it over to himself.

Axel, I have sent you an expedited letter that has all the paperwork you will need for this new job. It should be at your house this evening. It's your resume, which I have conveniently brought up to date and already forwarded to the CEO of Aortica. You should read it over and make sure that you memorize its contents, since they are not exactly your experiences. I added experiences related to your role as The Follower, but described them in a way that makes it look like you got the experience from confidential forays with the agency at other companies; similar to what I expect to gain from this stay with Aortica. I talked to the CEO (Howard Foster) the day before yesterday and told him I was sending you. I assured him that it had nothing to do with any deficiency the agency has found in the company, and the agency will continue to sponsor Aortica. I told him you would arrive next Monday and he said he looked forward to it. He later called me and said that he had read your resume. He was quite impressed and felt you would add some additional technical talent to the company.

Also included in the mail is a complete description of Aortica, and the reports they have issued to us from their start to the present time. This should give you a good feel of what work the company has done to date and where they are going in the future. It also contains their costs, their assets, and their last two Profit and Loss financial reports. They have lost money to date, which we expected, but they should reach a break-even position in about another year. Anytime you feel you need additional information or input from the scientists at the agency, give us a call. Included with the material is a top secret clearance that you previously received from the agency and is considered to be active as of this date.

When he got home, Axel read the resume and was quite impressed with how Kim had worded everything. *That makes me look good,* he thought. The schooling and experiences were accurate, except where Kim had taken some liberties with his experience as The Follower. When Tori got home, he showed her the paperwork, and she thought it was very well done.

"Sounds like someone I should meet," she said with a big grin on her face. "It looks like the two guys I know, although I never see one of them around the house. He's always cavorting around the world." She laughed. She was describing Axel and his role as The Follower.

Axel was happy she found everything acceptable. He gave her a big hug and said, "Let's go out and celebrate my new job and then come home and really celebrate."

Tori immediately agreed.

Before going to his new position in the little company of Aortica, Axel knew he had to brush up on anything that related to nanoparticles. Nanoparticles were particles that were between one and ten nanometers in size in at least one dimension, but preferably in all dimensions. Axel believed the ideal size and shape would be a sphere that was one to ten nanometers in diameter. His studies through the Internet provided him with a significant amount of general information. The one key advantage proposed for these nanoparticles was that they were so small; they could go through blood vessel walls without harming the walls. The one big hope for the nanoparticles was to use them like missiles to carry medicine to selected spots in the body. The scientists working on these particles felt too much damage was done to the body when a person with cancer was treated with chemotherapy. Aside from the side effects, the fact that the chemo was nonselective meant it not only killed the cancer cells or tumors, but all the cells. The scientists believed that if they found a way to control the production of nanoparticles and the method of providing this material to selective areas, such as the cancer cells, the chemo would be much more effective in eliminating the cancer without causing side effects and collateral damage.

The key about a nanoparticle was that it had characteristics that were quite different from the material from which they came. Axel did not know why, but the nanoparticles had their own characteristics. One of the challenges was to bring a material down to this small size and to determine what its new characteristics were. They were so small; their physical size put a great strain on studying them. Everything had to be done using electron microscopes or other equipment. One of the researchers he found on the web talked about copper and gold, and how much their characteristics changed when they got to these small dimensions.

Maybe there was some way of using nanoparticles to carry nitric oxide to Tori's fingers, Axel thought. He knew the treatment Tori had used that had provided her some relief from her Raynoud's Syndrome was a salve that contained nitric oxide. Nitric oxide caused blood vessels to dilate, since they produced localized heat. Ninety percent of the time she wasn't bothered by the Raynoud's, but that other ten percent was dramatic. Maybe while working at Aortica, he would find a way to have the nanoparticles they produced to contain nitric oxide, which could be shot into Tori's fingers and relieve or entirely eliminate her problem. That would be a great by-product of his work with Aortica, finding a cure for Tori's fingers. Those thoughts gave Axel more incentive to go to work with Aortica. It wouldn't be long now.

Axel arrived at Aortica on Monday and met with Howard Foster. As they shook hands, Foster told him how much he had been looking forward to Axel's arrival.

"According to Kim at USSA," Foster said, "you have a background that is broad and could help here. Our work is very complex, and technical problems keep popping up. Keep in mind that the people I have here are biased toward one goal and biased on how to achieve it. We have been working a couple of years on this issue and have made great progress, but we have not reached our specified goal. Sometimes a team gets stale on an approach and loses its innovation. Innovation is something that all good scientists are looking for. It takes innovation to be creative in one's thoughts. Sometimes when people are working a long time on the solution to a problem, they run out of ideas and get frustrated from bouncing against a brick wall. They try to overcome this with old techniques, and they don't work. I need someone to look at the work we are doing and give us a fresh approach. How about just watching and listening for a couple of weeks to see where things stand, and then I will give you a shot at providing me with a review and recommendations? What do you think?"

"I appreciate your confidence in me," said Axel. "I will try to dig into the details and see where the problems lie. It's not always obvious, but there may be some critical step you're missing, or maybe some threshold level we must overcome. I will do the best I can. While I believe I will be of some help to you technically, I want you to keep in mind my main reason for being here. I know Dr. Kim has talked to you about one of the things I need to achieve."

"Yes," Foster said. "Kim told me about the odd deaths and his concern that someone is leaking our research to a terrorist organization. I know you are here to see if that's true, and I hope you find that we don't have that problem here."

Axel said, "It's important that you know what I'll be doing. It may sound counterproductive, but it might smoke out any terrorists in your operation. I would like to start dropping hints about how these nanoparticles could be used as a biological weapon. I believe I can do this in a subtle manner without alarming anyone, and hopefully I can connect with any individual who has aspirations in that direction. From what I know, all of your employees seem quite dedicated to the success of your program. But some people come from cultures that endorse violence, while others are looking for an opportunity to make money. You never know until you get close enough to them to gain their confidence and they begin to talk."

Foster agreed that it was hard to pull the bad apples out of the barrel at times, and he had no problem with Axel's approach.

Glad to have Foster's agreement, Axel asked the CEO to give him a summary of where the company was with its research.

"We have tried several approaches that give us results in the right direction," said Foster. "We have made single nanoparticles, but when we try to collect them, they agglomerate into a ball and we lose the singular nanoparticles. A few months ago, after trying several methods that we thought would reduce the attraction of the particles for each other; we decided to go a different route. We decided to produce the nanoparticles in a liquid suspension in order to reduce the attractive force on the nanoparticles when they are in dry form. This sort of worked, since it did keep the nanoparticles separated, but when we tried to sinter the suspension, the sintering action failed. Our studies of what happened indicate that the uneven heating was such that at one point, there were free dry nanoparticles while many were still in suspension. As added heating was applied, the nanoparticles that were out of the solvent began to agglomerate, and that got us practically back to square one. Keep in mind that we are talking about something you can't see with a standard light microscope. Because of this we use electron microscopes or force field microscopes throughout the process. We need to use robotic action since the engineers and scientists cannot see or select the individual nanoparticles. Everything is done based on theory and on either controlled chemical actions or robotic actions, with minute robots to handle the nanoparticles. So, the engineers have to be a mix of electronic, mechanical, biology, and chemical engineers. That's how tough this problem is. When we arrive at the end of the process and have the nanoparticles in suspension, we can't see them. We know they're there. The proof, of course, is that when we dry the solution, we end up with clumps of nanoparticles; with thousands of particles in each clump. We can see them better, but can't use them. This has been very disappointing. That's how close we came, and yet we failed to complete the mission."

"Sounds like your people have come a long way," commented Axel. "I have to admit that is frustrating and demoralizing, but it shows you have been close to a resolution. I will watch and see what I come up with. I have good experience in technologies like yours, and hopefully I can come up with some good suggestions for the company. We will see in a few weeks. I won't string you along. If I am not a good fit for this program, I will tell you."

Foster introduced Axel to the team of engineers and scientists, saying, "We have decided to bring in a very experienced engineer and biologist to review our work and see if we are missing something. I expect you all to give Axel Tressler your complete detailed analysis of any step we use to make our product. There shall be no secrets. Axel has done this kind of work under top secret clearance for other companies, and I expect you all to give him your full support."

Thus Axel started his first week as an observer for this highly technical crew. As he observed, he also thought about how he could lay the groundwork for finding out if any of these people were responsible for the three mysterious deaths. Each day brought him in contact with the various steps of the process. Everything was brought to the almost complete phase of the process several times, and Axel was able to see, with the aid of high magnification equipment, the nanoparticles being hatched. He could watch the single nanoparticles being formed, and then their loss during the remaining steps in the process. The frustration among the scientists was overwhelming. Axel sat with them while they described what they were seeing, each giving his or her hypothesis of why this was occurring. Axel could see that the different approaches the crew was trying brought different intermediate results, but the final results were always the same. They had good technical suggestions, but the product wasn't buying them. When Axel gave some input, the crew chewed over his suggestions. They said they were good suggestions, but they either had already tried them, or they had some reason why his idea wouldn't work.

Axel respected their reasoning. He could see that some of his suggestions weren't employed for good reasons. The scientists were not just being negative; they were giving him the straight scoop. He would have to think more about this.

Meanwhile he talked to the various team members to see if he could find out if anyone had aspirations other than those of the group. He would sit beside one of the engineers or technicians and make comments like, "You know, if we can get to a single particle in this process, there are many dramatic products that could be made using the particles. They would be ideal as virus carriers to cause major illnesses, as well as directors for carrying bacteria into animals or humans exactly where one wants them." Sometimes he would make remarks that indicated that whoever got those particles could make a terrific amount of money from them. During the first week, no one rose to his bait. However, when he returned to work on the following Monday and joined a technician at his work station, the other man said, "Are you interested in making some big money off of this process?"

Axel was shocked at first, since the week before had been so mundane. He spent a moment composing himself, and then turned on his internal phone system, which was tied into USSA.

"It would be worth considering," he said. "I guess the first thing that has to happen is that we have to get this thing to work. Then it would be a miracle to take advantage of. There must be a thousand uses for this. I have some money problems right now that need to be resolved, or my wife and I are going to have to move."

The technician kept working on the step he was responsible for. "My name is Venky," he said quietly. "How about we meet somewhere after work today?"

"Sounds good," said Axel. "Is there a place that is not so close to this facility? I don't want to be caught talking about work anywhere near here."

"Yes," responded Venky. "There is a place called Bart's Fish House on the wharf in Redwood City. It's about fifteen miles south of here. I will meet you there right after leaving work."

Axel nodded and walked on.

When Axel arrived at the Fish House, there was a small line waiting for seats, but Venky already had a table. Axel joined him and they ordered their dinner, and then Axel turned on his internal phone. As they waited for their food, Venky asked Axel how he thought they were doing.

"Things are running smoothly," Axel said, "but we can't get over the threshold. I have a few ideas that would probably help."

"Like what?" Venky asked.

"There are things being done that are similar to what I've worked on before," Axel said, "and I was able to resolve them. I have to keep them private at this time, until I see where the Aortica team goes with what they are trying."

"I guess that is the best approach at this time," Venky said. "However, if you think you have a solution of how to get a large number of individual particles without their clumping into little balls, I have someone who would pay you quite well for that information."

"That's an interesting point," said Axel. "I hadn't thought about it as a separate step that I get paid for. Would they pay me without seeing the results?"

"I believe so," said Venky. "These are bright people I am connected with, and they would be able to tell if your ideas are valid. They probably would be able to envision the end result before Aortica."

"Maybe," Axel said. "However, they would need all the equipment that Aortica has and would have to have made something like this. It would take them a year or so to put all that together."

"They have the equipment and it isn't far from here. In fact, we have two lines similar to the line Aortica's running at this time."

"Are you saying you've made these particles before and had similar problems to what Aortica has?" asked Axel.

"Yes. We have had some hiccups, and this product can't stand hiccups."

"What do you mean by hiccups?" asked Axel.

"They have had the same problems as Aortica," replied Venky, "but they were content to see what could be done with a few of the nanoparticles. Aortica hasn't been satisfied with only a few particles. Their objective is to find a way to generate millions or billions without any major problems. Our team wanted to see what could be made out of the nanoparticles as soon as they had a few. Aortica could have ventured that way also, but they didn't."

"Is this where the hiccups appeared?" asked Axel.

"Yes," replied Venky. "They wanted to see several things. One of them was to place a superbug inside one of the nanoparticles to see if they could direct the superbug to where they wanted it."

"So, they had a problem with the directing, or a problem with establishing the superbug in the nanoparticles?"

"Yes," Venky answered. "They didn't appreciate that the nanoparticles weren't like the bulk material from which they were derived. They thought that injecting the superbug into the nanoparticles would be straightforward. But it isn't."

Axel asked what were the problems they had found when they tried to combine the two materials. Venky said he didn't think he could tell Axel that.

"That's bullshit," Axel said. "You must tell me this, so I can understand the problem and figure out whether my approach would work. You wouldn't want me to be working in the blind, would you?"

Venky was silent. He looked like he wanted to tell Axel, but he obviously felt it would betray the trust of the group he was involved with. Stopping just short of talking, he told Axel that he would check with the man running the other program and see if he is willing to provide the information. Axel agreed to that. He had felt this was going too fast anyhow, and he wanted to meet the people Venky was talking about. They ate their dinner, and then Axel drove home, thinking about this contact. This was the hit he had been sent there to find. Now if he could carry this further and find the people heading up this deadly line, it would be the culmination of a major find.

Axel felt this was too important to keep a secret, even though he only had hearsay from Venky. Venky might just have been stringing him along, hoping to get more information from him that he could sell to a third party. Regardless, Axel decided to call Kim as soon as he got home.

When Kim answered, Axel started right off by saying he felt he had found the right person. Kim agreed, saying he had heard some of the details on the phone contact Axel had made while he was talking to Venky. Axel covered everything that had gone on that day, adding that he might eventually find the location of the line that Venky had mentioned. That would be a real hit. He told Kim he wanted to find out first what problems they had run into. If it was something like the three dead bodies that had turned up, it would be a real win.

Kim told Axel that he should talk to Howard Foster, but to make sure Foster kept the information confidential. He should also make sure that Venky didn't get involved in anything new at Aortica. "Sounds like you are getting close to what may have happened in the past," Kim said. "That's exciting. Let's keep close to this guy, and hopefully Foster will be able to keep Venky from learning anything new."

Axel kept up with his job at Aortica, and each day he expected to get closer to solving the problem. Venky didn't talk to him, though, and after a few days Axel thought this had been a "wild hair," so to speak. Then, just before they were ready to break for the weekend, Venky gave him a signal. He started across the hall to the men's room, indicating Axel should follow him. Axel continued with what he was doing for a few minutes, and then went into the men's room. It was empty, but soon Venky entered the room. He went to relieve himself and whispered to Axel, "See you right after work." Axel went back to the processing line. When he was leaving work and walking toward his automobile, Venky walked by him and said, "See you at the Fish House." Axel waited till he saw Venky pulling out of the parking lot, and then he took off for the restaurant. *I think we have a winner here*, he thought.

Once in the restaurant Axel turned on his internal phone so the agency would be able to hear everything that was said. Venky wasn't there, so Axel went to the table they had sat at before. Venky joined him a few minutes later.

"Are we eating or are we talking?" asked Axel.

"We are doing both," replied Venky. "I am hungry and need some energy before we talk."

Axel didn't mind, since he was hungry too. He hadn't eaten even a candy bar all afternoon. They ordered, and then Venky began to talk, not bothering to wait for the food.

"I got an okay for you to meet with the top man. He will discuss the issues with you. He wants to find out what you know and what you are looking for in the way of compensation."

This made Axel's energy level go up almost to his Axelvation levels, but he remained cool with Venky. "So, when will we meet and discuss things?" he asked.

"He said he would meet us here. He probably won't be here till about six-thirty." The man hadn't arrived by the time they had completed their meal, so Axel decided to have a dish of ice cream to while away the time. He had no sooner started eating the ice cream, when Venky said, "Here he is. This is the top man that wants to meet you. Just sit still until he comes over to the table and sits down. We don't want to make an obvious commotion."

Axel continued eating his ice cream, and then heard a man behind him say, "Good evening Venky. Nice seeing you here. I didn't know you came to this restaurant to eat." With that acknowledgement, he sat down next to Axel. "Who's your friend?" he asked.

Venky introduced the man as Mr. Gordon Strong. "You can call me Gordy," the man said. Axel was a little surprised, since he had expected the "top man" to be a foreigner like Venky, who appeared to be from the Middle East. Gordy, however, was white and dressed like a prosperous businessman. Axel guessed he was in his late forties or early fifties. He looked like he ran a business. In fact, he looked like he owned a business. And it didn't take him long for them to start talking about nanoparticles and their application.

"Before we discuss any details related to my operation," he said, "why should I expect you to know something that Aortica or my group doesn't know? What kind of experience do you have that provides you an insight that Aortica and my team are missing?"

Axel put down his spoon and looked at the man. With a sort of arrogance, he answered, "I have a doctor's degree in biology and I have experience with microbiology." He went on to say that he had put in a stem cell line and was now running one at the university. He talked in generalities, making sure he stayed away from any details. He told Gordy he had taken off some time from the university to provide consulting duties with Aortica. At this point he was well versed on how Aortica's process worked, and he believed it could be improved.

"How?" Gordy asked. "How would you know how to correct the process that is being run by Aortica?"

"I am an experienced scientist." replied Axel.

Their waitress came by and asked if anyone wanted anything more to eat. Gordy ordered dinner while Venky ordered a dish of ice cream. Axel asked for an iced tea. He also opened up his internal phone system and called Kim's home phone in Virginia. Soon Gordy brought them back to the subject of the nanoparticles.

"So, what do you have to give us?" asked Gordy.

"I won't give you anything until I know you're in a position to use it," Axel said. "I understand you have a facility that would be able to put this into motion."

Gordy said he had an operation that was probably more advanced than Aortica's.

"I have a hard time believing that," said Axel. "There are a few companies involved in nanoparticles around the world, and I know who they are. I haven't heard you mention the name of your company, but I don't believe it exists."

"Oh, it exists all right," said Gordy. "When we get a little further downstream on discussing your qualifications, I will take you there."

"Let's change the subject a little," Axel said. "According to Venky, you've had some problems with the use of the nanoparticles." Axel saw that this comment shocked Gordy. He was visibly upset, but cooled down to keep his annoyance from being too obvious. He sipped his coffee while glaring at Venky.

"Oh, has Venky told you about our problems?" asked Gordy.

"No, he hasn't told me anything in detail. He said you had some problems, but didn't go beyond that. I can assume he was telling the truth, or we wouldn't be having this meeting tonight. Let's be candid about this. If you had some problems with the application, I wouldn't be surprised at all. This is a difficult problem to resolve. Any new application of nanoparticles in any way is difficult."

Gordy waited while the waitress brought him more coffee. "Yes, we have had some problems," he said as she moved away. "I would like to keep them confidential. We tried to take a nanoparticle and add a virus to it, to see what it did when we injected it into a mouse. We had no immediate reaction from the mouse, but in a few days it died. We couldn't determine the reason. Then we took a methicillin-resistant *Staphylococcus aureus* bacterium, attached it to a nanoparticle, and injected it into a mouse. It died within an hour, and its insides were completely torn up. We experimented with these two methods to try to find a way around our problems. In the meantime, two technicians got contaminated and died terrible deaths."

"What did you do with the bodies?" asked Axel.

"We found a way to discard them without notice," answered Gordy.

"Have you stopped your work on this?"

"Yes, we stopped trying to use the nanoparticle in these types of applications, but we tried to make nanoparticles in a way that is similar to how Aortica has been preceding. We have had no real success in achieving a complete method of generating the particles without the clumping of over 99 percent of the output. I understand from Venky that this is where Aortica is stalled also."

Axel agreed, and Gordy asked him why he didn't provide them with the answer to their problem.

"It won't make me rich, will it?" replied Axel.

It was quiet for a while as Gordy took out a cigar, cut off the end, and didn't light it because of the no smoking restrictions. He offered one to both Axel and Venky, but they shook their heads. Gordy took a couple of puffs, and then he looked at Axel.

"How sure are you that you have an answer to the problem?" he asked.

"I am positive," replied Axel. "You see, the nanoparticle is not like the bulk material it is derived from. It is a unique material with unique properties. You cannot use it in this condition. You have to bond the material in a manner that provides certain stability. It is like material was when the earth was first formed, looking for a closure. You will not be able to use it in that condition."

"Are you suggesting that you know how to stabilize these nanoparticles?" asked Gordy.

"That's exactly what I'm suggesting," Axel answered.

"Well, how do we prove that?" asked Gordy.

"We don't, until you show me that you have the capability that you say you have. Why would I give away this jewel without a positive feeling that I was going to get a big reward? If you can't fulfill the end result, you will find a way to avoid the payment one way or another. What if I sell it to you and you sell it to another bigger buyer, like one of this country's enemies, for example?"

It was quiet for a few seconds, and then Gordy said, "It looks like we are at a standstill at this point. Let's abandon the subject tonight and get together some time early next week." He didn't even wait for an answer, but turned and waved at the waitress, telling her to give him the bill. Looking back at Axel, he asked if he had a cell phone that Gordy could call without anyone knowing about the call; a private cell phone number. Axel said he did, and gave Gordy the number. With that, the meeting was over and they all went on their ways.

At home, Axel asked Kim if he had heard everything and if he had any suggestions.

"I heard the whole thing, Axel, and I believe you played it right. He will be back. In the meantime, I will have the agency review the companies in the San Francisco area that might have capabilities like Aortica's. There are a number of companies working on micro-logic and bionics in that area. They could possibly do this, if someone like Venky gave them the details from Aortica. I will get back to you. Meanwhile, how are you doing with Aortica? Do you really have some ideas that could help them out?"

"I definitely do," replied Axel. "The question is whether I give it to them now, or wait till we get over this problem with Gordon Strong and his company?"

"I suggest you go see Howard Foster. Tell him what took place this evening and see what he suggests. I will call him myself and give him my recommendations. If you talk to him Monday morning, I will call him around noon on Monday. You can tell him I will be calling."

Axel spent the weekend thinking about two things, the meeting with Gordon Strong and what could be done to improve the product being made by Aortica. He knew he had some good ideas. On Monday, he would give Howard Foster his full critique and his suggestions to get them over their hurdle.

With these thoughts rolling around in his mind, Axel spent the whole weekend thinking and ignoring Tori's exasperation with him over his lack of attention to her. Each day began with Axel making his breakfast of cereal and bananas, with a slice of winter wheat toast and a glass of V8 juice. But as he ate, his mind was focused on nanoparticles, despite Tori's attempts to get his attention.

Something is missing, Axel thought. *It's obvious and I know what it is, but it won't come to my mind. I keep thinking this thing out and I keep being frustrated. I know what to do because of some past experience or because of something I read. What is it? As I go through the steps, my brain keeps wanting me to think of something that I know is there, but it won't come out. What is it?*

Finally, he gave up on thinking his way through the problem, and decided to go back and read through some books. He knew he read something some time ago that would help him to solve this problem. In his office, he scanned his bookshelves with his large array of books. Then he remembered a book he had read years ago, *The Microbe Hunters*. Like a light bulb being turned on in his brain, he knew the answer was in that book written in 1926, eighty-three years ago. He had read that book several times, because it was so interesting about how the microscope allowed scientists to see bacteria—"beasties," they called them—which they had never even known existed. Axel knew there was something in that book that was the solution to Aortica's problems.

He pulled the book off the shelf and rapidly ran through it, taking only a few seconds with each page. When he came to the right page, he would know it. Finally, he came to the part where Pasteur was trying to see under a microscope what caused rabies. He had some saliva from a rabid dog on a glass slide, but even with the microscope he couldn't see what it was. Then Axel came to the sentence he had been searching for. A swift chill passed through the hairs on his head and throughout his body. He read that Pasteur realized why he couldn't see the "beasties" on the slide. They were too small, even for the microscope. So, he poured fluid from the rabid dog's brain into a porcelain bowl. The porcelain was so dense, the only thing that could go through it would be these "beasties" that couldn't be seen by the microscope. They would pass through the porcelain bowl and be caught in the container below it. This was the clue that had been hiding in Axel's brain. This was the direction he had to suggest for the solution to Aortica's problem.

Monday came, and Axel eagerly drove toward South San Francisco and Aortica. He had thought this through and he knew it was a good suggestion; and maybe it would be the right one. When he got to the lab, he went to the desk they had provided him and anxiously awaited the call from Howard Foster. Soon it was nine o'clock, and no call from Foster. Then it was ten o'clock, and no call from Foster. Just as Axel began to think that Foster had forgotten about him, Foster's secretary came and said that Mr. Foster had been delayed coming in that morning, but he was on his way and should be there soon. This relaxed Axel. Not long after that, the secretary called and asked him to come to Mr. Foster's office.

As Axel entered Foster's office, the CEO greeted him with a big smile. "I hope," Foster said, "that you have thought out some suggestions that will get us beyond our failing point. I have seen the morale of the team go down, and it is reaching the point where our guys don't know what will save this project."

"I have some suggestions," Axel said. "But first I have to apprise you of some events that have occurred over the past two weeks, and more specifically what happened last Friday evening." With that preamble, Axel told Foster about Venky and the meeting with Gordon Strong on Friday. He also told him that Dr. Kim knew about the meeting, and would be calling Foster around noon to give his recommendation. "I would hope," Axel continued, "that I can carry this outside concern through to its logical ending. I want to find out what this company is, and I want to find what problems they had and why. All of this must be done without anyone at Aortica knowing, except you and maybe one or two of your most trusted individuals. This is important not only for Aortica, but for the security of the country. My first question is whether you know anyone named Gordon Strong in the area."

Foster sat back in his chair. "That's hard to believe and hard to digest," he said. "We thoroughly screen all the people working in this company, and now I find out that one of them has set up with a competitor and is helping them surpass our research. I could go out and shoot the guy right now. I know I can't do that to the little bastard, but I sure would like to. It is going to be hard to see him out there on the line every day, knowing what he has done and knowing that we have to be very careful to keep everything away from him for the time being. I hope it is not too long. That's interesting information about their problems of trying to attach a virus to the nanoparticle, and trying an MRSA with those hideous results. It's odd. We were going to do something like that ourselves, but we felt it was more important to get the process ironed out before getting into a new set of problems."

The phone rang, and Foster's secretary told him that it was Dr. Kim. Axel could only hear part of the conversation, but he could tell that Kim was giving Foster his recommendations. After they had talked for about half an hour, Foster said good-bye and hung up the phone.

"Kim told me the same thing." he said to Axel, "and made the same recommendations. I will go along with those recommendations until you put a closure on Venky and this Gordon Strong episode. We will keep Venky doing something menial for the time being. Kim asked me if I had heard of Gordon Strong also. I told him I hadn't. Kim said they have been looking it up and can't find anyone with that name heading up a company. My guess is that he gave you a fake name. You will probably find out his real name when you find the name of the company he is involved with.

"Meanwhile, did you think over the weekend about our process and how to solve our problems?"

Axel was happy to get on a subject that was more positive. He explained to Foster how he had been certain he had read something once that would lead him to finding a solution for Aortica's problem. After perusing the hundred books on his shelves, he had found *The Microbe Hunters*.

"Here is my suggestion," he went on. "In the present process, you have nanoparticles in both the dry and the emulsified state. Neither state works well because of the agglomeration that occurs with dry particles. My suggestion is a simple one. Keep the nanoparticles in suspension in the solution as you presently do. But instead of trying to dry the solution, let the solution fall into a porcelain or ceramic bowl. A porcelain or ceramic bowl, with its very small pores, provides an answer to the problem. In your case it is probably easier to obtain a ceramic bowl. Once the solution containing the nanoparticles enters the ceramic bowl, you have to keep the solution agitated. As the material is agitated, there is a tendency for very small particles to go through the ceramic and fall into whatever is below the bowl. In the case of your process, the only constituents in the solution that will go through the ceramic are the nanoparticles, leaving the liquid solution behind. This has them separated by a very simple process of filtering.

"However, if left like this, they will tend to agglomerate after passing through the ceramic filter. To solve the agglomeration problem, we must bind the nanoparticles to something that stabilizes their surface. To do this, we'll put a glass tube beneath the ceramic bowl, and then another container below that is capable of holding the nanoparticles. We'll have a gas of warm nitric oxide flood the tube as the nanoparticles fall through the ceramic and into the tube. The nitric oxide will react with the nanoparticles and this will tie up the nanoparticles' surface states, keeping them from agglomerating. You will therefore have a bowl of nanoparticles that contain a nitric oxide coating, which are stable and won't agglomerate. The tube containing the nitric oxide should be long enough to provide another function. The free-falling nanoparticles will be slightly cooled as they fall and will take on a spherical shape.

"You would now be able to process these spherical and stable nanoparticles as they are. In addition to your intended use, there is a need for nanoparticles that contain nitric oxide in medical applications. The body's immune system contains nitric oxide, which generates heat and causes blood vessels to dilate. Nanoparticles impregnated with nitric oxide could be used in applications in which blood vessels need to dilate and take on more healing oxygen, to be available for the body's cells."

Axel went on to discuss a paper that had just been released that past week by scientists and engineers at the Albert Einstein College of Medicine. "They took nanoparticles that contain nitric oxide and made a salve. They placed the salve on skin abscesses on mice caused by methicillin-resistant *Staphylococcus aureus*. This Staph infection can be deep in the skin. The salve penetrated deep enough to overcome the abscesses where other medical methods had failed.

"So, let's assume that this will work and you now end up with nitric oxide nanoparticles. This could be your first product. But let's assume that you also would like to have nanoparticles without the nitric oxide coating. I believe that once they are in this NO form, you can work on the nanoparticles to make what you want. You remove the NO under controlled chemical conditions, while simultaneously adding what you want to add to the nanoparticles. You would now be in a position of working with a stable end product, rather than all the steps that are now being pursued. I believe if you produce millions of these nitric oxide coated nanoparticles and provide a certain amount to each of your top scientists and engineers, these members of your team would come up with the means of converting these NONP into other products. Think about that; having millions and maybe billions of these nanoparticles that your team could now experiment with. That's exciting."

When Axel was finished, he looked at Howard Foster. He saw either amazement or disbelief in Foster's eyes. For a long moment, Foster just stared at Axel, not saying a word. Finally he said, "Mr. Tressler, I have just heard a remarkable presentation, the likes of which I have never heard before. You have taken the complex problem we have and made it sound simple to resolve. To tell you the truth, I believe what you have just presented makes the problem seem simple. I read that book, *The Microbe Hunters*, years ago, and I remember how a porcelain bowl was used to filter out the very small rabid material taken from rabid animals. Wouldn't this be incredible if it's a simple as the porcelain or ceramic bowl approach used years ago?

"If you present this to our team, they will eat it up. They will like it and they will find some ways to refine it. Even if they completely discount your method, it will make them think about other approaches. It will open their minds. I will sit back and enjoy your presentation to them. I want to see their faces and their responses. I don't care what the results are. I am going to call Dr. Edward Kim and thank him for sending you to review our process.

"If you don't mind, I'll set up a presentation for this afternoon. Is that okay by you?"

"No problem," Axel said. "But how do you keep Venky out of this?"

"That's a good point." Foster paused, thinking it over. "At times we have sent Venky out to procure material that we need. I will have his superior instruct him to get certain items tomorrow morning. So instead of this afternoon, you can give your presentation tomorrow morning, when we know he will be out of the building. I will have our top scientists and engineers come to my office, and you can saturate them with your ideas. I know they will be excited.

"It will probably take a few days for us to find the materials we need for your experiment. That will give you some time to find the answers to the Gordon Strong group. I know this is asking a lot of you, after all the technical input you have given me today, but I believe you will succeed with this Gordon Strong problem."

"The agency will be working on the Strong problem as well, "Axel said. "And I will be ready the first thing in the morning to give that presentation."

The next morning, Axel was called into Mr. Foster's office, along with six of the top technical people. Axel told the Aortica team what he had told Foster the previous day. In general, the team was pleased with the presentation, and found Axel's suggestion of an old approach was a possible solution to the problem. Several of them had some good questions to ask Axel, and most of them he could answer. Some were more hypothetical, and all he could say was, "We may find the answer as we go along."

To clarify his approach, he said, "I know that during most of the process, the product is not seen except in certain key points, when there are electron microscopes to take samples, or atomic force microscopes for the same reason. With the process I am recommending, you won't see anything till the nanoparticles are tied up with the nitric oxide, which will enlarge them slightly. At that point, you will see whether we win or lose."

Axel was happy with the general acceptance and the attitude of the scientists. Foster assigned different tasks to the different team members. One of the suggestions that had come up was that they should heat the mouth of the glass tube and shape it so that it fit exactly with the contour of the bottom of the ceramic bowl. The close fit would keep other gases from entering the tube. The pressure of the nitric oxide gas was another critical parameter. Too much pressure would cause one problem, and too little, another problem. Foster instructed one of the engineers, who had a master's degree in mathematics, to work out the optimal length of tube.

"You know enough about the physics and mathematics of the particle as it goes through the nitric oxide gas," Foster said, "and you know the pressure of the gas and its characteristics. You therefore should be able to mathematically figure out how long the tube should be; too short or too long can cause results that we don't want."

That afternoon Venky came back with the material his supervisor had sent him out for. Axel talked to him, and there was no indication that Venky knew that anything different was happening. The people on the standard line kept him busy with things that he had done previously. During a mid-afternoon break, Axel got to talk to Venky again, and he asked if had heard anything from Gordon Strong. Venky shook his head and said, "No, I keep waiting to get a call from him. I am anxious since he had promised me a nice sum of money if I brought anything in that would help their situation."

Axel asked if he knew the name of the company that Strong headed, and Venky again shook his head. "I went there when they were first setting up the line like Aortica's, but they didn't do it in their standard company building. It was set up in a small place that was close to the building, but that was as far as I got. I know Strong didn't want me to know the name of the company."

"I understand," Axel said. "I guess I would do the same if I ran a company that was stealing from another company." Venky looked shocked at the word "stealing," and Axel asked, "Would you call it anything else but stealing?"

Venky said, "I would have called it technology improvising."

Axel shook his head and went back to work.

It only took three days for the engineers and technicians to set up for new experiment. During that time, management made sure that Venky was stuck on some remote problem, distant from this new approach. The experiment began with tests on the ceramic bowl, which indicated that particles greater than ten nanometers would not pass through the bowl. The tube had been shaped to fit the bottom of the bowl fit like a glove. Initial experiments showed that particles indeed were making it through the tube and into a separate container. The engineers varied the pressure and flow levels of the nitric oxide gas. The shape of the particles was distorted from exactly spherical, depending on the flow or the pressure.

By the second day of experiments, they had adjusted the flow and pressure so that the particles were coming out in almost perfectly spherical shape. By the third day, they believed they knew the right flow and pressure of the nitric oxide to provide the proper shape of any particle. They then took the standard process that had been processing for several weeks and was about to go into the suspension stage. They passed it through the new process, and had results by the end of the day. Howard Foster asked the top engineers and scientists to stay when everyone left at five. This meant Venky was out of the building. Foster asked Axel to attend the meeting as well. The team's senior member, Martin Author, provided a summary of their results of the three days.

"First of all," he began, "I want to thank Axel Tressler for his proficient recommendations. After only spending two weeks reviewing our process, the recommendation he provided gave us the results we had hoped for." He then reviewed the various steps they had taken and their results. He showed a graph of the nanoparticles' size and shape within a given range of flow of nitric oxide. Then he displayed a curve of nanoparticles' size and shape versus nitric oxide pressure, using the optimal flow determined from the first graph. The second graph showed that there was a flat range of pressure that gave good results. Anything above or below that range gave poor results. Knowing the ideal pressure range, they then shifted the rate of flow, and found a much narrower flow, which gave the exact results they wanted.

Martin Author passed around a printout of the results of the experiment. Axel read his copy.

1. The general approach works almost 100 percent of the time.
2. The optimal flow range and pressure range of the nitric oxide for producing the exact size and shape we want has been determined.
3. The nanoparticles with their nitric oxide impregnation are stable.
4. It is believed that the nitric-oxide-impregnated particles provide a marketable product in this form alone.
5. It is believed that the Nitric Acid Nanoparticle (NANP) can be used to provide us with a solid experimental device. We can take these and determine how to stably remove the nitric oxide and add any other dopant to provide different nanoparticle functions.

The stability of the NANP is obtained by the combination of the oxidation of the nanoparticle by the reaction with the nitric acid gas, as well as the containment of the nitric oxide.

6. This process and its final form show that nanoparticle carbon does not act or have the characteristics of its carbon ancestor. We could never take bulk carbon and provide an oxidized carbon containing nitric acid as we have done here. This is a unique molecule.

Martin Author asked for everyone's attention again and said, "The group as a whole extends their thanks to Dr. Axel Tressler for his recommended process to this group. We wish to extend our appreciation by asking that top management and the financial supporter of this company's program grant Axel Tressler a number of shares of Aortica stock, so that he might benefit in the future from his timely and enlightening recommendations."

Howard Foster stood up and began clapping. The clapping was contagious, and even Axel started to clap.

"That is fantastic news," Foster said, "and I support the team's recommendation that Dr. Tressler be awarded stock shares in the company. I am also glad to see that a biologist knows something about chemistry and the working of the simple man." He turned to Axel and said, "I said this to you a few days ago, but I am going to say it again. I have never seen such good and simple recommendations to solve such a tough problem. Your ability to take this difficult problem and provide an employable, simple, and swift solution is remarkable." He gestured to the other people in the room. "I hope this provides you with an example of how sometimes you have to step back from the problem and examine it in a different light. Sometimes we get tied up with our own thoughts and can't get out of the ditch. Sometimes we have to get out of that ditch and try another ditch. We worked on a total process that gave us good results, until we got down to that last point. Thank goodness for someone else's fresh look at the problem."

He turned back toward Axel again and began clapping again. Everyone stood up and clapped as well. Axel got a big lump in his throat and some tears in his eyes. He nodded toward Foster and the others, and then shook everyone's hands as they filed out of the room.

Smashing the Terrorists at the "Bad" Silicon Valley Company

Now that things were working from start to finish, the team of engineers and scientists began taking their research to the next level. Axel spent eight to ten hours each day watching the progress and talking to each of the participants about what they were seeing, hoping that talking would help relieve any of their anxieties. After a few days, though, he reminded himself that this was not why he was there. He was there to see if there was or had been a leak out of Aortica. He speculated that there might be people there or in the Boston company that wanted to find a way to use the nanoparticles to do harm. Certainly, he had a strong lead with Venky and Gordon Strong, but he didn't know what to do about them. He believed Venky should be removed from Aortica before he provided any more information to anyone else.

Axel called Kim a call and explained the situation with Venky, saying that something should be done to get Venky out of the Aortica building and away from the improvements they were making in the process. Before he got too far, Kim said, "Hey, Axel, I have heard nothing but praise for how smart I am to have sent you there. They think you walk on water. Thanks for the effort, and thanks for helping the company. If I had thought about it, I would have sent you earlier. We have money in the company and want it to succeed. Howard Foster called to tell me you provided them with a simple but well thought out solution to a major problem they have been experiencing. In fact, they are now getting the results they were searching for during the past year. I was very pleased with that phone call from Howard. You and your brother Adam have been real finds for USSA. I might not have told you, but Adam has been doing a super job here in the agency, and we just promoted him last week. If I know Adam, he won't tell you about it, so I am passing the word to you."

They talked for a few more minutes about the progress Aortica was making, and then Kim shifted back to the problems that Axel had outlined on Venky. "I will have someone pick up Venky after work tomorrow and take him to a secure place for the time being. We can hold him on theft if nothing else. But we probably will eventually arrest him on espionage, especially if we find out that the process he stole and passed on was to this country's enemies. At least we will get him out of the way. I will call Howard when we hang up and tell him what we're doing. I'm sure he will be relieved."

Axel asked if the agency had found out anything about Gordon Strong and got a negative answer. "If that man is running a sizeable company, it's not with this name," said Kim. Axel said he hoped to be making contact soon with Strong, and would let Kim know what he found out. With that, they ended the conversation.

Two more days passed, and then Axel's internal phone tried to contact him. He answered over the unseen phone. The voice on the other end was Gordon Strong.

"Is it okay to talk to you now?" Strong asked. "Are we on a private phone?" Axel answered in the affirmative on both questions. Strong continued, "How about we meet this evening at that fish restaurant around six o'clock?"

"That's fine by me," responded Axel. "Is there anything I need to bring with me?"

Strong laughed. "Yes. You could bring me the process steps you would like to sell me, but I know you won't do that until you see my company and our operation on the nanoparticles, as you already pointed out."

"Yes, that's correct," Axel said. They hung up, and Axel thought, *I think we have the weasel by the tail. Tonight I will solve most of this mystery. Once I see his company, his real identity will be exposed.* He called Kim and told him about the conversation. Kim was excited, and asked Axel to keep his internal phone working while he was with Strong.

At six o'clock, Axel arrived at the restaurant and saw Gordon Strong sitting at the table they'd sat at before. As Axel sat down, Strong signaled to the waitress. He asked for a beer while Axel ordered an iced tea, and then they ordered their meals. After the waitress left, Strong asked how things were going with Aortica.

"They are improving," replied Axel.

"Oh. Did they try some of your suggestions?"

"As a matter of fact, they did."

"And they worked?" Strong asked.

"Yes. In fact, they worked perfectly."

Strong grinned. "Great, now we are on to something. This will make our trip to my company that much more enjoyable."

After they had finished their meal and Strong had paid the bill, they walked outside. "Let's go in my car," said Strong. As they were getting in, Strong added, "I would like your cell phone. I don't want it to be available to you while we are on this trip to the facility. I want this to remain private." Axel gestured vaguely toward the parking lot and said his phone was in his car. Strong believed him, and started the engine.

He drove out to where the road met with highway 101, but instead of turning onto the highway, he made a left hand turn, heading away from the highway. It was an uninhabited road, and when they had gone about two miles, Axel could see the lights of a good sized building in the distance. He asked if that was Strong's company, and Strong said it was. They drove about another half mile, and there before them was a large building with a name on it, Antigenics Technology.

"Antigenics Technology," Axel said, knowing Kim would hear him on the other end of his internal phone. "That's a good name for a company working on solving problems using antigens to overcome pathogens."

"Yes, I thought of that name. It's hard to find a name that is unique; seems like they are all used up."

Strong parked, and as they walked toward the front entrance to the building, Axel's internal phone gave him a message from Kim. "His real name is Michael Philips," said Kim. "His company has been around for a little over five years. They make some unique products in the bionics world. I can't believe this guy would ruin his position to steal from another small company unless it was for no good. He must be tied into the Taliban or Al-Qaeda, or some other new terrorist group. I am going to research him some more."

As they walked through the front door the woman at the desk said, "Good evening, Mr. Philips."

"Good evening, Margaret. How are things going?"

"It's been quiet tonight so far," she replied.

As they walked down a hallway, Gordon Strong extended his hand and said, "You probably know by now my name is not Gordon Strong. My name is Michael Philips, and I am the CEO and Chairman of the Board of Antigenics. I'm sorry I had to use that alias, but I had to cover myself."

Axel didn't respond to that, and Philips took him on a tour of the building, passing many ultra clean rooms.

"This is a great building and facility you have here," Axel finally said. "What kind of revenue is this company bringing in a year?"

"We continue to grow. Last year we did two hundred and thirteen million dollars, and this year we expect to come close to doubling that."

"That's a really great start from nothing not too many years ago. You must make some fantastic products for the world."

"Yes," said Philips. "We might hit a billion dollars in another five years if the industry continues to grow, and we continue to come up with new and exciting products. Most of our products support the medical industry."

"Where is your line that is processing the material that's like Aortica's?" asked Axel.

"I will take you to it when you have seen enough here to be convinced that we know what we are doing, and convinced that we could take Aortica's product and mass produce it."

"I have seen enough already," Axel said.

"Good. We have to go back to my car and drive to the other production line." Philips drove Axel about a mile behind the Antigenics building. His destination was a small concrete building that looked like a lonesome bunker from World War II. After parking, Philips walked with Axel to the front entrance. As they entered, a man at the front desk told him to sign in. He acknowledged Michael Philips, but made him sign in as well. As Axel leaned over to sign, he saw a shotgun leaning against the desk, next to the man's legs.

This is unusual, he thought. *This sure isn't set up like Antigenics.*

When they entered the main hall, he saw a man standing at each corner of the different hallways they came to. Axel said to Philips, "This surely isn't a friendly place like your other building. It's cold and secretive, and I don't like the guys that are standing around the halls with sneers on their faces."

"Yes, it's a different world," Philips said sadly. His tone and expression made Axel think differently about the whole situation.

I don't think this guy wants to be doing this. I have to press that issue and find out what the real scoop is. I think I can do it by acting like a hard ass about this whole thing. But right now, I better look at their line and see what they are doing and if it is exactly like the line being run at Aortica.

In fact, the line looked almost identical to the one at Aortica, except for the recent changes he had suggested. That was a relief. And the line was first class. He noticed that all men were running the line. *Unusual here in the states, he thought. Most fab lines are mostly women if not all women.* It didn't take many people to run a line, maybe fifteen or so; but why all men? He put that question to Philips.

"They felt that this was the fastest way to check out the process," Philips answered. "These are all engineers or chemists. They felt they could get the line working faster with these skilled people, rather than bringing in operators to train."

"You mean, they didn't want anyone to know they were stealing this process from Aortica, right?"

Philips looked stunned. He stuttered some comments, but none of them made sense.

Axel stared into Philip's eyes and said, "I can't believe you would stoop this low, to steal another company's process and product when you have a successful line running and you're making money. That is really a low blow."

"Let's drop the subject," Philips said. "I don't want to go there."

"I guess you don't want to go there, but you are there," said Axel. "I bet your family would be proud of you for doing something like this."

"Don't bring my family into this," shouted Philips. "That's a low blow. Let's just forget about it."

Axel looked at Philips and continued the pressure. He knew he was getting to him. *It's funny,* he thought,, *how quickly a soldierlike appearance can change to the appearance of a beaten man. An hour ago this guy looked like he owned the world, and now he looks like he is going to jail, or worse. Something is wrong here, and I have to keep pressing him to find out what it is.*

"Are you one of those people," he said to Philips, "who said to himself, 'I am going to make half a billion dollars by the time I'm forty-five'? And you think you aren't going to make it by the time you are forty-five unless you steal."

Philips cried out, "No, no. I am not like that. I am forced to do this. What about you? You are going to give us a process that would have made Aortica's process a winner. Aren't you some kind of a thief too?"

"You know what?" Axel said. "I am not going to sell you those process improvements. You couldn't pay me enough to get those process steps."

Philips looked shocked. Then he recovered and said, "What if I said you could have a million dollars?"

"It won't work," said Axel.

"How about five million in cash and unmarked bills?" asked Philips.

Axel looked at him again and said, "No deal. No amount will get me to change my mind about you and Antigenic. That's a dead deal."

With that comment, the expression on Philips's face changed. His jaw dropped, and Axel could see tears welling in his eyes. He looked up at Axel and said, "Please. It's a matter of life and death. I wouldn't do this unless it was that important."

I think I believe the guy, Axel thought. *I think he is up against it somewhere. I wonder if he gambles and has a debt so big that this is the only way out. I have to keep pressing this issue to find the answer.*

"What's the problem?" he said. "Lose too much money on the horses or Vegas?"

"No, no, it's nothing like that. It really is a matter of life or death."

"How about we take a ride back to the restaurant and talk sanely about this," Axel said to Philips. Philips nodded, and Axel added, "Give me the keys to the car. I'll drive."

As Axel drove to the restaurant, he used his internal phone to ask Kim what he thought. Kim said, "You are doing the right thing. There is something up and you are doing a beautiful job of bringing it to the surface. I will keep listening." As they pulled up to the restaurant, Axel got out of the car and handed the keys to Philips. "Let's have a good cup of coffee or a glass of wine and talk about this."

Once they were in the restaurant and having a glass of wine, Axel decided to push. "Look, Philips, I don't think you want to do this, but you have some problem that is making the choice for you. If it's a gambling debt or something like that, I can see what I can do to help." Philips sat in his chair like a cloth doll; no longer the straight-up character that Axel had thought he was. "You have a problem, buddy, and I am going to solve it for you."

Philips shook his head, "I don't think anyone can solve it. You are right. I have a problem, but no one like you can solve it. It isn't money or a tangible thing. It's like I said, life or death."

Axel looked him straight in the eye and said, "I solve life or death problems. I have been doing it for several years now, and I am going to tell you that there is no one on earth who can solve your problem better than I can. Do you hear me?"

This woke Philips up a little. Axel could see some response coming to the surface. "How can you solve a life or death problem?" he asked.

"What do you have to lose by telling me the problem?" Axel said softly. "If I can solve it, you win. If I can't solve it, what have you lost? Tell me the problem."

Philips shifted around in his chair and looked like he was thinking. Axel waved at the waitress and held up two fingers, indicating he wanted two more wines.

In a few minutes she brought their glasses. Axel took a sip of his wine and told Philips to relax, drink his wine, and tell him his problem without getting too upset. "Let me be the one to get upset, okay?"

Philips smiled for the first time in a couple of hours. Then he began to pour out his troubles. "About a year ago, I met this man at a party, and we talked shop for about an hour. He evidently knew me and knew the kind of business I ran. It was obvious he was a well-educated person, and he knew a good bit about bionics and other technical things. Near the end of the evening, he asked if we could meet sometime and talk about a venture he was just starting. He wanted to see if it matched some of the things my company was doing at the time. He gave me his card. It read, Sumar Nalithy, Professional Consultant, Bionics & Microbiology. He told me to give him a call and set up a time to meet.

"I called him the next day, and we set up a time and place to meet that evening. We spent an hour or so talking over dinner. What I didn't know at the time was that I was sitting with the devil himself. Then he began to spell out what he wanted. He said, 'I bought a building just about a mile from yours. There is a technical company down the way in South San Francisco that is working on something that I want. I would like to run it in your company, but only at the building I just bought.'

"I asked him what the name of the company was and what were they making. He told me it was Aortica and they are working on the development of nanoparticles. He smiled and said, 'I want to copy their line and make the nanoparticles.'

"I told him my company didn't make nanoparticles, and he said that was why he picked me. He said, 'I am sure you would like to add nanoparticles to your line of products.' I told him I knew nothing about nanoparticles other than what I had read in technical journals. It would take me years to reach the level that Aortica had probably already achieved.

"He laughed a hideous laugh. He said he knew it would take a few years if we used the normal method of learning something, but he had hired someone who knew the Aortica process. He could provide us with all the process specs, and even come in the evening and help to make the product.

"'But that's stealing,' I said. He laughed again and said, 'No, it's not stealing. It would be stealing if we made the product and competed against them, but we won't compete against them. I want the process for other reasons and it won't harm their company at all.'"

"By this time I realized I was with a shyster," said Philips, "who didn't care what I thought or anyone thought. I figured I'd better get out of the conversation by saying I would think it over." Then Sumar said, 'Don't you think your company could handle the process? Do you think it's too tough for you? I've already ordered all the equipment, and it is being installed as we speak. This is a winner. You don't have to do anything except help us technically to make sure we are doing the processing properly. I will pay you two million dollars for this. At some point we may have to run one step or another at Antigenic, but that's it; any problems with that?'

"I told him the main problem was ethics. I believe in good business ethics and this didn't sound like good ethics to me. I told him he'd picked the wrong horse and got up to leave. As I walked away, he said, 'I will call you tomorrow. And don't forget about the two million dollars. That's a lot of money.'

"The next day I was worried he would call me, and all day I was on edge. He finally called late in the afternoon and said, 'Did you think over the good thing you are going to do and the good money you are going to make?' I told him I wasn't interested. I had too many issues to worry about at my own business without getting involved in some new technology. His voice lost its laughter and dropped an octave as he said very seriously, 'I know where your two kids are going to school, Syracuse and Pittsburgh, and I have three men watching each of them twenty-four hours a day. You have one week to change your mind or change the lives of your two children. If my men don't receive a signal from me at a given hour, they are to go into action. If another hour goes by, you can say good-by to your son and daughter.'

"When I heard those words, I knew it wasn't a joke. I couldn't say anything. I lost my voice and just sat there. Then he said, 'I think I got your attention with that last bit of wording. Yes, I know about Stephen and Janice, where they room, what classes they take, and when they are to be in those classes. So, not only do you have to handle my technical business, you also must make sure that your children do not miss any of their classes. Are we in agreement?'

"I was shocked. I couldn't conceive of anyone ever putting me in that position. It didn't take much more in the way of discussion until I agreed to his terms. Just to make sure I keep up my end, he calls me every couple of days to tell me that he knows everything I have done since the last time we talked on the phone. So, he not only has my kids tied up, he has me tied up. This has gone on for a year, and I've lost twenty pounds. Now you understand what I am talking about and why I have to do this, don't you? Now you know why the men at the facility you saw in the hall and running the process are not smiling. They are Sumar's men.

"When something doesn't work on that line of theirs, I go through hell. They bring me in and have me review the issues. You know that Aortica hasn't got their process to work completely, and this has been a terrific burden on me. The longer they take and the bigger their problems, the heavier the pressure on me. It's a wonder I can function under these conditions. I have thought and thought about how I could get out of this. I've thought about talking to the police, but I'm afraid there is no way the police can get by the guards watching my children without Sumar Nalithy nailing at least one and probably both of them. One is twenty-two and a senior now, and the other is twenty and a sophomore. They don't know their lives are being monitored, day and night. Now I know why Sumar wants this technology. I have seen death here as a result of being too close to the process, or by doing something slightly wrong while processing this potentially helpful—and potentially harmful—technology. So, I am caught between giving up my children's lives and developing a potential weapon that might cause many deaths. Now you know the burden I am under. You also can see that you cannot resolve this problem. You may be able to help by getting the process to work, but I doubt you want that on your conscience. Besides, there is no way you can help me free the terror that exists around my children."

"Yes, I understand and also am in shock," Axel said. "I know there are these kinds of enemies of this country. I know that they would like this technology to do harm to our people and they will stop at nothing to fulfill their goals, whether they are driven by religion or simple greed. I think I am the only person you could have confided in that might be able to help you under these circumstances."

"I don't understand," Philips said. "How can you help me? You're just another tech expert trying to make a process work."

"I can be of a great help to you," Axel said. "But first I need to find out if what you have told me is the truth. Is this the true story, or just one you made up to get me off your back. Do you have any suggestions on how I can verify your story?"

"No," Philips answered honestly. "I will think about it and get back to you. Should I call the same cell phone number you gave me before?"

"Yes. But you will have to get a new phone, since your cell phone is probably monitored. Perhaps you can borrow a phone from someone at work. When you call my number, make sure you erase it after using the borrowed phone."

"But I still don't know how you can help me. What power do you have that could overcome all this web I'm tangled in?"

"I can't tell you now, but I will eventually let you know. Give me a call tomorrow."

As Axel drove home, thoughts bounced around in his mind. If what Philips said was true, he had to figure out how the agency or he could stretch their arms out as far as Syracuse, New York, and Pittsburgh, Pennsylvania, to protect Philips's children. In addition, he had to assume Philips and his wife were in danger as well. The whole family was caught in a spider web. In fact, Tori would be on that list if Sumar saw him with Philips and believed something was going on. He'd better call Kim.

Kim was home, and answered Axel's call immediately. He had been listening in on Axel's internal phone, so he knew what Philips was claiming.

"I can't believe," Kim said, "these people and the levels they will go to in order to procure weapons for killing. They must do this twenty-four hours a day, and now you know why our CIA has so many things to watch out for and why mistakes can be made. They are only human. This deal that just happened a couple of days ago, where eight CIA agents got killed by a 'would be recruit'? It turned out he was a counterspy. They didn't check him for weapons when he came to talk to them, and the next thing you know, we lose eight of our best CIA terror agents. There is no justice, no sanity, no regard for human life."

"The biggest problem here," Axel said, "is that it is not an army we're talking about. An army is easy for our country to fight. It is hard to fight when there are only a few here and a few there, and the next thing you know there are a few dead here and a few dead there." Axel paused. "Sorry, Kim. I didn't mean to cut you off like that. But I want to know what we're going to do on this case. I believe the first thing the agency must do is find out if it's a true story. You have to send agents to Syracuse and Pittsburgh and find Philips's kids. Your agents should know everything Philips claims this Sumar Nalithy knows where they live, their school schedules, and their friends. Then your agents will have to watch the kids and see if they can spot anyone else who's monitoring their activities. If you don't find that they are being tailed, then I have to hold back any actions here. If you find they are being watched, I believe your people know what to do. I need to know right away. In addition, your guys should go into the kids' apartments or dorm rooms and check for bugs. We need to know how closely these people are monitoring the kids. Knowing how these people work, I believe that once they see me with Philips more than a couple of times, they will find out where I live and will do the same thing with me and Tori. I don't care about me, but Tori won't be able to defend herself against these maniacs. I would suggest the agency finds a place for her to live by tomorrow. If we get her out of there and they start monitoring me, they won't know I have a fiancée. And then I hope they do try to give me a hard time. It will be the last thing they do.

"I guess the other thing you can check is the financial status of Philips. Check Antigenic's annual report. That will show his earnings, including bonuses and stock options. Then you can check his account at his bank and see if it corresponds. You can get his IRS report for the last three years and see if there is anything funny in those reports. Your guys have to find this out within the next two days. The one reason we need to act quickly is that I don't want them to learn that Aortica has found the method for producing the single nanoparticles. If they find that out, they will apply even more pressure on Phillips. Somewhere along the way, I want them to figure out that I am the one that provided the information to Aortica, so they will focus their efforts on me. I sure hope you find that Phillips is telling us a straight story. If we find that out, then we can figure out how to handle this big guy, Sumar Nalithy. Naturally, the agency should check him out too."

Tori was still up when he got home that night. Even though he was late, she was in a good mood, since he was now home almost every night and they could enjoy their "almost marriage" together. Axel told her about the events of the day, and then he told her that the agency was going to find a place for her to stay for a few days.

"Are you kidding me?" she said abruptly. "There is no way I am going to leave this place because of some big dude that thinks he can run me around."

"Listen, Tori, this is for my protection too. If they know you exist and start watching you, I'll have to step back a little from this assignment. I can't do a good job if I know that some slight slipup will get you hurt. I can't have any threats hanging over me. I have to come home tomorrow night knowing that even if they follow me, they will see a bachelor living at this place."

Tori kept shaking her head back and forth. "I can't believe this. We finally get settled down to a reasonable life together, and your job takes you away again. But this time, the agency is taking me away from you. This just isn't fair."

"I understand how you feel," Axel said. "But can you imagine how Phillips feels every day? If he slips up, one or both of his kids are dead. Maybe even his wife. I have to have a clean slate, so I can work the way I want and not the way they might want. Believe me; I will take whatever swift actions I can to get this over with, as long as it doesn't expose the people involved. I hope I am through this in less than a week.

"This bogus processing plant is run by a man named Sumar Nalithy. I haven't met him, but from what Phillips says about him, he may be the devil in disguise. I intend to one day pull his tonsils out through his nose, just to start. I will show him what disregard for human life is like. Before he leaves this earth, he is going to see hell, even if he isn't the devil."

With that emotional cry out of his body, Axel quieted down. He and Tori held each other, talking about how much they loved each other and how much they would miss each other. Then they both got up and started walking toward the bedroom. The next few hours were full of love and more love. Afterward, as he lay in the bed looking up at the ceiling, Axel thought, *Boy, it's almost worth getting her shook up when I get that kind of payback afterward. God is she beautiful, with or without her clothes on. I sure am lucky.*

The next morning, Axel was awakened by the phone ringing in his body. It was Kim. "Axel, I got a place for Tori to stay in San Mateo not far from the bridge. It is a great new apartment building, and I have a nice suite picked out for her. She should drive there the first thing this morning with whatever she needs for a week. We don't want her going back to your house for anything during the next week. After that, we may decide to go for another week. It's all depends on what happens with Sumar Nalithy and his crew. When she gets there, tell her to ask for the private suite set up by Brian Adams. She is not to e-mail you, and she can only call you on your private phone." Kim gave Axel the directions to the apartment and warned Axel that he was to stay away from the place.

With that settled, Axel was able to breathe a sigh of relief. Now he was free to put himself straight into the plot. The first thing he had to do was seek out Phillips and just stay with him, asking questions. Sooner or later Sumar would want to know why they were spending so much time together.

After Tori left, Axel went to Aortica to see how things were going. He was only there for a short time when he got a call on his internal phone. It was Philips. He had borrowed a phone and wanted to give the number to Axel. Axel told him he was working on verifying Philips's story and would get back to him. Only a few minutes passed before his phone rang again. This time it was Kim. He told Axel three agents were watching each of Philips's children. They hadn't spotted anyone else watching the kids, but hoped to do so in the next day or two.

Axel felt like the plan was coming together quite rapidly. *I hope they make connections by tomorrow,* he thought. *I have to find out from Phillips more information on how Sumar's people keep each other informed, as well as how Sumar contacts them.* Axel was too excited about his plan, so he decided to leave work and contact Phillips, start the ball rolling in that direction. He called Phillips on his new phone and told him he would like to drive over to his lab and talk to him a little more about the subject they had discussed the night before. Phillips agreed, saying he was glad he was able to pour this thing out of his system. He had not been able to talk to anyone about this issue for the year it had existed.

Axel gave his name to the receptionist—different from the night before —at the front desk. She directed him to Mr. Phillip's office, saying he was expecting Axel. Actually, Philips's office was empty, so Axel sat down and waited. After a few minutes, Phillips walked in.

"Hi there, Axel," he said. "I don't know how you want to handle this, so maybe you can let me know."

Figuring the office might be bugged, Axel winked at Phillips and waved his arm toward the door. "I just want to go over the process steps with you, so I know where you are on the Aortica process."

Understanding the hand signals, Philips points toward the door leading to the hall. "Yes, Axel. I will be glad to review that with you."

Out in the hall, the two men walked toward the process area. Axel whispered to Phillips that his office was probably bugged. Phillips asked if Axel was going to help him get out of this problem without any harm to his family. Axel replied that he was taking some steps, but he couldn't tell Philips what they were.

"I think you should go on with your work and anything else you are doing with these people. You should treat me like someone who probably knows how to solve the problems on the nanoparticles, and you are trying to get that information from me. I want you to bribe me or do anything that you would normally do, and let's see how this plays out. I want them to eventually believe I have the secrets to their success. Then I'll let them make the first move."

That said, Axel asked quietly, "How does Sumar signal the guards watching your children?"

Philips explained that Sumar carried a small electronic device that automatically sent out a signal every hour. When the signal was sent, a small LED light turned on in the face of the electronic device. The guards were supposed to signal back within fifteen minutes. When they did that, his device recorded it and automatically turned off the light.

"If the guards don't get a signal from Sumar," Philips went on, "they are to wait one more hour. If they still don't receive a signal, they know something has happened to Sumar and they are to … to …" Philips faltered, and then said, "They are to kill my children. If Sumar wants them to take action, he hits the signal four times. In addition to this automatic signaling, Sumar also sends out a different signal at noon, four, eight, and midnight to let them know he is okay."

Axel nodded to show that he understood. "Now we should go back to your office, and you should push me for information on the process changes required to get the Aortica process working here at Antigenic."

Once they entered Philips's office, Phillips said, "Look, it seems like you know the Aortica process quite well, but you still haven't given me a clue that you know the steps to take to make the process a complete success."

"That's right," Axel said. "I haven't given you a clue about the process changes, but I haven't heard anything from you yet on what I would get out of providing you that information."

"I have to research that a little to see what I can get for you. I am sure it will be worth your time. You won't be disappointed," Phillips said.

"Well, when you get a better feeling on what you can do for me, call me. I will be interested to find out. I guess I'll be on my way."

"I thought by now we had a mutual understanding of what I need, and that you would be justly rewarded."

Without further comment, Axel left the office. While driving back to Aortica, he got on the phone with Kim and told him about the conversation with Philips, especially the signals he used with the men watching Philips's two children.

"Now that we know this combination of signals, we can handle this several ways. First and most important, we have to wait to see what actions Sumar takes against me. I am sure Philips's office is bugged, and they will be sending someone to see me soon. I haven't figured out how I will handle that yet. Anyhow, I will go to my internal phone so you know what is happening at the time. One thing I know for sure is that we have to handle it from this end first. I need to find out what Sumar wants the nanoparticles for. In the meantime, if your agents make the three men at the two schools, and if at any time we want to take an action against them, it has to be done simultaneously at both sites. I gather only one agent watches each child at a time. So if we decide to take them out, whatever agents are on duty at that time must be taken out simultaneously; in Syracuse and Pittsburgh, and their signal systems taken. Then your agents have to be prepared to take out the number two agents at the two schools simultaneously when they come on duty. Then they have to take out the number three agents in the same way. The sequence of these actions is very important. We must be able to nullify any actions by those guards."

"I understand what you are saying," Kim said, "and I will let you know when my people are in position to take any action. Now what about you? What happens when Sumar takes his fifteen men or so from their facility and assaults you?"

"Don't worry about that. I'm warming up to that issue. I know eventually I'll have to deal with these people while you take care of the men watching the kids. Keep me up to date."

After Axel left Aortica at the end of the day, he went to eat at a restaurant not far from his home in Palo Alto. On his way back to his place, he saw that a car was following him. *It didn't take them long to get on my ass,* he thought. He wondered if he should nail these people now, or let them take him to Sumar. He'd have to go sooner or later, but he'd prefer to delay it a day or so. That would give Kim's people more time to get their thing done. *When I hear from Kim that we're watching the watchmen,* he decided, *I can afford to be a hard ass; but not tonight.*

He continued on to his place. When he arrived, he said to his internal control, "Axelvation two, hood down." and felt the energy rush. As he got out of his car, the car that has been following him pulled up behind him. Two men got out and walked over to him.

"Okay, guy with the answers," the bigger one said, "Sumar wants to see you."

Axel looked at the two of them and asked, "Who is Sumar?"

The second one stepped up and said in a nasty voice, "Sumar is your new boss."

Axel studied the young man and the ape who was with him. "I don't know Sumar, and he's not my boss."

"He's your new boss," the bigger guy said, moving closer.

Axel stepped back. "I think you have me mixed up with someone else. I don't know anyone named Sumar. It sounds like a name you guys made up. If I were you two dingalings, I would get back in my car and go find another person to bother. I just want you guys to know that I have taken karate lessons and I am dangerous."

The two guys looked at each other and started laughing. "He takes karate lessons," they both shouted.

Axel held one finger up to his mouth. "Quiet. Some people are sleeping around here."

The two guys were still laughing, but then the big man tried to grab Axel's arm. Axel slapped his arm down, but not too hard.

"Is that all you got, karate expert?" the big guy yelled. He tried to grab Axel's arm again, and Axel pounded his arm a little harder this time. The big guy growled. "Oh, so the little boy wants to play patty cake. Well, let's see what you can do with this."

He reached out to grab Axel with both his hands, but Axel swiftly grasped his arms and pinned them to his sides. The big guy laughed, apparently thinking he could easily break loose from this hold, but when he tried to pull his arms free, nothing happened. His arms were held tight against his body, and he began grimacing from the pain.

Axel leaned close and whispered in his ear, "I think you and your punk friend ought to go on your way and find some little kid to do battle with."

As the big guy continued to struggle, his buddy finally realized he really couldn't move his arms. He started to pull out his gun, but Axel picked the big guy up and threw him against the other man before he could get his gun free. The two fell to the ground with a painful sounding thud. Yelling and angry, they get up. Before they could charge Axel, he grabbed each one by an arm and snapped it downward. He could hear bones cracking in each arm. They screamed in pain. Axel took the gun from the smaller guy, and reached in the inside pocket of the big fellow's jacket and took his gun.

"I don't think you need these now. If you're quiet, I'll go in and call 911 and have them send an ambulance out to take care of you. I don't think you want to be trying to do anything with those arms for a while."

While he talked to them, he called 911 from his internal phone and told the dispatcher that two men had been attacked, and their arms looked like they were broken. As he walked toward his house, he told the men the ambulance should be there within minutes. "I will tell them you were attacked by a gang of teenagers, and I expect for you to leave me out of the conversation. Good night to you."

Sumar had sent two of his bodyguards to pick up this new guy in the game, but the two men did not return with him. Sumar asked another bodyguard, Rummel, to see if he could find out what happened. About an hour went by before Rummel told him the two guys were in the hospital with broken arms. Sumar told Rummel to go to the hospital and find out what happened. When Rummel called from the hospital, he told Sumar that the new guy had used some karate on them and had broken an arm on each of the two guys.

Furious, Sumar called Philips. "Philips, this is Sumar. I know there is a new guy you're trying to get information from. What's his name?"

"His name is Axel Tressler. He has a doctor's degree in biology, and Aortica hired him to consult with them. I've been trying to find out the details from him of his work with them. I don't think they've incorporated any of his ideas yet, but he is smart and I think he will help them."

"I want you to call him tomorrow," Sumar said, "and have him come out to your office. Then bring him to my facility. I want to get to this guy."

"I'll bring him to you tomorrow. I think he is breakable, but he is smart, so don't let him outfox any of your guys."

"Don't waste any time with him tomorrow. Don't tell him about anyone in my group. If this guy gets word from you and tries to protect your two kids, I will know and I will take action against them."

Philips said he knew that, and he wouldn't do anything to deter Axel's getting to the facility. After he hung up, Philips thought about what had happened so far. He still didn't see how Axel was going to be of any help. What could one man do against so many?

The next day Philips called Axel at Aortica and said he wanted to see him right away. Axel told him he would be there in about an hour. Philips called Sumar to tell him that.

Sumar had already been busy on the phone that morning. He had called the hospital and talked to Bruta, the big guy who had confronted Axel the night before. Bruta told him exactly what happened, and advised Sumar to warn his other men to be cautious around Axel.

Sumar made a few calls, but no one he talked to knew anything about Axel Tressler. *The guy was just lucky last night,* Sumar thought. *We will see what happens when he comes to the plant today. I will be ready for him.*

As Axel drove to Antigenics, he was fairly certain what was going on. Philips was going to try to convince him, in his bugged office, to go to the lab where the nanoparticles were being made. Sumar probably had got to him and was pressuring him to make that move. That was okay with Axel, because that's what he wanted to happen. He needed to meet Sumar and get a better feel for him and his whole organization, so he could figure out how to take them down without Philips' kids getting harmed.

Wondering how things were going on that end, he called Kim on his internal phone.

"Things are going well," Kim said in answer to his question. "We have all of Sumar's watchmen under surveillance on a twenty-four hour basis. We are doing everything except getting in bed with them."

"That's great Kim. I am on my way to meet Sumar. I intend to take it easy today and let him try to bargain with me. I don't think they will try any rough stuff today, but tomorrow they will, because I will push the issue. So tomorrow you should plan to have your men take these watchmen like we discussed."

"My guys will do their part," Kim promised.

Axel explained his plan to Kim. "If I take Sumar tomorrow just after his noon call to the guards, it will be three in the afternoon in Syracuse and Pittsburgh. Your guys should be ready to move in then. I will take Sumar's electronic device and send the next hourly signal. If the light stays on, I'll know your guys have done their job. They will just have to stay on the job for each shift change, so they can nab each of the three guards at both schools. If things go right we will have put this to bed by tomorrow evening."

"That sounds like a good plan to me. I will get hold of each of the six men on this and give them this schedule. They will be happy to put the cuffs on these six guys."

When he arrived at Antigenics, Axel proceeded directly to Philips's office. "You wanted to see me?" he asked Philips.

"Yes. I wanted to know if you've thought any more about the money you could make just by providing us the key to the nanoparticle processing," Phillips said.

"I've thought about it," Axel said, "but I haven't seen anything material to make me believe it's a fact."

"It's a fact," replied Phillips. "I want to take you to see the man who is going to make this offer real. He's at the new building I showed you the other day. Let's get my car and take a ride over."

Axel agreed, and soon they were at the small concrete building. As they walked toward the building, Axel gave his internal energy control the Axelvation two signal and felt the energy surge to his body. He then decided to have his hood also come down. As they entered the building, they were met by a large and rather ugly-looking Asian man. He let out a large roaring laughter and a loud greeting.

"Hello there! You must be the man who is going to solve my problems."

"And what problems are those?" Axel asked mockingly.

"Why, the ones that are keeping my nanoparticle process from being a success," the big man said.

Philips interrupted to introduce the two men. "Axel, this is Sumar Nalithy. I told you about him. He is the one who wants to purchase the process fixes from you. Sumar, Dr. Axel Tressler."

"Oh, yes," Axel said. "Two men last night told me that a man named Sumar wanted to see me. That was rather an awful way to try to get me over here. This way is much better. By the way, do you have a candy machine here? I need some energy and I would like a soda. I am hungry and dry."

Axel had a grin on his face, and he could tell that Sumar wasn't happy with his antics, but Sumar said, "Yes, there are a candy machine and a soda machine here. My secretary will take you to them, and then she will bring you to my office so we can talk."

Axel bought some candy bars and a soda, and then the secretary took him to the office. As they walked, Axel decided to call Kim on his internal phone so he could listen to everything that went on. When Kim answered, he said, "I want you to listen and record what goes on in this office. Get every word of it," pleaded Axel. "I also have to tell you that the guy not only sounds like the devil, but he looks worse. He is big and round, and has his hair glued down and over his forehead like Hitler use to wear his. He has a grin that is mean looking. He could win a dog fight with those teeth. It is going to be a pleasure to jam that mouth of his closed when the time comes."

In Sumar's office, while Philips remained quiet, the conversation quickly turned toward the subject of the nanoparticles

"Do you really know what it takes to make this process a success?" asked Sumar.

"Yes, I know what it takes to make that completion. I have watched the process at Aortica and I can see what needs to be done for a single nanoparticle to be derived from the process flow."

Sumar tried to coax the details from Axel, but Axel refused. Finally he said, "I understand that you will pay me handsomely for the process changes."

Sumar smiled and said, "Yes, we would pay you handsomely if those changes work."

"What does handsomely mean?"

"We would be willing to reward you with a million dollars," Sumar said with that evil smile on his face.

I sure would like to bash that smile off his face, Axel thought. *Sooner or later, I will.* "Why do you want this process so much?" he asked. "It makes nanoparticles. What would you do with nanoparticles?"

"I am sure you know where these nanoparticles would have a major impact," Sumar said. "I think you are playing a game with us when you make those remarks."

"No, I am not playing a game," Axel said. "I would like to know where you intend to use these nanoparticles."

"I will pay you a million dollars, and that is what you will get from me," said Sumar. "I don't have to tell you where I am going to use them."

Axel knew he was getting under Sumar's skin, and he liked the way the conversation was going. So he continued. "Where are you going to use these? Are you going to do good or bad with them?"

"We don't know where we are going to use them. We know there will be a big market for them. That is why Aortica is working so hard on this process and being supported by the government. That is why they are paying you to consult with them. These devices have a terrific market."

Again Axel tried to push Sumar's button. "Good or bad?" he repeated.

"Everything is relative when it comes to good or bad," claimed Sumar. "What do you call good or bad, Axel?"

Axel picked up a candy bar, tore the wrapper off, and took a big bite. He drank some soda, taking his time. He was ready to say something, but decided to have another bite of the candy bar. "I guess," he finally said, "I consider it good when I get two million dollars, and I consider it bad if you use the nanoparticles to do something against my country."

Sumar squirmed in the chair, and then got up and walked around the room. "I am losing my patience with you," he said, looking at Axel.

Axel finished his candy bar and reached down to pick up another one. "This is good candy," he said, biting into the second one. "You should try some to soothe your nerves." He chewed and swallowed, and then said, "You want these nanoparticles so you can harm people, don't you?"

Sumar looked ready to burst from frustration. "Yes," he shouted. "I am going to use them as a weapon. What do you think of that?"

"I think you should have said that to begin with instead of beating around the bush. If you want them to hurt people, that is your business. But how do I know that I am going to get two million dollars? How about showing me some money now?"

Sumar's body instantly went from tense to relaxed, as if he were a puppy that had just been given a promised treat. "You want to see money? Is that it?" he asked.

Axel smiled. "That's what this is all about, isn't it? Where's the money?"

Sumar sat back down behind his desk. "I will show you the money tomorrow. I won't show you two million, but I will show you one million dollars."

"Now you're talking," Axel said. "You will pay me two million dollars to provide you with the information you need so you can kill people with these nanoparticles. You will pay me one million of that two million tomorrow. Is that correct?"

Sumar looked up at the ceiling and purred like a cat. "Yes, I will pay you one million dollars to start and the other million when I see the results."

Axel kept egging him on, so that Kim got all the details. "What do I have to do tomorrow, and what do you mean by seeing the results?"

Sumar looked at Axel, his expression dead serious. "I will list this out for you. One, you bring the process changes that will allow the present process to put out individual nanoparticles, and two, I will pay you one million dollars. Then three, we will see if the process makes single nanoparticles. Four, we will see if we can inject something into the particles. Five, when we are successful in injecting what we want into the particles, we will, six, experiment to see if the doped particles do what we want them to perform. And seven, if that is successful; you will get the second million dollars."

"I don't know what items four through six mean in your list," Axel said.

"They mean exactly what I said they mean," said Sumar. "Just having nanoparticles is not the name of the game. It goes beyond that."

"I guess I thought I was going to get two million dollars for providing you with a process that makes singular, individual nanoparticles. We never talked about doping them with anything. Sounds like you're roping me into something I didn't agree to. Am I going to get two million dollars for providing you the information on how to get singular nanoparticles?"

Axel watched as Sumar's face turned red. He obviously was not used to being challenged. Sumar paused for a moment before answering, as if he needed to control himself. "I am not going to pay you two million dollars just to gain the way to produce singular nanoparticles. I want all the information I just listed."

Axel took another candy bar out of his pocket and started eating it. "Are you going to pay me one million dollars tomorrow to have the process for making singular nanoparticles, and then another million dollars to help you develop a way for you to kill people? Is that what this has been about?"

"Yes, that's what it has been about, Axel. I will pay you one million dollars tomorrow for the process to generate millions of singular nanoparticles, and I will pay you another million dollars to show me how to add ingredients into the nanoparticles that will make them deadly and able to kill humans. Now, is that clear enough?"

Axel took another bite of his candy bar. "It sounds like we started out where you were going to pay me two million dollars to provide you the process to successfully produce singular nanoparticles, and then you changed it to adding those other things, and I still only get two million dollars. Seems to me I need an extra million dollars to take this to the level where it can kill people. Now that makes sense."

Sumar stared at Axel for a good five seconds before he said a word. Then he calmly said, "Yes, you are right. I will pay you one million dollars tomorrow for you to provide the means for obtaining singular nanoparticles. Then I will pay you another million when we actually produce singular nanoparticles. After that, I will pay you another million dollars when you provide us with the means of injecting material into the nanoparticles that makes them deadly enough to kill people. That's a total of three million dollars. Are we clear on that now?"

Axel knew he had enough on record at Kim's office to make his case that this creature, Sumar Nalithy, wanted to develop a biological means of killing people.

"I think we have an agreement," he told Sumar. "I will come tomorrow and deliver the process for producing singular nanoparticles. I would expect that you will be able to prove this within a few days."

"A few days?" Sumar repeated.

Axel explained that he would have to procure certain equipment and set it up. He estimated that would take four days. Producing the singular nanoparticles would probably take another two days.

"Finally!" Sumar exclaimed. "Finally we have an agreement." With that he jumped around and almost danced around the room. Then he turned to Axel and asked, "What time tomorrow will you bring the process changes?"

"I will bring them at exactly twelve thirty in the afternoon. Will you have one million dollars tomorrow at twelve thirty in the afternoon?"

Sumar looked almost shocked, and proclaimed, "I am a man of my word. When I say I will have a million dollars at twelve thirty in the afternoon, I will have your million dollars."

Perfect, Axel thought. He had Sumar committed to twelve thirty, which was what he wanted. It would be after he had given out his noon signal, so Kim's men could start moving on the watchmen in Syracuse and Pittsburgh.

Axel stood up and walked over to Sumar to shake his hand. He made sure he squeezed his hand so tight that Sumar winced, almost crying out in pain.

"My God," he exclaimed when Axel released his hand. "You sure do have a strong grip. That must be how you broke my men's arms last night."

"Oh," Axel said. "I always forget that my hands are strong from training. I've had many a person tell me that I shake hands fairly roughly. Sorry about that." He walked toward the door. "I get to see the million dollars before you get to see the process tomorrow. So have it ready." With that he smiled and walked out.

As Axel got in his car, he began to talk to Kim, who was still on the line. "Did you get all of that on tape?" he asked.

"Yes, we did," replied Kim. "You did a great job of dragging that out of him. It amounted to a confession of what he intends to do with the nanoparticle program."

"So I am set to go back at twelve thirty tomorrow and put an end to this whole deal. This should be after he gives his noon signal to the watchmen at the two universities. It'll be three thirty your time when I meet with Sumar. Are you ready, or do I have to get any additional information from Sumar?"

It was quiet for a few seconds. "I am thinking," Kim said. The silence continued for another minute. "Axel, the only thing you might want to do is make the one million dollar payoff evident tomorrow, so that it is known that he really wanted to pay for the stolen information. You know that he is going to try to kill you when you don't give him the information he wants?"

"Yes, I know they will try to kill me tomorrow, and I will have to defend myself. The threat to kill me will be recorded by you, and that will be another piece of evidence against him. I will be able to take care of myself. However, I want to make sure you are holding up your end and will have the watchmen taken care of. I will probably have time to ask you on my private line just before the twelve thirty debacle whether the action has started out there."

Again it was quiet for a few seconds, and then Kim said, "I just got an idea. I will have the men that are arresting the watchmen have bugs on them. That way you can listen in. Can your internal computer handle listening to them while going on with what you are doing?"

"My computer will handle two lines at the same time," Axel said. "I just will hear the one that you mentioned as an incoming signal, and you will be handling my output as an outgoing signal. I will listen to what is happening and I don't have to listen to what I am doing. You do."

"I hope my guys can take these watchmen without any shots being fired. I'm the lucky one. I can have you on your line coming into one phone, while I can be listening to my men arresting these watchmen on another phone. I'll record both calls, and one of these days, you and I can sit down and listen to them being played simultaneously. Won't that be a laugh?"

Axel laughed. "And I agree. I hope the only guns fired are the ones on my end. I'll call you tomorrow and see if you've thought of anything else I need to do."

The following day Axel prepared to go to Sumar's facility. He had never considered taking the process changes to Sumar. He was going to play a ruse on Sumar, just to have some fun with him and, he hoped, embarrass him in front of his men. He had considered taking Philips with him, but decided it was too dangerous. Sumar was going to be very irritated. Still, Axel called Philips to tell him he was going to be at Sumar's at twelve thirty.

"Today," he added, "your concerns about your children and family will be eliminated."

"I don't understand," Philips said nervously. "How can your visit to Sumar's facility affect my children's safety?"

"I can't tell you the details at this time, but I promise to tell you this evening. Is that okay?"

Philips said it was, and then added, "I still don't see how you can have that effect on my children, but I can wait till this evening to find out. I have suffered through this for a year now, and I can wait another day. I wish you luck for whatever you intend to do today. I will pray for your safety."

"Thank you very much." After he hung up with Philips, Axel called Kim and asked him how things were going.

"As planned," Kim answered. "In the next hour or so you will be listening to what's happening with my men at the two universities."

"That's great. And you'll be listening to me in Sumar's office, getting his goat, so to speak."

"That's one scenario I wish I could watch, but I am happy that I am going to hear it. While we're on the phone," Kim continued, "I wanted to ask you how things are going at Aortica."

Axel explained all the things he has seen there recently, and he believed the scientists loved the new process. "They are making good singular nanoparticles, and they're considering new experiments to try to add new features to the process."

"That all sounds good," Kim said. "Remember, after you're done there, I want you to visit the start-up in Boston. There was that death on the East Coast that might be explained by the nanoparticle program they have going, and some rogue group that has confiscated their process and mishandled it."

"Yes," said Axel. "I have been so involved with what I'm doing here, the Boston company slipped my mind. We'll have to discuss that later. By the way, when can we have Tori return to our house?"

"That's up to you," Kim said. "You should know after your visit to Sumar today whether you have completely eliminated him and his men as a threat."

"No one has asked me any questions about my private life," Axel said, "so they may not know about Tori. I think she has been out of the equation, and the only one who can include her is Sumar, and he will be out of the picture soon. If I continue to believe that, I will probably bring her back tomorrow."

Kim agreed, and they said good-bye. All his loose ends tied up, Axel headed for Sumar's. He arrived at the facility about a minute before the twelve-thirty meeting. As he parked the car, he commanded, "Axelvation two, hood down," and felt the energy flow through his body. He was about to get out of the car when he heard the phone click on. Two men were talking about this being the time when they should now approach the watchmen and take them out. Carrying a small brown paper bag, Axel listened intently as he entered the facility. The receptionist told him to go directly to Sumar's office. He thanked her and handed her a folded piece of paper. Written on the outside of the note was, "Don't open till 12:45." Inside Axel had written, "I want you to leave the building immediately. Do not talk to anyone. Do not inform Sumar. This is for your safety. A legal and government action is about to take place."

In Sumar's office, Sumar asked him if he would like to have anything before proceeding. Axel held up his brown paper bag as he sat down, saying that he had picked up some candy bars and didn't need anything more.

"Then why don't we begin?" Sumar said. Axel nodded and said, "Let's see the money."

Sumar didn't like the abruptness of Axel's remark and said so. He picked up the phone, dialed a number, and said something in a voice too low for Axel to hear. Then Sumar hung up the phone and said that two of his men would bring in the money in a few minutes. Since they had to wait, Axel took the opportunity to listen more intently to the conversations going on at the two university sites.

"Excuse me, sir," he heard one of Kim's agents say, "we're with the U.S. government and that is a pistol in your back. My partner is going to frisk you for weapons. Please do not try to stop him or I will shoot you. Go ahead, James."

It was quiet for about thirty seconds, and then James said, "Just this one gun in his inside vest."

"Cuff him, James. Now tell me," the first agent continued, "when is your partner due to arrive? You might as well tell us, because we know what you three men have been doing here and we will get your partner sooner or later. It's best for you if you cooperate with us."

"My partner is due within the next five minutes," Sumar's man said. "He's meeting me here."

"Good. Now I'm putting a cloth over your hands so he can't see the cuffs. We're going to move away, and I want you just to stand still and say nothing. Do you understand?"

"Yes, I understand."

"We're going to step back, out of sight, but if anything wrong happens, we have a sharpshooter on the roof across the way. He has a direct sight on you, and he will shoot to kill if you try to communicate with your partner in any way. Do you understand?"

"Yes."

It was silent for about a minute, and then Axel heard, "Here comes the other guard, James. Let's go."

Axel heard a muffled exclamation from another man, and then James said, "Do not move, sir. We are government agents. Put up your hands while we frisk you for any weapons."

Another thirty seconds of silence, and then James again. "I found a gun in his shoulder holster, one in his ankle holster, and a switchblade in his rear pants pocket."

"Wonderful," the first agent said. "Sounds like you were ready for a war instead of just shooting a student, little man. Cuff him, James.

"Dr. Kim, we have both of the suspects in custody. Are there any other actions we need to take at this time?"

"Great," Kim said. "Just transport them to the jail. After that, I want you to get Stephen Philips and take him to a safe place until I get back to you. I don't want anything to go wrong while getting the third guy."

"Yes, sir. We look forward to your next commands."

"Did you hear all of that, Axel?" Kim asked.

"Yes, I did," replied Axel.

"The other situation at Pittsburgh went off just as well. I recorded it and will let you listen to it when you have the time."

"That's reassuring to me. I've got to go. My million dollars just arrived."

Two men brought three boxes into Sumar's office and set them down on his desk. "There's your one million dollars in unmarked hundred dollar bills," Sumar said. "Take a look."

Sumar took the lids off the boxes, and Axel peered at the most money he had ever seen in one place.

"It looks like money, it smells like money, it must be money," he said.

"Yes, it is, a million dollars worth. Now what do you have for me?" asked Sumar.

Axel picked up the brown paper bag he had set on the floor next to his chair. At the same time he pulled a candy bar from his jacket pocket, unwrapped it, and took a bite. Of course, this got on Sumar's nerves, which was what Axel wanted, although Sumar managed to stay fairly calm. Axel reached into the brown bag and took out a ceramic bowl. He placed it on Sumar's desk and said, "There's your answer."

Sumar looked at Axel and began to laugh. "I know you are just pulling my string, as you say in this country. That is not what I am paying you a million dollars for. Now let's get serious."

Axel looked at Sumar. "This is serious."

"What do you mean by that?" Sumar shouted.

"I mean, this is the answer to your problem. This is it."

Sumar got up and walked in a circle. He turned and shouted, "I want to know what this shiny bowl has to do with solving my problem. Do you think I am nuts?"

"No, I don't think you are nuts, you are crazy with terrorism. That's your problem. You want to see people get killed. I want to stop you, but it seems like I can't."

Again, Sumar walked around the room, his face almost glowing red with his anger. "All right, I will play your silly game. How does this solve the problem?"

Axel took another bite of his candy bar. "When you have the nanoparticles in suspension, you let the suspension fall into this ceramic bowl. The nanoparticles can fit through the minute holes in the bowl, and they pass through it one by one. They, therefore, become separate nanoparticles."

Sumar stared up at the ceiling as if he could find answers there. When he turned back to Axel, he had a look of superiority on his face. "This doesn't solve the problem. If the nanoparticles fall through the ceramic bowl, how do I catch them without them losing their characteristics?" Axel finished his candy bar and threw the wrapper in the wastebasket next to Sumar's desk. Looking at Sumar, he smiled. "I told you I would solve your problem. Your problem is getting singular nanoparticles, and this will do that. How you handle them after that is your problem."

Sumar pounded his fists on the desk. "I know you know more than that. I have informants who tell me you have added several steps to the Aortica process, and they have stable nanoparticles. Now, either you tell me or you don't get the million dollars."

"I didn't ask for the money to tell you how to do anything more than I've told you, including how to pound your fists on the desk," Axel said calmly.

Sumar smacked the desk again and shouted, "Tell me the rest of the story! Tell me the rest of the story!"

"Look," Axel said. "You can thump on that desk until it falls apart and it won't get you anywhere. You have my bowl and I have your money." With that, Axel stood and replaced the covers on the three boxes, as though he was going to walk out of there with the money.

"Just what do you think you're doing?" Sumar yelled.

"I thought you wanted to give this money to charity. In fact, they just had an earthquake in Haiti, and I thought you wanted to grant this charitable donation to that country to help them out with their terrible problems."

Sumar laughed. He laughed so hard, he had a hard time staying upright. When he had the laughter under control, he looked at his two henchmen and told them to take the boxes of money out of the room. When they reached for the boxes, Axel pounded his fist on the desk. The desk split in two, and the boxes slide toward the middle of the broken desk. Sumar stared, looking like he couldn't believe his eyes.

"That," Axel said "is how you pound on a desk when you want someone's attention."

As the two henchmen stared in awe, Sumar put his hand in his inner jacket pocket.

That must be where his electronic device is located! Alex thought. He grabbed Sumar's wrists, holding one arm immobile as he pulled the other hand out of his pocket. As he suspected, Sumar was holding an electronic device. Axel released the other wrist and grabbed the electronic device. He slipped it into his pants pocket while smiling at Sumar.

"What are you?" Sumar shouted. "Some kind of magician, or what? What is going on here?"

Axel released his hand. "I just wanted to make sure your watchmen at the universities don't take any actions against anyone. I wanted this to be just between you and me."

"What do you mean, between you and me?"

"Just what I said. This is just between you and me. No children in this game."

"Do you think that taking that device from me keeps anyone safe? Do you think I would be so dumb as to rely on that device alone? Do you think that without that device, anyone I have in my sights is safe? In fact, without the device, in a given time frame, those two kids will be killed."

Axel nodded. "Right; if four hours go by without a signal from your electronic device, Stephen and Janice are supposed to be killed. But that's not going to happen."

Sumar frowned. "What are you talking about?"

"Your thugs at the two universities have been taken into custody. And both Stephen and Janice are being held in a safe place, away from any harm from you. All your cards have been trumped. You have lost. You have no leverage over me or over Philips."

"And why do you think you are safe?" Sumar asked. He gestured to one of his bodyguards, who left the room. "When he comes back, it will be with fifteen other men, and they will be armed."

Axel smiled. "Thanks, I've been waiting to get all of your assholes together in one place. Now we'll celebrate lunch break together."

Sumar smiled as well, a nasty smile. "You are a smart-ass, and I am going to enjoy the next couple of hours."

"What makes you think you're going to last that long?" Axel asked, just as the door to the office. The first bodyguard walked back in with four guards Axel had seen on the first day. He took another candy bar from his pocket and started eating it.

Sumar gaped at him. "Aren't you being a little cool when you see six of my men in here, ready to take you apart little by little?"

Axel took another bite of the candy bar. "You haven't seen me running anywhere. I'm surprised that by this time, you're still that dumb and think that six guys will be able to handle me. I think you better call in the rest of your crew. I'm going to get them sooner or later. But maybe it is smart. Those lab guys probably aren't part of your killing scheme. They're just good technical people earning a living."

Sumar ignored that comment. "Grab this asshole," he commanded. "Take off his clothes and stretch him out over on the conference table. We'll take our time with him to make sure he realizes the ignorance of his ways."

Axel allowed two men to grab him and flip him onto the table. He didn't struggle as they pulled off his shoes, pants, and shirt, and then held him down, his arms and legs stretched out. Sumar walked over and smiled down at him.

"Axel my friend, we could stop all this if you decide to tell me exactly how to make this process for singular nanoparticles a viable one."

Axel looked up at him. "I wouldn't give you the time of the day if your life depended on it."

"You haven't understood, Axel," Sumar said, his voice rising. "It's your life that depends on it!" He walked over to his desk and pulled out a whip from a drawer. "Maybe this will help to open your mind and your mouth."

Just to show Axel a sample of the power of the whip, Sumar snapped it at a statue in the corner of his office. The head of the statue fell to the floor. He walked back to the table, where Axel was held down, spread-eagle. "You have ten more seconds to think about this whip slicing into your skin. I will enjoy this, and I believe you will be spitting out those candy bars you have been downing in front of me."

The ten seconds passed, and all that has happened was that Axel's gaze at Sumar became more intense. Sumar reached back with the whip and snapped it across Axel's chest. Nothing happened. There was no mark on Axel's skin. He didn't even flinch. Puzzled, Sumar stuck Axel again, whipping Axel's chest three more times. Then, as if out of desperation, he struck at Axel's legs and his feet. All that happened was the sound of the whip snapping. Sumar shook his head in disbelief while the other men stared in confusion.

Sumar threw the whip against the wall and asked for the AK-47 assault rifle one man had across his shoulders. Holding the rifle by the barrel, he raised it over his head and brought it down as if it were an ax. The rifle smashed squarely on Axel's chest and snapped in two. Sumar couldn't believe it. Running out into the hall, he yelled, "All you men come in here. I need some help."

In less than a minute, eleven men had run into the office. They all stopped and stared at Axel, stretched out on the table with four men holding his arms and legs.

Sumar pointed to the newcomers. "I want two of each of you to hold this man's legs or arms down. He is an enemy of our country. With three of you holding each limb, I want you to pull until his arms come off and his legs are torn from his body."

The men looked at Sumar like he was nuts. None of them moved. Sumar grabbed another AK-47 from a different henchman and pointed it at the eleven men. "If you don't do what I just said, I will begin to shoot each of you. Do you understand? At the count of three, I will begin shooting. One …"

Apparently believing Sumar meant what he said, the men all but run to the conference table.

Axel decided it was time to end this charade. He didn't want innocent men hurt because of him. He pulled his hands and legs from the grips of the men holding him like they weren't there. As he leaped off the table, toward Sumar, Sumar began firing. The AK-47's bullets bounced off Axel's chest. Sumar emptied the clip and tossed the assault rifle aside. Screaming in frustration, he grabbed another AK-47.

"If you come toward me," he shouted, "I will start killing the men who just came in!"

Four men still had AK-47s, and they aimed those weapons at Axel. The other two men pulled out pistols and took aim as well.

Axel took Sumar's threat seriously. He leaped in the air, over Sumar, and landed behind him. He grabbed Sumar's arms as the six men who had been aiming at him opened fire.

"Don't shoot!" Sumar shouted, but it was too late. The bullets tore into Sumar's body while the eleven men ran out of the room. Axel dropped Sumar's body and dove at two of the henchmen, his arms outstretched. His fists hit the men directly in the chests, and they fell, their chests crushed. Axel leaped over the table as the other men continued to fire fruitlessly at him. Grabbing two of the men's heads, he twisted them completely around. Their bodies fell to the floor like two damp cloths. That left two more men, who were still firing at him. The bullets were no more deadly than the previous shots. They ricocheted off Axel's chest and flew directly back at the men, piercing their bodies. All of a sudden it was quiet in the office. Axel picked up his clothes and started putting them back on.

"Did you hear all of that?" he asked Kim on his internal phone.

"I sure did." replied Kim. "That son of a bitch was evil from his head to his toes. I'll send some of my men out to clean up the place and close the line immediately."

"I think you should have the eleven men who work on the line sent back to their home countries. I don't believe they knew what they were involved in, but we can't take any chances. A couple of them may have similar grievances against this country. Of course, you know how to handle this better than I do, so I am out of this. I'll go over and see Philips and tell him his kids are safe. I assume you are taking care of the third watchman at each of these college locations."

"Yes, you go ahead and talk to Philips. We'll have the last of Sumar's men in custody by midnight. As usual, you did a great job on this, Axel."

"About those eleven men," said Axel. I think I will go tell them that we want them to return to work tomorrow. That way your men can take them as a group, and then you can decide what to do with them. They know a great deal about this process, and you might not want them carrying that information back to other areas. You might have your men talk to them and see if something could be worked out as an extension to the Aortica line, or they could add some qualified ones to the Aortica line. That's another thing to keep on your plate and for you to decide."

Axel was feeling good as he walked into the Antigen building and asked for Mr. Philips. The receptionist called Philips's secretary, and within a minute the secretary came to get Axel and take him to Philips's office. As he walked into the office, Axel smiled broadly at the other man.

"You and your family are now free of Sumar. The thugs who were watching your children have been apprehended. Your two children are being held in a safe place till tomorrow, just to make sure everything has been taken care of and all threats are eliminated. Your business is your own again."

"That's tremendous!" Philips exclaimed. "But, what about Sumar and his men?"

"They're taken care of also," Axel said. "Sumar was killed by gunshots from his own men. I sort of hated to see it end that way, but that's life. He gambled and lost."

"I underestimated you," Philips said. "I don't know how you did this in such a short time. What is your source of confidence, energy, and power?"

Axel considered his answer, knowing that Philips had never seen him display his physical power. "I was sent here by the United States Scientific Agency. They were concerned that some dead bodies had shown up with inexplicable medical issues. After months of investigation, the agency became concerned that the deaths might have to do with nanoparticles, and suspected that someone at Aortica was trying some experiments with these particles. They were particularly concerned that terrorists might be using nanoparticles, planning an attack. So, they contacted me. I have a doctorate degree in biology and have worked as a consultant for them in the past.

"When I found out about your company, and then about Sumar Nalithy and his hold over you, I contacted the agency and they began to monitor your children. They soon found out that they were being watched twenty-four hours a day, as you had said.

"As soon as I told the agency that I was going to put Sumar out of business today, the agents watching your children were able to apprehend Sumar's men. You can thank the USSA for that, and your kids can go on living their lives. You take care and give your kids a call."

Philips started to reach out his right hand to give Axel a handshake, but changed his mind and put his arms around him instead and thanked him. As tears began to roll down his cheeks, he said, "There is nothing in the world I could do to thank you for your efforts. I want you to know that I will always be thinking about you and what you meant to me and my family."

Axel knew it was time to go.

Back in his car, he called Tori on his internal cell phone and waited anxiously for her to answer.

"Hello, this is Tori."

He laughed and said, "You mean, the good-looking woman who goes around with those two funny guys, Axel and The Follower?"

"Axel!" she shouted. "How good to hear you speak those words. Yes, I am the woman that runs around with those two guys. I haven't seen them lately, so you can come over and see me while they are gone." She laughed. "Are you coming to take me home, I hope?"

"Yes, I am coming to take you home. I am coming to take you home and to love you to make up for the many days that I have been away from your lovely presence."

"Yippee! I'll start packing now so that we don't waste any time when you get here. How long will you be?"

Axel looked at his watch. "It's 5:30 now. I'll pick you up at 6:30. Can you be ready in an hour?"

"You bettcha, honey." She replied.

It took Axel a little over an hour to take care of things and be on his way. He pulled up at the apartment building where Tori was staying, and she was already outside, waiting for him. She ran toward him and when she was about six feet away, she leaped in the air and landed on his broad shoulders. She began hugging and kissing him.

"Wow," he exclaimed. "I've never been met by a flying bird before. I like it." He hugged and kissed her back, and then broke away long enough to suggest they go get some good Italian food at a restaurant they liked in Los Altos.

"I don't care where we go and what we eat," said Tori. "All food tastes good as long as I'm with you."

"Now that's what I call a compliment." He stowed her bags in the car and soon they were off toward Los Altos and that good Italian food. When they were settled in the restaurant and had ordered, Tori asked Axel if he was now free from the job he had been on.

"Yes, I believe it is completely finished. I may have to go to Boston for a similar situation in the near future. Do you think you could get a week off and go to Boston with me?"

"Oh, that would be nice," Tori said. "I think I could. I've only worked there for a few months, but I haven't taken a day off yet."

"You know," Axel said, "it's possible you could use this as a work assignment. This latest venture was all biology in nature. Since your business is bionics related, I might be able to get the agency to approve of a person like you going with me, sort of as a separate entity that is not related to me, even though you would be. If you could work on the line, you would be able to see things I don't and it would be a good experience for you. Maybe it's too big a stretch. I will have to think about it. There's still time. Dr. Kim hasn't asked for me to go there yet, but I assume he will. He may want me to help them get their product into a production stage. I have some familiarity with this kind of processing now, even if their process is different from Aortica's. Anyhow, it would be nice if you were there while I'm working. We could have a good time in the evenings around Boston."

Their food arrived, and Axel dropped the subject. Later, they went home and made love until the middle of the night to make up for not seeing each other for a while.

Axel returned to the university and attended the classes his substitute was teaching, so that he'd know where to pick up. His classes went on without skipping a beat. He was fortunate that he had a willing and excellent substitute. The students liked Mr. Bromberg and his soft spoken but direct method of teaching. Things rolled along smoothly in the weeks that followed.

Axel's stem cell lab was highly respected at the school, and there was money coming from the government's administration office that supported stem cell work. Advances were being made in labs across the country every week, and Axel had a web of correspondents who kept him up to date on their work. Stem cells were found in most, if not all, multi-cellular organisms. They were unique in their ability to renew themselves, and could be used to replace functions lost by the human body through disease or birth defects. The two basic types of human stem cells were embryonic stem cells from the body of a pregnant woman, and adult stem cells that were found in adult tissues. When embryonic stem cells were used, they could differentiate into all of the specialized embryonic tissues throughout the body. In adult organisms, adult stem cells acted as a repair system for the body, replenishing specialized cells, but also maintaining the normal turnover of regenerative organs, such as blood, skin, or intestinal tissues.

More and more findings related to adult stem cells were being found in the body instead of in the embryo. They played an important role in solving problems related to organs in the body. The one advantage of using adult stem cells to cure an organic problem was that the body didn't reject it, since the cells usually were derived from the same body that was being fixed. Adult stem cells were being used for many functions, just as they had been used for people with blood cancer.

For about thirty years, doctors had cured blood cancer by using the adult stem cells of donors, taken from the bone marrow of donors whose blood type matched the recipient's. The recipient did have to take medication for the rest of his life to prevent his body rejecting that blood source. Using adult stem cells from the bone marrow of the person with the cancer didn't raise that issue. After removing the adult stem cells from the person's body, their body was heavily radiated to destroy all their diseased cells. Then the person was supplied with their own stem cells. This method was being used more and more, as doctors found better ways of performing this function.

Axel's lab was being taught how to look for adult stem cells in the body. These cells were not obvious. About one in every ten thousand cells in a given area was an adult stem cell. It was as if the body provided these as spare parts in case of trouble. However, for many years no one knew about stem cells, and particularly adult stem cells. So, they were spare parts that no one knew how to use. Axel's main objective was to eventually establish a lab that not only found adult stem cells, but found better ways of employing them. He was very happy with his progress in this area. He had a couple of outstanding students who pressed him on finding better methods of discovering and using the stem cells. Like every advanced class in school, there were always a couple of students that helped the teacher to learn, and that was true in this case.

Tori has a Medical Problem

Axel and Tori lived a normal life for a short time, away from any strenuous duties. Axel continued with other things to keep his energy levels stressed and his body able to handle them. As for Tori, she began to have a unique problem; every once in a while, her hands would feel like they were burning. When Axel would look at them, he could see that her middle three fingers were discolored for almost the full length of them. He made Tori make an appointment to see a dermatologist to determine the cause. After many visits, they finally diagnosed the problem as Raynoud's Syndrome as had previously diagnosed; a medical problem that was more likely to occur in women, and usually between the ages of thirty and forty. It usually happened at the extremities of the body, such as the fingertips and the ends of a person's toes. It was brought on by cold weather, stress, or something that was cold to the touch.

Tori's doctor visits provided information, but no cure. She was supposed to stay away from things that were cold, and keep her hands warm during cold weather. Axel bought her some special gloves, and these helped to keep her hands warm when it was cold outside. He also read everything he could find so he could understand the problem and maybe come up with a solution. His studies showed that people with this syndrome could be helped by the same medicine that helped men who had erectile dysfunction. The medicine caused the blood vessels in the penis to dilate and allow more blood to flow into the penis. Axel asked the doctor about this, and he agreed it could be a short term help for this problem.

Another medicine that helped was Arginine, which increased the nitrous oxide in the blood vessels, therefore acting as a vasodilator. This worked but the patient could only use it three times a year, since it tended to have unpleasant side effects. Axel had thought that the problem was that blood was unable to get to the extremities, but found that the opposite was true. The blood in the fingers couldn't get out, since the capillaries become reduced, thereby trapping the blood. Since the area couldn't be re-oxygenated, the blood lost its oxygen and its color changed from blue to red. Pictures that Axel found on the web looked like Tori's hand when she had this problem. At first they thought it was an autoimmune disease, but it didn't happen in warm weather. Axel kept hunting, since he felt he could find some clue as to how to overcome this problem. As far as he and his health were concerned, he took hikes out into the open areas around San Francisco, the Bay, and beyond, so that he was able to release some of his special energy.

For Axel, it was fun to see three men racing along, trying to beat each other, and he would call out "Axelvation two." That brought his energy level up two levels and allowed him to go on a tear, whizzing by the three joggers, who couldn't believe their eyes. He did this, or he dove into the cold water of the Pacific without a wetsuit on, swimming rapidly by those who were wearing wetsuits and believed they were great swimmers. They found it hard to believe that anyone would want to swim in fifty degree water without some protection, let alone swim as fast as this man could. Axel had found he could swim about thirty miles an hour on the top of the water, and thirty-five miles an hour underwater. He also had found that he could remain underwater for a little over ten minutes while keeping up this speed. He had to make sure he maintained his food intake to help supply the energy. The food plus a good input of oxygen paved the way. In water, he felt he had to receive an extra amount of oxygen, since his body covering seemed to allow the oxygen from the water to enter his body.

As he was swimming one day, Axel thought, *I certainly am fortunate that I was born with these unique capabilities. However, they are of no importance unless there is a need for their use. I am fortunate that I was born with the mind I am blessed with. It allowed me to obtain my education. The knowledge I have or will obtain never needs a unique capability, and it never runs out of style. It's there day in and day out, and it's used day in and day out, and it doesn't require special events such as I encounter as The Follower. Most people would love to have either of my capabilities, and I am fortunate enough to have both. I thank my mother for this.*

Axel's thoughts turned to Tori's problem and a possible solution. He recalled the article he had read by some scientists at the Albert Einstein College of Medicine, back when he was working with Aortica. The researchers had taken nanoparticles that contained nitric oxide and made a salve. When they applied the salve to abscesses on mice that had been caused by methicillin-resistant Staphylococcus aureus, the salve healed the abscesses.

If Tori used a salve like that on her hands, Axel thought, *it would penetrate her skin. The nitric oxide would dilate her blood vessels, and the trapped blood would be able to flow again. Once the blood was released, her fingers would return to their normal state. Nitric oxide is an ideal solution for her. I must keep this in mind, and perhaps have her visit the Albert Einstein College of Medicine and discuss this with them. They probably hadn't thought about using their salve on a person suffering from Raynoud's* Syndrome. In fact, thought Axel, *the nanoparticles that received the nitric oxide treatment that I recommended to Aortica should be able to help Tori.*

When the phone rang the next day, Tori answered. It was Dr. Kim calling for Axel. She turned and looked over at Axel, and he knew by her expression who it was. He got on the phone and asked Kim how he was doing. Kim said he was fine, but he was concerned about something that he had been seeing.

"Two more men have turned up with the same strange symptoms we saw before, and they died within hours. Your work at Aortica showed us that the West Coast issues were related to improper use of the nanoparticles, and we think we have the same problem at our Boston facility. There is probably 'a loose cannon' in the East Coast nanoparticle company. More definitively speaking, we found the victims in the Boston region, within thirty miles of the company we're financing there. We haven't decided if this has anything to do with the nanoparticle work being carried on there, but I have hypothesized that it may be related. Since you resolved the issue with Aortica, we think you could use the same approach with the Boston Company, Nanico. These two entrepreneurial private companies have been working on nanoparticle research for two years. We thought maybe we should use the same routine with Nanico that you used with Aortica.

"There is a company in Germany," Kim went on, "that has developed something like this. And, like us, they intend to use it for medical purposes. Imagine if you could pinpoint a location in the body, and then use the nanoparticles to send medicine to that one place rather than to the whole body. Consider chemotherapy. It not only kills cancer cells, but it kills many cells in the body. Rarely does a person get cured of any kind of cancer without some side effects from the treatment. Wouldn't it be fantastic if one of these small elements could be programmed to carry the treatment to only the cancer cells? This would open a whole new field for the medical and biological fields, plus some others that we can only hypothesize about at this time. We have had recent good news from Nanico, and you know how Aortica has progressed. Both of them have been able to produce nanoparticles using totally different approaches. The key is being able to produce them using improved processing and attaining higher yields. Right now Nanico has been able to produce them about one tenth of one percent of the time. This doesn't sound like much, but it is a good start. These types of technologies are difficult at best, and making one out of a thousand shows it can be done. Nanico has been working on reducing the number of steps while being able to produce the results we have wanted. The simpler they can make the process, the better the chance of reducing the cost and improving the yields.

"As you know, all technologies at this level have a learning curve. Nanico has smart engineers, scientists, biologists, and chemists that have been on a learning curve about nanoparticles. I believe Nanico has been stopped in their progress at about the same place in the process where you found a solution for Aortica. They make some nanoparticles, but not in large quantities. Many times they have found that the product was very close to what they were looking for, but then troubles have popped up. We think you could help to resolve their technical issues, plus find out if someone is taking nanoparticles outside the company and using them incompetently. Everyone thinks they're a doctor when they have some new tools or toys to play with. The problem could be one of that nature. However, like Aortica, the problem could be terrorists trying to take a step outside the company and using these nanoparticles improperly with deadly intent.

"Anyhow, that is enough preaching. The thing I want to get across is that both of these start-ups have found how to make a small number of nanoparticles, but not in volume yet. It looks like your input had a major impact at Aortica. Now we want you to take on the same role with Nanico. What if there are the same types of culprits at each location that want to do harm to this country? Terrorists with microbionic experience who are able to find a way to do harm to great numbers of people is scary."

Kim paused, and Axel asked, "What does this have to do with me?"

Kim was quick to answer. "What it has to do with you is the same thing that you accomplished at Aortica. We want to send you to the Boston area and have you involved at Nanico. We're going to give it a few months, though, to make sure we're not overreacting. So consider this your warning. We hope we won't have to take it any further than this. We also want you to keep thinking about any possible actions we might take that would help to resolve this issue."

"Okay," Axel said. "I have been warned, and I will think about any ideas that come to mind. You will be the first to know if I come up with anything. Have a great day."

Boston and the Russian terrorists

A couple months went by, and Axel heard nothing from Dr. Kim about the situation in the Boston area. He thought that Kim must be busy working on something else. But one day Axel received a phone call from Kim.

"Hi Axel, how's it going?"

"Everything has been going well here at school. I've been learning as much as I have been teaching. I have some very bright students here, and they keep me on my toes. I haven't heard from you for a while, so I thought the problem must have gone away."

"That's what I am calling about. The problem was gone for a few weeks, and then appeared again two months ago. We have seen three cases like the ones we saw many months ago. It looks like something has crept into action again. Either that, or there have been some unfortunate mistakes. Just to check it out, we have gone to Nanico and looked through their roster to see if the victims were workers within the company. We felt if these were accidents, they would show up as the loss of personnel. There are fewer than thirty employees at this company, so it would have been easy to see if anyone was missing. We didn't find anyone missing from work. We also looked into the relatives of the employees in the company and didn't see any connection there. I am about ready to bring you in on this one."

"I would be glad to help," replied Axel. "But I would like it to be about a month from now. School is off for the summer then. Besides, it would be warmer up in the Boston area by then."

"Okay," said Kim. "I will keep that in mind. We will work on getting you there about a month from now. That should be okay, unless we see a dramatic increase in the problem."

"By the way, is there any chance that Tori could make the trip with me? I miss her when I am on these trips. She could probably get a week off, and I would like to show her around the Boston area. It's also a possibility that she could take a temporary job with Nanico, since she is majoring in Microbionics and could fit in. This would give me an inside person who might pick up some information I wasn't privy to. What do you think?"

Kim said he would check with his superior. "At this point in time, I would think it's a good idea, but we have budgets and I would have to get the okay from my boss. I will let you know."

When Axel went home, he told Tori about the conversation with Kim. "You could go even without the okay for the job. We have enough money. So, you should plan on it and put in for a vacation four weeks from now.

That excited Tori and made her day.

A couple of weeks went by, and then Axel got another call from Kim.

"Axel, we have seen two more of these awful deaths. I'm going to line you up for two weeks from now. I checked with my superior, and he thought it was a good idea to have someone inside the company, so Tori is a go. Start making plans to leave the day after your school lets out for the summer. We will take care of the plane tickets from San Francisco to Boston, and reserve a motel room for you and Tori. I will get back to you on the final details. I talked to the CEO of Nanico, named James Morgan, and advised him of what the status is, and that you will be out there the last week of June. This works out, since Tori probably takes off work on the Fourth of July. So she could have about eleven days with you."

"That's great," replied Axel. "I will tell my department head that I will be away for a while. I'm sure he didn't expect me to be around this summer anyhow, but it's always good to keep him informed. Let me know if anything changes."

That night, at home, Axel told Tori of the plan. Excited, she immediately sent an e-mail to her boss asking him for a week off. She wanted to make sure he had time to think about it, and so she could clean up anything she was working on. After sending the e-mail, she started talking with Axel about the good time they would have together in Boston.

Axel dampened her enthusiasm when he said, "Keep in mind that I am going to be there on assignment. There may be days when I can't take you anywhere."

"I expected that," Tori said, "and it's not a problem. Remember the girl Evelyn you saved when you met me? She works in the Boston area, and I've told her I might be able to get off work and be in the Boston around the last week in June. So, on the days when you are stuck with your work, I can plan to go somewhere with her. I have wanted to see her, anyhow, since we graduated from school. She will be excited to see you too, Axel."

"That's great," he replied. "You are always thinking and organizing and making plans. This time it will work out. Does she have a boyfriend up there?"

"Yes, she has been dating a guy, and it seems pretty serious. I expected her to be married by now, but it hasn't happened."

"That's good that she has a boyfriend. We might be able to share some time with them both, and then you can give her your opinion of her boyfriend and I will have someone to talk baseball with. I suppose he is a Red Sox fan?"

"Yes, I heard her talking about how much he liked to watch Red Sox games."

"Good, go make arrangements. The plane tickets will be taken care of by the agency, as well as the motel accommodations."

The last week in June came fast, and before they knew it, both Axel and Tori were on a flight to Boston. Tori was all excited and couldn't wait for the plane to land.

"Keep cool, my dear," said Axel. "The plane has to land before you can do anything. Just think, it was just a little over thirty years ago when my mother was flying to Boston to see my dad, when the plane wrecked. Adam was born in the woods beside the plane wreck, and I wasn't born till three days later in a Boston hospital. The doctors believe that because of that wreck and the delay in my birth are the reasons why my mitochondria became so abundant. Thank goodness my mother wasn't killed. Everyone died in the crash except my mother and three men."

"Don't talk about a plane wreck," Tori said. "That scares me, and the people on this plane might hear you say something about a plane wreck and start a panic."

Axel smiled and nodded his head in acceptance. They watched a movie, and soon the plane began descending as they approached the airport in Boston.

Evelyn met them at the baggage area. Tori was excited to see her, since they hadn't seen each other for a couple of years. There were a lot of hugs among them. Tori told Evelyn the name of the motel where they were staying. Evelyn drove them to the rental car pickup and then led them to the motel. Once they got there, the two women spent time talking about things that had happened since they last had seen each other. Meanwhile, Axel called Kim on his internal phone and told him they had safely arrived. He also asked for some input on what his actions should be. Kim told him to take the next day off and then go to Nanico on Monday. The CEO, James Morgan, would be expecting him then.

"He's a young guy for a CEO, only thirty-four. He was very excited about your visit, and he hopes that you can shed some light on those bodies. He also hoped your review of their process might see some areas for change."

They talked a little longer, and then Axel joined the women and their happy excitement.

On Monday, Axel left Tori with Evelyn and proceeded to the Nanico building. As he entered the building, he was met by a pretty receptionist's bright smile. He told her his name, and she called Mr. Morgan's secretary. In a couple of minutes the secretary came and took him to Mr. Morgan's office.

As he entered the CEO's office, Morgan extended his hand and said, "Nice to see you here, Dr. Tressler. Would you like something to eat or drink before we start reviewing the Nanico process?"

Axel told him he would like a candy bar and a cup of coffee, and soon they were discussing nanoparticles. Axel told Morgan he had seen another laboratory that was producing nanoparticles. Morgan asked him what their starting material was. Axel told him they started with carbon.

"We looked at using carbon when we got started," said Morgan. "The problem with carbon is that it tends to make nanotubes instead of particles. We believed that would give us some problems in obtaining the nanoparticles. We chose to use graphite. One would think that the problems with graphite would be the same as those with carbon, but when one takes the material from the bulk to the nanoparticle level, those things don't follow the normal characteristics. This proved to be quite evident as we worked on the graphite. We didn't obtain nanotubes as we got to the small size, below twenty nanometers. We got spherical particles, true nanoparticles. Our problems since then have related to the fact that the nanoparticles are unstable. Any time you try to move them, they move toward each other and form clumps. So, most of our latest work has been in trying to resolve this clumping problem. I think if you spend some time on the line, you will see this effect and you might have some suggestions. There may be parts of our process that you might see as causing the problems and come up with some suggestions."

Axel said he would review the process and see what he came up with. "In fact, I would like to start right now."

He felt very confident that he would be able to help them. He had learned a lot at Aortica. Morgan took him out to the process line and introduced him to the various engineers. In about an hour, Axel was unattended and walked around the lab. He followed the process, finding various places that could use some of the same help he had offered Aortica. He thought about that and decided to call Kim.

"Kim, I am here on the line at Nanico, and I can see various things that could be changed, similar to the changes I recommended to Aortica. What I wondered was whether I could tell them about the corrections I made in the Aortica process. or is that considered confidential?"

There was silence on the phone for about a minute, and Axel asked Kim if he was still there. "Yes, I am still here. I was thinking about your question. I believe what you gave to Aortica was your input. Your input is not Aortica's property, even though they are using it and applied for a company patent on the process. So, I believe you are free to use anything you come up with that you don't consider Aortica's private material.

Axel told Kim that Nanico's process was somewhat different than Aortica's. "They start with graphite instead of carbon, and it makes the process easier from what I can see. That is not where I see the problems."

"Yes, I know," said Kim. "Remember, USSA has supported both of these programs, and both companies had to give monthly reports on their technical status. Once this is done, the reports are available to each of the companies, so they will soon see reports that show some of the changes you made. You will get credit for those changes."

"That's great," Axel said. "That leaves me free to work with them on changes I can recommend on their process. In fact, I am going to go and talk to Morgan when I am done talking with you."

"Go have at it," said Kim.

Axel went to Morgan's office. He had to wait for about ten minutes, since Morgan was on the phone. When he entered the office, Morgan asked if he had some suggestions already.

"Yes, I believe I do," said Axel. "You do a good job bringing the process along till you get near the end of the process. At that point; you produce singular nanoparticles, but they don't stay singular. As you had mentioned, they clump together. I was impressed that you are able to obtain these nanoparticles without using a solution. You are able to provide them in the dry form. But in this singular form, they're acting almost like magnets. They need to be stabilized. Have you tried to oxidize them?"

"No," replied Morgan. "Carbon and graphite are not oxidizeable."

"Yes, I know," said Axel. "But these are no longer graphite or carbon. When they are in nanoparticle size and form, they no longer function as either carbon or graphite. They have new characteristics, and they are able to be made stable if they are surrounded in a sea of nitric oxide gas. The nitric oxide reacts with the nanoparticles and should form a stable material. That is my experience with carbon generated nanoparticles. The fact that you get singular nanoparticles this early in your process is a great jump. I have to think of a way to take your singular nanoparticles and introduce the nitric oxide to them. I will think about it tonight and come with a recommendation tomorrow morning."

"That's fabulous," Morgan said, grinning with excitement. "The problem is," he added, "that we don't want nitric oxide singular nanoparticles."

"That may be true," Axel said. "But once you have stable, singular nitric oxide nanoparticles, you have something you can work with. Your people know what you want to end up with, and working with these stable nanoparticles will allow them to achieve their goal."

"That's a very perceptive thought," remarked Morgan. "You are right. If we have stable singular nanoparticles to work with, we can find ways to go from an oxidized nanoparticle to one we might desire more."

Axel told Morgan about the medical paper put out by the Albert Einstein School scientists. "They used a salve of nitric oxide nanoparticles and applied it to problems with mice who have trouble with receiving the proper amount of oxygen to their extremities. The nitric oxide dilates the vessels in the ends of fingers or toes and allows more blood flow and the resultant increased oxygen. I know you don't want to use your nanoparticles in this manner, but if you read through their work and results, it may give you some clues on how to work differently with your singular nanoparticles."

Morgan thanked him for the information, and Axel left for the day. As he exited the building, he called Tori and Evelyn and asked them what they were doing and where could he meet them.

That evening, Axel thought about the process being run by Nanico. He felt that if the singular nanoparticles were being formed, then they should go through a curtain or volume of nitrogen to keep them in their relative position with respect to each other. The nitrogen gas should be at atmospheric pressure, so as to not disturb the particles. They could use a quartz tube that was flooded with nitrogen, like he had recommended for Aortica. The quartz tube would be perpendicular to the ground, and the singular nanoparticles would fall through a volume of nitrogen. This part of the tube would be approximately five inches in length. This five-inch length of tube would be surrounded by a box, whose walls would be almost against the outside of the tube. The box would be flooded with nitrogen, and the nitrogen would flow from the box through the holes in the side of the tube without causing agitation among the falling nanoparticles.

The tube would be terminated by another section of quartz tubing that would be in the shape of a T, set at ninety degrees to the first section. The center of the T-shaped tube would be open to, and connected to, the output of the vertical tube and would receive the falling particles. Heated nitric oxide gas would be fed through the T-shaped tube at a pressure higher than atmospheric. The nanoparticles would fall into this river of hot nitric oxide gas.

The hot nitric oxide would serve several purposes. First of all, its flow would create a negative pressure region at the bottom of the initial five-inch tube, which would help direct the singular nanoparticles to fall downward while maintaining their respective positions, so they don't clump. Second of all, the hot nitric oxide hitting the falling singular nanoparticles would cause a rapid reaction and almost immediately convert the singular nanoparticles to stable nitric oxide nanoparticles. Third of all, it would carry the converted singular nanoparticles out of the T-shaped tube to another container that would store the nitric oxide nanoparticles. At this point, it wouldn't matter if the nanoparticles collided since they would be stable.

Axel was quite happy with this resolution. It might not be detailed enough, but he felt the scientists and engineers would be able to solve any other problems. He was eager to take this to Morgan in the morning. He wanted this to solve their processing problems, and then he could spend his time resolving the deaths that had occurred in the area.

On the next day back at Nanico, Axel headed directly to Morgan's office. He had to wait for about fifteen minutes before Morgan arrived. He apologized to Axel for having him to wait, but he had been tied up with some issues on the process line. He led Axel into his office and told the secretary to get Axel a coffee and some candy bars. He was already used to Axel's morning routine.

"So, what can I do for you, Dr. Tressler?" he asked.

Axel told him he had thought about the method being used in the Nanico line, and had some suggestions on how to have the singular nanoparticles maintain their singular characteristic. Morgan seemed quite surprised, and asked if Axel needed any material to give his presentation. Axel suggested having a whiteboard and different colored markers so he could draw his suggestions.

"No problem," Morgan said. He pushed a button on his desk, and a whiteboard came down on one of the side walls. The secretary brought in markers, and Axel was ready to go.

Axel began drawing a schematic of the flow of the material in the line. At the output, he drew a vertical tube in green. He surrounded this with the side view of the box that encased the tube. He showed where nitrogen came into the box, and marked where holes would be in the vertical tube for the nitrogen to flow through. He drew the connecting

T-shaped tube, and showed where heated nitric oxide gas was generated and entered this tube. He explained how the singular nanoparticles would drop through the vertical tube into this flow of nitric oxide. He drew where the now nitric oxide nanoparticles would flow into a "catch basin." for these particles. He finished by saying, "You will now have stable singular nitric oxide nanoparticles."

Morgan was very interested in the whole concept and asked many questions. Axel either knew the answers or thought that Morgan's chemists would.

"I would like to bring in my top technical people," Morgan said, "and have you given them the same presentation while we have the drawing on the board. Do you have any problems with that?"

"No, I have no problems," replied Axel.

"They may ask you many questions. Are you prepared to discuss any questions?"

Axel gave him the same answer. Morgan got his secretary on the phone and told her the names of the technical people he wanted to see in his office. "While you are at it, bring in a camera and take a picture of the drawing on the board," he said.

While they waited, Morgan told Axel that he was very impressed by the rather simple approach to the problem. "I think my technical people will like what you have here. They may suggest some changes or suggest something besides nitric oxide as the stabilizing element in the process."

The secretary came in and took several pictures of the drawing on the board and downloaded them for Morgan. One by one, six of Morgan's technical people entered the office. Morgan asked where Max Alter was.

"Max has something that is running and he can't leave it right now," was the response.

"Well, we are going to proceed without him. Whatever we discuss in this room is confidential and company private. Dr. Axel Tressler has provided us a possible solution to keeping the nanoparticles we generate as singular, and I want you listen carefully and ask him anything you wish. I would suggest that you allow him to go through the whole presentation before asking any questions or making any remarks. I don't want anyone to miss any of the material that Axel will present."

With that introduction, Axel went to the board and began to repeat what he had presented earlier to Morgan.

Axel's presentation to the technical people was received well. They had a few questions that precipitated some constructive conversation. They liked the idea of tying up the nanoparticles with the nitric oxide and stabilizing the particles. The discussion then revolved around how they could then take the nitric oxide singular nanoparticles and work with them to provide a myriad of other nanoparticles. This was a very rewarding part of the discussion for Axel, since he hadn't thought much about deriving other nanoparticles for different applications. He sat back and listened to this intriguing discussion. He was amazed at the ingenuity of these people and how their minds worked. Several patentable ideas came out of this discussion, and Axel made them aware of it. He told them to make sure they wrote these things down in their notebooks and applied for the patents.

"The strength of a company comes from the technical foundation formed by patents within the company."

When the technical people left the room, Axel told Morgan that he felt fortunate to have been there and to see how the minds of these people work. "That was very exhilarating."

Morgan said, "Remember, this was the result of your presentation today. It got their minds working in a new direction and got them excited about their work. They haven't felt that way for several months. Thank you.

"Now I guess you will be pursuing how any of the information from this facility got out and caused some deaths," Morgan speculated.

"Yes. In fact there is something I would like to ask of you," said Axel. "My fiancée is working here on the line. She is a graduate student, having received a degree in Microbionics. I want her to try to fish out some information from your people. To do this, she must take the role of a potential terrorist. She must be able to quietly talk about her disagreements— she doesn't actually have any—with this country and various things that make it hard to live in this country. This is a ruse to try to pull out anybody who works here who has similar feelings. We have found that this maneuver normally leads us to the culprits we are searching for. For her to do this without being arrested, she must have your permission to quietly voice these opinions. Do we have your permission?"

"This is a tricky situation," Morgan said. "If done poorly, it could cause morale problems in the company."

"Yes, we know this," Axel agreed. We believe we can handle it in a very subtle manner and not cause any problems within your company. I will keep you abreast of what she has said and how it is being received. We normally do this kind of thing during lunch, when people often talk about things besides their work or the business of the company. It is done as a subtle opinion. The comment is usually about the country or the people leading the country. If the employee doesn't bite on it, Tori will talk to someone else who she believes will be receptive to this kind of talk. She would normally pick a person out by something he or she said previously. We will do this professionally."

"I was warned about this from Dr. Kim, who thinks very highly of you and your professionalism. So, I have thought this out and decided to let this go on in the hopes of finding a culprit. We do not want people dying from something that we have done in this company. Bottom line, keep it professional, and I believe it will pay dividends."

Tori Makes Major Contributions against Terrorists

Axel left Nanico that evening with Tori. Now that they were at the same company, this worked out on using one car. On the way to the motel he told her about his conversation with Mr. Morgan and that her actions were approved, as long as she kept them professional and subtle. He gave her a few hints on things that she might say. Tori was excited about this. It gave her a chance to play the game with Axel in his role as The Follower. Axel said he would be trying the same tack with the professionals at the company.

"You never know who the trouble maker is," he said.

The next day Tori was eager about going to work. She had thought about her assignment a good bit the night before, and was looking for candidates to try it on. On her first break, she saw one of the women who seemed to talk tough about things, and she decided to get a cup of coffee and begin a conversation with her. As she waited for her coffee to cool a little, she stood next to the woman. Her name was Gayle.

"How's it going, Gayle?" she asked.

"Oh, it's going fine. I like working here," she said.

"I do too," said Tori. "It seems like this company is progressive compared to what the federal government is doing."

"What do you mean by that?" asked Gayle.

"Well, here we are in a hole, and the administration is increasing the number of soldiers going to Afghanistan. Seems like a dumb move to me."

Gayle took a sip of her coffee and said, "I don't pay much attention to what the government is doing. It's too complicated. I have a hard time keeping my life straight, let alone what our government is doing. I am sure that they believe what they are doing is right."

"What about the health bill they passed?" asked Tori. "Just gets us in more debt, don't you think?"

"Oh, I don't know," said Gayle. "It seems that they are trying to help more people with their medical issues. There are a lot of people in this country without any medical assistance."

"But what about the costs?" asked Tori.

"Well, someone has to pay for the insurance for those people. There are 85 percent of the people covered in this country with some sort of medical insurance. Maybe they are happy, but they should help the 15 percent that aren't insured. That's what this country is about, isn't it?"

Tori couldn't argue with those opinions. She downed her coffee and said, "I guess we should go back to work and let our president worry about those things. That's what he gets paid for."

As Tori walked back to work she thought, *Boy, I misjudged her. I thought she would be a tiger about those issues, and it turns out she is just an innocent citizen of this great country.* Tori had a few chances to bounce these things off other workers during lunch and her breaks, but there was no grumpy feedback from anyone she talked to. When she rode home with Axel she told him what she had tried, and that it hadn't resulted in anyone jumping up and crying, "Down with America," or "Down with the president."

Axel laughed. "Keep trying," he said. "You are hitting the right note, and somewhere along the way someone will probably begin singing with you. You never know who."

"Isn't that the truth?" commented Tori. "I picked the women I thought would be the most outspoken and got nothing in return. I guess I will keep trying."

The next day was almost a repeat of the day before, as Tori took her breaks and continued her comments about the government and the president. She didn't get anywhere. Just the opposite, it would seem, as if everyone who worked at Nanico were liberals or backers of the Democratic Party. *Boy,* Tori thought, *if the president were to come here and ask for support, he sure would get it. Of course, this company is just south of Boston, and Massachusetts is a democratic state. This is where John Kennedy, Bobby Kennedy, and Ted Kennedy came from, and they were greatly loved by the people of this state. So, I guess I shouldn't expect anyone to shout them down. Also, health care was a big thing with Ted Kennedy. Maybe I need to try a different tack. Maybe I should push a little more on the war and sending our good men to fight in a country that we don't know anything about. Why are our men dying to help a foreign country?*

As the day proceeded, Tori tried to put more emphasis on the loss of lives in the Middle East. This got a little more action, but nothing important. When they drove home, she brought Axel up to date on what had occurred; telling him that she had decided to put more emphasis on the war.

"That's a good point," he said. "That was one of the points that was stewing in Britain when I was there trying to find those who were against the government."

That night, Tori thought about her conversations with the ten or so people she had talked to over the last two days. She remembered one of them had an English accent, and she decided to try the new tactic on her. Driving to work with Axel the next day, she asked him if he was making any progress with the professionals he had been trying to rouse up.

"No, Tori," he said. "I have found them to be like you have found the women. They are patriotic, and they seem content with the way the government is going and the world in general. I was surprised."

On the first break of the day, Tori went to get a coffee and looked for the women she had talked to the first day. Her name was Margaret.

"Hi, Margaret," she said. "How's life treating you?"

"Same ole same ole," Margaret said.

"Are you from England?" Tori asked.

"All the way," Margaret bragged.

"How do you like it here?" Tori asked.

"Oh, it's a lot like England. It seems we have the same kind of thoughts against the government about sending men to war." Margaret replied.

This got Tori's energy up. Here was a sort of attitude she had been looking for. She tried to encourage the discussion by saying, "I am against sending our men to fight the Afghan's fight. They wouldn't do that for us, would they?"

"Definitely not," Margaret said in an exaggerated tone of voice. "I am for bringing back the good men from this country and letting those 'rag heads' fight their own battles. They have been fighting them for thousand of years and getting nowhere. Where do we expect to get? Besides, why do we lose lives against something they have been arguing about for years? It's more about religion then common sense. And it's not even our religion. This sucks if you ask me."

"I agree," said Tori. "It sucks!"

They had to go back to work, but Tori knew she was onto something. She couldn't wait till lunch, when she sought out Margaret again.

"What are you having for lunch?" she asked.

"Oh, I don't eat a lunch," Margaret said. "I have a cup of coffee to keep me going. I can't afford to be spending money on lunches."

"Do you mind if I share a cup of coffee with you?" asked Tori.

"That would be fine," said Margaret. "You and I have some things in common, it seems. I meant to tell you on Monday that I am against the things the government is doing here, just like I was against the things the UK was doing when I lived there. My husband and I were against the UK sending troops to Iraq and Afghanistan. We had a friend that got killed in southern Iraq, and that made my husband even more irate at the government. At one time, my husband was pretty close to tying in with the Russians in the UK, who wanted to do physical harm to the country to make a point about British troops being killed. It seems the Russians wanted the U.S. out of Afghanistan so they could continue to take advantage of the opium crops there that get converted into heroin. I talked him out of getting involved with the Russian, and then we decided to come to the United States. My husband, Earl, has a good education, and since there were jobs available here in the States, he decided to take one. Then when we came here, it seems he got back in the same groove about this government."

They continued drinking their coffee and talking.

"I have liked it here," Margaret continued, "but my husband seems to never be satisfied. Each day when he comes home from work, all I hear is the problems with this country and the war in Afghanistan. If this keeps up, I will divorce him. I'm sorry to spill all this out on you. I have had it in my system so long, and I've felt like I was going to explode. I had to let it out on someone and get it out of my system. I hope you don't mind. I feel a little better since I talked to you."

Tori took in all that Margaret was saying, and in fact, encouraged her to say more. She wanted to know how far this had gone and whether this was the weak spot in the company. She knew if she sounded too interested, Margaret might get suspicious and clam up. So she left Margaret spill it out, and tried to calm her down a little by saying things like, "Don't let that get to you. Things will change. Your husband will start to like this country more and more as he lives here." She also tried to urge Margaret on by saying things like, "I am disturbed at times also, because we are fighting wars in two countries that don't have anything in common with our country. It costs us taxpayers a lot of money, and I wish that more of the money would go toward improving the economy and helping on health care."

After lunch, they went back to their work. When they were leaving the facility at the end of the work day, Margaret waved at Tori and said, "See you tomorrow."

Tori couldn't wait to see Axel and tell him about her experiences that day. Axel had known he'd have to stay late that day, and had got a ride to work with another engineer who also had to stay late. Axel had to stay to help solve some problems that had popped up. He didn't get to the motel until after nine that evening, and he hardly had got in the door when Tori was all over him, telling him about her conversations with Margaret.

"She's like a loose cannon that is full of shells to shoot. I don't think it is so much her as it is her husband. I am going to play on her tomorrow and see where this takes me."

Axel thought there was something there, and he went over his experience in Aortica in more detail, suggesting different avenues Tori could take with Margaret. Tori felt good, because at last it was her input that was being listened to, instead of Axel's.

The next day when Tori went to work, she was excited to see if the conversation with Margaret would continue. When she got coffee on her first break, Margaret hunted her down. Tori could tell that she was in a talking mood. In fact, she couldn't talk fast enough to get out all the things she wanted to say. A lot of it was similar to what she had said the day before. When the break was almost over, Margaret asked if Tori would have lunch with her. Of course, this played right into Tori's hands.

At lunch Margaret really let things out of the bag, as she spilled some very confidential information. "When Earl met with some of the Russians working in this area, he became more agitated," she said. "He talked about some actions the Russians wanted to pursue. They felt if they could carry out some terrorist actions, it would arouse the American people to speak out about things, as if to say, 'Why are we off fighting terrorists that don't affect us at all, while here in our home country no one is keeping terrorists in check?'

"You know, Tori," Margaret continued. "There are times when I begin to think he is right. I am beginning to see his visions."

Tori wondered if Margaret had said that as bait, to check how Tori thought. She didn't take the bait, but just said, "You know Margaret, its one thing to talk, but to walk the walk is another thing. Those things your husband talked about were just that, talking. Don't you get tired of it?"

Margaret looked at Tori. "I used to get tired of it, but then I began to be swept his way. See me after work in the parking lot and I will tell you some things that happened that will blow your socks off. You won't believe what I have to say."

Tori could hardly wait until the day ended. When work was over, she walked out to the parking lot. Margaret was already there, and Tori could see she was raring to go. As she approached, Margaret said, "How about getting in my car and we will go down to a coffee shop down the road? I don't want anyone to hear what I have to say."

Tori nodded and got in Margaret's car. Margaret started talking as fast as she was driving. Tori had to tell her to slow down. "We aren't in any hurry." she said.

When they got to the coffee shop and sat at a table, Margaret began to talk in a low voice. "Earl kept telling me about these 'Ruskies,' as he calls them. They wanted to cause some violent acts in the country to do three things. Leave off steam, arouse people, and take steps against the government here. The Ruskies kept thinking about ways that would get the biggest results and strike hard against this country in retaliation for sending soldiers to Afghanistan. Earl felt they just wanted the U.S. out of Afghanistan so they could continue their dope running businesses over there. He kept arguing with them about this, but putting all things aside, he was against this country sending soldiers over to fight other people's battles. I used to say to him that they aren't really our people that are being sent over. They are Americans and we are British. That would make me mad and I would correct myself.. I used to say to him, we are American now and they are our people they are sending over. What I said was like lighting a fire. He realized they are 'our' people and it only made him angrier. Now he really wanted to stop them.

"Anyhow, this went on for a while, and one day when Earl came home, he said the Russians were trying to figure the best thing they could use to make a big impact. They figured they could do it with IED—you know, an improvised explosive device—a bomb made from ammonium nitrate and a fuel like kerosene called ANFO. Or they could make it from high grade hydrogen peroxide and acetone to make an explosive material called acetone peroxide, or TATP. These types of approaches were used in past major events, with ANFO being used in the Oklahoma City bombing, and TATP used in the London subways a few years ago. There were two other approaches that were more dangerous but resulted in broader damage. They included the use of nuclear material for a dirty bomb, or the use of nanoparticles that were contaminated with a type of virus. They knew where they could get the material for the dirty bomb, but it would take some doing to get it into this country. They thought they might be able to get hold of some nanoparticle material more easily, so they decided this would be their first approach. The more they thought about it, the more they became interested in using the nanoparticle method.

"Earl knew that Nanico was trying to develop nanoparticles, but he didn't think I would be able to get any out of the place. Besides, at that time Nanico still wasn't producing singular nanoparticles. They produced some randomly, but that was it. However, he felt that soon the company probably would be making them in high numbers. Either that, or the government would stop funding the program. So, he kept bugging me on seeing what I could do about getting some. Well, I didn't know from a horse's ass how to get any nanoparticles, but I decided to keep alert and see if I could.

"A couple of months went by without me finding anything about getting any nanoparticles. In fact, I was beginning to worry I'd lose my job, because Nanico couldn't produce the particles. Then one day while I was at lunch, I heard one of the managers talking to another manager about using the nanoparticles on mice. I heard a little thing here and a little thing there, and that led me to believe they were trying to get some people to offer themselves as volunteers for medical experiments with the nanoparticles. They were offering a good sum of money to anyone who volunteered. I went home and told Earl about that, and he got excited. He told me to try to sit near those men as often as I could while going to lunch, so I would hurry to get to lunch before the place was crowded. When I saw them come in and sit down at a table, I would go and sit at the table next to them. One night when Earl came home he told me he had brought me something that would help the situation. He showed me a little gadget that when you put it in your ear, you can hear things at a much higher volume. He told me how to use it, and then he went to the other end of the family room and whispered something. By God, Tori, I couldn't believe it. I could hear every word he whispered.

"So, now I took this to work with me and put it in before lunch. At lunch I made sure I sat next to the two managers in charge of volunteers. Eventually I heard them say that Mr. Morgan would pay someone to volunteer for that experiment. When I went home, I told Earl what I had heard and this got him all excited. The next evening when he got home, he told me he had called Mr. Morgan and told the secretary it was a private thing he wanted to talk about concerning nanoparticles. This got him to talk to Mr. Morgan. When he got on the phone, he told him that he'd heard from one of Nanico's managers that Nanico would pay for someone to volunteer for an experiment concerning nanoparticles. Morgan tried to put him off, saying he knew nothing about this. Earl told him he was from England and had been in the states for a few years, and that he'd like to do something to help the country. It was quiet on the phone for a while, and then Morgan said, 'I don't know where you got your information. We are in no position to do any experiments with humans at this time. Maybe one of these days we will.' So, Earl said fine and gave him his cell phone number. Earl bet he would call him one of these days.

"Sure enough, one day several months ago he got a call from a person who works for Morgan. He said they were interested in talking to him, and they set up a meeting for the following day at eight in the evening. The next day when I came home from work, I asked Earl if he was still going to the meeting that evening. He said he was. At around seven in he evening, he took off, excited as a puppy.

"When he got home that night, he told me an interesting story. He said the guy from Morgan's office, who wouldn't give him his name, said that they had an experiment they were ready to try. This guy was with a few other guys, and they gave him an inhaler, like people with asthma use. They said they had loaded it with a nanoparticle and a medicine like what people with breathing problems use. They explained to him that the lungs have a large number of alveoli at the end of the bronchial tubes, and that these alveoli are where the lungs take in oxygen. The oxygen gets squashed in the alveoli, which causes the oxygen to be pushed into the tiny blood capillaries. The capillaries carry the blood into the arteries, and that sends oxygen throughout the body. When the veins carry the used blood back to the lungs, the carbon dioxide gets squeezed out of the alveoli and is exhaled by the person. The oxygen that is provided via these alveoli is what gives the body energy. When a person has a disease such as asthma or emphysema, their alveoli are damaged. The damage could be that the tubes that feed the alveoli are too narrow. Or the alveoli can be damaged. The alveoli are like a bunch of grapes on the end of the bronchial tubes, and with one of the diseases there are less of them. It's almost like a branch in a grape vineyard that has a bunch of squashed grapes at the end of the stem. Anyhow, the inhalers that people use has a medicine that dilates the alveoli, which makes them look like balloons that have been blown to bigger than normal. This helps the person with the disease to take in more oxygen.

"This guy told Earl that there were just enough nanoparticles with medicine in the inhaler to last Earl one day. He gave Earl one thousand dollars in cash, and a cell phone number. He told him to call that number and leave the results. Earl was supposed to use the inhaler for a day, wait a day, and then tell him how it worked. Earl was all excited about this experiment. He didn't know anyone who had a breathing problem, but he talked to his Russian friends. It turned out that one of them had a wife who suffered from emphysema. He gave the inhaler to the man and told him to have her use the inhaler two times, once in the morning and the second time in the evening.

Two days later the guy called Earl and said his wife had died. She started bleeding from the mouth the day after using the inhaler, and when they got her to the hospital, they found that her lungs were all torn up and bleeding, and there was no hope for her. She died without speaking a word. The doctors wanted to know what had happened to her, since they couldn't explain her condition. It was like her lungs had been torn apart by a buzz saw. The husband swore to Earl that he was going to kill him for what he had done to his wife. Earl was all shaken up. He tried to call the phone number that had been given to him by the man from Nanico, but no one ever answered and there was no voice mail. Earl thought maybe the guy from Nanico already knew what had happened. He tried to call Mr. Morgan, but the secretary always said he wasn't available. Then Earl asked Mr. Morgan's secretary if she knew the man who had given him the inhaler, and she said she didn't know anything about it. Earl gave her the cell phone number that he had been given, and she said it wasn't listed anywhere in the company. So, Earl got stonewalled at Nanico.

"From the time of this woman's death until now, the pressure from the Ruskies has been really bad. One of their leaders, Arisol Spersick, came to our house to talk to Earl. He told Earl that his comrades wanted to kill him, and he needed to know what had happened. Earl told him that the whole episode had been done in the best interests of the group. He told Spersick that he had made an indirect contact to Nanico to try to get some nanoparticles, so he could see how they would fit the group's needs. The inhaler he got was supposed to contain the nanoparticles with some advanced medicine tied into them. It turns out that the results were terrible, and then he told Spersick that he had not been able to make contact with Nanico since then. He begged the group's forgiveness and hoped they would understand that it had been done with the thought of helping, not hindering. Spersick said he would get back to Earl after talking to the group."

Margaret stopped, and Tori stared at her, mouth agape. It was so hard to believe, but she could tell from the details that Margaret had not made this up.

Tori said, "My fiancé was hired by Nanico as a consultant to show them how they could improve on their process. If you don't mind, I will tell him, confidentially, what you just told me. You might not believe this, but he is against sending our soldiers to foreign countries, many of them never to return. He might be sympathetic to your cause and be able to help you. He is smart, and previously worked with some people in another country who were against their country sending its soldiers to war. Do you mind if I tell him?"

Margaret was quiet for a few seconds and then said, "If you think he can be of help in this cause against the government, then you can tell him what I told you. See if he is willing to work with the group in some way."

Tori could hardly wait to go to the motel and tell Axel. She got there before him and started to make a quick dinner for herself and Axel. She called and asked when he would be home, and he said he was on his way. When Axel walked in, Tori couldn't wait a moment before she began spilling out what she had learned from Margaret.

"If you want to do something about this, you have to let me know this evening, since tomorrow is the end of my temporary work with Nanico. I have to fly back home in a couple of days."

Axel was excited about this for three reasons. It provided information about the dead body Kim had said had been found in the Boston area; it showed that the nanoparticle could kill when used improperly; and last of all, it gave him input about the group of Russians he needed to stop. He told Tori how proud he was of her and her findings. "I guess I am going to have to bring you more often with me on these escapades," he said.

Of course this made Tori's day.

While eating, Axel discussed the possibilities with Tori of how to handle the information she had received. They agreed that the first thing to do was to contact Kim.

"He will be somewhat happy," Axel said, "since it resolves the issue of how this person died. He had been excited about the fact that there had been similar deaths on both the East Coast and West Coast without any explanation. Now he will have the reason. It happened on both coasts because there were two nanoparticle start-up companies on each of coast that were in proximity to where these sudden deaths occurred. Then he will have to recommend how to handle the group of Russians. Maybe he will only want this group monitored. After all, they really have done nothing but talk, and in this country that is not grounds for a legal action. The Constitution grants that freedom to whoever may choose to use it. Talk is cheap and safe in this country. We have to find out if the Russians are planning on doing anything before we can take some action."

Tori asked Axel if he wanted to take advantage of the offer she had made to Margaret, that Axel use his consultant skills to help direct the Russian group.

"I have been thinking about that," replied Axel. "I think you should say I turned it down. Then you tell them you know at least three Russians who would like to do something against the country. You ask her if Earl would like to know these men, since you believe they would be a big help. All three of them are well learned and greatly experienced men. The names are Adrian Gomanski, a Russian biologist that knows a lot about nuclear material that is used in bombs. Then there is Yaro Patraska, who spent much of his time in Mexico with the drug cartel, and also worked the last couple of years in Afghanistan exporting opium and morphine into Pakistan. There is also Jacob Teratov, who worked on missiles in Russia, and then went to North Korea to help them with their missile program. When they ask you how you know them, you tell them that you belonged to a Russian club in college, and a man you were dating knew them. When they came to the States over about a four-year period, you met each of them and know how to contact them. If they are interested, say you will see which of them you can contact. You tell Margaret that you will be leaving and going back to the West Coast on Saturday, so you need to know which one they would like to talk to. Give them the phone number of the motel to contact you. I will not answer the motel phone at all on Saturday or Sunday, in case they call. When you talk to them, tell them the one man that would be the easiest to take on this deal would be Yaro Patraska. Then you give them one of my internal phone numbers and tell them it is Yaro Patraska's number here in the United States. The good thing about me pretending to be Yaro Patraska is that I can get them over anything that bothers them about Yaro, since they could call Bene Zuri in Afghanistan, or contact Vasco and Vina Pasteranski in Pakistan for references. All of these people know me as Yaro Patraska, and they loved what I did for them in Afghanistan and Pakistan."

Kim had been listening to this conversation, and he interrupted. "I think that is great thinking, Axel! The people in those two countries know you as a Russian who helped them in their time of need. Plus, you can come off as a 'strong guy' who has had great experience with handling major problems. It's a winner!"

With all that put to bed, Tori knew what her position would be with Margaret the next day.

The next day, Tori was excited as she entered Nanico to complete her last day of work. She knew she had made a hit with Axel and Kim, and was eager to pull this thing off. She could hardly wait for her first break. Before taking the break, Tori called Axel on his internal phone and asked if he would like to listen to her conversation with Margaret. Axel said that he didn't need that; she was on her own.

During the break, Tori discussed the fact that she knew some very powerful Russians. She mentioned their names. She and Margaret didn't have time to go into details during the break, but they agreed to go over the details at lunch. A couple of hours later, they sat in the corner of the lunch room. Tori went over the names of the three people she supposedly knew, providing some background information on each and how they would help Margaret and Earl in their efforts.

After she had described to Margaret the great experiences each had, she said, "I know that Yaro Patraska is in this country. In fact, he is on the West Coast. He is also the one with the experience that best suits the Russians" needs. He has worked in the drug cartel in Mexico, the opium trade in Afghanistan, and the morphine and heroin trade in Pakistan. This guy is not only smart, but he is tough. He has experiences the Russians in the Boston area wish they had."

Margaret said that she would call Earl and tell him about this during her break in the afternoon. "Then I will be able to tell you what Earl thinks about this," she remarked. "He will probably call the top guy in the Boston Russian group and provide him with the background of Yaro. He will probably call me back before quitting time to keep me updated. I will let you know by the time we are ready to go home. You said you can get Yaro's phone number in the States, and I will tell him that. If he gets the number by this evening and he is up to it, he will probably call the guy this evening or tomorrow morning, since there is the three hour difference in time between here and the West Coast."

With that decided, they went back to their work. Tori thought she had handled it well. When quitting time and Tori was heading toward the parking lot, she knew full well that Margaret would intercept her with some information. She hadn't gone twenty paces when she heard Margaret call her name. She turned and saw Margaret wave toward the right side of the parking lot. Tori headed in that direction and soon joined Margaret at her car. They got in the car, and Margaret began talking very fast.

"Earl was excited about this man Yaro. He called the top guy in the Boston area and filled him in with the information that you provided me. He was also interested, but wanted to have Earl talk to Yaro first and get some first impression about him. If it goes well in that phone call, he will call the top guy back and let him know. After that, assuming it goes well; the top guy will call Yaro and size him up."

"That's great," Tori exclaimed. "I called my friend in California this afternoon and got Yaro's phone number. I wrote it down for you."

She handed Margaret a piece of paper with Axel's phone number. "We are going to get this thing going in a big way. The men will be proud of us before it's done."

Both women said they were sure glad that Tori had had a chance to be out there and that the two women had met and become friends.

"The friendship we developed in that short of time is amazing," said Margaret.

Tori agreed, and they hugged. Tori walked to her car and called Axel. She told him he could expect a call on the West Coast number that night or tomorrow. Considering the three hour time different, they thought Earl would call the next morning. If things went well, that would be followed by a call from the top Russian guy of the Boston area.

Axel Enters the Russian Den as Yaro

The next day, the phone with the West Coast number rang at a couple of minutes to nine. Axel picked up the phone and said in a Russian accent, "Hello, this is Yaro."

"My name is Earl," the man on the other end said, "and I believe you know something about what I am calling about."

"Yes," said Axel. "Tori called me about an hour ago and said that you might be calling me. What can I do for you?"

Earl described the general frustration of the Russians in the Boston area. "We are frustrated that America is fighting terrorists in Afghanistan, sending men over there and many of them are not coming back. We felt if we could unleash some terrorist event in this country, maybe the government here would look at that, realize they have a terrorist threat here in this country, and that they should leave the Middle East alone and bring their troops back. We are looking for someone with a strong background in fighting the system to come and lead our charge here in the Boston area. I don't know if you are aware that there is a big Russian population in the Northeast, and especially in the Boston area. You have been away from Russia for some time, but we thought that perhaps you could still think like a Russian and could provide your strengths toward that cause. In the end, America will benefit for what we do. We wanted to know if you are interested."

"Listen, Earl," Axel said, "I have been around this world for a long time, and I know my Russian friends better than you do. I know they have some other motive than to just get America to bring her troops back to this country. Now how about telling the whole story? How about telling me the truth? As much as I like this country, I am not going to create a terrorist attack just to bring the boys back home. What's the scoop?"

Earl hemmed and hawed, and finally said, "You are right. This is not for the sake of bringing the boys back home. My Russian friends want the American army out of Afghanistan, so they can get back to their opium trade. It's amazing how much money is involved in the opium, morphine, and heroin trade."

"You don't have to tell me that," replied Axel. "I spent years running one type of dope or another around. I ran cocaine and marijuana in Mexico. I ran opium in Afghanistan. I ran morphine and heroin in Pakistan. So, do you think you can tell me anything about the money in that business? It's like pouring dollars down the biggest drain you ever saw."

Earl was quiet for a few seconds, and then he said, "You are right. That is the big deal and you know what it takes to make all this happen. Are you interested?"

"Certainly," Axel responded. "As long as I get my share of the money to be made, then I am interested. Can you guarantee me a good pay up front and a percentage of the action on the trade?"

"I can't promise you anything. You will have to talk to the top Boston guy to get that kind of action. I will tell him you are interested, and if he thinks it is worthwhile, he will give you a call. How does that suit you?"

"Like you said, you have my number," said Axel, and turned his internal phone off. He then called Kim at the agency and told him what Earl had said.

Kim said, "Axel, it looks like you hit the big bonanza."

"No, Tori hit the big bonanza. All I did was answer a phone."

The next day the phone on Axel's western extension rang just before noon. He thought, *well, they are consistent. I hope this is not Earl, but the big banana.* He connected on the call, and a voice that wasn't Earl's asked, "Is this Yaro Patraska?"

"Who wants to know?" Axel asked.

"My name is going to be Nada to you right now until we get on better terms."

Axel almost smiled and said, "Okay Nada, I understand. You must be the guy that Earl said would be calling me. Are you the big one?"

"For right now I just want to talk about you and see if I can check your references. So, why don't you just cool it and tell me a little about yourself."

"Fair enough," said Axel. "I ran cocaine from Russia for several years, before I decided I liked pushing the various things from Mexico. After a couple of years I went back to Afghanistan, where I had previously picked up on the trade. I worked for a guy named Bene Zuri, who runs the opium and morphine trade in northeastern Afghanistan. Then I worked with Vasco Pasteranski to move morphine, and helped to direct opium from northern Pakistan to southern Pakistan. The man I worked for in Mexico got shot and died a couple of years ago, but you can contact either Bene or Vasco. I have their phone numbers and their e-mail addresses. If you want to know anything about me, you should check with those men. Bene is a Russian who got into the drug trade when Russia was at war with Afghanistan. Vasco is a Paki who receives opium from Afghanistan and manufactures morphine and heroin. Fortunately, no one in the U.S. knows that I did those things, so I was able to come over on a visa. I have relatives here and I have a degree in biology. Does that do it for you?"

"How about giving me the phone numbers and the e-mail addresses of the two contacts you mentioned?"

Axel gave Nada all the information he needed, after which Nada said, "Okay, Yaro. I will contact these people. If they check out, I will give you a call. If they don't check out, I wouldn't stand by the phone waiting."

Axel disconnected and thought, *I know that was the big cheese. I know he will check with those two. I know they love me and they will tell him that. When I was over there I did a lot of things to impress them. Now I am glad I was over there and I used a Russian name. This fits perfectly. The only thing that can stop this now is if Bene or Vasco got killed. Knowing them, I don't think they would be the victims of any killing. Besides, it hasn't been that long since I was over there. I don't believe anything could have happened to screw up their deals since I was there.*

Axel sat down, still thinking about Bene and Vasco. *Those were two interesting men, despite the trade they were in. I really liked them, but if Kim had told me to take them out, they would have been taken out. I hope Kim doesn't ever ask me to do that. If the drug cartels are going to be running for years, then I hope they are the ones that do it. It's the only trade they have. It's like they went to school to learn how to be drug peddlers and were the valedictorians of their classes.*

Two days passed, and the West Coast phone number rang in Axel's body. Axel was certain it was Nada. He picked up the phone and said, "This is Yaro."

The voice on the other end of the phone was the same voice he had talked with a couple of days ago. The voice said, "Yaro, this is Nada. I talked to the two men you told me about. You came out smelling like a rose. I could have sworn you were their son. They both think you have some power that you hide until you have to go into action. How about telling me about that?"

"I don't know what they are talking about. There were a couple of incidents that occurred, and I had been taught during my stay with the Mexican cartel how to react fast. I think they are referring to my rapid reactions to trouble. Is that it?"

"Well that is part of what they said," commented Nada. "However, they felt you did that and had something extra to spare. How can you explain that?"

Axel muttered something about swift thoughts didn't exist over there, and Nada said, "Are you saying that they just thought you were something extra because the other people around them were kind of slow?"

"Yes, I believe that may be part of it. Keep in mind that I am highly experienced and I have a degree in biology, so I had some things behind me that they didn't. Both of those two guys are sharp, and I would work for them anytime. I respect them. If I were on the other side of the law against them, I would have my hands full. They know how to run a tight ship."

"Well, I told you I would call you back if you checked out. I called, so you must have checked out. Now how about our talking about the needs of the Russians in the Northeast? We lead a good life, but we are always thinking about how we could be doing better, and how we might have enough money to bring some additional families from Russia to live in this country. We believe we could do this if the U.S. military would leave Afghanistan. With those forces gone, we could regain control of the opium trade. When you control the opium trade, you also control the morphine and heroin trade, since they are derived from opium. With this control, we are talking about billions of dollars coming into our hands. This is billions of dollars every year. Over a ten-year span, we are talking about close to a trillion dollars. With that kind of money, we would be able to do tremendous things for this country and for our families who live in Russia and the countries that used to be part of the Soviet Union. One of those countries borders northeast Afghanistan and the only thing that separates them is a river. At one time this river proved to be the biggest transporting means of carrying opium from Afghanistan's rich opium fields.

"Now we get to the point of what we need to do in this country to have this kind of wealth and power. We need to set off some terrorist events here in America, so that the American government would be under great pressure to bring the troops back from Iraq and Afghanistan. It's as simple as that. Do you see where I am going on this subject?"

"I certainly do," Axel said. "I also agree with you if there is an increase in terrorist events in this country, the president would be troops back from overseas. How do you propose on doing this?"

"I am glad you can see and agree with the approach. We have considered several ways to generate a terrorist scare in this country. I could have radioactive material, bomb grade, brought into this country, and we could do a lot of things with this approach. We also considered using nanoparticle as a means of providing this threat. We have considered using IEDs (improvised explosive devices), which are the simplest and easiest for us to manage. Each of these has a problem of one nature or another. Using nuclear methods is too drastic and less controllable than other methods. It is also too hard to bring the material into the country. But the biggest problem lies with the fear a nuclear approach will harm us as well as to the American people. Setting off something of that nature within a safe distance from our homes and our families is difficult. Besides, it might be unpopular for our mother country if the word got out that the material came from Russia. So, unless we change our minds, we are not going the nuclear way.

"We considered using nanoparticles. Nanoparticles have some interesting characteristics. Mainly, they are so small that we could easily carry them across the country without being caught. They could be put in water systems and air control systems, like ventilation systems in motels. The problems we see are several. We don't know how to handle them. We don't know exactly how they work yet. We don't know how the country would react to any problems caused by the events that we could initiate. They might not consider them a terrorist threat, but more like an industrial accident. We looked at the use of various types of IEDs. The good thing about using these is that we could pinpoint where we want the things to take effect. We also believe they would bring a high exposure level to the American public. If people see explosions occurring at several places at that same time, they know it is a terrorist act. So, this crude method seems to have the most popular appeal with my people in the Northeast. We can see this working. We know how to make these bombs. We know how to remotely control their effects. We believe they will give us the biggest bang for our bucks. Therefore, unless you have other ideas that could persuade us otherwise, this is the way we have been planning. What do you think?"

Axel responded by saying, "I have been on the East Coast this week doing business. I am in New York. I could drive up to Boston tomorrow and meet with you so we can talk face to face. In general, I agree with your plan. What do you say?"

"That's great that you are on this coast. Why don't we meet tomorrow night or the next morning?"

"Good," Axel said, "but I need your name and contact information. I can meet you at your work or at your home."

There was a quiet period on the phone for a few seconds before Nada spoke. "I will give you the address of my work, and we should meet tomorrow evening. I will leave a message at the front desk that anyone coming in the evening and asking for Nada should be directed to me. Is that fair enough?"

"Yes, I can work under those conditions for now. I will try to be at your office by 7:30 in the evening. Give me your work phone number, and I will call you if I can't make it by 7:30."

Nada gave Axel the phone number and the address of his work. With those conditions agreed to, they broke off the phone conversation.

No sooner were they done talking when Axel called Kim. He told Kim the phone number and address, and asked him to look up the company.

Kim was quite happy to receive this call from Axel. He discussed the thoughts that those at the agency had about terrorist threats on the West Coast and the East Coast. He believed the one that Axel had uncovered on the West Coast had eliminated a potentially big issue. Now with Axel on the tail of some East Coast terrorists, Kim said he was very excited.

"Axel, I believe you are on the right trail. There is no doubt that there is a building threat in the Northeast, and I think you may be on the right one. Keep us informed so we can help whenever anything comes up."

The next day Axel, who of course was already in the Boston area, only had to finish up other things he had to do with Nanico. They had been working on the procedure that Axel had recommended, and everyone felt quite confident that this was the right direction. Of course, the information that Morgan was involved with the death of a person who had been given an inhaler that contained nanoparticles was no help to Axel. He had to keep his distance from Morgan. However, he did stay close to the people on the process line to make sure they were incorporating valid material and methods.

That afternoon Axel went to Morgan's office and said he would be away for a few days. He told Morgan that he felt that the changes being made on the line were going in the right direction. Then he got on the phone with Kim and asked him about the company he was to visit in the evening.

Kim briefed Axel, saying, "The name of the business is Micromissions, and they make physical elements out of the same processes used by the semiconductor business. They are not chips like you are used to. They are physical elements that are made with those techniques to make miniature motors, generators, sensors, and other very small elements. The CEO is Vinder Laskovich, and he is a Russian who came to this country a little over ten years ago and got some financing from sources in Russia, as far as we can tell. They make good material, but their problem is that many of the things they make have a limited market with military applications, or advanced developments for companies that are working with the government. We don't have any bad news on the CEO, but you don't know yet whether this is the man you will be meeting with. Let us know as soon as you find out."

Axel went to dinner at 5:30, and afterward spent some time thinking about what direction he was going to take at the meeting. Before long it was time to head to Micromissions. When he entered the building, he told the person at the desk that he was supposed to see Nada. The woman picked up the phone and called a number. A man answered, and she said, "There's a man here that wants to speak to Nada."

"Fine, tell him I will be right down," the man said.

In a few minutes, a well-dressed and well-groomed middle-aged man came to the lobby. Extending his hand, he said, "Good evening, Yaro. You made good time."

"Yes," Axel said. "I got here around five and went to a restaurant for a leisurely dinner."

The man called Nada nodded and gestured for Axel to walk with him. They got into an elevator that took them to the second floor. From there they walked down a hall to a door with a sign that said Vinder Laskovich. Below that were the letters CEO. Axel now knew the man's real name, and it corresponded to what Kim had told him.

When they entered the office, Nada said, "Well, now you know who I am and my position in the company. You will soon realize that I have a big core of people in the Boston area who are ready to take some actions, such as the ones we talked about on the phone."

"Yes," Axel said. "Now I know why you chose to keep your name hidden. At your level, you have too much going for you to risk having people know that you have other plans. I think having only Russian people involved is also a good strategy. Loyalty is very important in risky undertakings. But how sure are you of their loyalty? Do you think any of them will want to drop out of this venture when we really put it into motion?"

Vinder sat behind his desk. "I make sure of everything I intend to follow. These people have been loyal to me in the past, and I don't expect it to change in the future. Why would it?"

"Keep in mind," Axel said, "that even though they may have come from your Mother Russia and have shown loyalty in the past, times change. Some of these people probably have gotten used to living in this country and like it. This may put them on the fence when it comes to committing terrorist acts against this country. Many of them would not want to go back to Russia. I know. I lived there and I don't want to go back. The only reason I am interested in this plan is money. I want to better myself, and the only way of doing that is to gain more wealth.

I expect to make money from this venture. I admit it will be a long way off. First, we must make this country want to pull their forces out of Afghanistan, and then our Russian buddies will reap the rewards of taking over the opium trade. And only after all that is done will I be able to enjoy some wealth. But I have significant funds, so I can afford to wait. Are all your people in this kind of position?"

Vinder was quiet for a while, and then said, "You have a good point. In most cases I would agree with you, but in this case these are people that have worked with me for a good while, and they have me to thank for the good life they live. They get paid good salaries and have good benefits. They have sworn to take on this mission, and I believe they are 100 percent behind this."

"Maybe so," Axel said. "But I bet that some of them have thought that they don't want to lose what they now have, even if you were the major reason they got what they have. Most people will follow a good leader, but there are times when they question whether that leader is being straight with himself, let alone with them. When this happens, questions appear in their minds. When that happens, their wife might say something like, 'I don't think this is a good idea,' and that might bump them off the fence."

"Again, I think you have a good point. What about you? Do you need more information of why this is worth doing?"

"You don't understand," replied Axel. "I am doing this because of the money. But I am also doing it because I think it is dumb for the American people to be over there fighting for something that they will never get. There is no way the efforts of this country are going to change the way Iraqis and Afghans will live out their lives. They are driven by religion and faith in certain things that the people of this country don't understand. Iraq is the easiest to work with, trying to make its people realize they can have a better life with the country being run different than before; even though the two major religious factions will kill or do anything to offset any gains the other would make. I give that country a couple of years, and then those people will be back to wanting a strong leader like they had before the U.S. invaded; someone like Saddam Hussein.

"As for Afghanistan, that is a lost cause. We Russians found that out when our country fought them for eight years before pulling out.

The reason is different than anyone could imagine. Here is a country without a government per se. Most of the people live in small villages far from the capital. They don't care about who is governing the country. They live their lives the same no matter who is in power. Why? Because a change in government in Afghanistan has no effect on the individuals who roam, fight, eat, grow opium, harvest opium, and sell opium. They only have to cross a river to sell to a country that was once a part of the Soviet Union. They only have to cross a territorial line and they can sell opium to Pakistan, which then sells it in the form of heroin. They go about this business no matter who is 'in charge.' They are probably happy the American troops are there, because it helps to keep the Taliban and Al-Qaeda from taking their crops. They make more money now than they did before.

"They also do not have a density of population like other countries do. Most other countries in the world, if you wanted to overcome them, all you would have to do is take over a few major cities, since those cities contain a high percentage of the population. Afghanistan is not like that. It is made up of a bunch of tribes that live their lives like their ancestors did. You take over the two major cities of Afghanistan, and most of the people in the country won't even notice. They don't care. They have lived this way all their lives. It's an individualist country. There is no way of fighting them, because you can't find a cluster of them to fight. You spend most of your time looking for them and wearing heavy gear and sweating and cussing because you are not getting anywhere. Being in the army is fun when you are doing something worthwhile and can see the benefits. The troops in Afghanistan will see some benefits in a couple of towns before it is all over and they decide to come home, but once they leave, nothing will change."

Vinder said, "That's the first time I ever heard that description of that country and its people that makes sense. Do you have any more of those general descriptions of any other country?"

Axel replied, "I didn't have to spend a day in that country to know that, and I have spent many days there. I am surprised that neither the U.S. nor the Soviet Union realized this. A lot of energy is wasted in chasing and killing a few bad Afghans, when all they need to do is set a couple of IED bombs and kill a bunch of people to make up for it. They are so religious; they feel good about wrapping their bodies with bombs and going into any location and blowing themselves up, as long as they take many others with them. That's insane. But I guess we didn't get together tonight to talk about that. Still, I thought you ought to understand that one of the reasons I would be for your plan doesn't relate to money. I like many Americans and I hate to see them wasting their time over there. I would do this just to bring many of them home."

Vinder kept looking at Axel. "You know, when I checked you out with Bene and Vasco, they told me you were different. Now I am beginning to understand what they meant. They had a hard time explaining why you are worthwhile for this venture. They kept talking about your physical strengths and trying to explain some other hidden features you possess. I think I just heard some of them. I would really like to have you join our group. We need some experienced leaders, and you appear to be one of those. You have experiences that not one of us has, including me. I would like you to meet my people. What do you think of that?"

"Do all the people work in this company, or are some of them in other companies?"

"Why do you ask that?"

"I don't know why I ask that," Axel said. I was just wondering if there were others people in other companies, and if they have the same strong convictions that you have."

"You hit on a very big point," Vinder said. "There are other people who work elsewhere, and some are the CEOs of their companies. They were the ones who came to me and asked me if I felt this way. Then they said they felt I was the only one who could successfully lead a venture like this. So, I was one of the recruited ones, and this makes me feel very strong about others being committed to doing this."

"It sure sounds like it," remarked Axel. "When do you think you can bring them together?"

Vinder thought about it for minute. "I know I could get about 80 percent of them here by tomorrow evening. Let me check on the others and see what I come up with. Excuse me while I make some phone calls. Would you please sit outside until I complete these calls?"

Axel left the office. He had contacted Kim on his internal phone just before he began to talk to Vinder. Now that he was outside, he asked Kim if he had heard the whole discussion.

Kim responded with, "How about that? You never know what people are thinking or how aggressive they can be."

"Let's see what happens when he gets his people together," Axel said. "Hopefully he can arrange it in a day or so."

They talked on the "silent phone" for about fifteen minutes, until Vinder came out of his office.

"Looks like I may be able to get all of them together tomorrow," he said to Axel. "I only have one that is questionable, and I probably confirm with him by tomorrow morning. Even without him, I think we can have the meeting tomorrow night at 7:30. How does this fit with your plans?"

"No problem," replied Axel. "The sooner, the better. I am here, and I can be here tomorrow night. You have my number, so if anything comes up to change the time, give me a call."

The next day passed rapidly, as Axel drove around Boston to see the sights. At 6:30 he headed for Micromissions, arriving there at a little before the meeting time. When Vinder came down to meet him, he told him they'd go to the conference room on the first floor. It could hold about thirty people, Vinder said, and there would be twenty-two of them, if everyone showed up. When they got to the conference room, several people were already there. Vinder sat, indicating that Axel should sit beside him. When everyone was there and settled, Vinder spoke.

"I am very happy that you all could come. I have brought a new person on board that I believe could be a strong leader for the venture we have discussed in the past. I have always held back on this venture, because I didn't think we had the right person who had the time, the energy, and the same drive that we all have. I want you all to meet a fellow Russian, Yaro Patraska. He has experience in working in the Mexican cartel, worked with Bene Zuri in Afghanistan in the poppy trade and morphine trade, and with Vasco Pasteranski in Pakistan on the morphine and heroin trades. He has expressed a desire to work with us. He believes that if there are enough terrorist acts in this country, the U.S. will pull back their troops from Afghanistan in order to bring more stability back home. Yaro believes our Afghan contacts will then pick up on their trade, and we should all be able to become wealthy. Yaro also believes this is good for America, since it will reduce the number of casualties for American troops. But probably his biggest reason for wanting our venture to wake up Americans is because he believes that this country will never be successful over the long term in Afghanistan. He feels we are simply playing with ourselves over there, and that the Taliban and Al-Qaeda will be there long after American troops leave that place. Does that sound familiar to you?"

The other men all clapped their hands and laughed. One of them shouted, "It took our comrades eight years to learn that. Maybe Americans are even dumber, since they've been there nearly nine years. And I wouldn't be surprised if they were there for another nine!"

Everyone laughed again.

Vinder raised his hands to quiet the group. "I know each of you are busy with your work and cannot spend the kind of time that is needed to make this a success, so I am asking Yaro to take the reins on this venture and, with your help, make it work. I am asking each of you to follow his lead." Vinder turned to Axel. "Yaro, the floor is yours."

Axel stood up and looked at everyone for a few seconds. Then he said, "Are you all committed to this? If you are not, then you should leave the room now. No one will think the less of you."

One man raised his hand and said, "I am going to excuse myself from this venture, even though I believe it is the right thing to do. My job doesn't allow me the time to participate as much as I feel I should. I hope you all don't think less of me for making this decision. I just cannot handle the risk. I wish you all the best, and as far as I am concerned, I have never heard anything about this. My mouth is sealed." With that he got up, wished everyone the best, and left.

You don't know how good a move you just made, buddy, Axel thought. *You are the only one in this room who has made a good decision. The rest will suffer sooner or later, I guarantee it.*

After the group had settled down from this disruption, Axel said, "I'm glad to see that only one doesn't have the necessary commitment. The rest of you will be the winners in the end. I want you all to know that Vinder and I have thought about the various methods that could be used for this venture. We have considered a nuclear dirty bomb threat, a special threat using nanoparticles, and the use of explosive devices. We believe that using nuclear or the nanoparticle approach in this country that you have adopted would not be appropriate. Even though they would be effective, they are too dangerous and not popular. Anyone using these methods really wants to hurt this country, and it would be very unpopular as a terrorist method. We believe that the use of random explosives makes the point and allows people to think about it.

"An explosion is a controlled event, and then nothing happens and the media takes over. A few days later, another explosive event would force more and more people to believe that there is a terrorist organization that hits and runs. They start believing that something could happen to them. These events can be pulled off without a large loss of life, but still making the point. It is something that people understand, and they believe they can find the culprits. But once the media has this and the people start being excited from their propaganda, this is a runaway train happening. The good news is we can stop and fade into the background, and maybe never have to come out and do anything more. Or we could wait a month, and just when people settle down, we can have a few more bombs go off. Does that make sense to you?"

Axel got good feedback on this approach. At this point he decided to discuss the supply of material to carry out these ventures.

"We will utilize two types of explosives for these events. There is the ammonium nitrate with fuel to make the kind of the bomb used the most in Iraq and Afghanistan by the insurgents over there. They take either oil or kerosene as the fuel to mix with the ammonium nitrate to complete the explosive mix. It is called ANFO, and would be used whenever highly explosive material is required. My suggestion is to use kerosene, which works quite well and is rather inexpensive. The other type of explosive is the one using good grade hydrogen peroxide mixed with acetone. It is called TATP. The TATP is quite sensitive to impact, temperature, and friction. This is used when the bomber has restricted space. Something similar to this was used by the 'shoe bomber' and the 'Christmas bomber.'"

Axel continued his presentation by asking who was going to get what material. "Gentlemen, I know we can get all the kerosene we need, and all the acetone we need. However, the high-grade hydrogen peroxide and the ammonium nitrate are harder to come by. I need to hear from each of you as to what you can do to bring in the hard to get materials, as well as the more easily obtained material."

Vinder spoke. "I have all the acetone, and will get all the kerosene we need. We use acetone in our process here at Micromissions."

"Good," Axel said. "Who will get the ammonium nitrate?"

Several people put up their hands, and Axel pointed to them one at a time. As each was questioned, Axel gathered that the fertilizer would be easy to obtain from the farms in northern New York, only about two hundred miles away.

However, one of the men stood up and said, "My name is Omar Simtenus, and I have a crate of ammonium nitrate from Afghanistan that is coming in on a Bulgarian freighter. That ship is due this coming week. I will let you know when it has arrived."

"Well, I have to say that's timely," said Axel. "Is there some particular reason why you have this arriving in the States?"

Speaking dramatically, Omar said, "I wanted to take some of these actions into my own hands. I was tired of waiting. However, with Yaro directing these missions, I am willing to give the crate to him when it comes in. I believe the rest of you that are able to obtain some of this material should go ahead and do so. We want to make sure we have an ample supply of good material. My crate is supposed to be one hundred and fifty pounds."

"That's great," Axel said. "All of you should let me know sometime in the next week how much each of you thinks you can provide. In order to coordinate this information, Vinder will supply you with the phone number you should use. I will monitor the phone messages. I also need to know which of you can obtain a supply of high-grade hydrogen peroxide?"

Several hands went up, and Axel asked each to give their source. Two of the people ran beauty parlors, and it turned out they used both off-the-shelf hydrogen peroxide and the higher-grade material Triacetone Triperoxide, that had been chemically stabilized. With some additives, it would provide a terrific explosive. One of the men ran a semiconductor production line, and they used methyl ethyl ketone peroxide in some of their processes. He said that it was stable, especially when kept below a certain temperature. He felt with a chemical additive, it could be used in a TATP.

There were two men who worked in places where silicone or polyester resins were formed. "Often this is used in producing fiberglass reinforced composites," said one of the men. "My company works with fiberglass for boats and repair of Corvettes."

Axel said, "This explosive was used in a couple of airplane incidents, the one with the 'shoe bomber' being the best known. This explosive works by the creation of gas at a terrific rate that can't be controlled, and results in a highly explosive combination. If kept under two grams, there is no danger of accidental explosion. But when the amount goes up in weight, the critical nature of the material goes up, especially if it is confined in a small volume container. It is best when it is wet after first mixing it. But the best way to use it is to let it dry. Although this is the best for explosive force, the mixture is also less stable, and a shock can set it off. The message here is that I want everyone to be careful with this stuff. We may decide to use the ANFO for every event and stay away from the TATP, unless some of you come up with a way of safely using it. I think that is what they tried to do with the 'shoe bomber,' and the more recent event with that flight going into Detroit at Christmastime. Both of those events fizzled when the bombers tried to combine wet material with the dry crystals. Instead of an explosion, they got smoke and some fire. This is a good example of how not to use this tricky material."

The discussion went on for a while, and at the conclusion Axel asked that each man sign his name in a notebook he had brought, along with the men's phone numbers and e-mail addresses.

"Also write what you are going to do about providing the materials we've discussed. Just write ANFO if that is what you intend, or TATP if that is what you intend. Also, if you think there are other materials to use, write them down by your name. Keep in mind that each of you should remember to call the number Vinder will give you to keep me up to date. I will be checking it about four times a day."

As the men left from the room, they said things like, "Good move, Yaro," or "Glad to see this is moving forward." Axel had the feeling that everything had gone smoothly, and he was surprised there weren't any antagonists in the crowd. After they had left the room, Vinder turned to Axel.

"That went quite well. They seemed to have accepted you without a lot of anger. Some of them are very forceful leaders, but they stayed in line today. That is a good sign. They probably feel that your experience is needed in this venture, and is beyond what any of them possess."

Axel agreed it had gone well, and added, "You have my phone number. If you want anything, just give me a call."

Axel went to his motel and talked with Kim on the phone.

"What do you think about the meeting?" he asked.

Kim said that he thought the meeting had gone well, if you want to have a group of men that wanted to do harm to the country. "To tell you the truth, Axel, I am shocked and demoralized that these men, who have been in this country for some time, would have this feeling. It is obvious they are greedy and just want to suck out the drug money."

"Yes," replied Axel. "Here were nineteen men in that room, and things went smooth as silk. You would think that you were just in a business meeting talking about strategy for the coming quarter, rather than about bombing people. I was confused about their single-minded attitude. They obviously are cruel people, but if you met them at a dinner party, you wouldn't know they held this kind of malice in their bodies. This reminds me, I am going to look at the notebook with their names, phone numbers, and e-mails, and send them to you via a fax. Is your fax machine on?"

Kim replied in the affirmative. Axel took out the notebook and looked at it page by page, and then sent the page via the new fax sending method that Kim had installed in him the last time he'd been at the agency lab. After waiting a minute, he asked, "Did you get the transmission?"

Kim said that he had, and he would have his men search down any data they could find on these people. "This is a great start," said Kim. "Having this list of names puts us in a good position to find out what we can about each person, and perhaps learn what they have against this country. It will be interesting to find out how long they have been here, and whether they are true citizens of this country or just here on a visa. Good work, Axel. Keep me updated."

It turned out that Axel was experiencing the calm before the storm. This storm was expressed by the various people who had been quiet in that meeting, but as the following week passed, it became evident that some of those people really wanted to inflict damage on the United States. One of the men came to see him, and said that he was quite concerned that Axel had got the wrong message from either Vinder or the people in the meeting.

"I am not interested in the opium trade in Afghanistan," the man said. "I am interested in creating damage in this country. I am pissed off at the loss of jobs and the unsettled nature of the country over the last ten years. I used to have a great job, but due to some bad decisions by banks and others, there was a complete financial collapse and I lost what money I had. I also lost my job, because my employer couldn't survive the hard times, and couldn't get any bank loans. Before we knew, we were being laid off. This was me and another of the Russians in the meeting last week."

Axel asked the man his name and the name of his friend.

"My name is Elias Mankov," he said, "and my friend is Paul Vanderhoff."

Axel told him that he understood his anger, but felt that many people in the country felt the same way, to a greater or less degree. "Many have lost their jobs and are searching for new employment. It doesn't pay to just complain. The past is what it was, and that won't change. The new president is trying to do things to improve the job situation. I am sure that your experience is such that just 'beating the bushes,' so to speak, will result in some payoff for you."

"No, you don't understand," said Elias. "I believe this is a plan that the politicians have. If I could get into a congressional meeting with explosives, I would bomb the whole place, even if it took my life! I don't believe there's a good congressman or senator in the country."

Axel was not ready for this kind of conversation after the rather quiet meeting the week before. "Why didn't you bring this up in the meeting?" he asked.

Elias was quiet for a while, and then he said, "I should have spoken up. I didn't because Vinder is always trying to do right by us. I didn't want to be the one who broke his bubble. I wanted to say something, but the meeting was constructive, and everyone seemed happy with what was being said. I gave it more thought and decided that the agenda at the meeting wasn't hitting my sore spot. I want action. I want to set off bombs everywhere I can. Do you understand that?"

"I guess I am just getting the drift of what you are saying. You are anti-American. Why don't you go back to Russia?"

"Look, Yaro," Elias said, "I don't like it here for the way things have changed. They are changing to be more like Russia. I don't want to go back to Russia and see this all over again. Russia is not the place to live if you aren't at the top of the government. No, I don't want to go back to Russia. I haven't given it much thought, where I would like to live.

This place has been much better than Russia. I just don't like the way its going, and I don't like what happened to me and my job."

Axel said he got the drift, and then asked, "What would you like to do?"

"If I could do it, I would like to get that shipment of ammonium nitrate and make a big bomb, like the one that shook Oklahoma City several years back. I don't want to piss around doing little things in the hopes of getting the government's attention. I want those folks in Washington to realize there are people that don't like the government. Where I come from, they try to eliminate the government they have. I would like to do that."

Axel tried to calm this man down with a comment about waiting until the other people in that meeting came forward with their thoughts about what should be done. "Maybe they will agree with you," he said. "Maybe Vinder and I were misunderstanding the focus of our Russian friends. Give this a week, and let's see what comes out of it. I will talk with you a week from today and let you know the general tone of the feedback I receive. Does that make sense to you, to give it one more week?"

Elias looked down at the floor and thought about it. Then he looked up and said, "You know, Yaro, you have only been involved with this a few days. You may find that the tone is much different than you think. You may find this is an immediate thing they want. I will give you a week."

"That's great," Axel said. "Maybe in a week you will find a job and things will settle down for you. At least I hope so."

The next day, Axel got a call from another member of the group, Joseph Meleshef. He wanted to talk to Yaro and asked if they could meet that evening at Micromissions. Axel agreed, and was surprised when three men showed up, not just one. He led them to the conference room.

"Well, gentlemen," he said, "I talked to Joseph and expected just him. Which one is Joseph, and please let me know the names of the other two?"

One man stepped forward and said, "I am Joseph, and I hope you don't mind that I brought two of my friends with me. They have the same story as I have, and you might as well know the members of the group that want to express a different view than was expressed the other day. This man is Albert and this man is Marcus."

Axel shook each of their hands and asked if they wanted a coffee or anything to drink. They all thought a cup of coffee would be fine, and Axel poured for all four of them. As he sat down he asked, "What can I do for you gentlemen this evening?"

Joseph took a sip of his coffee and said, "I mentioned to you on the phone that I had a different slant on where the actions should go. It turns out that Albert and Marcus have the same views as I have. I will give you our view, and if I say anything wrong, each of them knows to speak up to make sure you have the exact nature of their comments.

"At the meeting, we listened to what you had to say and what Vinder evidently agrees with. Afterward, the three of us got together to talk. All of us came to this country about ten years ago. Things were going quite well, and we got off to a good start. But soon afterward, we began to see there were ethnic pressures against us and our Russian ways. We were treated like the black people were treated a half century ago. But now it is the black people who are getting the good jobs and nice homes, and we are just running up against roadblocks. We finally came to the conclusion that we needed to do something to arouse the government about our situation. We sent letters to our members of Congress and told them that they should look into why we were being treated like enemies of this country. We never got a straight answer back. The few answers we did get indicated that what we were experiencing was just the normal reaction of people towards immigrants, and that given time, this problem would disappear. It hasn't disappeared. We want to do something to bring this to the attention of the U.S. government. We are tired of being treated unfairly. Supposedly, this is a country that treats everyone fairly. Now we think that is propaganda and not real. Each of us is educated and has a degree from the upper schools in Russian. This is not recognized by any of the companies we have interviewed with. It's a myth!"

Wow, Axel thought. *This is looking more and more like I have a bunch of dissatisfied people on my hand. I better find out where they want to take this.*

"What do you want to do?" Axel asked.

The man named Albert answered. "Maybe you don't know it, but there are about twelve of us who came from Russian about ten years ago, and we were very good at what we did in Russia. We ran rackets. We placed bombs in key places and blew up whatever we wanted to. We didn't know better. We had no trade, and being gangsters in Russia was a good living. We were what one would call terrorists now, and this is a popular trade in Russia. There are many people, sometimes over 50 percent, who want the present government overthrown. Over half our deeds were against the government, local or national. We got paid well to do this.

"Now we are in this country, and with the pull of several of our countrymen, we were able to obtain good jobs when we first came here. But we can't say we were the best of employees, and when times got tough; we were laid off or just straight fired. Now we are left with nothing to do and no way to obtain recommendations or references for new jobs. We are trained to do harm and we know how to do it well. If we have to kill someone while carrying out a robbery, we will do that without thinking twice. Before you came on the scene, we were ready to start robbing stores, robbing banks, robbing individuals, taking on hits for people like the mafia and things of this nature. That is what we are good at. Do you understand?"

Axel thought about this for a minute and then said, "I know where you are coming from, and I can see why you think that is your trade. That is all you have been successful at in your young lives. That is tragic, but I can see how you got there. We have mobs in this country filled with people like you. I have been involved with people like that in Mexico. They wander around and take on tough assignments that are difficult to handle, ones that most people wouldn't want to take. Are any of you married?"

"No," replied Albert. "But I have a girlfriend I have lived with for a couple of years."

"Has that made any changes in your life?" Axel asked.

Albert considered that. "I have had a good life since she's been around, although it is more difficult now that I'm not working. Fortunately, she has a job. But that is not the same. I am always fidgeting around with nothing to do. That is boring, and when I think about what I used to do in our homeland, the boredom is intolerable."

Axel considered that these men could be very dangerous. In order to try to come up with a solution, he decided to take a positive tack and see where that took this issue. "I understand the problem you are describing," he said. "I have been there myself at times. Usually, I have found that in a short time, I find something that takes my mind off my troubles and they fade away. Maybe we can come up with something to keep you active and allow you some time to recover from this feeling of worthlessness. How about giving me a week to think about the problem, and we then we'll meet and discuss it further?"

Albert looked intently at Axel and said, "You know the things we talked about at the meeting the other day? Getting off to a rapid start would do a lot for those of us who been feel this way. We have had some ideas of our own, and they're not the same as the ones you mentioned at the meeting. We believe that the actions you proposed might take some time to get off the deck. Do you have a time line in mind now?"

Axel said that he had a general time line, but nothing has been solidified as of yet. "Maybe by the time we meet next week," he said.

The three men looked at Axel as if to say, "Here we go again." Axel immediately took the initiative and said, "You mentioned that you had other plans. What have you considered? Maybe you have a better handle on this than Vinder has."

Now it was Marcus's turn to speak, and he said, "Botulism." This surprised Axel, and he asked what they meant by botulism

"We believe we could use Botox to create a problem immediately," Marcus said.

Axel stared at the three men. "What do you mean, Botox? That is used to suppress wrinkles on people's faces. What does that have to do with terrorist actions?" Axel knew the answer, but he wanted to understand what these three men knew.

"Botox has been used as a medicine in many cases," Marcus said. "However, it is produced by the bacterium that is the most toxic protein known to mankind. It takes very little to kill a person. People that use it for winkles don't realize how little is used to help them for about seven or eight months. In fact, the new series of a form of Botox is nothing more than using smaller needles or hypodermics to reduce the amount used. It only takes about two thousands of a microgram to kill a person if they ingest it in food or water."

"Yes, I am aware of that," Axel commented. "It is definitely a powerful form of botulism that can kill. But in most cases, it is ineffective. If used on food, it gets eliminated during the cooking process. Anyway, I will think about that during the coming week, and we can get together and see if anything pans out of the next session."

Joseph looked at Marcus and Albert. They sort of nodded their heads in agreement, but Axel noticed that they did not seem optimistic about what the next week would bring.

After the three of them left, Axel got on his internal phone and called Kim. He told him what the day had brought. "

It's hard to believe," Kim said. "They have been here for about ten years, and they haven't really changed their ways. I guess that's why so many criminals who eventually get out of jail normally end up right back in there. It's all they know how to do. Crooks remain crooks, it seems. It's a wonder when you see some of these people who were criminals actually end up doing good things and leading normal and happy lives. I guess that's why we have prisons. We are hoping that at least some of them will learn crime doesn't pay, and they come out with some knowledge or skill they learned in prison. And some of them do. Let's hope these three men change their minds between now and next week. If they don't, you need to delay them and find out where they intend to take their actions, so we can be prepared to stop them. I guess I don't have to tell you that. You are always on the ball and looking for ways to solve problems."

After he hung up with Kim, Axel kept thinking about botulism and Botox. *It's a wonder that more people don't get hurt while going through treatments with Botox,* he thought. *Botulinum toxin is dangerously powerful. It's a miracle that some doctors worked long and hard on using this dreadful protein to gain some good from it. The first fruitful results were for people who had cross-eye syndrome, and it helped to relieve them. Then there were those that had other problems with their sight and with muscle spasms, and treatments with mild reengineered forms of this helped for seven or eight months at a time. Then they had to get another shot to carry them through the next period. It took researchers hours and hours and years to find how to use this powerful toxin to create good. I remember that there was a problem with children due to botulism caused by eating honey. Now they don't allow children under one year old to eat honey for fear of getting this toxin. In general, there is no way the toxin can really bother people in its normal form. There was a company that used to sell canned goods. Then some people got deathly sick, and it was traced to canned food that had not been properly sealed, and this allowed the bacterium to enter and form its deadly toxin. That company went out of business. Even in that case, probably if the food had been properly cooked, they wouldn't have gotten sick. I don't know how these Russians want to use Botox or some form of it to do their dirty work. But I know I have to find a way to stop it.*

Botox Enters the Picture as a Terrorist Weapon

The week went by, and Axel made some progress in getting the ammonium nitrate that some of the Russians had promised. However, he didn't make any progress on the Botox issue, and that concerned him. He hoped the three men had gotten this off their menu and wanted to do something else. He didn't look forward to the meeting with them about the Botox. He hadn't thought of any good reason to stop their plan, other than the fact that it was difficult to hurt people with Botox, if they used proper procedures in their cooking habits. Finally the day came, and Elias (not one of the three men who wanted to use Botox) called Axel on the phone to confirm their meeting that evening at 5:15. Axel kept thinking nervously about the meeting, trying to figure out their angle. *I guess I just have to wait to see where they are coming from, so I can then make a judgment and hopefully figure a way around the issue.*

At 5:15, the three men were there for the meeting. Axel began by saying, "I have thought about the Botox proposal. Have you taken it any further?"

"We have thought it over," Elias said, "and we are convinced this is a very effective means to an end. We believe it would be a terrorist act that would really shake up the people."

Axel asked, "Do you have a source of Botox, and is it the kind that is effective for doing this act?"

"Yes, we have a good source of the material," Elias said. "It is now produced in China and Ireland as well as the States. It has become quite plentiful and easily available. We have a friend who runs a cosmetic business, and we know how to get into his supply."

"That's great," responded Axel, as he tried to show he was behind this plan. "But have you figured out how you can use it to do the harm you wish to do? This is not easy, since a good cooking of just over one hundred and sixty degrees Fahrenheit will kill the Botulinum toxin and eliminate its effectiveness. So, if you add it to food that meets these cooking standards, it can be useless."

"We know that," Albert said, "but we have figured a way around that. We will attack sushi restaurants first. They don't cook their food. We believe we would be able to apply the material in ample quantities to kill anyone eating the sushi. We have worked on a way of spraying the material. All we have to do is walk past sushi dishes being prepared for customers, and when they eat the food it would begin to take effect. The neat thing about it is that the botulism doesn't take effect for about a day or two, so those that ingest it will not die at the place where they ate it. The authorities will have a hard time determining how they were contaminated with the botulism. We could hit a few local sushi places one week and some other ones farther away from here the following week. The Americans will believe there is a mass serial killer on the loose, and in fact there will be. It would be our accomplishment. The media will pick it up, with a little help from our friends will report it as a terrorist threat."

Axel was deeply concerned. The men had thought of the right place to hit and how to hit it. "Do you have the proper spray bottles developed?" he asked.

"Yes," answered Albert. "We take window cleaning spray bottles, clean them out, and then refill them with diluted Botox. The dilution is not enough to reduce the power of the material. It just makes it easy to spray. We have tried it on the food of different animals and have seen it work. Animals eat canned or dry foods that don't need cooking. The diluted Botox doesn't seem to deter them from eating their food, and by the next day they are dead."

Axel hated to hear this, since he loved animals as much as he loved people. *How can I stop this plan?* He wondered. *What they had thought out would work if they didn't get caught before the fact. Their plan was simple and quiet, and it would be effective if he didn't do something about it.*

"So, what do you think Yaro?" Albert asked.

"I think this is a well thought out method of killing people," responded Axel. "The only problem I have with it is that it kills all kinds of people. You don't know who you are killing. Doesn't that bother you?"

"No," responded Elias. "If we used a bomb, we wouldn't know who we had killed. It's just the same. Why do you think of it as being different, Yaro?"

"I think of a controlled bombing as something we do to hit a known group of people. I also believe an explosion is a 'visible thing,' so to speak. It stands out and is immediately looked at as a terrorist event, until proven otherwise. This use of a rather slow method that kills people who happened to eat sushi one day is sort of savage. At the same time, days will go by while the authorities try to determine what killed them. Since they are not dying on the spot, like they would from a bomb, time will pass, people will lose interest, and just think it was because of some bad sushi. It doesn't stand out like a bomb. It takes this being done several times at several places for the authorities to figure out that it is a series of terrorist attacks that are happening. Even then they might not figure it out. It might be too subtle." The three men were listening intently. He hoped he could delay them long enough for him to figure out what to do about this. "How close are you to using this stuff, and where would you use it?"

"We could begin using it day after tomorrow," replied Albert. "We have picked out the sushi house, the biggest one in the area. It is located right here in downtown Boston. We have also considered using it in the drinking water at the restaurant, so as to have a double impact or a faster death rate."

Axel smiled and said, "I have to admit, you have thought this out very well. You have taken it further than I had expected. How many are you thinking of using?"

Again, it was Albert who replied; "Maybe twelve."

Axel figured Albert must be the brains of this technical approach, and directed his next question at him. "Tell me, Albert, how do you keep the Botox from getting in your system while performing these acts?"

Albert smiled. "I have taken the spray bottle approach and refined it. I made special belt buckles for the guys. Each buckle has an opening. The Botox is injected at a high pressure into the belt buckle. Pressing an electrical button on the side of the belt releases the Botox. It will spray out in a direct line at the food, rather than as a mist like from a spray bottle. In this manner, it is controlled more directly and more effectively. We don't have to worry about inhaling fumes through the nose or mouth. We have practiced this for the past week and see that it does a good job. We actually used water, went to the sushi restaurant, and effectively sprayed the water on the food. If we would have used the toxic material, we would now be talking about the super results we achieved."

"I am convinced," Axel said. "When do you want to do this?"

Elias spoke up. "How about tomorrow about five o'clock, so we can hit the place for dinner?"

"Sounds good to me," said Axel. "Where should we meet?"

"We could meet at my garage," Albert said. "That is where we load the belt buckles for the twelve men who will participate."

Axel asked where the garage was, and Albert said it was on Delaney Street. He produced a small map. "This map shows how to get there from the major roads. It is not a long distance from the sushi place downtown."

"I'll be there about four thirty so I can see how this is handled," Axel said. "One other thing, do you really think you need twelve people to go this time? That seems like overkill."

Elias took this as his signal to provide his piece about the effort. "The reason we are taking twelve is because only six will go into the Sushi House on Broad Street and do their thing. The other six will go to another restaurant about three blocks away. You were right when you said the police may just think this is a case of poor food control if it happens only in one place. But if we hit two places, they won't be thinking that way. This is especially true if the sushi in the two restaurants is not supplied by the same company."

"Good thinking," Axel said. "I will be at your garage around four thirty tomorrow afternoon. If you aren't home from work yet, I will just wait around. This should wake up the world, or at least the local police, especially when the media shouts, 'Terrorists Strike!' I can see it now."

The three men left and Axel immediately called Kim. He relayed the plan to him.

"I'll be damned," said Kim after hearing the gory details. "I have a hard time believing there are adults living around here with those kinds of lousy ambitions. They consider it a big achievement if they kill a large number of innocent bystanders, who have nothing to do with anything that is contrary to their lives. How do you want to handle this?"

"I think you should just leave it to me," Axel said. "This is happening too quickly for you and your people to do anything about it. I will find a way to make it look like an accident of sorts. I have a whole day between now and then to prepare. They may not have expected me to accept their plan so readily, so they may call and put it off. Who knows? But maybe it is good this came around so rapidly. When I'm done with them, it knocks the number who wants to kill Americans from twenty-two to ten. Is that okay by you?"

Kim was quiet for a few seconds, and then he said, "You know I have the utmost confidence in you and how you think and react. I don't believe that there is anyone in our agency that has the combination of technical and chemical background that you have. There is definitely no one who has your power and your armor to carry this out, not without a lot of police shooting their guns at twelve deadheads. So, go for it!"

That night, Axel thought about what the scene might look like tomorrow at the garage. He knew he wanted it to end at the garage and never make it to the sushi place. He also had to get rid of the toxin so no one else could be hurt by it, such as the workers at a crime lab. He knew he would be able to handle anything that happened tomorrow, and he had no problem going to sleep.

The next day, Axel called Vinder and told him that he would like to talk to him about some plans he had. Vinder was happy to hear that, and they agreed to meet at seven at Vinder's office. Axel had set this up so it wouldn't look like he had been at the garage with those twelve men. All day he thought about how things might play out that night. When it was time to go, he stopped at a candy store and bought a bag of candy bars. He immediately ate one of them, and then ate a couple more as he drove to Albert's garage. He wanted to make sure his energy level would be up when he called for it. When he got to the garage, five men were already there, including the three he had expected. He knew then that those three meant business and would be ready to go.

When he got out of his car, he waved at Elias, Marcus, and Albert. They waved back.

"Right on time," commented Elias.

"As are you," Axel said. As Albert led him into the garage, he gave his internal computer the words of action: Axelvation two, hood down. He felt the energy surge through his body and knew he was ready for the task at hand. Another car pulled up and three men got out of the car. He recognized them from the meeting in Vinder's conference room.

So, we have eight of them now, he thought, *and it's only a little after four thirty. That gives us about half an hour for the other four to arrive. I want them all to be together when I make any move. I want nothing left hanging—except them.*

Axel nodded to Albert. "How have things proceeded?"

"Things have moved right along," said Albert. "I have prepared all the Botox in a special container I made that allows me to fill all the belt buckles easily."

"Good for you." *I wish this guy weren't involved with this,* Axel thought. *He is a sharp man, and I could have gotten him a job doing something for the agency, or in some technical group around here. It's a shame that he wastes his talents on something like this, the killing of people. He is the one I will least like to eliminate from this party. But that is the way it must be. They must all go.*

Just then Marcus said, "Neal Boroffski has arrived with Frank Petrovick. We just have Mikale Borskanski and Adrian Gorgovich left to make our team total."

"Those two have always been the last ones to arrive," growled Albert. "They find different ways to get held up, and it all sounds so logical when they tell you what happened. But they aren't late yet, so I should keep quiet about them. They are both good guys to have on our side."

Albert showed Axel how the container worked for adding Botox to the belt buckle systems he had made. He had the twelve belt buckles on his workbench, and the container for filling them. He gave a mock demonstration on how he would fill each of them when the time came, and Axel was impressed.

He sure has his act together. These buckles he designed are truly artist and mechanical marvels. They can hold the Botox and not leave any out.

Albert loaded a spare buckle with water and held it against his belly. By pushing a button that was attached to an electrical wire, he made the buckle squirt out a fine stream of water into a dish sitting on the workbench. The water went out as a burst and stopped. It was almost like a jet ink printer that puts out bursts of color without any spillage and hits right where it is supposed to.

"That's incredible," Alex exclaimed.

Just then another car pulled up, and Marcus said that the last two arrived. Axel began to breathe a little more rapidly, knowing the time was coming for action. His heart was pumping as if he had just finished a long run. He pulled out a candy bar and began to eat it.

"Need my energy," he said as Elias looked at him.

The last two men walked into the garage, and Elias hit the button for the garage door to close. When the door hit the concrete floor, Axel felt his heart rate go up a little more.

They don't know it, he thought, *but this is their last day on earth. What they had planned to do to others is now going to happen to them.*

At that point Albert took over. "I am now going to fill each of these buckles. All of you need to remove the belt buckles you presently have on your belts."

All of the men did that, and Albert handed them the new buckles with wires attached to each of them. He told them to first place the buckles on their belts, and then slip the wire beneath the belt. The wire had a clip that allowed it to be attached. Also on the wire was a metal button. The button had a sliding cover, so that the button couldn't be pushed unless the cover was moved. This was to prevent an accidental activation of the switch. Albert told them that the cover should be over the switch until they entered the Sushi House, and then he would tell them when to remove the cover.

The men had the new belt buckles on their belts, but Albert told them not to buckle them yet.

"Now," he said, "I am going to go to each of you, push a point on the back of the buckle, and put this injector in the middle of the belt buckle. You all should watch while I do Elias's belt buckle. When I push on the back of the buckle, the orifice on the front of the buckle opens, so I can fill the buckle with my injector. When the buckle is full, I will let go of the point on the back of the buckle and release the injector. Then you will fasten your belt as you normally would."

He completed filling Elias's buckle, and the men all nodded their heads in approval and understanding. Then Albert went from one to the other, and before long there were eleven systems ready to go. He then took care of his belt buckle.

"All of you practiced this with water the other day," he said. "This time it is for real, and Americans are going to die when you push that switch on your right hip. Are you ready?" he shouted.

The others answered with a loud, roaring "Yes!" To Axel it sounded like a football game..

"One more thing," Albert said. "I think that Yaro should have one of these put on his belt. What do you think?"

They all turned and faced Axel, shouting, "Right! Three cheers for Yaro!"

When Albert came up to Axel with a buckle, Axel said, "First I want to shake the hands of all those here today and wish them the best."

He started with Albert, who was standing right in front of him and therefore a little hidden from the others. He grabbed Albert's right hand and snapped it, and before Albert could even cry out in pain, Axel raced from one man to the next, grabbing their right hand as if to shake them and then snapping each of their wrists. At he got to the eleventh man, the last man pulled out his gun and began to fire at Axel. This was worthless, and the bullets flew around the room. Axel grabbed the gun and in one move broke the man's wrist. It took only about twenty seconds to handle all men, and then he returned to Albert. Albert, however, had gained his senses, and he pulled out his a gun with his left hand.

"You asshole!" he shouted. "You didn't know I was left-handed, did you, Yaro?"

He fired the pistol, one shot after the next, but the bullets ricocheted off Axel's chest, falling onto the concrete floor throughout the garage. Albert stared, and before he could think of anything to do, Axel grabbed him by the back of his neck. He squeezed the nerve there, and Albert dropped to the floor unconscious. Axel immediately turned to the other eleven would-be terrorists, grabbing the backs of their necks and squeezing the nerves. Each fell, one by one, like a sack of potatoes. They went from pain to unconsciousness, almost as if this had been an act of mercy.

Axel stopped and looked around at the twelve disciples of death. He knew he had to take this to the next step, since the United States justice system was too lenient for what these twelve had been about to do. Axel pulled the belt off one of the unconscious men. Positioning the buckle over the man's face, he pushed the electronic switch. The toxic mix was injected into his mouth, and Axel knew the man would not last long. He probably would be dead before he regained consciousness. Axel went from one to another of each of these enemies of this country and performed the same function. Next, he collected the guns and the bullet shells that lay on the floor from the firings. He didn't want anyone to know that guns had been fired. This had to look like a mass suicide. He grabbed each of their rights hands and pulled their wrists

I hope that anyone who tries to find the cause of death doesn't look at their wrists. They would think it strange that all of them have broken wrists.

As Axel looked over the carnage, he felt sorry for them. He looked at Albert, who he had thought was a genius, and wished this didn't have to be. Then he shook his head as if to recover from a trance and called Kim.

"Kim, I have a problem. I have just taken the first step in eliminating any terrorist attacks, disposing of twelve of the twenty-two." He then described the events of the past half hour. "I need this to be a hush, hush thing. Someone from the agency must come to this garage and get the bodies out of here. You must find a way of making this look like a mass suicide, so we don't alert the remaining people in this Russian group."

"We will collect the bodies," Kim said, "and we will put them on a small boat and send them out to sea. At some point we will make a gash in the bottom of the boat, and it will sink. We will have someone in our agency find the bodies and report that it looks like twelve men of Russian decent had gone out in a boat, bore a hole in the bottom, and drowned themselves. Since this will take place in the next couple of hours, the toxin will not have completely taken effect, so it won't show the cause of death. Cause of death will be drowning. In order to offset any investigation into the broken wrists, we will tie a rope around their right wrists. It will look like this was done to make sure all of them kept their promise of suicide. This should work."

"That's a remarkable idea," Axel said. "It is now 5:30. I have a meeting with Vinder at 7:30. so I will be in his office when this is taking place. It probably shouldn't be released to the news until the day after tomorrow. That will give me time to take care of some other business."

As Axel was about to walk out of the garage, he decided to call Kim back to make sure he has the right house number, and to tell him that he would leave the remote control for the garage door in a bush by the left side of the door.

"Also, you better take several vehicles parked around the place. If all the vehicles are still there, someone will wonder how the twelve got from the garage to the marina. At least four of the cars should be found in the marina parking lot. Your people should take the keys from the four or five cars you use and put them on the bodies. This will close that loop. The news should relate that it is evident the men were depressed from losing their jobs about six months ago. If I think of anything else, I will give you a call."

The Follower Smashes the Boston Terrorist Group

At 7:30, Axel was in the office of Vinder Laskovich. Vinder had been awaiting his arrival. "What's the scoop?' he asked.

Axel said he wanted to bring Vinder up to date on what had occurred so far, and to make some recommendations. Vinder was very interested in hearing these details, since nothing seemed to be moving very fast.

"Two of your men brought enough ammonium nitrate to sink a battleship," Axel said. "I believe we should start moving on a plan to use of this material, set up a strategy until we hear from some of the others on their quests for the hydrogen peroxide explosives. I have the list of the people that were at the meeting. I have reviewed that list, and seven men said they wanted to bring in ammonium nitrate. The seven included the two that brought me the garbage can full of the ammonium nitrate. You already said that you would supply the kerosene fuel for this ANFO explosive. I believe we should call these seven and set up plans for tomorrow evening. If we can put them into action, it will be a great start."

Axel showed Vinder the names of the six who had indicated they wanted to go with the ANFO approach. Vinder looked over the names and nodded his approval.

"You should contact them tonight," Axel said, "and say the stage will be set for day after tomorrow, but that we should meet tomorrow to go over the details. Meanwhile, I will go out tomorrow and buy seven briefcases for computers from different stores, so we have what we need to load with the ANFO. It's common to see businessmen and college students carrying these computer briefcases, so they should not raise any alarms. We should talk tomorrow evening about the targets and go through some exercises to show the men how to handle the job. Everything will be set up, so it will be rather simple for them to accomplish each of their tasks. You should pick out the targets tonight and call me. Don't tell anyone else the list of targets. And pick which man will hit which target, but we won't tell them until tomorrow. We can tell them at 8:30 in the morning day after tomorrow. This will give them all morning to get to their targets and take them out. I will supply each of them with a cell phone tomorrow and show them how to use the phone to set off the explosives remotely. This should work like clockwork."

"At last there is going to be retribution," Vinder said. "Tomorrow begins our war against this country through terrorist attacks. These explosives should grab this country's attention. They think they have terrorist threats under control. This will provide them strong evidence that they are wrong. I love it."

The next day Axel prepared for his meeting with the six men who were going to be handling the ANFO explosive attacks. He decided to put ammonium nitrate in a small plastic bag, stuff it inside the briefcases, and rig the case to blow up from a signal from his phone. The briefcases would also hold five pounds of a non-explosive material. Along with the ammonium nitrate, he'd add a plastic bag that contained about two ounces of kerosene. This bag was tied at the top with a small wire that led to an insulated piece of fuse material, a small battery, and a small circuit board. When Axel gave the proper signal from his cell phone, this explosive device would go off. The bomb would be just big enough to kill the carrier.

Using a non-explosive material, Axel did a practice run to see if it would do what he wanted it to do. The signal from his cell phone was supposed to turn on the circuit in the small plastic bag. The current would run along the wire and burn a hole in the kerosene container, and the kerosene would flow onto the explosive material. In the meantime, the current through the fusible material would ignite it. The combination of heat supplied by the fusible material and the kerosene reacting with the ammonium nitrate would result in an ANFO. He sent the cell phone signal, and the kerosene was released to the powder. The fuse got red hot, and if the powder in the packet had been ammonium nitrate, there would have been an explosion. It worked like a charm.

So he would put into the briefcases the small plastic bags full of ammonium nitrate and five pounds of the white non-explosive powder. He'd tell the men that was the five pounds of ammonium nitrate. With these briefcases, the Russians carrying them would do no more harm than blowing themselves up. He would give them phones with a signal number that did not match the signal required to explode the briefcase, but they wouldn't know it. Then he would remotely explode each of the briefcases using a signal from his phone, and the Russians carrying them would be eliminated.

Axel got in his car, placing the briefcases in the backseat, and took off for his rendezvous with Vinder and the six Russian carriers. When he got to Vinder's place, he went in without the briefcases to make sure there was no one else in the office. Vinder was there along with the six carriers.

"Well, are you ready to go?" Axel asked.

All of the men said they were, and Vinder asked where the briefcases were.

"I left them in the car to make sure no one was in here but you. I will bring them in, but first I want to describe their functions. Each briefcase has a cell phone attached to it that has been pre-programmed with a signal that will remotely set the explosive off. Each briefcase is loaded with five pounds of ammonium nitrate, as well as a plastic bag with kerosene and a bag that contains the circuitry for dumping the kerosene and igniting the fuse. The briefcases contain enough ammonium nitrate to blow up a store or a two-story building. You can handle the briefcases rather casually, since nothing will happen until the kerosene is released into the ammonium nitrate. Everything is packed solid, and when you give the signal, you had better be far away from the place where you leave your briefcase."

"That sounds great," said one of the men.

"Yes, it is foolproof," responded Axel. "Perhaps two of you could come with me to bring in the briefcases."

Two of the men stepped forward and followed Axel out to his car. When they returned with the briefcases, Axel said, "I will open one of the briefcases so you can see how it is packed."

He laid one of the briefcases on the table and opened the case. They could see that the case was stuffed with a large bag of white powder. A smaller plastic bag was stuffed in the top of it. "That small bag," Axel said, "has another bag inside it that contains the kerosene, and the complete circuitry for releasing the kerosene and igniting the fuse."

Before they had a chance to check out the contents, Axel closed the briefcase and asked them if they had any questions. He wanted to make sure he diverted their attention away from the material inside the briefcase.

After answered their questions, Axel said, "I don't know what your targets are. That is between you and Vinder. I will be happy to read tomorrow's paper to know where you used these. Have a good trip."

With that comment, Axel said he was going to leave, unless they had other questions. They had none, and Axel left. He drove only about half a mile away, so he could watch to see when the men took off with their explosives. He waited about an hour, and finally he saw the cars driving away from the building. They all drove down the same road and past his car, which he had pulled over onto a side street. When the last of them passed, he pulled out and followed them until they started to take different routes from each other. This was perfect, and Axel decided to follow one of the cars. When the man had driven for about another mile, Axel pulled out his cell phone and hit the button to send the signal. He could see the car explode in the distance. He knew that the other cars and drivers had met with the same fate. He smiled to himself and drove back to his motel. On the way, he called Kim and told him what had been done.

"There will be six cars that have exploded. There shouldn't be anything left to show what caused the explosion. I need the agency to get hold of the local police and tell them that this is a federal situation, and that you will send the proper men to handle the whole scene. I don't care if there's some confusion about this. I am sure you can hint that it was a terrorist threat and that you want to keep it low-key for a couple of days. I need that amount of time to handle about another five or six of them."

Kim was quiet for about ten seconds, and then he said, "Axel, you sure do cause me a bunch of problems, but I know that you had to do something like this to prevent several terrorist acts. I will take care of this. You notice that there have been no leaks about the dozen men we found in the bay. It should take another day for that to come out. I wish you luck in finishing this devilish thing, so you can get back to your woman and your teaching. Let me know if you need some other help."

The next day Axel got a call from Vinder, and Vinder asked him to stop by his office that evening around seven. Axel asked if he needed to prepare anything for the meeting, and Vinder said, "No, just bring you. We need to talk about the terrorist program." Axel was a little concerned about that call and wondered what this was about. He didn't think anything had shown up in the papers yet, so he didn't think that was what Vinder wanted to talk about. He just prepared himself to talk about what he thought should be their next step. He had already been considering the hydrogen peroxide acetone program and how that would proceed. He felt he had a good plan for it. As he drove to Micromissions, though, he kept wondering about this meeting. When he pulled into the parking lot, he felt he should prepare himself for the worst and signaled his insides to action. Axelvation two, hood down. He felt the energy push through his body, and reached back into the car for a few candy bars. He stripped the paper from one and ate it. He unwrapped another on his way to Vinder's office. When he entered the office, he saw one of the Russians who wanted to use a acetone bomb, and that relieved him. However, there was another man in the office who was of a large build and had a police officer's uniform on. Vinder introduced Axel to the man.

"This is James Vrakoff of the local police, and this is Yaro Patraska." Axel shook the man's big hand and sit down to listen to what they had to say. "Yaro," said Vinder. "Officer Vrakoff is bringing me some stories that have me concerned about your loyalty to our cause."

"Oh?" replied Axel. "And what would that be?"

"It seems that twelve Russians were found in the bay, drowned, and Officer Vrakoff said that there is something about their deaths that doesn't make sense. He is in the section of the police department that handles criminal cases. You have probably heard of CSI on the television. Well, he is CSI here in Boston. He believes there is a group from the federal government that is trying to keep their cause of death a secret. Would you know anything about these twelve men? They are on your list of our people that wanted to take actions against this country."

"No," replied Axel. "I have talked to some of the people who have not yet taken any action, and some of them were kind of reticent about doing anything. Perhaps these twelve included them. But I don't know."

Vinder than brought up another issue. "Remember last night, the six men who left with the briefcases? According to Officer Vrakoff, six cars blew up yesterday almost simultaneously. These incidents also are being hushed by someone telling the local police to stay out of this because it is a federal matter. Are you aware of this?"

"No," Axel said. "I haven't seen anything in the paper or heard anything on the news. I can't believe that they didn't perform their tasks."

Vinder got up from his desk and walked around the room, mumbling something that Axel couldn't understand. Then he turned to Axel. "Did you set these men up with a booby trap?"

Axel began thinking there was no good way out of this thing, but he decided to remain calm and play it out. He looked up at Vinder and said, "What makes you think that?"

Vinder walked back behind his desk and leaned against the chair. "I believe you are setting us up. Vrakoff has data on eighteen of our people that have met death in the past several days, and you might have been the last one to see them. I know that the six last night were sent on their missions by you, and you and I were the last to see them alive. These things have become too obvious. I believe you are the rat in the woodpile, and you are taking our people out."

He reached in his desk drawer and pulled out a revolver. "Just sit there," he directed. Then he instructed Vrakoff and the other man, Grenden, to take Axel's arms and hold them behind him.

Axel sat still as the two men grabbed his arms and held them tight. Looking behind him, he asked, "And how did you come into this plot, Vrakoff? Are you another of the Russians who wants to turn things around in this country? Are you like the soldier down in Texas who shot and killed thirteen of his comrades because he was a terrorist? Who's the terrorist here?"

For the first time, Vrakoff spoke. "We are going to find out who is the spy here. I don't think you are in any position to question our motives. We are here to question your motives, and we will find the answer."

Vrakoff took his handcuffs and handcuffed Axel's right arm to the chair. "Fine way you treat your men," Axel said. Vinder walked over and slapped Axel across the face. Axel flinched as if it had hurt, then he looked at Grenden. "Where are your other buddies that wanted to use the acetone bomb? Did they wise up and drop out on you and all this terrorist stuff?"

This time Vinder punched Axel in the face. Axel didn't move a muscle, but Vinder cradled his hand as if he was in pain. "What do you have on your face?" he shouted.

"Let me handle this," Vrakoff said. "I will get the truth out of him. This is my kind of business."

Vinder nodded, and Vrakoff hauled back with his fist and hit Axel square in the face. Axel didn't move an inch, and Vrakoff stepped away, holding his hand in pain.

"See what the truth will get you," Axel said. "Yes, I was the one who stopped those dumb asses. They had ten good years in this country, and then they blew it. They took the ten good years and didn't even wait out one poor year before they decided to kill Americans. That is intolerable. First there were twelve who wanted to kill as many Americans as they could, who had nothing to do with the problems they thought they had, by poisoning sushi food. Then there were six more, who wanted to blow holes in buildings, killing more Americans. Well, I took out those eighteen, and now I am going to take out another three. I only hope the others who didn't show up with Grenden had second thoughts and decided to go work for a living."

Vinder aimed his gun and fired a shot at Axel. Seeing no result, Vrakoff took out his police pistol, put it next to Axel's head, and pulled the trigger. The bullet flew wildly back across the room.

Axel said, "I guess there are no means to prove to you people that you are on the wrong track. I thought things were bad, but now I see one of our trusted policemen is involved. That is terrible."

With that comment, Axel ripped the handcuffs off the arm of the chair and faced the three of them. First he went for Vrakoff. He grabbed him and threw him across the room, and Vrakoff rolled off the wall like butter off hot toast. Axel turned toward Vinder, who was firing shot after shot at him, and rammed the flat of his hand against Vinder's gun, shoving it back into Vinder's chest. Vinder's eyes opened wide, and then he dropped like a dead fish being thrown back into the water, the gun stuck in his chest. Axel swung his arm in a semi-circle, crashing it against Grenden's head. His head spun around like it wasn't attached to the rest of his body.

Vrakoff had sort of recovered. He picked his gun up off the floor and began drilling shots at Axel. With each shot, his eyes widened more and more in complete surprise, until Axel grabbed both of his arms, lifted him into the air, and head butted him. It was no contest, and the policeman, in name only, fell dead to the floor.

Axel sat back down in the chair and looked around. *Lucky there are no others in the building,* he thought. *I don't believe the guns were heard. Now what do I do? None of these deaths look like an accident. How do I keep this quiet without causing a major scare in the country? I am glad that some of the Russians didn't come. Maybe they will miss their fellowmen and realize that killing others is not worth it. I surely am done in the Boston area.*

Axel realized that none of the men had bullet wounds. Both Vrakoff and Grenden looked like they could have been in a car accident. If he took the gun out of Vinder's chest, he could replace it with something from a car that could have crushed his chest in an accident. He would have to make it look like Vinder had called the policeman to come arrest Grenden, and the accident occurred on the way to the police station. It would have to be a very bad accident.

Maybe, he thought as he picked up the bullet casings around the room, he could set it up so that Vinder was in the passenger seat of Vrakoff's car, holding a gun on Grenden during the ride to the police station. During the crash, the gun was jammed inside chest and it killed him.

After he picked up all the bullet shells, he cleaned up any blood stains. Looking around the room, he checked to see if there was any other evidence. *I am fortunate,* he thought, *that I can't leave a fingerprint on anything with my body covering on. I leave nothing to show I was here.* Then he saw the chair he had been sitting in. He had destroyed the arm of chair when he'd ripped the handcuffs off. *I will have to do away with that chair. I could take it down to the garbage room in the basement and put it with all the other trash. On second thought, I better take it with me and dispose of it someplace away from this building.*

He took Vrakoff's car keys from his pocket, and then placed Grenden in the chair, picked the chair and body up, and carried them outside. He unlocked the police car and placed Grenden in the backseat, shoving the broken chair in beside him. Back in the office, he grabbed both Vinder and the policeman, swung them over each of his shoulders, and carried them out to the car. He placed Vinder in the front passenger seat and the policeman temporarily in the backseat.

He went back inside to make sure there was no evidence that he had been there. No one had been at the reception desk when he arrived, so he hadn't signed in. He looked at the log book and saw that Grenden had signed in at 5:12, and Vrakoff had signed in at 6:45. *This is great,* he thought. *That showed both of them had been there.*

He drove his car about a block away and parked it. Then he ran back to the police car and drove it about two blocks away, to an area where there were other factories with Dumpsters behind the buildings. He saw one with no lights on. Feeling that was the best bet, he drove behind the building and threw the broken chair into the Dumpster. Afterward he checked to make sure there were no pieces of the chair left in the backseat, and then drove off toward the police station.

Axel now had to find a good place to wreck the car. The station was located about four miles away. He knew he had to wreck it somewhere out here, away from the city, but he had to be on route toward the station for this story to hold up. About half a mile down the road, he reached a highway. Since it was about ten o'clock at night, there wasn't much traffic. Axel knew there were some large oak trees along this road, and figured he could smash into one of them. He turned onto the highway, but as he approached the area with the trees, he saw the lights of a car behind him. He pulled onto the side of the road and let the car catch up and pass him. The driver probably thought he was checking for speeders. Axel waited till the car was in the distance, and then slammed down on the gas pedal and took off. Soon he was doing about ninety, and he swung the car toward a large oak tree, hitting it dead on. His head smashed against the steering wheel, breaking it; while Vinder, who didn't have his seat belt, crashed against the dashboard, forcing the gun even deeper into his chest. Grenden flew up over the front seat and smashed against the roof of the car. Of course, Axel was unhurt.

He crawled out of the wreck and moved Vrakoff from the backseat to the driver's seat. After putting Vrakoff's seat belt on, he arranged his head against the smashed steering wheel. *I can't understand why none of the air bags deployed,* he thought. *If I was a cop and found this accident, I would report the maker of this car for having an inferior air bag.*

Satisfied that it looked as though the three men had died in the accident, Axel headed back toward his car. He ran at his top speed of thirty miles an hour, and knew he could duck behind a tree or next to a building if he saw a car coming. In a very short time he was back at his car. As he drove toward his motel, he kept going over everything that had happened and making sure he had accounted for everything. *They will have a hard time with that wreck and having any suspicions about it,* he thought.

He called Kim and said, "Hi, Kim, I have to report an accident."

"What happened?" Kim asked, and Axel told him the events of the night.

"There was a bad cop up here and I had to take him out. Things like that will happen. In this case, the cop was being paid on the side by Vinder. I believe the wreck they find will show that something happened in the car on the way to the police station. Since the cop probably didn't radio in that he was going out to Vinder's plant, they will have no record of why he was there. This makes Vinder look good. His business will not be destroyed, and someone else will take it over and during the funeral they will say good things about him. They will say he found a group of Russian terrorists in his company and elsewhere around Boston, and did whatever he could to make them change their ways or report them to the police. I believe the few other Russian 'hope to be terrorists' will see this as an act of good luck for them, and they will go out and get good jobs, and do something worthwhile with their lives. I don't intend to hunt them down. The way I figure it, we found how the one person died several months ago from improper administration of nanoparticles. We found twenty plus Russian 'would be terrorists' and got rid of their leader and nineteen of them, plus we got rid of a rotten cop. That sounds to me like a good piece of work. I am going to fly back to California tomorrow and see my woman."

It was quiet for a few seconds, and then Kim said, "I had to do a lot of weird things to cover up the cleaning up you did. But I know it was for the good of the country. I would have had a hard time figuring out any better way of putting that terrorist group away than the way you did. You accomplished all this, and no one will know what actually happened, and no one will know how much better off they are. You saved the lives of many, and the odd thing about it is that you won't get any credit, except from me and a very few here in the agency. You will disappear back to your job in California, teaching biology, microbiology, stem cells, and a lot of new things we don't know about today. I will call the airlines and find when a plane is flying to San Jose, California, tomorrow, and make your reservations. Then I will call you and let you know the airline and the time. I wish you were flying to Washington and the agency. I would love to see you and talk to you about the things you learned when working with those terrorists. But I know there are other things in life for you. I need you to go to the school and learn as much as you can from your students." He laughed. "I also want you to go and learn a few things about Tori that you haven't learned yet. Thank her again for her part in this. I'll be talking to you soon."

When he and Kim were finished with their talk, Axel called Tori. It was only about seven thirty in the evening there.

"Hello?" she said in that lovely voice.

"Hello there. Is this the woman who works for the USSA and finds out who the bad guys are and what they are doing that is so bad?"

"Axel!" she shouted. "You bettcha. I'm the secret sidekick of a devilish character who keeps flying all over the world, and I am hoping that he's calling to tell me he is on his way to me."

"You have that right," said Axel. "I am finished here. I will be flying to you sometime tomorrow, and I am hoping for a ride home."

"Oh Axel, that is so great. I thought this was going to last a lot longer then this. Just the other day, you thought it would be weeks. What happened?"

"Well, I had a couple of lucky breaks that allowed me to finish up faster than I thought I would. In fact, the boss of the Russian group made the last move, and that was his last move. I will tell you about it when I get home, that is, after I love you up for about half a day."

"Only half a day?" Tori commented. Do you have another girlfriend out here?"

Axel laughed. "Okay, a whole day."

"Good."

Finding the Texas Supplier of Mexican Arms

Axel had returned several months back from doing battle with the Mexican drug cartels, and he wondered if any progress had been made on finding the source of their guns. He knew it took more than crushing one cartel leader in Mexico to put this major problem to bed. He thought, *I haven't heard anything about finding the sources of the guns that end up in Mexico. Of course, I wouldn't have been able to do anything about it anyhow. I was completely involved in finding terrorists in the Silicon Valley and the Boston area.*

The agency had been excited about not only reducing the drug trade, but also in eliminating the huge amount of guns that transferred across the border between the United States and Mexico. In his role as The Follower, Axel had been sent to Mexico to determine the main types of guns that were being supplied to the cartels. The agency hoped that this information would direct them to the suppliers located in the U.S. These weapons have caused numerous deaths to Mexican police, troops, and innocent bystanders. To Axel's mind, the collateral damage to the innocent was even worse than the intended damage. Families lost their fathers, their mothers, and sometimes their children. Besides these deaths, there continued to be significant deaths among the competing cartels, as they vied to control the drug business. Axel had found that there were five major types of guns being used by the cartels, with two types standing out as the major contributors. The two guns of high priority were the AK-47, which had been originally designed in Russia. Later derivatives of this gun were supplied by Romania and many other gun suppliers around the world. The other gun, the Uzi, was designed in Israel, and many of them were still supplied by Israel. But since the Uzi was made up of stamped parts, it was easy to duplicate. Therefore many more suppliers of this gun had shown up around the world. Axel had provided the agency with detailed reasons why these guns were the choice of weapon for the Mexican cartels.

The AK-47, Axel explained, was a lightweight, short assault rifle. Its bullets were supplied by magazines, which held anywhere from thirteen to eighteen bullets and which could be fired off in seconds. The shooter didn't have to be that accurate. He could spray the shots in the hopes of hitting his target, especially at medium to close range.

The other advantages of this weapon were its cost and availability. Over one hundred million of these guns had been manufactured over the years, and were used in guerilla type warfare in Iraq and Afghanistan, as well as the gangs in Mexico. This had made the weapon easy to obtain.

As for the Uzi, like the AK-47 it was an automatic weapon that was capable of firing off many shots in a very short time. It was also short, like a large pistol, with a much greater fire power. It was easy to handle and lightweight. It was smaller than the AK-47, but at short distances, it was just as deadly.

The Uzi was cheaper than almost any other comparable gun. It was most effective at short range fighting, which suited the cartels' needs. And as with the AK-47, the shooter could spray the shots around to insure hitting his target.

Axel had supplied this information to the agency several months ago with the hope that they could find likely suppliers of these two weapons. The agency had taken this information and paid particular attention to possible candidates in Arizona and Texas, where it was believed most of the guns had their origin. Dr. Kim had since assigned several people to investigate the suppliers in these two states. Since Kim had no new information for him, Axel returned to his teaching position at the university.

He was happy to return to teaching in the university in northern California, and to be with his fiancée, Tori. His past actions with the agency had been quite intense, and he was ready to settle down, spending his time teaching and running the stem cell lab he had designed. His background in biology had made him an ideal source of technical knowledge for his past missions for the agency, and Axel had derived satisfaction from those missions. But he also looked forward to providing the young people at the university with his knowledge. Teaching was another source of excitement for him, and tended to relax him. Like everything else, when he was teaching he was learning. He looked forward to this type of reverse learning. Also, the stem cell work that he headed up had never been done at the university, and his experience from a previous mission for the agency had provided him a significant start in that direction. The laboratory at the university was a duplicate of the one he had designed for terrorists on the east coast.

While the school and the teaching brought Axel a great amount of satisfaction and relief from the tense assignments with the agency, his greatest relief was Tori. She was a beautiful, smart, and well educated woman, and he loved and hoped to make his wife one day. He had met her at the university. One night he happened to save her and a friend from an assault by two men. Tori had just completed her bachelor's degree in biology, and when they fell in love, they made an agreement. They would live together for a year, and if any assignment came up for Axel, or anything came up for Tori, the two of them would decide together what to do. Tori had already agreed to several assignments that Axel had pursued, and the two of them had agreed on the company Tori would work at after completing her graduate work. This was with a start-up genetics company in Silicon Valley. The two of them decided to hold off on marriage and just live together until they were sure they were compatible under the constraints of Axel's assignments for the agency. Neither of them knew when he would be called upon, or how long an assignment would last. Tori had just recently learned of Axel's special talents, and she, Axel's twin brother Adam, and Dr. Kim were the only ones privy to complete knowledge of these extraordinary skills.

Whenever Tori met Axel at the airport after he returned from any of his missions as The Follower, she could not hide her great joy. Axel would lift her above his head and slowly allow her to descend for his kiss. This had become a ritual with them whenever they were separated for any length of time. Theirs was a true love, and later when they arrived home, they would complete the lovemaking. Life was good. However, multitasking like this was difficult for Axel, since he had to keep up with his teaching and provide his students with the best of his ability while away on an agency mission. he was fortunate in that he had found a retired professor who welcomed the chance to teach Axel's classes when Axel was on an assignment. This was Professor Marv Goodwin, who liked to attend Axel's classes as though he were a new student, which provided him with added knowledge and made him perfect for substituting. Axel and Marv each treated the subject matter slightly differently, and they worked together to make their individual approaches mesh. Marv taught with Axel's approach as much as possible. However, the laboratory was quite different, since Marv had never worked on stem cells. But the work was also new to Axel to a great degree.

Marv's presence relieved Axel's multitasking to a great extent and Marv was happy to receive the extra money and enjoy his retirement. Meanwhile, the biology department head knew that Axel had special assignments that related to the country's security, and he was more than happy to accept this arrangement, since he had a lot of respect for Marv Goodwin as well. While on assignment, Axel was paid by the agency, and the university paid Marv Goodwin.

One evening while Tori and Axel were having supper the phone rang. Tori answered the phone, and it didn't take long for her to turn toward Axel and frown. "It's the agency," she said.

Axel picked up the phone, and Dr. Kim was on the other end. "Axel, we have spent a good bit of time researching the possible sources of the two gun types you mentioned being used in Mexico. After a month or so, it became obvious that we should concentrate on the state of Texas. In the Houston area alone we have found over twenty five hundred dealers of all kinds of guns, many of them probably being sold to the cartels. We have been zooming in on the possible suppliers to these dealers. I wanted to review this with you here at the agency, but I know you're busy with Tori and your teaching, so I thought I would fax you our findings. After you have read this, you will have an idea of the massive amount of gun dealers there are in Texas alone. We are trying to pinpoint the major manufacturing sources, and we've got it down to five possible. They either make the guns or have them sent in from outside the country. In some cases, they purchase the parts and assemble them in their factories. I am not going to go over these possible sources with you until you've read the fax and we have obtained a little more definitive data. Do you think you can free up the time to review the fax?"

"Yes," replied Axel. "I can look at the information over the next few days. I think the fax is a good idea. It gets me on board without my having to spend time away from home. I am also sure Tori will like this approach better than my being away." He turned and winked at Tori, who was sitting at the dinner table. She threw him a kiss. "When do you expect to send the fax?" Axel asked.

"I will send it right after we finish talking. You don't have to start reviewing it right away; maybe sometime tomorrow. Does that sound reasonable?"

"Tomorrow is not a good time. Tori and I have something planned, but I can start day after tomorrow."

"That's fine," responded Kim. "You have a great night, and I will hear from you whenever I hear from you; take care."

Axel returned to the table and told Tori what the plan was. She was elated to hear he wouldn't have to take off again so soon. "You just got back two weeks ago. They don't seem to give you any time to cool your heels and enjoy yourself."

"Yes, I know. At least this is a different approach. And maybe by getting a leg up on the assignment while at home, I won't have to be gone as long when I do go."

The fax machine began printing out pages of data for Axel. He gave them a quick glance and then set them aside. Kim had told him he didn't have to look at the information right away, but he was curious and knew that he would read the fax before bedtime that night.

After he and Tori had cleaned up from dinner, and Axel had read the newspaper, he sat down with the printout. The report from BATFE (Bureau of Alcohol, Tobacco, Firearms, and Explosives) showed that significant amounts of firearms, especially assault weapons like the AK-47, were manufactured in America, and that a considerable number passed through Texas distributors to those that wanted to purchase guns; in this case, Mexican cartels. Both the United States and Mexican governments had loudly protested the amount of military type weapons that had made their way across the border.

These types of assault weapons were difficult for Americans to purchase in American gun shops, so it was a wonder to Axel that they had been making their way to Mexico. The official report of traced firearms by the federal Bureau of Alcohol, Tobacco, Firearms, and

Explosives indicated that at least 90 percent came from the States, and approximately ten thousand had crossed the border between the middle of 2008 and 2009. Most of the arms came from Texas, Arizona, and California. This data supported the data from the agency that Texas was the biggest supplier. The cartels used these guns in their war with Mexico's military and police, and among each other. The data also indicated that there had been a shift in the type of guns. Where previous data showed a preference for small caliber weapons, the latest data showed higher caliber attack weapons were being bought, and more AK-47s than any other type. A large number of the weapons were capable of "vest penetration" with armor piercing bullets. What was even scarier was that the numbers reported only represented a limited percentage of the actual guns in the Mexico. Most of the guns could not be legally purchased in the U.S. These weapons were coming from outside the country, as well as from manufacturing firms in the U.S., to traffickers between the United States and Mexico.

The report also indicated that some of the shops selling guns had misrepresented the number and types of guns actually sold. Many of the guns were purchased using "straw man" maneuvers, where several people were sent to the stores to purchase guns under one person's name. This maneuver allowed a large number of guns to be purchased in a couple of days.

Kim's report also mentioned a law called the Tiahrt Amendment, which banned the public release of data about weapons recovered from crime scenes. Without this information being available, it limited critical data reaching the public, the media, members of Congress, and most law enforcement agencies. This included data that the USSA had not been able to obtain. In most cases, traffickers were responsible for greater numbers of weapons than the data reported.

As Axel read through the fax, he was amazed at how much data was not being reported. What was reported represented a horrific number of weapons. *No wonder so many people are being killed or wounded,* he thought. *The cartels have huge amounts of money from selling drugs, so they can virtually buy as many weapons as they want. At the same time, the gun dealers in this country look at this as a huge opportunity to make a lot of money. In the same sense, the gun lobbyists have significant reasons—that is, money and power —to keep the laws lax, and not allow a stronger effort to catch the suppliers and criminals using this firepower. This is like a big circle, where money goes from America to Mexico as Americans buy drugs; and then money comes back to America as the cartels use the same money to buy guns. The money goes from the drug buyers to the gun sellers in this circle of terror.*

At the end of the report were a few sentences from Kim.

Axel, you can see by this information that trafficking has been so spread out, it has been impossible to monitor the action of all the dealers in the three states indicated. Our data show that we should do something in Texas to find the manufacturer and supplier of weapons to the dealers in Texas. By finding the manufacturers and suppliers, we can interrupt the flow of guns to the dealers. If we can do this in Texas, we can follow up in the other states.

At this time, we have identified two manufacturers as the largest suppliers of these guns to dealers. Both are located north of Houston. General Gun Chamber is about ten miles northwest of the city; and the other manufacturer, Gun Specialist, is located about thirty miles northeast of Houston. We continue to monitor these two. At this time, it looks like the BATFE is limited in enforcing any tough laws. As far as that goes, our agency is limited as well. Our hope is that if you go and find the culprits, you may be able to take action into your own hands. There's no law against defending one's self, and we know you are good at defending yourself. In the course of your actions, you may find information and a legal means we can pursue against these culprits. I will get back to you in the next day or so on with any further information we find on these two companies.

Axel laid the papers aside and thought about the terrible incidents he had seen in Mexico during two of his assignments. He thought to himself as he had thought before, *the drug addicts of this country are the culprits in this case. The more money the addicts spend, the more money the cartels spend on guns. We need to stop this circle of death and destruction. We have drug-addled people in this country and dead people on the other side of the border. We need to reduce both of these numbers. I will be glad to play my part, even though it will be rather small compared to this total picture. But Kim is right. There is no way to put all the small dealers in these three states out of business. That would take forever. We need these kinds of actions against the major manufacturers, and we need new laws to limit the sale of guns.*

Just then Tori called him to come to bed. Axel decided it was time to eliminate these thoughts from his head, and go and grab Tori and hug her.

I'll think about all this tomorrow.

The next day Axel called Kim to discuss the situation. "Kim, I looked at the information on the fax and I have one big problem. If you decide which of the manufactures might be supplying these big numbers of weapons, how do I get into the place to confront them?"

"I have been giving that a lot of thought. I know you could break into the place illegally with your special capabilities. But I don't know what purpose this would serve. This is a real problem."

"I have been thinking of different ways of doing this," Axel said. "I thought that maybe you could find a way of providing me with an authorization to represent the IRS and do an audit on these places. This would allow me to walk in the front door, but I don't know that you could get the permission for me to do a random audit. I also could try to find a way to get in and audit their shipments to see if they agree with their manifests. I could follow their shipments to see if they're going where the company says they are going. How about thinking about this and see if you can come up with a plausible plan?"

Kim said he would get together with some of his people and see if they could come up with an approach that looked feasible.

After they hung up, Axel considered his option again. He thought that maybe the last thing he'd mentioned might work. He decided to call Kim back and discuss it further.

"Kim, I was thinking about a way that would require the help of several of your agents. I would monitor the shipments leaving the plant at night. You would need to have about a dozen men with cars, and each of them would follow one of the truck shipments. By doing this for a week, your men could report to me by phone where these deliveries are going. Then I would find a way of getting in and checking the shipment logs to see if they matched. If there is a discrepancy, I would find a way of determining who the culprit is within the company. A week's shipments add up to a lot of guns. The shipment log should show not only the destination, but what was shipped. In addition, I could check their incoming logs, see if they are receiving any guns from other manufacturers. With this data, I could compare the total number they manufactured or received against the amount they ship. This combination should point us to the source of improperly logged shipments and where they went. If the trucks were followed, we could check to see if the recipients were equal to the shipments sent out. One week's data should provide us with enough information. What do you think?"

Kim said he would check to see what could be done at the agency to provide help for this type of solution. "I will also check with our contact at the IRS and see if we can send you in to do an audit. It may require doing this along with the other actions you suggested. I will get back to you tomorrow."

After he hung up, Axel thought, *it's amazing when two people talk to each other; they come up with things they didn't think of before the fact. I think Kim liked my suggestions. It would be like coming in the front door and the back door at the same time.*

The next day, Kim called Axel while he was teaching a class. Axel got the message when class was over and called him back.

"I have good news and maybe more good news for you," Kim said. "The good news is that the IRS could provide us a way to do an audit on General Gun. The other good news relates to your other suggestions. We like the monitoring of the outgoing shipments, but we believe the monitoring should be done all day long, not just at night. The good news for you is that the agency would provide the men to do the monitoring. We don't believe we need to use you for this broad an operation. This will take three or four men each day, since we believe that is the number of trucks that leave each day with shipments. We also may audit the books at the places that receive the shipments. We probably won't have any problems with the legitimate places, but the culprits will probably give us problems, and we can figure out how to handle that eventually. In addition, we may have to find a way for you to get in the shipping company and check their logs, to see if they have logged all the truck shipments or not. Then by checking their outgoing logs and the customers' incoming logs, we can see if there are any discrepancies. That's it. What do you think?"

"Sounds good to me," replied Axel. "This takes me off the hook for all that monitoring, and I will get involved when I must. But, believe me, I want to be involved when it makes sense. I want to track down these killers. I have a suggestion to add to this. You should check on the last seven shipping days of September, which is this coming week. September is the end of the third quarter for most companies. Companies ship everything they can on that last week. They will work overtime and scrape everything they have to ship, so as to show a high level of sales to their owners. So by checking on these seven days, I believe you will get the maximum shipments to check."

"That's a great suggestion," said Kim.

Axel went on to teach his next class. He was relieved by the phone call, since he had thought he might get stuck in Houston following trucks or monitoring trucks. That would have been a waste of his unique resources.

Axel and Kim talked again on September 28. Kim told him the agency had a complete complement of men on site at General Gun Company, and each man had been following truck shipments. A cumulative report on these activities would give the agency a list of destinations for shipments from General Gun. They would follow up with audits of those places to see if the shipments were recorded as received. This would close one end of the loop. This report would be completed in a couple of days, and Kim would be sending it to Axel in the first week in October. Hopefully the results would point them in a direction for subsequent action. As he listened, Axel's excitement over this assignment grew. As much as he liked teaching school, he found the agency's assignments invigorating, and he knew one would be coming soon.

On the second of October, Kim gave Axel a call. "Axel, we have one glaring discrepancy. We monitored General Gun's shipments for the last week of September, and we have matching shipments and receiving on all of the companies but one. That company, Chamber One, received a shipment from General Gun on September 30, but they have no record of that shipment. At this time, we don't know what types of guns were delivered, but I would suggest you get into that place and see what you can find. If they have received guns, especially something like an AK-47, it would give us our first hit. We can fly you to Houston on the last flight out tonight. It's an all-nighter and will get you in on Saturday. Saturday night or Sunday should be a good time for you to get into General Gun and look around. We don't know what you should to expect on a Saturday or Sunday, but we feel you can handle whatever shows up. We will secure your plane tickets and you can pick them up at the airport. We will have a man, Tony Marsh, meet you at the Houston airport. He'll take you to General Gun. As I previously mentioned, General Gun is located about ten miles northwest of Houston, so it won't take you long to get there once you arrive in Houston."

Axel's juices started to flow as he thought about the trip to Houston. Tori had been expecting this, so he didn't figure to have any big problems there. However, he crossed his fingers when he called her, because it had come up so rapidly and he had to move so fast on it.

"Axel," she said after he told her, "you would think they would give you more time on these things and consider our lives as well."

"I know what you are saying is right," said Axel, "but the key to this one is that they just got this shipment and haven't had time to do anything with it. Therefore, we have a chance to find it in their plant and confront them with their ruse."

"Yes, I understand, and it does make sense to catch them with the evidence. I understand and believe you should go. What time do I have to get you to the airport?"

"We can go out and eat tonight. I think if you get me to the airport by ten, it will be fine. So, maybe I can pick you up at work and take you out. What do you think?"

The phone was silent as Axel waited for the verdict. Then Tori said, "I would rather go home and get cleaned up and then go out to dinner. I will just drive home like I always do and meet you there."

"See you at home then," Axel said.

Axel was waiting at home when Tori arrived at six. He was so excited to see her before leaving for Texas. Just seeing his beautiful woman walk through the door was like opening a package at Christmas. He completely forgot about the mission, or even about eating dinner. The only thought that came to his mind was that he would like to join her in the shower.

"I've been thinking about it, and I think we both should take a shower," he said to her. Her eyes lit up, and he knew she approved. They both hurried to the bedroom and took off their clothes. Tori was quicker, and she was already in the shower and soaping up when Axel joined her. Axel's dick was already standing out in attention, and Tori laughed.

"That little fellow knows what he wants," she said, and reached down and began rubbing soap on it.

"Not too much," Axel said, "or I won't be able to hold back. I am already sexed up, and any soft motion of those beautiful hands of yours on my dick will cause an unwanted early explosion."

She laughed, and Axel grabbed her and pulled one of her tits into his mouth. "Boy," he said, "When these are wet, they are even better than when dry. I can see you are in a good mood for this too. Your nipples have doubled in size, and are just begging for attention."

And he gave them that attention. It wasn't long before he lifted her off her feet, holding her against the wall, and began inserting the knob of his dick into that wet tunnel of love.

"How come this feels better the more you do it? And nothing can replace it," he asked.

She moaned. "It's because it is unique. It's made for you and for me. Oh, that feels so good inside me. I've already had one climax when you put it in, and now I'm getting ready for another. Don't go any faster. I love it when you do it in slow fashion. We need to put a music system in here so we can have soft music playing when we are making love."

She began to have a dramatic orgasm, and Axel followed right along, surging back and forth to gain as much satisfaction out of lovemaking as possible.

He groaned. "Boy that drains as much energy from me as anything I know." He slowly let Tori down to her feet and gave her a big hug and kiss.

Later, after finishing a great dinner, Tori drove Axel to the airport at San Jose. As they approached, Axel said, "They've really made some big changes at this airport, and they are only about halfway through. I remember this airport about fifteen years ago, and it was like a small city airport. Things have changed. It's bigger and nicer than the one in the capital of North Korea I recently visited."

Tori dropped him off at the terminal and went to park the car. By the time she returned, Axel has his ticket and boarding pass.

"Just like clockwork," he said. "I'll say one thing about the agency, they have their shit together. They complete whatever they say they will do."

It was 10:30 and the plane was scheduled to start boarding at 11:30. Axel felt he better head toward the gate, since it might take him added time going through security. "Give me a hug and walk me to the security line," he said to Tori.

When the plane began to roll down the runway for his flight to Houston, Axel told the attendant not to awaken him for anything unless it was an emergency. She nodded, and he placed his head back on the seat and began to relax. He was asleep before the plane took off. Later, Axel was awakened by the attendant saying, "Sir, we are going to be landing in fifteen minutes." Axel nodded and looked at his watch. He thought, *I can't believe the time passed so quickly. Seems I slept five minutes, and here I am at Houston.* He rubbed his eyes to bring him to his senses and to make sure he wouldn't fall back to sleep. It was already early in the morning local time, since the plane was flying east, toward the rising sun. He didn't remember if Houston time was two or three hours ahead of California, but they were ahead, so he would have to change the time on his watch.

Tony Marsh, Axel's agency contact in Houston, met him in the terminal. Tony drove Axel to the rental car lot to pick up his car, and then Axel followed him to the motel where he would be staying. After Axel had settled down in the motel, Tony drove him to General Gun Company, so Axel would know how to get there. From there, Tony drove Axel to the company that hadn't shown any receipts from General Gun. This company was Chamber One Guns, which was located near Axel's motel. After that, Tony returned Axel back to his motel. Axel asked Tony if he knew the name of the president of Chamber One.

"His name is Weldon Pratt," Tony said, "and he has been at Chamber One since they opened in 1999. He gave Axel Pratt's e-mail address and cell phone number.

"If I need anything," Axel said, "I will give you a call."

Tony said that he would be around and would be happy to discuss anything about the situation with him. Tony told Axel he had worked as a field agent for the agency for several years, and he would be quite interested in any information that Axel might find at Chamber One or General Gun.

"Thanks for the information," Axel said, "and for driving me around."

"No problem, that's what I am here for," replied Tony. They shook hands, and Tony was on his way.

Axel thought about how he might approach this invasion of the two businesses, and decided to go to Chamber One first. *I think it is better for me to start with trying to account for the shipment from General Gun to Chamber One that seems to have disappeared. It would be better to go in the evening too. The building is two stories high. I probably could get in by going in one of the windows on the second floor. Once I find the shipping and receiving department, if anyone's there I'll tell them I want to know the status of the latest runs that came in. If they ask me why, I can say that Mr. Pratt is interested in knowing how smoothly things are coming in, and how they are getting along with shipping them out to the customers. This should get me the information I need. If not, then I may have to force the subject as an interested person. The more I think about it, the more I like that approach. I think I will go and buy some candy bars to carry around for energy.*

Axel considered calling the agency to tell them of his plan, but changed his mind. *I can't call the agency and tell them I am going to do this. It's against the law to break into a place like this, and I don't even have a search warrant. All I would get if I talked to the agency would be words to the effect that they can't sanction anything like this. So, I guess I am on my own on this.* He waited until eight to leave for Chamber One, and by the time he got there, it was dark outside.

He drove around the building and noticed that lights were on in the shipping area in the back of the building, and a truck was parked there. There were lights in several other areas of the first floor. Axel thought they were probably repacking some recently received guns to be shipped to their final destination. Several windows on the second floor had ledges. He could jump onto one of those ledges and make his way into the building through the window. He decided to use a window in the back of the building, but knew he had to park the car some distance from the plant, so no one would expect anything. He drove about one hundred yards away, parked, and ran back. He gave his internal signal for his second level of energy—Axelvation two—and felt the energy rise in his body. He moved closer to the building and leaped onto the ledge he had chosen.

The windows were locked, but were not barred. He punched a hole next to the inside lock, unlocked the window, and swung it outward. Axel jumped in. He found the nearest set of stairs and walked down to where he believed shipping and receiving was located. A man was sitting at a desk. Axel walked up to him and said in a sharp voice, "Let me see the shipping log and the receiving log."

The instruction shocked the man. He had been making entries into a book, and obviously hadn't suspected anyone other than the men working around him was in the building.

"Who are you?" he asked Axel.

"Mike Gant. I work for Mr. Pratt," responded Axel. "Mr. Pratt is interested in the status of everything received or shipped in the past two weeks, since he has been working on clearing the books for the quarterly report. September is a little confusing with all the increased inventory, and he wants to make sure of his numbers."

"When did you come into the warehouse?" the man asked.

"I have been here since five, when Mr. Pratt told me to get involved. Do you have any problems with that?"

The man still looked stunned, but he went over and pulled the books that showed the receipts and another book that showed the shipments.

When Axel looked through the receipt book, he didn't see any receipts for the thirtieth of September. 'Is there some reason why you haven't shown the receipts of the guns that came in on the thirtieth?"

"What guns?" the man asked.

"I know there was a shipment sent by General Gun Company that arrived here on the thirtieth," Axel answered. "Why aren't they shown as received, and what has been their disposition and, while you are at it, how about giving me your name."

The man answered, "Oh, I know which shipment you're talking about. I had orders to receive the guns and then send them to the production control department. Production control uncrates them and splits them into what we keep here and what will be picked up by an outside company. When they complete that transaction, I show the part meant for us as having been received in the log book. That will probably happen on Monday. As for where they are, they were probably split up today. To answer your other question, my name is Henry Wirth."

I bet this guy doesn't know any better, Axel thought. *He is just following orders. I have to go and find those crates before they get too far.*

"Who instructed you to follow this procedure?" Axel asked.

"This came straight from the boss, Mr. Pratt. You should know about that if you really have been sent here by Mr. Pratt."

"Yes, I knew about it," Axel commented. "I was just trying to see if you have been following Mr. Pratt's orders. I'm glad to see you knew what to do. Now, why don't you point me toward production control, so I can go and check on their progress?"

"Go through that door right there and make a left, and then go all the way back to where you will see another shipping and receiving dock. It's smaller than this one. Shipments from General Gun always go there first."

"Thanks Henry," said Axel. "I will tell Mr. Pratt you know what you are doing. Keep up the good work."

Axel followed Henry's directions and arrived at the secondary shipping and receiving area. He looked around and saw many crates sitting in the area. He began to look through them and soon found that they fell into two categories. Some were marked "Chamber One Gun" and others were marked "Marshall Pratt." *That's interesting,* Axel thought. *It looks like he is sending these to someone in his family.* He decided to look inside a few of the boxes and was not too surprised at what he found. The boxes marked for Chamber One Gun contained small caliber guns, like rifles and some handguns. The boxes marked for Marshall Pratt contained AK-47s.

Here's at least where part of the game is played, Axel thought. *I better take some pictures of this.* He pulled out his digital camera and took pictures of the receiving dock, the address on the outside of the door, the office of production control, the crates as he had found them, the opened crates, the addresses on the outside of the ones with the small arms weapons, and the address on the one containing the AK-47 assault rifles.

Then Axel decided to begin taking the AK-47 rifles out of their crate one by one. As he removed each one, he bent a small piece of metal inside it. When the weapon was fired, it would now blow up in the shooter's hand. As he proceeded through this routine, he counted forty-two assault rifles. When they were laid out on the floor, he took a piece of paper and wrote, "42 AK-47 assault rifles were found at Chamber One Gun on October 1, 2009 with the recipient being Marshall Pratt." He laid this next to the guns and took a picture of the guns and the note. Having completed his disfiguring of the assault rifles, he placed them back into the crates as he had found them, taking a picture of the crate and gun each time he added a gun. He wanted all forty-two guns accounted for. He then closed the crates and walked back to Henry's desk.

"You were right," he told the other man. "The guns are located in the receiving dock by production control. They have been separated into two batches. I guess they will log the ones for Chamber One on Monday, as you mentioned. So things are going according to plan. Keep up the good work."

"Thanks, Mr. Gant," replied Henry.

After completing his survey of Chamber One, Axel decided to go to General Gun Company and review how they marked their shipments. It didn't take long for him to drive there. Like Chamber One, all the lights were out, except a large light at the front door. Axel suspected that there was a guard at that door of this building, so he drove down the block to park his car. He ran back to the rear of the two-story building and surveyed the possible entry points. The shipping area was in the back, and it was dark in the rear of the building. He reviewed the windows on the second floor and decided to go for one of these as he had at Chamber One. This time he was lucky, since the window he had chosen was unlocked. He was soon inside and quickly found the shipping and receiving area. The area were closed and locked. He thought about turning the light on, since the guard out front would not be able to see it. Figuring it was a safe move; he turned on the light and checked the desk. All of the drawers were locked, so he took out the tool he used for to unlock drawers. He found the logs for shipping and receiving in the second drawer..

He opened the shipping one and saw an entry near the bottom of the last page that listed Chamber One Gun. The guns shipped to Chamber One were the small caliber ones he'd seen in the one crate. The log did not list the AK-47 assault rifles. There was an entry just below that one that read, "Lot #4700 received from rework area and rejected; and returned to shipper, total of 42 guns."

This is it, Axel though. *I must take a picture of this log, and then I need to find the rework area.*

He turned out the light and, taking out his flashlight, made his way to the offices located in the back of the plant. He soon found an office marked Quality and Reliability Control. The door was locked, so he pulled out his magic tool and unlocked it. Since the office didn't have a window, he figured he could close the door and turn on the light. His guess was that the quality control manual would be in one of the big desk drawers, and he proceeded to open them until he struck it rich. There were several quality and reliability logs in the drawer. He found one of the logs that listed everything by lot number. There was lot 4700, and it showed that three samples had been pulled from that lot. The acceptance criterion was to accept zero rejects. The whole lot had to be rejected if only one item failed. The sample from the 4700 lot failed, and the lot was shipped to "rework," to be determined if the guns could be reworked or had to be sent back to the supplier.

Axel looked through other logs for comments on lot 4700. Sure enough, the lot number appeared again not too far down another list. The comment written in the log was, "Lot rejected at rework as not reworkable, return to vendor." Axel continued to follow the paper trail and soon came upon another entry for lot 4700. "Reject lot 4700 sent to secondary shipping platform, instructed to return back to vendor." But he knew the lot hadn't been returned to the supplier.

This means there are several people involved in this scam, including the quality control manager, the reworks manager, and the shipper. This lot was disqualified at several locations, and this rejection was used as the ruse for shipping it to Chamber One without it being shown as a normal shipment for which revenue was expected. They didn't expect any revenue to show on their books. Any money paid by Chamber One is off the books and below boar; a crime.

Having obtained what he considered the full story for lot 4700, Axel needed to find out how the lot had made it to this plant and who had shipped it in. It hadn't been manufactured at General Gun, since they had never had the capability to manufacture AK-47s. Axel was pissed at himself. He should have looked through the receiving logs too. So, after he took pictures of everything he thought was relevant, he returned the logs to their drawer, locked the drawers, and locked the door as he was leaving. Returning to the first place, he began looking through the receiving logs. Sure enough, there was a receiving log entry for the shipments that had arrived at the secondary receiving platform. He looked through the log and found that lot 4700 was logged in the same day as it was rejected and was supposedly sent back to the vendor. However, the log also showed that the guns were sent in the care of Mr. Raymond Anzel, and were not supposed to go on the receiving logs of General Gun Company. Axel knew that Raymond Anzel was the president of General Gun. The guns were shipped by a company in New Jersey. As Axel took pictures of all this information, he thought about the implications what he'd learned. The president of General Gun had had guns shipped to him. The same day they were received, they were rejected at quality control and at rework, and shipped back to the vendor. However, they hadn't been sent back to the company in New Jersey. They had been shipped to Marshall Pratt at Chamber One.

After Axel had finished his review and was preparing to leave, he heard a noise and decided he had better arm himself. He said to himself, "Axelvation two, hood down," and turned rapidly around. He was facing six tough-looking men with Uzis in their hands.

"What were you looking for, mister?" one of them asked.

"Oh, I was just checking up on how your company pulled the wool over people's eyes," said Axel. "Nice game you have for yourselves here. I don't think the IRS would be happy with what I have found. I also bet the Mexican people that get nailed by these guns wouldn't think it's so nice."

"What makes you think anyone is going to know that?" asked the man.

"Oh, I have a way of telling people when I find something wrong and evil," said Axel.

"You don't understand, mister. You aren't going anywhere with that message or that camera."

"If I were you," Axel said, "I would go home to your families and be glad you had."

"Or what?" the man asked.

"Or I will jam those guns down your throats, and you will wish you had turned around and had gone home."

"Oh, this is a tough guy," the leader said as he looked at his buddies. "We are going to have fun with this one before we put him in a crate and ship him out."

The others laughed, and all half dozen of them began to walk toward Axel with their guns aimed at his chest. Just as they were about to shoot, Axel leaped up in the air in an arc that was about fifteen feet high ceiling and landed behind the six men. Their shots rang out, but there was only a wall to receive them. With his right arm, Axel made a swiping motion, smacking the back of each man's head. He counted as they went down— one, two, three, four, five, six. There were now six thugs lying at his feet, out cold. He could have killed them, as they had intended to kill him, but he had thought about their families. Maybe this would be a good lesson for them. It would certainly alert the company that someone was onto their game.

They will be out a couple of hours, he thought, *and by the time they wake up, I will be waiting at the airport for my flight back to my woman.* He picked up the guns and bent them each into a U shape. Then he went upstairs and left the building the same way he came in.

Axel returned to his motel and picked up his belongings. As he drove to the airport, he called Kim on his internal phone. He described what he had found during his short stay, and what he had done to the AK-47s at Chamber One.

"I have pictures of everything," he added. "Now you have to think about how you handle this from here on. I would guess that this one company ships out a couple hundred guns a month, and over two thousand in a year. That's a lot of firepower. Keep in mind this is only one company we are talking about. General Gun might be shipping guns to three or four good shippers each month, and this could add up to ten thousand guns a year. I don't know where they get them from, but this has got to be the next big question and the next big bust. As far as I can see, this suspect shipment of AK-47s was sent from New Jersey to the president of General Gun, but the quality control manager, the rework manager, and the production control manager of General Gun Company are accomplices in the carrying out of this fraud, and indirectly guilty of the murder of innocent Mexican people. The president and the production control manager of Chamber One are also accomplices in the same respect. That's a lot of high level people in those two companies that were carrying out this venture. I also believe they have been liable to the Internal Revenue Service for understating their shipments and receipts. There is no doubt the presidents of the two companies are guilty of tax evasion, and the financial head of each company might be involved as well."

Kim thanked him for his quick work, and told him to enjoy his trip back to California.

Axel was able to get a flight to San Francisco instead of San Jose. He could have taken a later flight to San Jose, but chose to get home earlier. He called Tori and told her he'd be in San Francisco around noon, and asked if she could pick him up.

"I'm sure I can get some time off for that," she replied. "That's exciting. I didn't expect you would get your thing done so quickly."

"Yes, I was lucky," he replied. "If you can't pick me up, then give me a call and I will find a way to get to the school."

Tori was able to get an hour off from work, and picked up Axel and drove him to his school. She wanted to know when she should come and pick him up from school, but he said he probably could get a ride from one of the students that lived near them. Axel went in and sat in on the class that was being taught by his substitute professor. It was nice to hear the lecture being given, rather than giving it. It was also nice to hear the different twist Marv put on the subject matter. Some areas needed better definition and discussion. He was happy to see the number of students attending, and they appeared to be enjoying the subject matter. Afterward, he attended another class being taught by a friend of his, since he knew there were students in that class who lived near his home. After the lecture, he asked around and was able to snag a lift to his house.

When he got home, Tori wasn't back from her work yet. She normally got home about six, and it was just five o'clock. He was tired, so he went into the bedroom, took his clothes off, and lay in bed. It wasn't long till he was fast asleep. While he slept, he a woman was softly touching his back. Only it wasn't her fingers doing the touching; it was the nipples of her breast. As unconscious as he was, he could feel the response down in his private parts. They were rapidly coming alive, and it didn't take long for him to open his eyes and realize this was no dream. No dream could be this nice. Against his back was the cool naked body of his beautiful woman.

"It feels like you took a cool shower," he whispered to her. "It feels wonderful."

"Yes, I took a cool shower to cool me down. When I think of you in this bed with me, my body temperature goes up and my nipples get hard and stand out."

"I know. I can feel them and they feel wonderful."

He reached behind himself and grabbed her butt. Beginning to massage it, he slowly worked his way to the magic area hidden between her legs. As he caressed this area, she began to coo.

"I think I found your cooing area," he said, "and it feels nice and wet."

"It is wet," she said. "It's waiting for you and you better hurry while I am able to hold back my orgasm." She reached around his body and began to stroke his hard dick.

"You don't have to wait any longer," he said, and turned around and began to suck on those beautiful nipples. "God sure gave women a wonderful and enjoyable thing when he gave them breasts. They have a feel of their own. There is nothing I have ever touched that feels as good as your breasts feel, and the nipples have their own feel, both to my hands and to my mouth."

As Axel continued his play, Tori mumbled that she wanted him inside her.

"I want to feel you inside me and our rhythm to start up."

Axel was more than happy to put his dick in that nice warm spot. What a great feeling. It was juicy from the foreplay and allowed his dick to penetrate and retreat, as if trying to keep from coming too quick. But soon her loud moaning and crying out that she was coming was like a trigger, and his come shot into her body, and she cooed and cooed some more. Axel surged back and forth inside her.

"No feeling like this either," he mumbled as they lay there in sweet splendor, the aftermath of splendid accomplishment. "Too bad it doesn't last longer. But I guess God wanted it to be short so we would come back for more. No use ruining a good thing by oversupply."

A couple of days went by, and Axel received a call from Dr. Kim. "Axel, this case has been turned over to the Bureau of Alcohol, Tobacco, Firearms, and Explosives, and they are going to make a visit to the General Gun Company today and follow up on the Chamber

One Company tomorrow. They are able to use the fact that we know a shipment went out of General Gun and was delivered to Chamber One, but not logged in. All the data you got is hidden data that we may use if this goes beyond these two companies. I believe they will cooperate as soon as they realize that the government is on their case. In addition, the IRS will be visiting the financial people of these two companies starting today. This means we have done our thing here, and we can sit back and watch the action unfold.

"I almost hope the guns that you ruined at Chamber One were sent out, since they'll turn out to be lethal weapons against the user. I would love to see the expression on the face of anyone trying to use those guns. That was a slick trick you pulled, and it will save lives. We are hoping that these actions on General Gun will bring out the information we need to show where the AK-47 assault rifles came from. When we find that out, we may need your services again. I will keep you updated on anything we learn. I am really excited about this, and hope you are too."

Axel had been holding his breath when Kim gave him this news. At last he was able to breathe, and gave out a shout of happiness. "Oh, that is so great. I am so glad I had a part in this, and I know that Captain Renaldo of the Tijuana police will be happy to hear about this. Let me know if they find out where the AK-47s have been coming from."

"Oh yes I will," Kim said.

Locating the Ship Carrying the Guns into the Country

Only a couple of weeks went by before Axel got another call from Dr. Kim. They had found out where the AK-47s were coming from.

"We almost fell into it," Kim said. "While the BATFE was going through everything at General Gun, a truck showed up with a delivery. They turned out to be AK-47s. They arrested the driver and found that he had driven the truck from New Jersey. A place called Salt Beach, New Jersey, was where the driver had picked the crates up. He had enough information, even though he wasn't connected with the group that was bringing in the guns. He works for a company that does odd pick-ups like this. He didn't know what was in the crates. They were marked Ironwear and were supposed to be ceramic dishes of some sort. The information he'd picked up was that a large ship had dropped anchor about fifteen miles outside of Salt Beach. Then a small craft picked up some crates from the ship, and the ship continued on its way. The small craft then made its way to a dock located on Salt Beach. It turned out to be a good place to do something like this. There aren't many houses or businesses along the beach. So, someone can make a landing there without being detected. The driver heard that the crates had come from Romania, but didn't know how. We are going to follow up on this, but we might need you on this to find a way to get on the big ship and find out more details. We know that Romania is now the biggest maker of AK-47 assault rifles. They have provided many guns to insurgents in Iraq and Afghanistan over the past decade. They have not been allowed to ship them into the United States. It is possible they were transported from Romania to another country in Europe, and that country shipped them to the States. I thought you would be excited to hear that we have obtained this amount of information. We want you to think about it and see if you come up with a suggestion over the next few weeks."

"The key," Axel said, "is to know when the ship is going to be in that position off the coast again. It would be easy if there was a regular schedule, but I doubt there is. Perhaps the agency can check what ships are due into New Jersey ports and their scheduled date. It might be an oil tanker, since there is considerable amount of oil delivered into that area of New Jersey. If it's oil from the Mideast, it's possible the guns came from the Mideast. They are groups in the Mideast that have a vested interest in disrupting anything they can in the western world, especially the United States.

"I suggest we put a submarine in that area to watch for the ship. It can alert us to the exact location of the ship. It's illegal to drop a shipment off without coming into a legal port, so we would have the right to board it. I can see us developing a routine, where the sub sights the main ship and sends a message to me, and I swim out and board the ship and take action. The alternative is to just keep an eye on the dock at Salt Beach, and when the sub provides the signal, I slip aboard the small craft and let it take me out to the ship. This is a good approach, since if I am on the smaller craft, I can wait till they are lowering the crates into it and stop the action right away. Then the Coast Guard can come in and board the big ship. This way we get both ships and the bogus freight all in one swoop. At that point, we might be able to find the paper trail back to where the guns were shipped from. What do you think?"

"I think that's good thinking," said Kim. "Both of those ideas could work, but I like the second one better. You are right about us being able to check the scheduled ships into the ports near Atlantic City. That should give us a broad picture of all the ships coming into the area. We can narrow it down a little, since the ships coming from a northern approach won't be the ships to worry about. They have to be coming from the south, so they pass Salt Beach before they enter the northern New Jersey area. If we review the scheduled ships coming in from the southern route, we will know which port they are coming from. Once we actually find the ship with the crates, we can then determine which port it came from. From that information, we may be able to follow the paper trail to how they might have made it to that country. After that, it is up to international intelligence to track it down further. I will get back to you when I find out all the information we talked about. This is a good start, and you made good suggestions. I guess that's why I call you so often. You take care, and I hope you and your lady are doing well."

"Yes, school is good, and Tori is better than good," replied Axel.

The following week, Kim called again. "Axel, we have the schedule of ships heading toward the East Coast from the southern routes this coming week. There are twelve ships arriving from that direction, but only two of them are putting into ports south of New York. We are going to cover those two and get more details on where and when they will head into port. We got some additional input from the truck driver that we caught making a delivery to General Gun. We have the name of the truck service that was contracted to make the pick up from Salt Beach. Agents are visiting that trucking place this week to see if they get any calls for deliveries from Salt Beach. Anyhow, that's the most recent information, and I will let you know if any additional information comes in."

"What if it is one of the two ships carrying the guns and you get info from the trucking service that they have a delivery to make? Where do I come into the scene? It would take me at least a day to make it to the East Coast and get down to that remote place."

"Yes, this could be a problem," Kim said. "I have contacted the right people in the Air Force, and if we find out enough information to give us a 90 percent probability that one of those ships is the right one, they are ready to fly you out here posthaste. We are talking about an Air Force jet that can make that flight in a little over three hours. They would fly into the Naval Air Force base just outside of Atlantic City and we would have some form of transportation for you from there. All together, we believe we can get you into the Salt Beach area in less than five hours from when they pick you up."

Axel was impressed. "That is really moving, and that would be great. I will be ready. Can I get a flight back as fast as that?"

"I can't promise you that," Kim said. "But I will do whatever I can to make that happen. I know we are taking you away from your teaching and your home life. All I can say is, 'It's for the good of the country.'"

Axel agreed and said he would be ready when they were.

Two days went by, and Axel got a call from Kim.

"Get your flight suit on, Axel. We have confirmation that one of the ships is headed toward Atlantic City, and the trucking firm received a call for a pick-up at Salt Beach. We are fairly certain this is a winner. The ship is supposed to dock tomorrow around one in the afternoon, and the trucking company got a pick-up time of noon. This makes sense, since it would take about an hour for the big ship to get to port from Salt Beach. We know you could handle both ends of this one, the small boat and the large ship. It is almost three o'clock here. When are your classes completed for today?"

"My last class today is at 3:00, which is 6:00 your time."

"How about we pick you up at 5:00 and fly you out here? You would get here about midnight our time. We would make arrangements for you in a hotel in Atlantic City, so you can get a good night's sleep. We would pick you up the next morning at 9:30, which would get you to Salt Beach at approximately 10:30. This gives you at least an hour to get squared away with the small craft. We have thought about it, and we believe that, with a warrant, you can take over the small craft while it is still sitting at the dock. How does that sound to you, Axel?"

"I have thought of a little change to this plan. I would like one of your agents to drive the delivery truck. Your agent could drive the truck close to the docking area. I would take over as the driver, and I would arrive at the dock earlier than they expected. The reason for this is we get the delivery truck out of the equation, and we arrive on site without any problems. Perhaps I could talk the guys on the boat into allowing me to go out to the ship with them. If they agree, then I have a ride to the ship without having to bang anyone up. After arriving at the ship, I could make the proper moves against the gang on the craft and handle any problems with the people on the ship. On the other hand, the guys on the small craft might not want me along. If that's the case, I would overpower them, but keeping one of them active to show me out to the ship. If not, no problem, I know how to run one of those crafts. There is one problem I can think of about nailing the group at the dock before going out to the ship. They might have a signal that they are supposed to send to the ship that would confirm with the ship that everything is going as planned and there are no problems. If I subdue the crew on the dock before they send that message, the ship is liable to take off. I guess I will have to play it by ear, and decide when and where I need to take action. Once I am on that craft, with or without the men that were supposed to be on it, our officials can move in on the dock, awaiting the return of the craft. Also, my leaving the dock on the boat should be a signal for the Coast Guard and whatever agents we want to board the large ship to head out."

The Air Force jet picked up Axel, and everything went according to plan. The next day Axel found himself driving a truck down to the dock at Salt Beach. Just before he arrived, he gave his internal system his energy orders—Axelvation two, hood down—and he felt the energy level in his body shift into a high gear. He took out two candy bars and made short work of them. I *may need that extra energy,* he thought. *Besides, I like those candy bars.*

When he arrived at the dock, six men hustling around the small boat docked there. They were surprised to see him. One man, who said his name was James and who seemed to be the boss of the crew, wanted to know why he arrived an hour early. Axel told them that when he had picked up crates from this site before, they had had problems handling of them, and he thought they might need some help. This seemed to satisfy James, and Axel helped them to get the craft ready to go. Axel kept his eyes and ears open in case one of them took out his phone and made a call. Just before they were ready to leave James did indeed do this. He turned to the other men and said that it was time to go.

The rest of the crew acknowledged this and began to board the craft. Axel did as well, but James asked him where he thought he was going. Axel said that he believed he would go out with them and help them with the crates.

"No use my staying here and doing nothing on this dock," he said.

James thought about and then waved Axel on. "What's your name?" he asked Axel.

"Jake," Axel said.

"Well, Jake, this is against my better feelings, but we have needed help in the past, and maybe you will be a help more than a hindrance."

Soon, they were on their way out to where the ship was expected to be. When they got out about ten miles Axel could see a ship in the distance. He called the agency via his internal phone.

"You should go to the shipping company and find out who ordered the truck to pick up this shipment. That is the culprit you want to catch. That's the master brain of this whole deal. Also, I assume you have sent the Coast Guard out to where this ship is moored. I will take care of preventing anyone getting away."

In a short while, as the craft approached the ship at a steady speed, the ship was only about a mile away. Axel saw the men on board the ship getting some crates on the port side. A crane had lifted one crate, positioning it over the edge of the ship as a crew member guided the boom and the boon had. He could see a second crate getting readied for the crane. At that point, Axel felt the ship's crew had committed itself enough that the Coast Guard could take legal action. He decided to get rid of the men on the small boat with him, so they wouldn't be a bother when he took on the ship's crew. He walked up to one of the men on board with him, picked him up, and threw him about thirty feet into the air, over the water. The fall into the water from that height would either kill him or knock him out, so the Coast Guard could pick him up.

"What are you doing, Jake?" James shouted.

"Getting rid of excess bad baggage," Axel answered.

James drew his gun and began firing at Axel. The bullets bounced off Axel, tearing holes in his clothes but not penetrating Axel's body. Axel dove toward him and jammed his fist against the gun just as James fired again. The gun blew up, and the bullet ricocheted off Axel's armored hand and rammed into James's chest. That was his end. Axel turned to the others, who all faced him with guns in their hands. They began to fire away at Axel, and were astounded as they saw the bullets bounce off his body. Axel leaped at one of them and hit him in the chest so hard his fist penetrated his body and got stuck in his chest. In order to rid himself of the body, Axel swung it like a club at one of the other men. Both of them flew in the air and into the water some twenty feet away. This left only two more of the crew, and both of them knew better. They dived over the side of the boat and began to swim away.

The craft was only about a hundred yards away from the ship by this time. The crew of the ship had seen what had happened, and they scurried to get the first crate back onto the deck. They were too late. Axel had cut the engine on the small boat and leaped high in the air toward the ship. He landed softly on the deck, not far from the man running the boom. Axel reached over and slammed the guy across the head, and he fell like a rock. That took care of anyone being able to bring the crate back on board the ship. After that, Axel ran around and knocked men to the deck before anyone could do anything. Since they were aboard a oil tanker, none of them could shoot guns at him for fear of igniting the fuel. Not that it would matter to Axel, but it mattered to all those aboard the ship. Just as Axel had cleared the deck, the Coast Guard cutter came alongside.

"This is the Coast Guard," a voice announced over a loudspeaker. "Remain in your position and drop any weapons you might have in your hand. Surrender and no harm will come to you."

Axel collected the weapons from the crew, and then went o see if there were other problems that needed to be handled. As he opened one of the double doors below the main deck, he was surprised to see eight men who were obviously not a part of the crew. Knowing that they would fire their guns, he rapidly ran toward them. As they reached for their guns, he slammed his hands against their arms. Once they were hit, their arms and hands became useless. He then corralled while asking them in various languages where they were from. They were in great pain, which made it hard to interrogate them.

Finally one of the men spoke in Russian. "We are Russian, and we are from Iran."

"What were you doing on this ship?" Axel yelled in Russian..

"We paid money to be brought to this country. We were supposed to be let out of this room when the ship dropped off some crates. We were told about an hour ago that we would soon be let off the ship. We were told that the boat that picked up the crates would bring another boat that would take us ashore."

"What was you intention once you got ashore?" asked Axel.

"A truck was supposed to transport us to Boston, where we would find friends."

"But how would you make your way in the U.S. without proper paperwork?" asked Axel.

"We have proper paperwork," the man replied. "We have driver's licenses from the state of Massachusetts, and visas that allow us to be in the country."

Axel shook his head. "You are going to have the shortest stay in the States of anyone I know."

He grabbed the leader and nodded to the others, gesturing in the direction of the door. He led them up the ladders to topside, just as men from the Coast Guard were coming aboard. Ten of the Coast Guard personnel boarded the ship and advised the men of their rights, including the Russians. The Coast Guard captain had gone to the pilot house and directed the captain of the ship to drop anchor.

"You are under arrest for delivering property to an unauthorized point of the sea and within the United States territorial waters. In addition, if the delivery contains assault weapons, you are further charged with delivering illegal arms to this country. You have Russians aboard, which represents illegal immigrants being brought into the country. I don't think you will be taking this ship anywhere."

Axel introduced himself to the Coast Guard captain.

"Glad to meet you, Axel Tressler," the captain said. "I am Lieutenant Justin Markel, and I am impressed by your performance today. I don't understand how you accomplished what you did, but it was one of the highlights of my career. I hope you carry this further and find who was behind the whole deal."

Axel thanked him and told him he was going to take the small boat back to the dock. He assured the lieutenant he was available if needed for future information or as a witness against the men they'd arrested. He told him that the USSA would have his complete write-up of this event, including his part in the action.

Axel got on his phone with the agency and soon was talking to Dr. Kim. He gave him a verbal report, and told him that he not only found the guns, but had found eight Russians who were heading for Boston.

Axel said, "I don't know how they were going to make it from the ship to shore, since the only boat that had gone out was the one I was on, and I didn't hear anyone talk about another boat to pick up fugitives. I wonder if there was no intention of getting them to shore. The captain of the ship might have taken their money and figured that when he delivered the crates he had been paid to deliver, he would figure out how they were going to make it ashore; or not. Maybe he thought his crew could handle the problem physically. Anyhow, the Coast Guard has them now, and hopefully they will find out the total story. What bothers me is that they were prepared to go to Boston and meet other Russians up there. They had all the proper paperwork to get away with it. I wonder if this is the first of many excursions into this country, or if they represent something that has been happening for some time. We saw how many Russians were in the Boston area when I broke up that terrorist gang there. Maybe this is where they got many of their people in the past. I will be heading back home as soon as I can make arrangements, and I will write up a complete report. Now I have to give my woman a call."

Soon Axel was talking on his phone to Tori, letting her know he soon would be home. "I am so happy," she said. "I always worry when you are on one of these assignments. I know you can handle almost everything, but I worry."

"Keep cool, my dear," he said. "As fast as an airplane can get me to the western shore, I will be hugging you.

Axel returned home, but he talked with Kim every day. He wanted to understand more about the gun trafficking, and wanted to know how things worked out with the fugitives that were picked up. The crates on the ship were found to have four hundred AK-47s in one crate and three hundred Uzis in the other crate. The ship's captain and crew were being held for illegal trafficking of arms and for illegal shipment of cargo in an unauthorized docking location. The truck that was supposed to pick up the guns had been leased by Raymond Anzel, the president of General Gun. The agency initiated action against him, as well as the president of Chamber One and the other people that Axel had found to be part of the scheme at the two companies. The agency was also in the process of determining where the guns had been shipped from. The AK-47s were manufactured in Romania and shipped across the Black Sea to Turkey. From Turkey, a plane flew them to Saudi Arabia, where they were secretly stored aboard the oil tanker carrying oil to a refinery in New Jersey. The U.S. government had been determining what action should be taken against whom in this case. So far, Kim told Axel, they had not found where the Uzis came from, but a review of the flight path of the plane that had carried the AK-47s from Turkey revealed that it flew near Israel on its way to Saudi Arabia. The various government agencies involved felt this was probably the logical source for the Uzis. Israel was a major manufacturer of the Uzi, and the agency was checking to see if the plane had stopped in Israel; or if the Uzis had made their way down Saudi

Arabia. The tanker's route from Saudi to New Jersey was just one of many possible routes that had been used to deliver guns to this country.

Finally, Kim thanked Axel for his findings. The government knew of his actions, and he was to be commended on the results. Kim added that the BATFE was picking up the whole action up, and the USSA was no longer involved.

This shift of responsibility left Axel somewhat disappointed. He had wanted to follow it through to completion, but he knew he had other responsibilities. He understood that this gun trafficking was a huge undertaking and would take more than his actions to resolve it. It probably was being pursued by hundreds of agents across various continents, where the key item was solving the Mexican issue as fast as possible.

Axel returned to his teaching and his life with Tori. He felt good about what he had accomplished. He felt that it might affect only 10 percent of the guns that made it to Mexico, but every little bit helped.

I hope, he thought, *that one batch of guns I altered was sent out, and some of those cartel members fire them and have them explode in their hands. That would serve them right.*

The Follower Receives New Powerful Communication Capabilities

It wasn't long afterward that Axel started to get little hints from Kim about some other actions that were occurring in various parts of the country. One day he would get a call from Kim, and he would talk about terrorist groups in New York. Then a few weeks later he would mention potential terrorist activities in Chicago. Mixed in with these conversations were other elements that related to terrorist threats in the UK. There was nothing solid in these conversations that required any action by Axel. They were like little pinpricks at his skin, first one thing than another. He started to get paranoid about these conversations. He thought, *it seems like Kim wants to keep in touch with me and keeps bringing up these intangible things that are happening in different areas, but nothing solid that the agency might want me to get involved in. Maybe Kim feels the need to get involved in some action somewhere, so he has been looking at all these possible things and talking to me about them. It's like he has bait on the end of a fishing line, and he wants me to take a bite. Yet, there isn't any bait on the line for me to grab hold of. Maybe it's me and I'm reading too much into these conversations. Yes, I guess I am paranoid, or something like being paranoid.*

But as the weeks rolled by, the discussions that Kim was having with Axel took on a shape that looked more and more real. Axel could almost see his involvement coming. Then one day Kim called and told Axel that the terrorist activities in these different places seemed to be related. They discussed it for over an hour, and Axel could see from the details that something common about the occurrences was happening. He could tell that eventually he would be involved in hunting down terrorists of one sort or another. Near the end of their conversation, Kim brought up an entirely new subject that was a surprise to Axel. He informed Axel that the transmitter they had installed in his teeth over a year ago was giving out weak signals.

"We have to get you back here to bring your transmitter up to speed," he said. "You will be happy to know, Axel, that we have developed an even better one. You will be surprised when you get here to see what we have come up with. What's your schedule look like?"

"I wouldn't mind coming out after Christmas. The school will be closed for two weeks, and I have been thinking about taking Tori back east to meet my twin brother and his wife and son. Also, we would hope to stop in and see my mother in my hometown of Monessen, Pennsylvania, over by Pittsburgh. How would that work for you?"

Kim thought it was a good time, since he would be free then. He also wanted to meet Tori, since he has heard so much about her from Axel. Axel told him that he would get back to him about dates, and that he was excited about the new transmitter.

When Axel got home from teaching, he hurried to tell Tori about his conversation with Kim.

Tori got all excited and said, "Thank goodness you have thought of something we can do at that time of the year. I would love to meet your family, and maybe it will snow while we are out there and we can have a white Christmas. I have never been anywhere where there is a natural white Christmas."

"Great," exclaimed Axel. "I will check with the school on the exact dates we have off. Then I will contact Kim and my brother. I haven't talked to Adam for months. I know he and his wife will be excited to meet you, and maybe we can stop to see my mother while we're out there. She has wanted to meet you for some time now. She would be in her glory."

Axel called the school and learned that he would have off from December 18 to January 5. Then he called Kim and gave him that information. Kim thought that was a great window of time for him to set something up at the agency. Finally, Axel called Adam. Adam was surprised to hear from him, but he had known something would be coming up, because he knew about the new transmitter for Axel.

"Adam, I will be bringing Tori with me. Do you think Laura would mind if she stayed at your house while we are there?"

"No problem, bro," Adam said. "We have been waiting to meet the woman who has turned my brother's head. That would be great. Laura will be excited and happy. We may bring Mom down here for a while, and that would give you and Tori time to spend with Mom."

"Terrific," said Axel. "I will get back to you when I have dates and times of arrival. You take care, and tell Laura I love her."

A few days later Axel got a call from Kim. "Axel, we will be ready for you anytime from the eighteenth on. The transmitter is about complete. It needs a few checks, but it will be ready in a couple of days. We will look for you and Tori around the eighteenth. If you give me the exact dates, I will have the agency pick up the tickets at our cost, since you will be out here on duty as far as we are concerned."

"Oh, that's terrific," Axel exclaimed. "I never meant to get a free ticket out of you, but it is business, and we will be there to transact it. How about looking for a flight out on the morning of the nineteenth? Also, while I am thinking about it, what about the battery for this new transmitter? Do you have to change the battery I have now?"

"Yes," replied Kim. "We will be doing the whole thing. We have a new type of battery that is longer lasting and very efficient. You will be getting the complete dental treatment, and we have for you another surprise for you."

Kim wouldn't tell him what the surprise was. The conversation left Axel wondering about the other thing they would be doing when he was out there. He knew it would be something new and exciting, so this gave him another thing to look forward to in late December.

On December nineteenth, Tori and Axel flew from San Francisco to Dallas, Texas, and from there to Dulles International Airport in Washington DC. They arrived at seven thirty in the evening, and Adam and Dr. Kim were there to meet them. Both Adam and Kim ignored Axel and went straight to Tori, as if she were the only one that had arrived.

Axel stood back and said, "Hey guys, what is this? Aren't I welcome here?"

They both laughed and said Tori looked better than he did. Tori laughed as well, enjoying the joke on Axel. After Axel and Tori got their bags, Kim said good-bye, and Tori and Axel got in Adam's car for the drive to his house. It was only about a half hour ride. When they arrived, Adam hit the garage door opener. Up went the garage door, and there on the other side was Laura and her son Justin. After greetings and introductions, Laura said to Axel, "Now I know what you mean when you say she's beautiful. She is gorgeous."

Tori blushed, but Axel could tell she was happy to hear that from his sister-in-law. They spent the rest of the evening talking and telling stories about Axel when he was growing up, and what it was like for Adam to watch his twin take on all that energy as he got older. It was a fun evening. Later, Adam told Axel that Kim wanted him at the agency the next day around ten in the morning. Adam said Axel could take his car, since he was off for the Christmas holiday. Axel asked Adam if he wanted to go in to the agency too. Adam said, "No, I think they are going to be spending the time with you, and it would be like another day at work for me. I don't want that on my holiday time off."

The next day Axel drove to the building that housed the USSA. Kim was in the front lobby, waiting. In Kim's office, Axel asked for a cup of good hot coffee, and then before long they were deep in discussion about the new transmitter that would be installed in Axel's back tooth.

"It's a new design," Kim said, "and you can almost whisper and send a signal. But the exciting thing I have you out here for is something that you and I have been wanting. I have always had to send faxes and things with pictures to your office computer or your home computer. That is going to change. You have always wanted to be able to receive and send diagrams and circuit schematics. Well, we think we have solved that problem. We have designed a system that works with your internal computer and supplies that capability. We have to install a CCD chip in your body that is similar to the one that is used in cameras. It is somewhat different, since it will be installed in your body and therefore will not be able to see an image. However, since it is inside you and isn't going to be picking up an optical image directly, we can design it to use much less power. As I will explain later, we will be able to use your eyes and an analog-to-digital converter to provide a low level signal for the CCD. We will have to operate on you and get into your internal wiring. We will set the system up so that when you want to send an image, you have to say 'Axelvation See.' and the computer and the CCD chip will know they are to receive text or a picture. You will not say 'Axelvation See' until you are ready to send an image. To do this you must be staring at the image you wish to send. The circuitry we will install will send the analog signal from your eyes through your internal wiring to two converters located at two places. One place will be extra electronics on the CCD chip, and the other is a modification that has it in the computer chip. When the information is converted to digital, it will be placed in two places, on the CCD chip and in the computer memory. The 'Axelvation See' statement provides an automatic address code that automatically makes it available to the computer memory. The electronics on the CCD chip or on the computer will take this information and convert what you are seeing as an analog view to the digital format. The CCD chip is able to see images, or it can simulate those images with digital information, and that is what we will do in this case. This simulated information on the CCD chip will look like the picture you were viewing, but in digital format. To send this information to the agency, you must state 'Axelvation send.' The output of the CCD is then decoded. The information is sent to the new transmitter we will be placing in your tooth, and a signal is sent to the agency that contains the image you were looking at.

"This image is received at our intelligence office and my office as a fax. That is what will happen when you want to send us an image with some details in it. For this to work you must stare at the drawing or whatever you want to send, give your internal code, and then maintain your stare for only a second. As soon as you blink, the system is turned off and will not come back on till you state 'Axelvation See' once more. If you want to send ten pictures, you have to go through these processes each time for each image. We have simulated this type of sequence in our labs, and you should be able to send ten images in ten to twenty seconds. The electronics are very fast, and if they were a person, they would think you were doing this in slow motion. Isn't that great?"

Axel smiled. "I knew you would come up with something for me to send images. This is tremendous. I think about it and my eye becomes a camera. I am a walking picture machine; that's hilarious."

"I haven't finished," Kim said. "Remember, you have all of these images in your computer memory. This is only for redundancy purposes, in case we didn't get an image clearly. If we send a message back to you, saying we need you to resend, you just call up that image from your computer memory and send it again. The images only stay in the memory for twenty-four hours, after which they are erased. We don't need to clog up your computer memory, when we have a fax at our office that we can send back to you at any time. The hard copy fax provides us long term memory here at the agency."

"But I have a question. What happens if you want to send me an image?"

"That's sort of like the same thing in reverse, but maybe a little harder. First, we have to tell you that we are going to send an image. So, you will get a message from us through your internet phone system that an image is going to be sent. After that, you close your eyes at the count of five. We will send the image, and it will be collected by your transmitter, which we'll have coded for our messages. You must keep your eyes closed till everything is complete. Your transmitter will receive this coded message and signal your computer to pick up the image. The image will be in digital format, and will go directly from the transmitter to the CCD, and an image will be simulated. This simulated image will then be decoded and converted from digital to analog. The analog signal will go to your part of the brain that allows you to see. It will be there for at least a full second, since we have programmed the CCD to hold the image and the analog signals from the computer to your brain. The image will be held in a frozen position for one second. Actually, the image will persist as long as you keep your eyes closed. If you want to retain the image, you must say 'Axelvation store.' The image at the CCD will be downloaded into your computer memory. The computer and the system will be set up so that as soon as your eyes open, the signal is switched off and the image is gone. So, you have to practice this, get used to not hurrying and taking everything in a rhythm. Think of it as a picture that you will observe as for as long as you need to look at the details. Keeping your eyes closed will allow this to happen. Storing the image in memory allows you to look at that image later if you need to review something. All you have to do is go to your internal internet system and say, 'Pull from memory store,' and the computer will show you this image. During this time, you must keep your eyes closed. When the image comes up from the memory, you can review it for up to three minutes. Anytime you want it back in storage you just say, 'Store.' and it will go into the memory. If you forget, the image will automatically go back into storage after three minutes. When you want to eliminate or modify the image, you follow the same routine that I just reviewed for bringing the image up. When it is up and you want to eliminate it from your computer memory, you just say 'Eliminate.' If you want to modify it, say, 'Modify.' and then make comments about what you would like to modify. The image will be modified. Anytime you want to send an image to another address besides ours, you call it up from the computer memory and say, 'Transmit to …' and give the computer the fax number. You can only send it by fax, and not e-mail. Does this make sense to you?"

"Yes, it does," replied Axel. "How about giving me a printout of all these directions, so I can review it and make sure I have it down pat?"

"I will give you a printout of everything related to this capability. It will include other options for its use as well. If you have any questions about this, just bring them to me.

"No, I have no questions, just the urge to shout out loud that I have added to my repertoire of capabilities. This is a fantastic advantage, Kim. I could have used these capabilities in North Korea when reviewing the missile drawings. But now that you have surprised me with this new concept, how do you propose installing this capability?"

"We will have to do it in several. First of all, the CCD can be placed anywhere under your skin, since its output will be connected to the proper places by titanium nanowires. However, because of your body covering, we can't just cut anywhere. We have to find a spot that is available to us. We have decided to put this just beneath your collarbone. Your neck doesn't have the spiderweb-titanium body covering when you have your hood up. So this will be rather easy, only requiring a small slit in the skin at the neck. The other electronics, such as the digital converter, is already on the computer. The electronics that allow it to know that an image will be sent is included in the new transmitter that will be installed in your tooth. It will also contain the analog-to-digital decoder, which will convert the analog image to a digital image. The signal that decodes the digital image at the CCD is included in the electronics that go in the tooth. This converted analog image is transmitted to your brain through the titanium nanowires. At the same time, this information is forwarded to the computer and awaits your signal to store it or not. So, to summarize, you will have a slit in your neck to receive the CCD. You will have a new transmitter, which contains other electronics, inserted in the tooth, after we remove the old transmitter. This will also contain the new battery that includes a new technology.

"Getting into your computer is a little trickier. We will have to use a diamond blade to put a small slit down by your belly button, so that we can go in and route the proper nanowiring from the neck to the computer, and other wiring that allow the transfer of signals to the proper places. We have to use a diamond blade to do this, since we have found no other means of cutting into the spiderweb–titanium nanomaterial. We have practiced this type of cutting on the limited amount of this material we have, and we found that it works quite well. Our biggest problem has been finding a way to reattach material we have cut. We can't use standard stitching, and we eventually developed a special glue that allows the material to be mended together, and still be as strong as the original material. That is it. As you can see, it is not very complex as far as the operations are concerned."

"I would say that those are minimal invasions of my body, especially for all the complexity it brings to my system. So, when do we do this?"

Kim said that they were ready to go, but needed to schedule the operations according to Axel's time available. Axel told him he was ready for anytime they wanted to schedule it, "But the sooner the better, so Tori and I can get on with our vacation plans."

"Great, how about tomorrow morning?" commented Kim

"Let's do it!" exclaimed Axel. "Can I bring Tori?"

"We would rather not," Kim said. "We like to keep these things as secret and private as possible. Not that there is anything wrong with Tori, it's just the way we like to handle these things."

Axel didn't like that answer, but he realized the agency had its priorities, and they had been doing these things longer than he had experienced them. "Okay, but I want her to be the first one to witness the results. I want her to send me an image from her laptop while I'm here in the operating room. She should be witness to what I am going to be carrying on my body."

Kim agreed to that. "She can come around noon, since we should be done, and then afterward we can go to lunch and celebrate its success. However, if there is a problem then you"—he pointed at Axel—"pay for the lunch."

Axel laughed and said, "This was a win, win bet for the agency. They win if it works, and they get a free lunch if it doesn't work."

"What if we turn it around?" Kim said. "If it works, you pay for lunch, and if it doesn't work, we pay?"

Axel laughed again, and Kim said, "Tell you what, Axel. You have proven your ability to use what we have provided for you over this past year. The programs you have been involved in have been very successful, and the agency would like to buy you, Tori, and Adam's family dinner tomorrow at the nicest restaurant in Washington. We will be celebrating, also, the success of what we will do tomorrow, since we are very confident we will be successful. How's that for a winner?"

Axel stuck out his hand, and they shook on it. They took care of some other minor things, and then Kim said the head of the agency, Samuel Hall, wanted to see him. "Do you mind if we check to see if he is available now?"

Axel didn't mind, even though he thought he would be kind of embarrassed by any congratulations. "Let's do it," he said.

Kim escorted Axel to Hall's office and told his secretary that Director Hall wanted to meet Axel. She escorted them through the large door of the office. As they entered, the director got up from his desk and walked toward them. He stuck out his hand and said, "I am very excited to meet you, Axel. Your accomplishments for the agency are legendary, and I only wish that we could tell the public about them, so that you could receive your just due."

Axel shook the director's hand and said, "Thank you, Mr. Hall. Your agency took something I was born with and allowed it to realize its full potential. Without the agency, I would just be a biology professor, teaching in a college. With the value it provided to me, I was able to see the world and experience events that still ring in my mind. It has allowed me to see how much of the world works, and compare that to how much this country possesses. The poorness and strife I have seen should be seen by everyone in this country, so they would count their blessings for living here in America. I know that is impossible, but I know I helped some of the people in other countries, and showed them how an American can help them."

Hall told Axel that he looked forward to the next accomplishments of "The Follower." "I know what Kim and his men are going to be adding to your arsenal of capabilities, and I look forward to how they impact future actions by you for our country."

They shook hands again, and Kim and Axel left.

"That was really nice of him," said Axel. "It sent cold chills down my spine and the hair on my head stood up."

"Don't underestimate yourself, Axel," said Kim. "The comments you made almost blew my mind. I didn't expect that to come out of you. I have not seen that side of you."

"Well, Kim, you must remember that I am a doctor of biology, and I give speeches every day to my students. Some of that has to rub off."

As Kim walked Axel back to his car, he said something that took Axel completely by surprise. "If you think meeting the director of the USSA was something, the President of the United States wants to see you. We have to work it around his schedule next week. Do you think you will be up for that?"

Axel stopped walking. He turned to Kim and said, "You are kidding, right?"

Kim shook his head from side to side. "I am not kidding. He knows what you did to that terrorist group in Baltimore, how you broke up one of the cartels in Mexico, your actions in North Korea and Iran, as well as helping find out where some of the guns are coming from that make their way to Mexico. He knows about your significant efforts in taking down the Silicon Valley and Boston terrorist groups. He has been impressed, and has asked our director to make sure you make it to Camp David while you are out here."

Axel almost stopped breathing and tilted his head back, looking straight up at the clouds above. Kim was silent as tears filled Axel's eyes and rolled down his cheeks. He closed his eyes and whispered something. After a few seconds, Axel lowered his head and looked at Kim.

"I have been blessed since I was born. I was given gifts that were somehow pulled from my mother's body as she lay by that wrecked plane thirty-one years ago. I have received the gifts of adventure that the agency has supplied to me. I need no special accommodation from anyone, even alone the President of the United States. My rewards have been seeing the results of my efforts. No one on this earth should feel more appreciative than I am. What I have done has been a pleasure that no one on this earth could experience. I have received all of this, and need receive no more, other than whatever future adventures these capabilities of mine will bring to me in helping our country. You know that, Kim, and you know that I would be honored more than you can think to meet out president, whom I believe is doing everything he can to help the American people and the people of the world. There are no other words I can say to express my gratitude to you, the agency, my mother, and all that allowed me to receive this honor. I wish my mother, Adam, and Tori could be present at that meeting."

Axel shook Kim's hand and walked on to his car.

The next day Axel and Tori got up early. She knew Axel was going to the agency to have some new work done on him. She didn't know what it was, but she was concerned that something might happen to him. Axel could tell she was shook up, since he had told her the night before that he wasn't allowed to eat any breakfast before going to the agency. She had asked him several times what they were going to do to him. He tried to calm her fears by saying that they were only going to do a small incision in him, and that he probably could stand it without an anesthetic. This seemed to quiet her worst fears, but he knew she still was upset. Before leaving, he told her that they all would be going out to lunch. Adam was going to bring Laura and Tori to the agency at noon, and once he was ready, they would go to lunch at some nice Washington DC restaurant.

She smiled as he was leaving, and said, "See you in a few hours. Hope things go like they want them to go."

"Thanks. I will tell Kim that you are going to be after him if any harm comes to me."

When Axel got to the agency, it was just before eight in the morning. Kim and several of his team were waiting for him. They had already prepared the operating room by cleaning it with an anti-virus cleaner. Axel took a shower and put on a hospital gown, and then lay down on a operating table that was wheeled into the operating room. He looked at all the special gear they had, the video scope and all the screens awaiting signals from his body while he was operated on. He thought he wouldn't worry, but sure enough, his brain started to imagine all sorts of things as they began to inject an anesthetic into his neck. This was the only place they could apply the shot, since he was essentially impenetrable in any other part of his body. He didn't get to think another thought, as the anesthesia took effect and he went rapidly unconscious.

While Axel was unconscious, Kim watched the doctors and technicians as they went about their work. First, they removed the old transmitter from an upper molar on the left side of his mouth. Then they took from a stainless steel bowl the new transmitter, which contained not only a new generation battery, but some of the new and very small electronics that Kim had discussed with Axel the day before. Once the new transmitter was inserted, they checked to see if it was working. They sent a signal to the transmitter; it responded, sending an answer to the computer in the room. They all smiled, since if this hadn't worked properly, they would have had to stop and complete the operation on a later date.

The surgeon proceeded to cut a slit in Axel's neck, next to his collarbone and next to the wiring that had already been installed in his body, connecting the tooth transmitter to the other electronic gear in his body. The CCD chip and the new electronics were placed in the slit and connected to the wiring. The slit was not closed, as they wanted to make sure everything worked properly, after they completed the remaining work down near his belly button. Everyone had been nervous about the step that followed.

The special diamond scalpel was handed to the doctor, and he viewed the area through special glasses. The lenses allowed him to see every pore around the area he was operating on. Using the diamond scalpel, he cut a very thin opening line in the protective covering. He smiled and looked around at the others, and they smiled also. There beneath the thin material was Axel's skin. He could see the scar from the previous operation, and he knew he had picked exactly the right spot for the slit. He cut through the skin, and there was the computer chip and other electronics, including the nanowires. The doctor rapidly completed the electronic connections with a special tool. At that point, he gestured to Kim. Kim sent a signal from his computer via the Internet, and the doctor saw that it was received properly by checking the status of the internal computer. He gave Kim a 'thumbs up' signal. Then Kim sent a phone signal to the internal computer, and the doctor gave the thumbs up signal again. Now Kim took a map and placed it on his fax machine, and faxed it to Axel. The doctor knew where he was supposed to look to see if the CCD had picked it up. Again, he gave Kim the thumbs up sign. That was the only time Kim smiled during the whole procedure. Then he shouted, "Yowee!" Everything had worked without any problems, as far as they had witnessed.

The doctor told the anesthesiologist to waken Axel. They needed to check with Axel to determine if he felt everything was working properly, before they closed up the two holes in his body. The anesthesiologist injected the proper medicine, and Axel began to awaken. When he was somewhat lucid, they told him that everything had worked as they had expected, but they needed to find out if he felt it functioned properly. Axel lay still and waited for the signals. They checked most of them out, and they all functioned properly. Then they came to the new one, which required Axel to view the map they were going to fax him. He waited and got the signal that told him to close his eyes and count to five. He counted, and when he got to five, he saw a map behind his closed eyes.

Keeping his eyes closed, he said, "This is a map of Northern California."

"Right!" exclaimed Kim. "Now give the signal to store the map." Axel gave the signal and Kim said, "Now, open your eyes and then close them, and the image should be gone."

Axel did as he said, and there was no map. He opened his eyes and said, "The map is gone."

"Great," shouted Kim. "Now close your eyes and address your computer memory. Ask for map of Northern California."

Axel closed his eyes and said, "Axelvation, computer memory, map of Northern California." He immediately saw the map. "It worked," he said.

"Open your eyes and the map should be gone," said Kim. He waited about ten seconds and then asked nervously, "Didn't it work?"

Axel laughed. "Yes, it worked."

"That's it," Kim said. "You can close him up now, Doc."

"Wait one moment," Axel said. "You haven't checked to see if I can send a fax."

"You are right," Kim replied. "I got so excited; I forgot to check that thing out. Is there something you would like to send?"

"Yes. I would like to send that map of California to Tori and to the agency, but with a mark on it that shows where Tori and I live."

Kim took the map and marked where he thought should be close to where they live. He handed it to Axel and asked him if he knew the instructions.

"I think so," replied Axel. He took the map, staring at it as he said, "Axelvation See." Then he said, "Axelvation Send," and the image was automatically sent via fax to the agency. Axel then repeated, "Send to" and included the fax number of Adam's house, where he knew Tori would be watching for this signal. Axel then blinked; the image was gone. Satisfied that they were done, Kim instructed the doctor to close the incisions. The doctor put several dissolvable stitches in the skin slit in Axel's belly. Then he went to the neck and stitched that closed. Last, he turned to the opening in the special covering at Axel's belly. A technician prepared the special glue in a small ceramic dish. Using a piece of ceramic shaped like a toothpick, the doctor spread the glue along one cut edge of the special material. Then he took the other edge and pushed it against the glued edge, and held it for five seconds. It was supposed to set in less than five seconds, but he held it for another ten seconds just to make sure. He then viewed the slit with his special lenses, but the slit was gone. The glue essentially chemically melted the two edges together, leaving no residue and no evidence of the incision.

The doctor stepped away from the table and told Axel to wait a few seconds, and then sit up. Axel did so, and everyone in the room watched for any problems. After a couple of minutes had passed, the doctor told him to stand next to the table. When he did, the doctor asked Axel if he felt okay.

"Yes, I feel fine," he said. "Is there any reason why I shouldn't feel fine?"

The doctor told Axel that there was always a concern when a person had been given an anesthetic, that they might feel dizzy or faint. "Some have a hard time gathering their balance," he added. "One of the things we don't want is to have a successful operation, and then have the patient fall over and crack his head."

Axel felt fine, and said he wanted to call Tori to see if she got his fax, and to let her know that things went well and their lunch was on.

Later Tori, Laura, and Adam joined Axel and Kim to go to lunch. While they were driving into DC, Kim told Axel that he changed his mind about lunch. "Since I won the bet, you are supposed to buy the lunch. But I am going to renege on that bet. I will pay for the lunch, since the results were so good and you did such a great job on achieving our goals."

"That's great," said Axel. "You aren't going to get an argument from me on that."

They all had a great lunch, and everyone was in a good mood. During the wait for dessert, Axel mentioned that now that this was over, he assumed Tori and he could now start enjoying their vacation and visit some tourist sites. Kim said he felt that this was almost true.

"Remember Axel, I mentioned that the president is trying to set up a time to talk to you. We don't know when that will be, but it means that maybe you have to stick close for the next few days."

Axel said that he thought Kim had been joking with him about that. "What if I go up to Pittsburgh and visit my mother? That's only a couple hundred miles from Washington. And Camp David is in Maryland in the Catoctin Mountains, right on the border with Pennsylvania."

Kim said he thought that was reasonable. "I will always be in close contact with you by phone, e-mail, and even fax now. It seems that anything that comes up should be able to give us at least a day's notice, and from Pittsburgh, that's plenty of time for you to make it. We will take care of any transportation that will be needed."

Axel quietly reminded Kim that he had would like Tori and his mother and brother to be included in any visit to the president. He didn't want Tori to hear this.

"Yes, I have checked that out," Kim said, "and that was met with an 'okay' by the right people. They feel that those people should receive their due also."

"That's great," said Axel. "I won't be as nervous if they are there. They can share the nervousness with me."

Later, while driving to Adam and Laura's house, Tori asked Axel what Kim had been hinting around about with his subtle comments. Axel thought about how he would tell Tori what they had been talking about. The more he thought about it, the more he realized he should just tell her the truth.

"Kim told me yesterday that President Hargrove might want to talk to me at Camp David. The president wants to extend his congratulations and thanks to me for the achievements made over the past year and a half. At the time, I asked Kim if you and my mother could attend this meeting, since I believe you two have been more than helpful for me to carry out these ventures. I also told him I would be less nervous if the two of you were there, and I thought that Adam should be there, since he was the one who recommended the changes that the agency made in me. That's it."

Tori was speechless. It was like she was stunned. Then she began to ramble. "Do you mean that I would get to go to Camp David and see President Hargrove, the President of the United States? That's unbelievable. I didn't realize that what you were doing was that significant. You have never talked about the details only that you were going. And then you would come back and still not tell me about the details. I think that is wonderful that the president thinks you have achieved good things for this country. Aren't you proud, Axel?"

Axel was quiet, and then he said he was more than proud. He was humbled. "What I have done goes back to what my mother was able to provide in me, and what the agency has done to enhance me even more. Some of the achievements relate to my own accomplishments. I developed the computer that took voice instead of a keyboard. I was able to provide my computer with ROM codes that allowed me to speak ten different languages as though they were mine. These things I am proud of. These are not available to anyone at this time, and I have worked with the agency through Adam in the past to have them placed in my body. Adam was quite perceptive, when you think about it. He recognized the advantages I had, including the computer. He was the one who got the agency to install this unique capability that I developed onto my body. Kim was instrumental as well, since he made a computer model of my body and figured out how to integrate my capabilities and interconnect them inside my body, and have them play like an organ. All of this came together, and that is why I want several people at this presentation. But don't get your hopes up yet. They haven't set a date. That's what Kim was talking about. He doesn't know when this might happen. I am going to take you up to see my mother and he may call while we are there. So, that's it in a nutshell."

"Wow," said Tori. "You sure got a lot off your mind there. I haven't heard you speak that much about it since we were almost married." She laughed.

Axel had called his mother, Virginia, and made arrangements for the trip up there. Adam loaned one of his two cars to Axel, and the next day Axel and Tori drove to Pittsburgh. When they got there, all his mother could do was hug him and tell him how beautiful Tori was. Tori was embarrassed, but not for long. It didn't take the two women long to be comfortable with each other, and Axel was surprised that they could talk about so many things. It was like they had known each other for years.

"I haven't seen Axel for a few years," his mother said at one point. "He looks older, of course, and he is a little heavier. Of course, I see Adam more frequently, since he brings his family up every so often around the holidays. Adam and Axel look so much alike, that it is like seeing Axel more often then I do. They comb their hair differently. Adam's hair is more formal and Axel's is more West Coast. Maybe that's what makes Axel look heavier."

"Mother," said Axel. "I am about five pounds heavier than Adam, and I have been heavier than him since I was about fourteen years old. Remember what the doctor said about me. I have some extra things in me that the average person does not. And now I have some other extra things in me that I am going to tell you about later."

That perked Virginia up. "What are you going to be telling me about?" she asked.

"We will talk about it this evening after dinner. Tonight I am going to take everyone to Carbones to have Italian food."

"Oh, that would be wonderful," his mother said. "I haven't been there to eat in years. They have the best Italian food in the world."

Axel took the two women to Carbones that evening. They had a great meal, and Axel didn't have to talk much. His mother and Tori keep chatting the whole time they were at the restaurant, and even in the car heading back home. They got to the house about nine o'clock, and about five minutes after nine, Virginia was questioning about what he was supposed to tell her.

"Are you going to tell me about how great a biology teacher you are?" she asked.

"Well, I could say some things about that, but what I have to tell you about is more basic than that. Remember what the doctor told us about my internal organs being different? That was when I was seventeen, and that got me interested in biology. While working on my doctorate, I designed a computer chip that could take directions verbally instead of through a keyboard. Adam later had the agency he works for install that chip in my body. This allows me to call up the extra energy levels the doctor had told us about. This internal computer also allows me to converse in ten different languages. Later, the agency made a cover for my body that is impervious to all external forces, like a bullet or a knife. The body covering is made of spiderweb and titanium nanotubes, and is transparent so you can't tell my body is covered with it. They later made a hood that can be called on by my internal computer. It drops from a seedlike source on top of my head, and covers my head and neck. And this hood matches my face so well, you cannot tell when it is covering my face. With these capabilities, I have been able to carry out some special missions for the government that no one else could do. I made this trip up here to especially thank you for what you went through in that plane crash thirty-one years ago. I have always believed that your travail made this possible for me."

While he spoke, Axel's mother looked like she was in a trance. When he was done, she remained silent. Axel looked at her and waited for a response. It was like she was dumbfounded and couldn't think of anything to say. Then she spoke.

"You're kidding me, right?"

Axel said he hadn't been kidding her. What he had told her was the truth.

"Do you have the body coat on now?"

Axel told her it was always on. She looked like she didn't believe him. He picked up her sewing scissors and handed them to her. "Here, Mom, try to stab me with these."

She said she couldn't do that. So Axel handed the scissors to Tori and told her to stab him in the chest as hard as she could. Tori grabbed the scissors, looked at Axel's mother, and then jammed the scissors into Axel's chest. Axel's mother almost screamed, but the scissors were stopped like they had hit a steel wall.

Virginia shook her head. "Don't do anything else to convince me. I believe you, but I don't want any more proof about the other things you told me. I will accept them without any demonstrations. I want to think of you just the way you naturally exist."

Axel knew he had to change the subject, so he started to tell her about the president. "Mom, one of the reasons we are up here, besides just seeing you, is to tell you that President Hargrove might be calling us to go to Camp David and see him. This would be you, Adam, Tori, Dr. Kim from the agency, and me."

"What in the world would he want me to go see him for?" she asked.

"It turns out that some of the things I have done over the past year have impressed him, and he wants to tell me personally. I told the people involved that what I have done was the result of what you went through during that plane crash, and if anyone is to get credit, it should be you."

Axel's mother smiled at him. "This brings back memories of when you were a young kid and your dad was alive and we used to talk about you. We knew there was something different about you, but we could never figure it out. I wish you dad were still living and could hear what you have told me. He always said that you gained something from that long wait after the crash before you were born. Those were tough days on me. I never thought I was going to live. I was at least happy that Adam was born, but I knew s something else was going to happen. When I had you several days later, it seemed like the culmination of the crash and that it was all over. It was like I relaxed. It was like closure. Now, when I hear you talk about the extraordinary outcome of that crash, I can say that I expected something all these years, but I didn't know what. Here we are more than thirty years later finding out the outcome. That's extraordinary. I have always been proud of the way you took to schooling, advancing to reach a doctorate of biology. I tell all my friends that my one boy has his doctorate and teaches at a college in California. I have always been proud of that. Now I am learning about your extracurricular activities."

"Hey, how about me?" Tori asked Axel. "I thought you were coming up here to show me off."

Her words lightened everyone's mood. They laughed and started talking about less serious things.

Axel and Family at Camp David with the President

Axel and Tori were enjoying their stay in Pittsburgh, when Axel got a call from Kim. The president wanted to meet Axel, as well as his mother and brother, and Tori and Kim, at Camp David the next day. Would Axel have any problem getting there?

"Not at all," Axel said. "We'll drive to Carlisle today, which is just outside of Harrisburg, and stay at a hotel. We'd only be about a half hour from Camp David then, so there'd be no rush the next day."

"That sounds good," commented Kim. "Camp David is not far from here, only about sixty-five miles northwest of Washington DC. Adam and I should be able to make it in an hour and a half."

After he hung up, Axel became nervous. He told Tori the news, and she got nervous. Then he went to see his mother to tell her what had occurred. She got nervous as well. Axel felt that he could relax and let them be nervous.

Kim called again about an hour later. "The president would like you there at 12:30. We'll have lunch with him and his wife, Sarah. I thought that was a good idea. It makes it less formal, and should relax your mother and Tori. I know you will be relaxed once we are talking. How about you and the others meet Adam and me outside the entrance to Camp David at 12:15?"

"That sounds like a good plan to me. We can leave fairly early this afternoon and be at the hotel in Carlisle by dinnertime."

"Okay," said Kim. "When you get to the hotel, give me a call and I will give you the directions to Camp David. It's not as easy as it might seem."

The drive to Carlisle was simple. They got on the Pennsylvania turnpike, and in a couple of hours they were there. During the trip, they talked about the state they were driving through. Western Pennsylvania was rather rolling with hills that led on to more hills. Nearer Pittsburgh the hills grew to mountains, and there was skiing there in the winter. Axel said they ought to visit Gettysburg after they saw the president. They'd have to stay over an extra day, but it would be worth it to see that extraordinary place. His mother and Tori agreed. Although she had lived in Pennsylvania all her life, Virginia had never been to Gettysburg or the Pennsylvania Dutch area, where the Amish farmers lived with their buggies and old-fashioned ideas. They found a nice hotel outside of Carlisle. Axel called Kim and told him where they were, and Kim gave him directions to get to Camp David from there.

The next morning, they had breakfast and spent some time looking around the area. They left for Camp David on time, and it was good Kim had given them detailed directions. Camp David wasn't that easy to find. As they approached the area, they began to see Navy personnel and Marines. After some driving around, they got to the main entrance of the part of Camp David that was restricted to personnel that had not been cleared.

There at the gate were Kim and Adam. Kim pointed to where they should park. Then all of them got into Kim's van, which handled five people easily, and Kim drove up to the guarded gate. He showed his pass, as did Adam. These other three, he told the guard, are guests of the president today.

The guard asked for their driver's licenses, and then made a phone call. Axel noticed a video camera pointed at the interior of the van, and knew their faces were being run through a security system. It didn't take long before the guard was back, signaling for the gate to be opened. He gave Kim directions of where to park.

They all got out of the van and walked toward the building. Another set of guards had them go through metal detectors, and then they were escorted by two marine guards into a fenced-in area that contained Camp David. Here in this isolated sanctuary, they saw several beautiful buildings that anyone would like to call home. The cabins had been given names of the various floras that grew wild in that area of Maryland. The buildings had a sense of privacy, while embracing the joy of the outdoor beauty. Here, a couple thousand feet above sea level, was the home of many deer, bears, and other creatures. This gave the place a sense of seclusion, even though it was only sixty-five miles from the White House, and less than sixty miles from Philadelphia. It was no wonder Franklin Delano Roosevelt had nicknamed the place Shangri-La. President Eisenhower later called it Camp David, in honor of his grandson, and that name stuck. Many famous meetings had occurred at this secluded place, but one of the most famous outcomes was an agreement between Egypt and Israel that had occurred at this place.

As they approached the quaint setting of the main house, they were surprised to see President Hargrove, Sarah, and their two children coming to meet them. They all shook hands as Kim made the introductions. Rather than stroll immediately back into the house, the president walked with Axel and Kim toward an outdoor eating place. The others followed. A cute little black dog, his tail wagging, trotted along with them as if he was going to eat lunch also.

"I thought you might enjoy eating lunch outside. We have been lucky the last few days the weather has been behaving for us, and the sunshine just takes the nip off the temperature. One couldn't ask for more than that."

"Indeed," said Kim. "It's breathtaking here, and we might as well take in as many of those breaths as we can. It's not often that one has this opportunity during a lifetime, especially with the company we will be enjoying."

"Amen," said Virginia.

Tori just looked around, taking in the beauty of the place and looking a little stunned that she was having lunch in this beautiful place with the President of the United States and the First Lady. As they reached the table, the president gestured for Axel to sit at the one end of the table, and then he Virginia's chair for her. As they others sat, the children ran off with the dog to play while the older folks ate their lunch.

The talk during the meal was about the weather, the trip down to Camp David, and other things the president asked about. At one point as they were eating the wonderful food, the president said to

Virginia, "I hear it was through your heroics that Axel was able to claim his wonderful energy. Kim has told me about that, and it was an extraordinary experience for you. I guess it was only about one hundred miles north of here, in the Pocono Mountains."

"That's correct, Mr. President. I certainly am surprised what came of that experience. I just learned about the outcome of this. Axel has kept this a secret until he and Tori came to visit me. I understand that this has been done for his protection, but to tell you the truth, I was always proud of him, even without knowing that. I was always proud of his doctorate degree and his teaching in a great college. What more could a mother ask for?"

"Indeed," remarked the President. "That is a wonderful combination of accomplishments. Most people would consider having reached that level of academia as the pinnacle of success. Only your son has reached two pinnacles that I know of. All of you are here to bring some private praise to Axel. Here is a man who has served this country as only he could. It's ironic that we cannot praise him in public. We have to hide his accomplishments to allow him the freedom to keep doing what he's been doing. We must keep his identity a secret, so he can continue to mingle with the potential enemies of this country and provide results that cannot be obtained in any other way. Virginia and Kim, what you have done for this man is a miracle."

Both Virginia and Tori wiped away tears.

Kim stood up and lifted his wineglass. "Here is a toast to Virginia and Axel. There is no doubt that Virginia was the originator of this miracle, but his man was very creative before he received further gifts. He invented a computer that his voice controlled, and with this computer he is able to control the extra energy levels that Virginia supplied during his birth. He can call them up without speaking out loud. He included in the chip the ability to communicate via phone or Internet, again without speaking out loud. He only has to think, and his thoughts are communicated. Last week we added the ability for him to receive or send faxes, using no equipment other than his eyes and brains. He has yet to use this added capability, but we are sure it will add a significant extra level of power of communication to his repertoire." He held his wineglass higher. "To Virginia and Axel." he said.

Everyone echoed the toast, and then Axel stood up. "I appreciate all that has been said, but we have not covered all the contributions. With what I have done myself, much could have been accomplished, but it would still be limited. It was the agency and, more specifically, Dr. Kim who was able to take me and make me invincible. Dr. Kim developed a special material using spiderweb and titanium nanotubes that was essentially indestructible. Then he was able to design and build, at high cost, a covering for my body with that material, except for my head. Later he developed a method of placing the material in a very small structure on top of my head, which drops down and covers my head and neck, and connects with the rest of my body covering. He was able to model my computer and my body, and develop a composite model to study how everything would be connected in my body. He was able to debug this until he found the proper way to have it orchestrate in my body. Then he provided the doctors and equipment needed to install the computer and the wiring that would allow them to work together. These things were not minor achievements. They are outstanding achievements. So here's a toast to Dr. Kim."

Everyone raised their wineglasses once more and gave a toast to Dr. Kim.

President Hargrove was silent as he looked at the people at the table. Then he said, "I didn't realize the full complement of Axel's capabilities. I don't know how you can return from one of your adventures and be able to teach biology and keep your body energy at this lower level without an extreme adjustment."

"It is an adjustment," said Axel. "However, that beautiful lady sitting there"—he gestured at Tori—"brings me down to earth. I return from those sorties with only one thing in mind, and that's her. And when I am with her, I am back home and loving life and her and ready to teach, which excites me almost as much as these adventures."

This brought a big blush to Tori's face, and a big smile. She winked at Axel and mouthed, "Thank you."

The rest of the conversation was light-hearted, and everyone enjoyed themselves. After being about one and a half hours, President Hargrove said, "I am sorry to break this up, but I have a busy schedule, and I want to talk to Axel and Kim before I take off. You are all welcome to enjoy yourselves here for the rest of the day if you like."

With that he got up from his seat and nodded toward Axel and Kim, who followed him into the house. The president led them to his office and asked them to have a seat. After they had settled, he brought up a problem that had been brewing.

"You probably have read in the papers that some terrorist threats are escalating.. What I am going to discuss is something that Prime Minister Benson of England discussed with me. He is quite upset by these terrorist threats, which seem to be brewing at a higher pitch in Great Britain than here in this country. As I'm sure you recall, in July 2005 there were terrorist attacks on the London subway and bus systems. Those terrorists used peroxide-based explosives, and there have been rumors of these type of attacks might happen again in several places, including here in this country. We have evidence of one group here in the states that were stockpiling peroxide. As you know, a peroxide bomb is fairly simple but quite effective, depending on where it is deployed.

"Mr. Benson believes the people of England are going to be exposed to more serious bombings. When you think of terrorists and their means of harming people in large numbers, the things that come to mind relate to transportation. For example, on 9/11 terrorists crashed planes into the World Trade Center and the Pentagon, creating an effect more terrifying than a bomb. More people were killed in that terrorist act than in the attack on Pearl Harbor in 1941. Isn't that amazing, that a few people could cause that much damage, compared to the Japanese Navy attacking Pearl Harbor? Think of that—greater than a bomb. Then think of the subway systems in cities like London, and here again, there were a large number of people involved and the terrorists used a large transportation system. When you consider the possible places where a terrorist can do the most harm without using sophisticated munitions, transportation systems top the list. Whether it's airplanes, trains, subways, buses, or ships, a large number are gathered who can be greatly harmed at the same time. And it only takes a few of these idiots to have this effect. Mr. Benson assured me that Scotland Yard is busy trying to strengthen security on their transportation systems. Other than transportation, the next big place to find a large group of people where an incident can cause a large amount of casualties is at sporting events. Soccer matches in Europe regularly attract tens of thousands of people. Imagine if a plane hit a soccer stadium.

"In his efforts to stay on top of terrorist threats, Mr. Benson has heard that we Americans have a secret weapon for working against these terrorists, and that secret weapon is Axel Tressler, alias The Follower. I don't know how he got this information, but if he can get it, I am concerned that terrorists can get it, and maybe negate any effort we might make to use Axel to help fight terrorism. To my knowledge, Mr. Benson doesn't know that it is Axel who is our secret weapon. He just knows there is someone who has had success against terrorists.

"This brings me to one of my main purposes for today. I believe that whatever is being planned in England is also being planned in Boston, or Chicago, or New York. I want to use Axel to overcome this problem. I just don't know how. I want you two, and whoever else you think you need to bring into this, to think of the places where this kind of thing could take place. When Benson and I discussed this, he thought if our 'weapon' could come to the UK and somehow blend in with the culprits, he might be able to force them to show themselves and thereby eliminate them. He believes, as I do, that our 'weapon' might be able to obtain information that will not only help the British, but help the American people. I want you to think about this. If Benson calls asking for our help, I will be calling you.

"The one major advantage that terrorists have is that there need not be a lot of them to cause a lot of harm. You have seen what happened in Iraq and Afghanistan. It is the few that harm the many. If we had to fight a real war against the countries of Iraq or Afghanistan, it would be no contest. But the insurgents are few in number and scattered around, and they fight only when they find the right time and can do the most damage. This is basic guerilla warfare. The one advantage we have is that we are not in Iraq or Afghanistan, and they cannot hide like they do in their own countries. The key is making the American people sensitive to this danger without causing more harm than good. When you think of Osama bin Laden and 9/11, it would appear he has achieved what he wanted. The terrorist acts on that day by only a few men have caused this country to spend billions of dollars on wars that are somewhat fruitless. We are not at war with the Iraqi people or the Afghan people. We are skirmishing with bands of Al-Qaeda and bands of Taliban. They pick the fights where and when they want them. We do not want that to occur in this country. You have my message. Do you have any suggestions at this time? I will understand if you don't, since this is such short notice."

Kim was the first one to speak, and he said that they would think this over. They needed time to digest what the president had said.

Axel agreed. "I will think about this also. I know where you are coming from, and I believe I could help. But we need additional information. When you talk to Mr. Benson again, you might ask him if he has a suggestion on how we could get involved."

At that point, one of the president's staff came in to remind him of his next appointment.

The President stood up and shook hands with Kim. "I know you will come up with something to provide us leadership in this worrisome problem." Then he turned and held his hand out to Axel. "Now watch it, young man. Shake gently," he said with a smile."

They shook hands, and the president said, "To look at you, it's hard to see that you have the capabilities you have. I can see how you could fool many people."

With that, he was on his way. Another staff member walked Axel and Kim out to where the women and Adam were waiting. The others had decided to take the president up on his offer to tour the grounds. They spent the rest of the day strolling around. A military guard walked with them and tried to answer their questions. As darkness fell, they decided to begin their trips home. Axel, Tori, and Virginia had already decided that they would go up to Gettysburg and view that area the next day. Since Kim and Adam were heading back to Washington, they all said good-bye in the parking lot.

As Axel drove the winding roads from Camp David, he had to be careful taking the curves. He also was being careful because when they were on their way to Camp David, he had seen many deer along the way. The car didn't need to be given a push on the gas pedal coming down those hills, and the car was being pulled by the curves. He had just completed one bend and began to approach another one that curved the other direction, when he saw a car stopped on the road with its emergency lights blinking. He applied his brakes, announcing to Tori and Virginia that it looked like there was trouble ahead.

He pulled off the road behind the car and ran over to it. It was then that he saw the real problem. Another car was in front of the first. It had gone off the road, hit a tree, and was upside down. A woman stood beside the first car, and she yelled to Axel, "They tried to miss a deer that ran out on the road. My daughter and her husband are in there." Axel saw that the roof was caved in, and as he got close he saw the two people trapped inside the car. He directed his internal energy—Axelvation two—and felt the energy level lift in his body. He waved to Tori, and she ran over to him.

"I have to lift the car," he said, "and you have to pull the passenger out."

Axel ran to the back of the car, grabbed the rear bumper, and pulled the car backward so that it wasn't jammed against the tree. He smashed his fist against the window on the passenger side, grabbed hold of the door, lifted the car, and rolled it back into an upright position. He yanked the door off and hollered for Tori to pull the woman out before there was a fire. Tori got the woman's seat belt unbuckled and pulled her out of the car. Fortunately, the woman was coherent enough to help. She cried, "Get Dan out of the car."

By this time another car had arrived. The driver came running toward them as Axel ripped the driver's door off its hinges. He reached in and lifted the injured man out, carrying him over to where the woman was lying. Virginia and the first woman had taken some coats from the cars, laying two on the ground, one for the woman and one for the man. Axel laid the man down, and then they covered the injured people with more coats. Axel then grabbed hold of the material that was under the two of them and dragged them to the other side of the road, away from the wrecked car.

"That car might catch on fire or explode," he said. "You better move your cars back away from this car," he told the other woman and man. Tori said she would move their car.

Only a few minutes had gone by, and they heard the sounds of an ambulance approaching. As a military ambulance appeared, Axel turned to his mother and Tori.

"We have to get out of here," he said, "before that lady starts talking about me lifting the car and brings up a lot of questions. Let's get in the car and let them do their thing. When the time looks right, I will pull out."

They all got in the car and Axel watched closely. There was enough room for him to get by, but this might bring their car to the attention of the military personnel. He waited until first the woman and then the man were lifted into the ambulance. He slowly pulled out, making it look like he was just moving out of the way. The other man also pulled out slowly, behind Axel's car. Axel just kept on moving, driving around the curve, and then pushing down on the accelerator.

"Oh, Axel," his mother said, "do you think you should be leaving the scene of the accident?"

"Yes, Mom, you don't know how all my actions get major attention. If they call back to Camp David and report my leaving, we can always explain why. The president knows why I need to avoid any kind of exposure."

They didn't speak during the rest of the short trip, except when Virginia said, "I am so proud of you, Axel, and how you handled that car accident. I now can believe all those things they have said about you and your strength. What you did back there was like watching a movie. You were wonderful."

Axel smiled and thought, *I am glad that Mom finally got a glimpse of what my capabilities are that she supplied many years ago.*

The next day Virginia, Tori, and Axel walked around the beautiful Gettysburg grounds and took in the wonderful statues and plaques. Tori said, "You know, this place is so beautiful, it doesn't even need to be a place to visit to review the Civil War things. Just walking around here is wonderful. I can imagine it without the statues and other Civil War memorials and just be enchanted by the freshness of the area. It is simply gorgeous."

Virginia agreed and said she wished she had come there before. "But as beautiful as it is, it is even more beautiful with the memorials. It's terrible that such a beautiful place could be a 'killing ground,' and yet it is also one of the places where this country was able to come together and be whole."

Since Virginia was in no hurry to head for home, and Tori and Axel were on vacation, they decided to stay another day and visit Amish country. That also was a day of beauty.

As they headed back home, Virginia said, "You know, the past three days have been the most pleasant days of my life. Camp David was wonderful and more than a person could expect. Watching my son do his thing, helping those people in that car accident was awesome. Gettysburg was like living history over, without the actual war. You could almost see the soldiers fighting on the fields. It was wonderful to see the statues and read the plaques that described what had occurred in the various places. It was wonderful seeing President Lincoln's Gettysburg Address and taking in the full meaning of it. Then we finished this off by having a pleasant drive around Amish country and seeing how those people live. I have always heard about Lancaster County, but never got there. Here they are driving around in horse drawn buggies, happy as could be. Not using the modern conveniences, and not hurrying. Maybe they have the right idea. Modern times have their advantages, but so did the old times."

Tori seconded the motion. "This has been just wonderful. The amazing thing is that we didn't plan it, and didn't go through all the pains you normally go through when you are planning a vacation."

After a couple of days with Virginia celebrating Christmas and visiting other relatives, Tori and Axel decided to drive up to Buffalo and Niagara Falls. Tori had heard about the falls since she was a little girl, and while they were out here it made sense to see these wonders of the world. They spent two days viewing the area, and crossing over to Canada to see how one of the other countries of North America lived. They had a wonderful time. Tori said, "This is the first time I have ever left America. Just crossing over the border into Canada seemed different than just the physical act itself. I had the feeling that I was going to a new world, even though it was only a matter of a couple hundred feet away." Time flew fast as they enjoyed themselves, and before they knew it they were driving back to Pittsburgh. They wanted to spend a belated New Years celebration with Virginia and other relatives and friends before heading back to California.

Back in California on the third of January, Axel decided to go to the college library and look though some recent newspaper articles he remembered reading. They had described some terrorist type events that had occurred during September and October. He went to the computer and called up the *San Jose Mercury News*, starting with the first of September 2009. He found a relevant article in the September 23rd edition. It read in part:

As FBI and New York police counterterrorism agents investigate a Denver man who authorities say received Al-Qaeda explosives training and recently traveled to New York, law enforcement officials around the nation have been advised to be on the lookout for any signs of bombs built with hydrogen peroxide. That kind of weapon killed 52 people in the London transit system four years ago. During the morning rush hour of July 7, 2005, three men carried backpacks that exploded within 50 seconds of each other on three London Underground trains. A fourth bomb exploded on a bus nearly an hour later. The same chemical components were allegedly used in a failed plot to blow up a passenger jet leaving England for America. The accused carried chemicals necessary to make a bomb in quantities small enough to fit into soda or water bottles. Now, according to law enforcement officials, authorities are concerned that 24-year-old Afghan immigrant, Najibullah Zazi, may have been organizing a plot to detonate similar devices in backpacks, possibly on crowded commuter trains in New York. Zazi has been charged only with lying to authorities, and has told reporters he has nothing to do with terrorism.

Dan Watts, a research professor at the New Jersey Institute of Technology, said a bomb made from hydrogen peroxide is "more effective in a confined space. When you hear about them being particularly horrific, it's a railroad car, a situation like London, rather than trying to bring down a big building like the 1995 attack on the federal building in Oklahoma City. When mixed together to make a bomb, the material is so unstable, it can be triggered accidentally by heat or shock."

Axel remembered what President Hargrove had told him about the problem in London. He thought, *that's amazing how inventive a person can become when they are trying to be aggressive and cruel. Not many people would think about using hydrogen peroxide this way.* He continued reading the articles, and came across one on the same case in the *Wall Street Journal* on September 24. It stated, "Current and former U.S. officials say the allegation in the case embody their worst fears, that a legal U.S. resident could leave the country, receive explosives training from Al-Qaeda in Pakistan, and then return to U.S. soil."

They forgot the shoe bomber, Axel thought. *Here was a guy that left England on a flight to the U.S., and he had an explosive in the heel of his shoe. When he tried to ignite it, it didn't work. One of the attendants smelled the smoke, and the man was constrained, the explosion never happened. If the bomb had worked, the plane would have gone down and killed everyone on board, and maybe many people on the ground. It's a perfect example of what one person can do if we are not alert*

Axel found another article in the *San Jose Mercury News* dated September 25. It was entitled "Bomb-plot arrests in Illinois, Texas." He read:

A man who idolized California Taliban soldier John Walker Lindh and a Jordanian national who frequented extremist Web sites are charged in unrelated cases after attempting to detonate what they thought were bombs outside an Illinois courthouse and a Texas skyscraper. Federal officials said Thursday that the cases are not connected to each other or the major terrorism investigation underway in Colorado and New York. Michael Finton, 29, who also went under the name Talib Islam, was arrested Wednesday in Springfield, IL, after federal officials said he attempted to set off explosives in a van outside a federal courthouse in the Illinois capital. Hosam Maher Husein Smadi, 19, was arrested Thursday in Dallas. According to federal officials he placed what he believed to be a car bomb in a parking garage beneath the 60-story Fountain Place office tower. In both cases, decoy devices were provided to the men by FBI agents posing as Al-Qaeda operatives. Both men are charged with trying to detonate a weapon of mass destruction and face up to life in prison if convicted. Finto also is charged with one count of attempting to murder federal officers or employees.

When Axel finished reading that article, he was convinced these articles represented what Prime Minister Benson and President Hargrove were relating to. As he left the library, he thought, *Thank goodness this has only occurred at this limited level so far in this country. I can see why Mr. Benson and President Hargrove are concerned. It is easy to make these limited levels of explosives, but I have seen what the road bombs have done in Iraq and Afghanistan. I can look back at my own experience with the terrorist threats in the Baltimore area, the Silicon Valley terrorists, and the Boston Russian terrorists. If any of those plots had succeeded, they would have made what I just read about look sort of insignificant. But, in fact, none of them are insignificant as far as the morale of this country is concerned. Each of these episodes might kill or injure fewer than ten people, but they would have a significant impact on the confidence and morale of the people of this country.*

When Axel returned to teaching and running the stem cell laboratory after the Christmas break, he felt like he received a fresh surge of energy. The students seemed more enthusiastic, and he personally felt more spirited in his teaching. However, every once in a while he would get antsy and call up Kim to ask him what was happening. So far, Kim has not been contacted by anyone about any terrorist threats. Just to keep things refreshed, Axel sent faxes to Kim that included some drawings of his stem cell lab. Likewise, Kim sent some drawings to Axel to show what he had been working. None of it, however, related to anything Axel would have been involved in.

He and Tori took a few trips up to South Tahoe to go skiing. They had fun, but there were no snowmobiles flying uncontrolled down any of the hills, so Axel could not recreate his previous exploits. He became a much better skier since, with his body protection, he could try radical things on his skis. He probably could compete in some ski events, but he felt that he had an advantage other skiers didn't possess.

The winter months in California were their normal selves, raining much of January through March in the areas around San Francisco, and snowing in the Sierra Mountains. Both helped to fill the reservoirs, and the snow in the upper regions of the Sierras piled up to tremendous heights. Axel remembered what they called heavy snow back in Pennsylvania when he was a kid. Heavy snow was a two foot snow buildup over a week or so. Sometimes it randomly would snow a foot or two in a day, but that was rare. In the Sierras, the snow could get thirty feet deep in many places. Sometimes it snowed five feet in one night. The thing that Axel was always wondering about was how the trees and most plants around the Bay Area, including San Francisco and San Jose, stayed green all year long. He felt part of it was the type of soil, which held the water for long periods and allowed growth when there was little rain April through December. Also, the cool nights allowed for condensation on the grass and trees in the early morning during this rainless period. People loved the cool nights anyhow. It could be in the nineties in the daytime, and when night came, it was anywhere between forty-five and sixty-five.

The rain made it tough to go anywhere, since the traffic tie-ups for rain could be dreadful. This was partly because of the heavy commuter traffic around San Francisco, San Jose, and the Los Angeles area. Also, many people who visited California didn't know there were a lot of hills to navigate. It wasn't flat like in the Midwest.

During the winter, Axel made the most of it by going skiing and using the weather for Tori and his benefit. Soon the spring season began and the rains stopped. Then as May and June neared, classes were completed and students and professors alike looked ahead to the summer break. It seemed that the first half of the year was a lull, a cautionary period waiting for the end of school, because when the end of June came around, Axel started to get calls from Kim.

The Follower Helps to Fight Britain's Terrorists

From late June through early July, Kim kept calling Axel about terrorist activity that was going on in the United States and Great Britain. Just after the Fourth of July, Kim called to say he'd received a private call from the president, who told him that Prime Minister Benson was seeing increasing activity among the "a-holes," as he called them. Some small bombs, not much bigger than firecrackers, had been set off. Only a few days went by before Kim got word that the president wanted 'The Follower" to travel to London to meet with Mr. Benson. Axel told Kim he was somewhat concerned that nothing was specific.

"Everything has been innuendos and maybes with no definite actions recommended," Axel said. But a day later there was a definite assignment. In two days, Axel was to fly from California to Washington DC, where he would get for further instructions.

"You will only be at the agency for a day," Kim said, "and then you will fly to the UK under a different name, Matthew Wilson. We're processing the paperwork, now it will be ready when you get here. You'll fly from Dulles to Heathrow. A Mr. Alter will meet you at Heathrow and take you to Mr. Benson. Mr. Benson will explain the situation and outline possible actions."

Axel got hold of Tori at her workplace and told her what was happening. "It looks like they waited till school was out and you were on your break," she said, echoing his thoughts.

Next, Axel contacted the head of his department and told him he would be taking off for a while. School was out for the summer, but certain classes were offered during the summer, and Axel taught one of them. He told his boss he could contact his substitute and get him up to speed.

Tori took the next day off so she and Axel could enjoy the day together before he left. He told her he was sorry he had to leave, since they had hoped to get some private time during the summer, and go to different places on the weekends.

"I would like you to come to London with me," said Axel, "but it might get too dangerous. While I am there, I will assess the situation and see if there are times when you could fly over. I will tell Kim, so he could take care of getting you the plane reservations and paying for the trip. He owes me at least that much."

They had a pleasant day, enjoying and loving each other a few times during that day.

Kim met Axel at Dulles Airport and drove him to the agency headquarters. There, he reviewed the paperwork that had been made out for Matthew Wilson. "We will be calling you Matt on any communications from now till when you get back, so get used to it. What we know so far is that Scotland Yard is setting you up to join one of the rogue gangs that are making things a little tough for them in South London. Evidently, they have some contacts inside this gang and they want to keep them undercover. They believe with your various capabilities, you can be more effective than they are and at the same time, keep them current with the gang. That's all we know at present. You can keep us up to date once you are involved. Our government wants you involved, because they want you to learn as much as you can about these groups, so we will know what to do if anything starts popping up around the States. Although the problems may be big ones for the English, their country is a lot smaller country than ours. It puts a hell of a load on this country just to cover the much larger area."

Axel agreed that any techniques used in England would probably mirror the ones that any terrorists might try to employ in the States. Kim's staff worked with Axel for that rest of that day, providing him with large maps of London and what background material they had.

When Axel, alias Matt Wilson, arrived at Heathrow and went through customs, Mr. Alter was there to meet him. They introduced each other, and that was all that was said until they arrived at 10 Downing Street,

London. Once there, Mr. Alter turned Axel over to a member of the prime minister's staff, who ushered him directly into Mr. Benson's office.

"Glad you arrived in one piece," the prime minister greeted him. "Have a seat and let's talk. I had you brought over as Mr. Wilson, but that name is going to change fast. The Commissioner at Scotland Yard, who is overseeing this mission, wants you to have a German name, but we can discuss that. The word we have is that the suspected rogue gang is made up of a cosmopolitan group of citizens of our country, several of which are German. Others are Russian.

"Of course, it's not surprising that different nationalities are involved, since we have quite a mix here in Great Britain. We have Indians, Chinese, Americans, Russians, Germans, Jews, and Arabs. Rather like your country."

Axel listened and nodded and got a word in every once in a while, but he soon learned that the prime minister liked to talk. Fortunately, he was an interesting person to listen to. Axel hoped they would soon get to the main topic of why he was there.

"Enough about that," Mr. Benson finally said. "I am glad you're here. I have heard a lot about you from your president, and I hope that you can work your magic here. What do you think?"

"I think I could do as much as anyone you could pick, sir," said Axel. "I have many advantages over the average person."

"I understand you have the ability to send e-mails or phone messages without speaking out loud. Is that correct?"

"It is, sir."

"Can I have a demonstration of that capability, Mr. Wilson?"

Axel asked the prime minister to give him his cell phone number and e-mail address. No sooner had Mr. Benson given these to Axel, when his phone rang. He picked it up, and Axel said,

"Hello, Mr. Benson." Mr. Benson looked at him with his eyes wide open. "I understand your first name is Casey but most people call you Benny. Is that correct?"

"That is correct. My name is Casey and the media call me Benny, but most of my friends call me Casey. I am sorry I haven't introduced myself properly. Please call me Casey and leave out the 'sir.'"

"You should check your computer, Casey. I think you have a message," said Axel.

The prime minister walked over to his computer and checked his messages. Sure enough, there was one from AxelTori.com. It read, "Nice to make your acquaintance, Mr. Prime Minister. I will be calling you Casey. Thank you, Matt Wilson."

The Prime Minister was impressed. "That's amazing. How do you accomplish that feat?"

"I have a computer in my body that works off direct voice or my internal voice. This is a powerful tool that I have used often. When I want someone to listen to a face-to-face conversation I'm having, I turn my internal phone on. You would then pick up your phone and listen to the conversation without the other party knowing."

After Axel and the prime minister had finished talking about Axel's various attributes, Benson got down to talking about the problems he had seen. "I am not concerned that this terrorist group is planning a catastrophic thing. I don't believe they have the power to set off an atomic bomb, or even a dirty bomb. What I am concerned about is that they can frighten the citizens of this country. It can develop a situation where no one trusts anyone. Not that it would get to the level it has in Iraq or Afghanistan, but you might remember when we were dealing with the IRA. It was not only dangerous, but it was frightening, and people began to not believe in their government. It's amazing what a disruption even the threat of terrorism can be. When the planes smashed into the twin towers in New York, what was horrifying was not just the number of people killed. It was the thought that anyone could do anything so terrible to innocent bystanders. One gets used to living and bitching and enjoying the good and bad that life brings. Then it is interrupted. If it continues, it changes things all around you. You have to go through security to get on an airplane. You have to take off your shoes so they can be checked. You can't carry liquids on with you. You stand in lines where before there were no lines. And the list goes on. I don't want that to add to that list. I want this stopped before it becomes a big deal.

"Yesterday, someone took a hand grenade, pulled the pin, and put a rubber band around the grenade to prevent it from going off. Then they stuck it in the petrol intake of one of our cars here. If it hadn't been found, the gasoline would have loosened the rubber band's tension and the grenade would have exploded. And since it was in a tank of gasoline, it would have been a huge explosion. I am hoping that this was just a crank getting his rocks off; an isolated incident that won't happen again soon. But if this and other things start happening over and over, it would begin to break the morale of the general public. Morale is where it starts, and then it becomes bickering among people, and then bickering with one's public servants. I am sure you understand where it can go from there."

"Yes, I understand. People's minds can get screwed up with things like this going on. I guess that is why I am here, to make sure people's minds don't get screwed up. What do I do next?"

"I will call Mark Wilkinson, the Commissioner of Scotland Yard," said Casey. "He is the guy you will be working with. You will like him. He's sharp and tough, but fair."

Benson picked up the phone and made the call to Scotland Yard. Mark Wilkinson got on immediately. "I have a surprise for you," Benson said. "I made a deal with Hargrove, and he has sent his secret weapon here to help us out. His name is Axel Tressler, although he's traveling under the alias Matt Wilson. I want to make sure this gentleman is kept a secret. Either you come and get him personally, or have your best person come. If you send someone, then only you and that person will know this man's true identity."

Benson paused, and then said, "Yes, I know that you know how to handle these types of things. I just wanted to make sure you knew where I stand. So, when will someone come? About an hour would be fine. E-mail his name and photo to me, so I can make sure the man who comes is the man you sent. Yes, we can't get too careful on this person on this person's identity. That's what I promised President Hargrove."

When he hung up, Benson winked at Axel and said, "You heard what I told him. He is a good man, and the two of you will do some good for this country."

Axel was impressed by what he had heard and the attitude of the prime minister.

Commissioner Mark Wilkinson came himself to pick up Axel. As they drove back to New Scotland Yard, Axel assessed this man who had such a significant job in this magnificent country. He guessed he was in late forties or early fifties, which seemed young for his position. He still with a full head of hair, and was a handsome sort of guy. Axel could see him playing James Bond in a movie. He was rather trim, so he probably ate well and exercised daily. Axel had been expecting someone more like Sherlock Holmes. Mark Wilkinson, on the other hand, looked like he didn't have a worry in the world, as if he was going home to watch a soccer match.

As they drove, Mark pointed some famous buildings and landmarks, but since it was dark, Axel couldn't see them. He knew he would get his chance when he was settled in and Mark got him a car.

When they arrived at New Scotland Yard, Axel noticed several armed officers patrolling the outside of the building. "Ten years ago," Mark said, "we only had a few guards. Now they seem to be everywhere. Indicative of the world we now live in.

When they were in Mark's office, he had one of the men bring them each a coffee and roll, and then they settled down to discuss how Axel could work with the Yard. Mark handed Axel a passport with his picture in it and the name Donner Poole. Mark told Axel that he wanted the paperwork made out for a German citizen who had migrated to England some ten years before and had become a British citizen.

"I know you can handle the German language. You should probably bone up on some basic facts about German popular culture, just so that you sound authentic when you are with other German immigrants. And we want you to mingle with other immigrants, particularly the young and bold talkers. They may lead you to others who are parts of gangs that are angry with this country and angry about the wars in Iraq and Afghanistan. These seem to be the ones that are most likely to become terrorist threats.

He handed Axel a packet. "Here is a driver's license and an owner's certificate for a 2002 Honda. Keys to the car and your flat are in there too. You have a flat at 2703 Lilly Lane, which is on the outskirts of London, in the suburbs. This is where many lower and middle class citizens live. Some of these people lost their jobs during this recession. They're just surviving, and they are bitching a lot. Our profile on terrorists include recent immigrants from the Mideast and those from our country that are either upset about losing their jobs or about the wars in Iraq and Afghanistan. We figure if you live among these people, you might find some who are more than upset and actually want to do harm.

"There is no timetable here. Take however long you need. Money will be deposited in a bank account at the British Royal Bank for you every week. You will have plenty, but obviously you won't want to flaunt it. I'd like you to check in with me on the phone every Thursday afternoon and let me know how it's going."

A sergeant led Axel to his car, and then Axel followed the sergeant to his new apartment. It wasn't anything to brag about, but he knew he shouldn't have an elegant one. It had basic furniture, a TV, and a computer that he might want to use besides his internal computer. The next day Axel drove around Surrey County, which was where the apartment was located. He found some interesting information about Surrey. At one time it had been much bigger, but in the 60s the northern part of Surrey had become part of Greater London. Surrey was not a farming area, far from it. He found it was the most wooded area of England, with nearly a quarter of it covered in forests, nearly double of the rest of Great Britain. The part that bordered Greater London was less wooded. Although still not a farming area, it had rolling hills and bridle paths and that makes it very scenic. It had the second tallest hill in southern England. The land was ideal for horses, and Axel saw many horse stables as he drove around. The biggest town was Guildford, and the area was one of the most affluent in all of England. Second in population density only to Greater London, Surrey had the highest GDP per capita of any county in the UK, and the highest cost of living outside of London. Many businesses were located in the area, including giants from other countries, such as Kia and Toyota UK. Procter and Gamble, Nestle, Kimberly-Clark, SC Johnson and Colgate-Palmolive also had headquarters in Surrey. In some respects, Axel found the area like parts of California. He enjoyed driving around Surrey, and made it a point of doing it as often as he could.

Axel found Surrey a wonderful area to burn off energy. Almost every day he went to the hills to run. Aside from wanting to burn off energy, he wanted to keep testing his ability to take energy leaps. He would call up Axelvation One, or two, or three, and let them take him where he could. He would leap, with joy, over many of the branches that hung out over the beautiful land. Sometimes he would race the animals he met, like a boy playing with his dog. He wondered to himself, *How could there be extremists or terrorists that would want to bring anything bad to this land? It surely isn't the people who have lived here for many years. It is surely not the people who defended this country during World War II, when the bombs were bursting around London and sometimes as far south as this land. Even the businesses that are located here are clean businesses and well entrenched, and they would not want anything to disturb their sanctity. I must keep a lookout for those who are disgruntled, who always seem to find something to complain about. But in this case it is more likely to be someone from outside the country, who finds a way to indoctrinate young people to follow him. This will not be easy. It won't be like my past endeavors, where I knew the enemy.*

On occasion Axel drove around the southern parts of London, or along the Thames River to the center of London. He had thought that he would see a lot of docks along the Thames, but they had been torn down over the years and shopping centers stood in their place. There were expensive boutiques, shops for men and shops for women, sporting goods shops, jewelry stores. The sporting goods shops were loaded with shirts that represented the various soccer teams in the UK. They also had a tremendous array of fishing gear, which was somewhat different than the gear he would find in the States. It was obvious the English were excited about fishing. As he drove along between Surrey and London, he saw many fishermen along the Thames River. At least it looked like they were fishing. Sometimes Axel thought they were just doing something to keep from being bored.

For driving in and out of London, Axel often took the M25 and the M4. They were the most traveled highways around London. He spent many days driving these routes, making sure he knew them well in case the subject of his life came up. He had to speak like he had lived here for years and was familiar with all the things a man in his early thirties should be interested in. ere.

His first several days were rather uneventful. He made it an objective to meet as many of the men and women that lived near him. He went into the pubs in the evenings and talked to as many people as he could. Since he was new to the area and good looking, he may draw many young women to him. He talked to them and tried to not lead them on. Whenever there were women around him, men seemed to follow. He found one pub he particularly liked and where he made many contacts. The good thing about the pubs was that a person could sit around and bullshit about almost anything in the world, while drinking a pint. As the night wore on, the drinking made the talking more open, and that seemed to bring out the bitching. Axel tried to enter those sessions as much as possible, adding his own dissatisfaction with the economy, or the wars in the Mideast. It didn't take much for those subjects to attract others. Axel had thought that the open opinions that he had heard in the States were unique to that country. But conversations among the English were almost the same. One man named Rick was overly excited about the fact that he had lost his job, and he felt it was due to the war in the Mideast.

"Why in the hell are we there anyhow? So, they nailed a couple of buildings in the U.S. Why not let the U.S. fight the assholes? We not only lose some of our guys in those damn wars, but we lose the war with the economy here at home. If we still had the money we've spent fighting those wars, we wouldn't have anyone being laid off. We pay taxes to support those wars, and this takes money out of our economy. The next thing you know, we are being laid off and have to stretch for a war that won't be won. It will just go on and on, like when the Russians were in there. They finally got wise and pulled out of Afghanistan. All Russians are not dumb, just most of them."

Rick's words found some support from others in the pub, and soon there was talk about who was for and who was against the war in Afghanistan. Axel said, "I am in agreement with you Rick. We should get out of Afghanistan. If we stayed there for twelve years and then left, it would take the people of that country about two years to return to their present ways. It's their culture. They don't like government. They like living in those hills over there and growing poppies and enjoying themselves. They don't like us or the Americans in there. As far as they're concerned, the troops they see are just like the Russians. They want the Americans, the British, the Aussies, and everyone else to go and leave them alone."

Axel waited to see if his words aroused those against the war, and those who might want to take some overt action to protest the war. His comments hit some raw nerves, and the conversations became louder. Soon it was a mixed-up jumble of words, and Axel couldn't make anything out of it. Eventually, the talk settled down to other things.

I know I have laid the right egg here, Axel thought. *There are those who will be expressing their beliefs over the coming days. It doesn't take much to spark people like that. I bet as the nights go on, they will separate into groups of pro and con on a couple of major subjects. I must be alert to those that are just expressing their opinion, and those that are trying to induce a growing anti-government sentiment. From my early understanding of the British, they have always complained about their government, but then were always the first to go and fight for their country. So, I have to try to separate the wheat from the chaff, as they say.*

One of the blond, good-looking girls kept coming over by Axel and sort of rubbing against him. She told him her name was Sally, and he introduced himself as Donner Poole. She could tell by his accent he wasn't from England, and asked where he was from.

"I live here and am a citizen of this country. I came here from Germany. I guess I am an English German." Axel continued talking to see what came of it. After about a half hour of small talk, he offered to buy her a beer. She said she would enjoy a beer, so he went to the bar and ordered two beers. After picking up the beers, he headed back toward Sally, only to find a big, rough-looking character sitting at the table with her.

Axel set the beer down beside her, and the guy said, "Oh, you have a new servant tonight, Sally." He looked at Axel and insinuated, "And what might your name be, servant lad?"

Axel sat down and asked Sally if this was one of her friends or one of the village idiots. She laughed; the other man didn't.

"You're a little small to be making those kinds of remarks," he said.

Considering he was over six feet tall and a little over two hundred pounds, Axel was not small. He looked at the man and said, "No, I am a little bigger than the guys you normally pick on."

"Keep it up, little one, and you will be eating that instead of just drinking the beer."

"Why don't you go and bother someone at another table? There are a lot of smaller guys than me that you might be able to intimidate tonight."

This really got the guy's goat. He reached across the table, meaning to grab Axel, but his hand only got about halfway there, when Axel grabbed his arm and stopped him. He turned to Sally. "What is this ugly guy's name?"

"That's Ike," she answered.

"How about telling Ike that if he doesn't go away, I am going to throw him away like a used handkerchief?"

Again, Sally laughed and Ike didn't. He reached for Axel with his other hand, but Axel grabbed it too.

"My name is Donner," he said to Ike, "and if you don't go away, you are going to be a goner. Why don't you leave and save yourself an unpleasant night out?"

Ike seemed willing to take that advice and stood up, but Axel still held his two hands. He couldn't move. Realizing he was being shown up in front of the crowd, Ike made the next move. He spat at Axel's face. Instantly, Axel pulled Ike across the table and flipped him onto his back. Then he grabbed Ike by the shoulders and pushed him. Ike flew about ten feet onto another table. Ike jumped up as fast as a wounded animal and stared at Axel, obviously surprised at what had just happened. He yelled and ran at Axel. Axel grabbed him by the arms and lifted him off the floor. Ike was helpless, and the crowd was impressed.

"Takes a lot of strength to hold a man that way," one man said.

"Must lift weights," another one said. "You have to be strong to hold a man the size of Ike like he was a wet blanket."

Ike started hollering, "Leave my arms go! You're killing my arms!" Axel kept holding on, until Ike said, "Please Donner, please let my arms go."

With that plea, Axel released Ike, and the other man fell to the floor. *I better leave now,* Axel thought. *If I stand here, he'll be required to continue this until the end, and I don't want that to happen.*

He turned to Sally and said, "Let's go someplace to get a beer without all this noise."

She jumped up, holding his arm as they walked out of the place. They only had to walk a few doors down the street before they came to another pub. Axel had decided that, pubs in this country were as plentiful as grocery stores in the States. As they sat, Sally immediately began talking about what had just happened.

"How were you able to do that to Ike?" she asked.

"I took special courses in Germany and here on how to handle situations like that. I also lift weights. After a few years of that, my adrenaline reaches high levels whenever something like that happens."

"Oh, I think that's wonderful," Sally said. "I was so glad you didn't take it any further than you did. I bet he goes home and thinks about it and realizes he owes you an apology."

"I am glad you said that," he said. "Some less mature women would want that to have gone further. It went far enough."

Axel knew that the situation he was in now could go much further than it has. *How do I handle this with her? How do I walk away from her now? This is tough, especially since she is so attractive and so nice. I better think of Tori and figure my way out of this.*

He had one more beer and then gave Sally an excuse for why he had to leave. He knew Sally didn't want him to go, but he had to focus on his mission. He knew he had made one of the impressions he wanted to make with the local crowd. He just had to wait and see if he'd caught anyone with his bait. Meanwhile, he had a good-looking woman who probably would keep looking for him each night. He had to find a way for this to continue without any sexual problems. This would be tough.

As he returned to his apartment, he considered how this situation differed from his previous experiences. Before, he had known the enemy and had known he could encounter them the way he wanted to. It was no problem for death to occur in those cases, since those people were enemies of his country or of the world. In most of those cases, he was attacked and simply responded to the attacks. All lives lost were fair in those cases. And it didn't matter if his enemies knew his face, because when he was done, he would leave those places.

Here, he didn't know the enemy. He was in a friendly country at the request of its government to see if he could find the enemy. The enemy might be one or two individuals who were dissatisfied with the direction the country was going. If he stopped them and that was observed by others, then his mission in this country was over. He had to find a way to protect his identity during any sorties that might arise, so that he could continue to connect with other enemies.

How would he do this? He wondered. He could wear a mask, but his clothes or his shoes of his physique might be recognized. He needed something that was simple but effective, and that he could do rapidly. He considered and discarded several ideas. After a couple of hours of thought, he came up with what he considered an easy approach. Picturing himself in action mode, he thought, *I don't need shoes, since my feet are protected by my special covering. I could wear sweatpants over my normal clothes, and that would be a partial disguise. Jumping into a pair of sweatpants would be very fast. Add a hooded sweatshirt, and the only thing recognizable would be my face.* Axel gave that some more thought, and decided he could use a plastic shield, such as was attached to the front of motorcycle helmets. He could attach it to the hood of his sweatshirt, and it would cover his eyes and most of his face.

He envisioned what he'd have to do to his moves to bring him the anonymity he sought. First he would put his shoes into the trunk of his car, and then take out the sweatpants and sweatshirt. The whole action would take only seconds. His only concern was that he had to be near his car to take on this masquerade. *Most of the time that would be the case,* he thought. But what if he had to make sure any law enforcement officials knew it was him.

He scribbled some ideas on a piece of paper, finally drawing a *T* and an *F*. He combined the two letters, so that the cross on the *T* was also the lower cross on the *F. That's good,* he thought. *This insignia will represent The Follower.* He would sew the insignia onto the chest of the hooded sweatshirt. He would also print business cards on his computer, using the insignia and the words "The Follower." He'd leave the business cards at the scene of an event, so other enemies would see it. The card will be where I want the "bad guys" and the government to see it. I want the bad guys to start fearing The Follower. Tomorrow, he would call Casey Benson and Mark Wilkinson and tell them what he was doing so they would know who was involved in any incidents.

The next day in London, Axel went to various shops along the Thames to pick up the various things he needed. He decided to make two of the outfits, so he had one for his apartment and one for the car. When he had accumulated the things, he used his internal phone to call the prime minister. Unfortunately, the prime minister was in Berlin, celebrating the twentieth anniversary of the fall of the Berlin Wall. Axel left a message on the prime minister's private voice mail, explaining his plan for remaining anonymous and the business cards. He then called the Commissioner of Scotland Yard. Mark Wilkinson wasn't available either, so he left the same message for the Commissioner.

It only took Axel a couple of hours to get his outfits together, most of that time was spent sewing the insignias on the sweatshirts. After he was done, like a kid, he hurried to see what he looked like in this outfit. He kicked off his shoes, jumped into the sweatpants, and pulled the hooded sweatshirt on over his head. The plastic shield, which he'd stapled to the head, fell easily over his face. He looked in the mirror and was surprised at how good it looked. He couldn't see his own face, and he was pleased with the insignia. He had timed himself, and the change had taken less than a half of a minute.

This is great, he thought. *I am now ready for some action.*

Axel's visits to the various pubs around the area became a daily routine. Soon he knew more and more people and their feelings about various subjects. They also knew more about him and his apparent feelings and aspirations. When he called Commissioner Wilkinson's office on Thursday, he told him he was making good contacts. He expected he would soon be getting more tangible information about those who were disgruntled enough to take some bold steps against Queen and country.

"That's great," commented Mark. "That's the way to make contacts here. The people love their beer and they love to talk. If you egg them on, they will talk about things they want to say but normally hold inside. Keep it up."

When Axel visited the various bars and talked to his new friends, he made a point as the nights wore on to talk about how discouraged he was with things.

"I didn't leave Germany to come here and not be working and wishing we would get out of the war with those rag heads over there."

When he made remarks like that, he could feel the temper of some of the people he was talking to begin to rise. He wasn't trying to rouse the general public, so he had to watch himself. He began to notice that the crowd around him most nights was more of the muscle type. Sally kept coming around, too, and Axel did what he could to keep her at arm's length.

One evening he was approached by two of his new friends, Arnie and Maxie. They said they wanted to take him for a ride the next day and show him some of the sights. The next day, as they drove around, Maxie said to Axel, "You know, Donner, we have the feeling you aren't all that happy with what's going on in this country."

Axel just nodded his head.

"We feel we should do something about it,' said Arnie.

"What can you do about it?" asked Axel.

"We know a bunch of guys that want to take some kind of actions to show we aren't happy with the government or the government's direction."

Axel asked what kind of actions, and Maxie asked if he'd heard about grenades being put in car gas tanks and blowing up.

"Yes, I read about that in the papers. It's terrible for the people who are in the cars."

"Most of these things have their negative effects," Maxie said, "but that is what makes it positive steps against the government. These things get written up in the paper and are on the Telly, and people start voicing out against the government. Some of the media that don't agree with our men fighting in the foreign countries take up the fight and start printing complaints against the government."

"I understand, but that is like being a terrorist; isn't it?" questioned Axel.

"Not really," answered Maxie "You might call it an agitating position more than taking direct steps to prevent something. We know we don't have the power to stop any of the things that we've been talking about. We can only agitate the rumbling that goes on. Sooner or later, the media picks up on it and this applies more pressure. If we can get more and more people involved in this, we may be able to get Parliament to make some better decisions."

Axel was silent for a minute and then said, "I am all for bringing this to the attention of more people and hoping it catches on. However, I don't think that sticking hand grenades in the random people's gas tanks is a good way to go about it. I would try to think of a better way to get the message across."

They rode for a while, and Arnie began talking. "We have been thinking of making bombs from hydrogen peroxide. We have ways of obtaining hydrogen peroxide, and acetone is quite easy to come by. We can get fairly large sums of the various components to allow us to make thousands of bombs."

"You can't just use any old hydrogen peroxide," Axel said, "since three percent medical peroxide is not concentrated enough. You might consider using TATP, which is made with acetone and requires the same kind of acid that is used in swimming pools. You remember the shoe bomber, who was caught on a flight out of England toward America?.

He had a special shoe that contained this TATP in the hollowed-out heel of his shoe.

"Acetone peroxide has an action that most explosives do not have. Most explosives contain nitrogen. The scanners used in airports and other places can detect explosives containing nitrogen, but this stuff passes by without being detected. Most explosives generate heat, but this explosive does not generate heat. Essentially, this substance causes its damage by rapid creation of gas from a solid source. Heat can be generated as a secondary reaction by the high pressure gas passing over other solids, and the friction causes heat. The funny thing is, this is what is used in air bags in cars. In those cases, the amount of material used is less than would be required for an explosion, but it is a mini explosion of sorts. Anytime there is over two ounces of this material, that is enough to detonate and cause an explosion. So, this stuff is nothing to play with. It is very risky, but a great explosive. If any of your guys has access to a plant that makes the air bags for cars, they that would have access to this material. Why don't you check that out? But as I said, this material is tricky to work with."

Axel sat back waited for a reaction from the two men. It was a long time coming, but finally Arnie spoke. "I know a man who is an expert on this material. If we decide to do anything with this approach, I will invite him to have a meeting with us and discuss this further. He also has access to all the ingredients required, and in volume."

"That sounds like a plan," Axel said. "This method is better than most of the other approaches. If the man is from Ireland, he will probably be an expert, because the IRA used explosives of this type. They are also being used in Afghanistan."

As they discussed this further, Axel thought about this scary situation. *I better ask a few questions. I need to find out if this is something just these two are thinking about, or if there are a large number of people who think this way.*

"How many people would be involved with this kind of an approach?" he asked. "Or is this just you two guys?"

"There are a significant number of people interested in taking some kind of action," Arnie answered. "Ask around the pubs and I bet you'd come up with at least fifty people that have it against the government and want to see some changes. They are disturbed enough to fight a war. And this doesn't count the Irish." He laughed. "If the Irish were involved, we could come up with an army."

Axel said, "You let me know what you're thinking of doing. The people you know may be ahead of our discussions today. They may have already planned some kind of action. Try to get a total picture, so we know where we stand. This is not something one takes on lightly. You have to be prepared for the consequences."

They arrived back at Axel's apartment and left him out. Axel thought about the conversation as he entered his apartment. *These guys are serious and this problem is serious. But I won't call Mark at this time because it might blow over and I don't want to be jerking his string on this. I'll call him when I know something is tangible and actions may need to be taken.* He would, however, call Tori.

"Hi there sweetheart," he said when she answered the phone.

"How's the world treating you?"

"Oh Axel, I was just thinking about you. I am still at work. I miss you and haven't heard your voice for a couple of days. What's going on?"

"Not much, so far. I have been going to the pubs over here each night and trying to meet as many people as I can. So far, there is an undertone of resentment among the people here, but I haven't really found an insurrection going on. I am going to try some ethnic pubs tomorrow. I would think there may be some different cults that might pop up that are in the planning phase of something over here. If I don't find something within a week, I am going to request coming back home."

"Yippee," yelled Tori. "That would be wonderful; wonderful for a few reasons. It would mean there are no problems over there and it would mean you could come home. It would mean my man would be back and we could continue our love affair."

"Yes, I have been thinking about that," replied Axel. "I miss you twenty-four hours a day. That's including the dreams I have about you. I hope it works out that way."

After talking to Tori, Axel thought about going to one of the pubs he'd heard about that was favored by the Russians. It was called The Russ Out. When he arrived, he said hello in Russian to a man standing by the entrance. That was like throwing a switch. Within minutes there were a group of Russians surrounding him as though he were their long lost brother. One man slapped Axel on the shoulders and said, "You are new here. Where are you from?"

"It's a long story," Axel said.

The man led him to a table where a few other men were drinking vodka. "My name is Ginsky," the man said. Axel introduced himself as Donner.

"That's an odd name for a Russian," he said.

"That's a long story also," said Axel.

He seated himself next to Ginsky, and the men immediately started to grill him on his Russian heritage. Axel told them he had been born in Russia, but had gone with his dad to Afghanistan when the Russians had invaded. He and his father had been held captive there for years. When they finally got out, his father got him papers that changed his name to Donner Poole. His father thought he had a better chance for a good life in Germany. He had migrated to England ten years earlier, with his German name and papers. "So, you can call me anything you want, but I am a Russian."

It didn't take the men long to start talking about Afghanistan. The discussion centered on wishing the Americans and their allies would leave Afghanistan so it would be easier for the Russians to start trafficking the opium out of the country again.

"There's a gold mine there," said Ginsky. "How about you, Donner? What's your feeling about that?"

"You are probably right that the armies have made it more difficult to take part in moving drugs out the way we used to. They have practically given Al-Qaeda and the Taliban free rein in owning that trade. If those two terrorist groups don't get the drugs in Afghanistan, they get it in Pakistan when it makes it over the border. There are probably more of those two groups in Pakistan now than there were before Afghanistan was invaded. The problem is that now there is an organized trail that leads from Afghanistan to Pakistan. Not too many years ago, under the Soviet Union, the drugs would travel north to Tajikistan, crossing the river in the northern part of Afghanistan. In those days our people controlled that drug trade. Since the breakup of the Union I don't know how much is still going over that border and through Russia."

One of the men said that there still is some trade going that way. "The river runs a long distance along that border, and the armies in

Afghanistan can't keep their troops along all the length of it. If the U.S. troops were to withdraw, there would be open season for picking up the drugs and moving across that river. I know a lot of the people here would like to see all the troops leave so they could have access to those drugs."

His comments were met with great acceptance, and the evening was spent talking about how to get at least the British to pull their troops. Axel sure was glad he had programmed Russian into his computer.

For the following two weeks, Axel continued making his nightly visits to the pubs, shifting between the ones with the locals and the one with the Russians. It became more apparent as time proceeded that the Russian faction was more likely to do more harm than the locals; maybe not sooner, but certainly a more damaging approach. The Russian group kept dividing into those not so violently opposed to the war in Afghanistan, and those who were ready to take action. This action group numbered about eighteen. Axel thought of them as the Russian Mafia. They wanted the war to end so they could gain more control of the drugs being shipped around the world. Axel became more alarmed as they discussed methods of making explosives out of ammonium nitrate. Axel kept thinking about the explosion in 1995 that had destroyed the Federal Building in Oklahoma City in 1995. Timothy McVeigh and Terry Nichols had made a six-hundred-pound bomb using fertilizer by Timothy McVeigh and Terry Nichols. They had loaded the bomb into a truck that they parked outside the building. When it went off, it killed 168 people and completely destroyed the building.

Axel knew ammonium nitrate could be exploded by shock or by a detonator. Some people used it to rip holes in the earth when looking for coal or other useful material. They exploded by using a couple sticks of dynamite as the detonator. An even more destructive device was formed by the fertilizer and a fuel oil, such as number two fuel or kerosene. This was called ANFO. This was the type of IED used in Iraq and Afghanistan as destructive road bombs.

Axel kept the discussion going by asking where they thought they were going to get the ammonium nitrate. Ginsky said that they are able get it from the farms in the southern part of Surrey. "We already have a bunch of the stuff stored away. We can pull it out on a day's notice. Worse case, we can bring some in from Ireland. This stuff is outlawed in this country, but we have a direct line to a good bit."

Axel was shocked to hear that they already were in a position to use this ANFO, and he decided to try to find out the timing and the target. Several of the Russians felt they should start the program right away.

Ginsky said, "It's one thing to explode this and cause a lot of damage, but another to get the British people to realize it as a signal to stop the use of the British troops in Afghanistan. How do we get that message across?"

After some discussion, they decided that the best approach was to start small. Even a small explosion could have a big effect if they could get the word through the media that they wanted to demonstrate that the country was tired of the Afghanistan war. They were tired of losing soldiers for nothing. They decided they would think about what would be the first attack against the system.

When Axel went home, he decided to call Mark Wilkinson to let him know how dangerous this situation has become. He left a message on Mark's voice mail, and Mark called the next morning at six thirty. Axel relayed the discussions of the night before.

"I am glad you are on this," said Mark. "I can't take any action at this time, but if you keep me posted, perhaps we can prevent an incident before the fact. I want to be able to stop the early incidents to keep them from considering the greater issues. It would be terrible to have an ANFO incident."

Axel said he would try to keep him advised on a real time basis. He told Mark that he sometimes was late in learning what they were planning or actually doing.

"Give us your best effort, is all I ask," said Mark. "I appreciate what you are doing to help us here, and I will keep Prime Minister Benson and President Hargrove advised of our appreciation."

After a couple more evening meetings, the Russian Mafia decided to start off by advising the media of their intentions. A letter was sent to the London newspapers with the message that the people of this country were tired of the wasted lives, wasted time, and wasted money on a war that showed no good conclusion. The letter ended with the message that there would be some demonstrations against this fruitless war. When he read that, Axel thought, *I wonder if they don't trust me yet, and they are doing things without my knowing them. I will push tonight to be kept aware of their actions.*

That night, Axel voiced his concern that not everyone in the group knew what was going on. He referenced the letter in the paper.

"I didn't know about it, and I am an expert on these kinds of explosives. If you don't trust all of us, you are limited in what you can do. This is not a small effort, and it requires the thoughts and actions of all of us."

Ginsky said he thought that Donner was right. "We must use all of us. Donner has had some schooling in chemistry, as well as other things we need to know in order to handle these actions intelligently and get the most out of them. I believe the message in the paper was a good one. I know people have been talking about it. The day after our letter was published; there were three letters to the editor that agreed that we should get out of Afghanistan. This is good. Now we need an incident to really bring it to their attention and get us more support. We have some plans to release some acetone peroxide explosives over the next couple of days. They will be rather small, but will give us more visibility, especially with the media coverage we'll get."

"Where is this going to happen?" one man asked.

"We're looking at some of the shopping centers along the Thames," said Ginsky "Incidents in those shopping centers will not go unnoticed, and they will put an instant scare into the public as well as the government."

Axel spoke up, saying that this type of explosive was dangerous if not handled properly. "These explosives can be initiated by heat, shock, or just by mixing them improperly," he said.

'Donner is right," another man said. "I used those in Afghanistan about fifteen or sixteen years ago, when our army was in that country. We had two guys lose their hands."

"Yes, we know," said Ginsky. "The guys doing this tomorrow have handled these explosive before, and they know what they are doing. Isn't that right, Frizel and Stanski?"

Two of the men stood up and said they had worked with these explosives before. While they were talking, Axel decided to take a fax picture of them. He stared at each of the two long enough and said the right words to generate and store their images.

Axelvation See, he thought to his computer. Then he thought, *Store in memory.*

"Good luck tomorrow," he said. "But I wouldn't use the common way of carrying the material, such as in a backpack. Too many police and guards are on the lookout for that, since the London subway bombing a few years back."

"We will be using a computer case to carry them," Stanski said. "Everyone is carrying those things around. The police would go nuts if they started to search all of them. The good news is that the scanners used by the police and the military cannot detect these kind of explosives."

"That sounds like a good plan," Axel said as the other men all raised their drinks in a salute.

After the meeting, Axel decided to follow Stanski to where he lived. He was surprised to discover that he lived only about a block away from Axel's apartment. Axel drove on to his apartment, and once there, planned on what to do the following day with Frizel and Stanski. He would have to find a way to blow them up with their own explosives. He would eliminate a terrorist threat and the papers would report it as an accident. With these thoughts in mind he sent a fax to Commissioner Wilkinson.

Mark, here are pictures of two Russians who that intend to set off explosives at two malls tomorrow. I intend to take care of the situation by having them destroyed by their own bombs. You can play that whichever way you want as far as telling the media what happened. I am hoping that by the explosives going off before they are supposed to, you can just say the men killed themselves before the police could take action. The police can take credit for preventing a terrorist attack, or just two loonies from trying to do something crazy. I will let you know as soon as I find out which of the shopping centers they intend to hit, and keep you up to date on what is actually happening.

After he sent that message, Axel directed his computer memory to bring up the pictures of the two Russians. He faxed those along as well. As he got ready for bed, he decided he would head over to Stanski's house around noon the next day, on the pretense that Ginsky had sent him to make sure everything went as planned.

Axel arrived at Stanski's just at noon and rang the door bell. Soon Stanski came to the door. When he asked why Donner was there, Axel said, "Ginsky got hold of me. He wants me to go along with you to the mall and help you if you needed any help."

Stansky looked surprised. "I don't know why Ginsky would do that. He trusts me, doesn't he?"

"Yes, he trusts you," Axel said. "He knows I only live about a block from your house and I know a lot about explosives. So, he just wanted me to go along and make sure everything went well."

Stanski asked Axel to come in and have a cup of tea or coffee. "Tea would be nice," Axel replied, stepping into the house.

As Stanski put a pan of water on the stove, he said, "Looks like it's going to be a good day to do this. The sun is out and it doesn't look like any rain."

As they drank their tea and some crackers Stanski had set out, Axel asked which malls they intended to hit that day.

"Two of the busiest malls around the Thames," replied Stanski. "I am hitting the Newton Plaza and Frizel is going to hit the Kirkoff Plaza."

"Have you selected which shop to hit, or are you just going to hit whichever one is convenient?"

Stanski said that he had chosen the Hanson Sporting Center at the Newton Plaza, and Frizel had selected Friedman's Women's Wear at the Kirkoff Plaza.

"Those ought to be great targets, lots of customer at both," said Axel. "Are you going to hit them at the same time to raise the level of excitement?"

"We thought about doing it that way," said Stanski, "but it seemed that I should do mine at around five in the evening, when the crowd begins to get big, and Frizel is going to do his one hour later. Frizel felt that while the fire trucks and police cars are at the Newton Plaza trying to figure out what happened, he would do the Women's Wear. This would have them going around in circles."

"That's a great idea," said Axel. "I can watch the excitement at the Newton Plaza and then motor over and watch the action at the Kirkoff Plaza. Those are good times, because the traffic will be at its peak with people getting off work. This will help tie up the emergency vehicles and police."

"Yes, that's what Frizel and I thought. It will be like a merry-go-round out there on the highways."

"So, do you intend to leave here about three in the afternoon to give you plenty of time to get there and set things up?"

Stanski agreed that three would be a good time, since it was only about a half hour drive.

On the way to the Newton Plaza, Axel asked Stanski how he intended to trigger the explosion. "I have armed the system with a detonator that is responsive to a signal from my cell phone. All I have to do is flip the cell phone open, hit the on button, and that's it."

Axel smiled and said, "That's the way to do it. Make it simple. You have to be careful when you add the acetone to the mix. Once mixed, it becomes sensitive to shock and heat. I hope you measured out the proper amount of acetone to be added. Too little is a problem, and too much is a different problem."

"Yes, I know. I have done this numerous times. I am positive I have this set up right. I will be some distance away from it before it goes off, and I will be careful when I add the acetone and set the package."

They arrived at the Newton Plaza around 3:45 pm and parked in the main parking lot. Stanski took from the trunk of his car the computer case and a smaller package. He put the smaller package in the case. They walked back toward the Hanson Sporting Center, which was at the end of the plaza near the Thames River. Axel mentioned to Stanski that they should walk down to the edge of the river, and he could add the acetone there. That would give them plenty of space with not many people around. Stanski agreed.

As they reached the river bank, Axel hit Stanski in the back of his neck with his right hand and grabbed the case with his left. Stanski fell to the ground and didn't move a muscle. Axel took cell phone and car keys. While he was at it, he pulled his driver's license and faxed the information from it to the commissioner's office. He returned the license to Stanski's wallet and put it back in his pants. Then he opened the case and took the small acetone bottle. He poured the acetone into the container of peroxide and rapidly closed the computer case. He slipped it under Schultz's body, stepped back about thirty feet, and turned on Schultz's cell phone. There was a loud explosion, and Axel would have been knocked unconscious if it weren't for his protective body covering. The bomb tore Stanski's body to pieces.

As he walked away, Axel called Mark on his internal phone and told him what had happened.

"We'll take care of it from here," the commission said as Axel made his way through the throng of panicking people. "We have been watching you and your friend since you entered the plaza. I instructed the police to keep their distance until they heard an explosion or if we saw that you didn't have control of the situation. You handled this quite well. We hope your next 'adventure' will go as well. We will be watching you when you enter Kirkoff Plaza. We have already seen Frizel. He is parked in the main lot. I can direct you to his location once you reach the plaza."

"That's great," exclaimed Axel. He was the people from Scotland Yard had been watching him.

Axel drove to the Kirkoff Plaza. As he approached the main parking lot, he got directions on where to turn right or left, and soon he was passing by Frizel's parked car with Frizel in it. Axel parked about twenty car spaces away and walked toward Frizel's car. He tapped on the driver's window, and Frizel stared at him in shock. He rolled down his window and asked what he was doing there.

"Ginsky told me to go and make sure that Stanski was in good shape with his deal at Newton Plaza. Stanski is almost ready to ignite his system, and he told me to drive over here in his car and see if you need any help."

"Really; the bugger doesn't believe I know how to do this without help. I am waiting till 6:00 pm when the plaza is loaded with people, and then I will make my way to the target area."

"The Women's Wear business?" asked Axel. "Right," said Frizel. "How did you know that?"

"Stanski told me." He walked around to the passenger side of the vehicle and got in. "Are you going to set it off with your cell phone also?"

"Yes, after I prime it with the acetone and place it. I will probably just drop the computer case in one of the aisles and walk out."

"Sounds like a good plan to me," said Axel.

All of a sudden Frizel pulled out a gun and pointed it at Axel. "Why are you here?" he demanded.

"I told you," responded Axel.

"I don't believe you, Donner; if that's really your name. I haven't trusted you since the day you showed up. That was a kind of wacky story you got Ginsky to believe. Plus, I don't think you have earned the right to be with us. What is your real name?"

"What's it matter what my name is? I am here to help you," said Axel.

"Get out of the car immediately or I am going to feed you some lead," Frizel shouted.

Axel simply looked at Frizel. "I think you are overestimating the power of that pistol and underestimating what you think about me," said Axel. "I am going to take that pistol from you and do what I came here to do."

Frizel shot the pistol three times. Each bullet bounced off Axel, and one ricocheted right back at Frizel, plunging into his left shoulder. Frizel stared at Axel with eyes filled with pain. "What kind of man are you?"

"I am the kind of man who doesn't want you to hurt the English people," Axel said, and reached over and snapped Frizel's neck.

Axel turned and looked around the car for the computer case holding the bomb. The case was sitting in the backseat. He opened it and saw the bomb looked just like the one Stanski had attempted to use. He took Frizel's cell phone and driver's license, and faxed the license to the commissioner's office so they would have that information about him and then he returned it to his wallet and put it back in his pants. He mixed the chemicals and got out of the car, leaving the case open. He walked back to Stanski's car and backed it up so he could see Frizel's car. He watched as a man and a woman walked by the car. He waited till they were about one hundred feet away and then turned on Fritz's cell phone. The explosion blew Frizel's car about ten feet into the air and severely damaged all the cars parked around it. Axel felt bad about the cars, but it had been a safe and easy way to detonate the bomb. Something had to happen so the other terrorists would see that a bomb went off and feel that Frizel made a mistake. Axel swung his car around and drove toward the exit. As he left the parking lot, he saw the police racing toward the shopping center, their sirens wailing.

He was still on the phone with the commissioner, and he said, "There's another Russian Mafia enemy of the state that you don't have to worry about."

The commissioner hung up without saying a word. *Tough, these British,* he thought. *Good people and tough. Now I have to find out what other mischief these Russian Mafia guys want to get into. There will not be a happy bunch at the pub tonight. I believe I have held my anonymity with them through these two issues with the explosives. We shall see what comes up next. This is getting exciting now. I must return this car to the Newton lot so it is accounted for. I can get a subway from that plaza to a stop by my apartment.*

That evening, Axel went to the Russian pub as if nothing had happened. As he sat down at the table, one of the Russians passed a mug of beer toward him. "How's your day been going?" he asked.

"Fine;" replied Axel. "And how about you?"

Just as the guy was going to answer, Ginsky said, "We had some bad luck today. Both Stanski and Frizel failed in their assignments. They both must have done something wrong and their explosives went off and killed them. I can't believe this. These screw-ups were supposed to be familiar with these types of bombs. Do any of you know anything about this?"

It was quiet at this normally loud table full of excited Russians. Axel waited for a minute to pass, and then he commented, "My experience with these kinds of things is that the person arming the bomb must be careful that the right amount of acetone is added. After priming the explosive with the acetone, the bomb is activated and sensitive to shock and heat. This is especially true if the peroxide is over two ounces. I would assume these were well over two ounces. Perhaps their experience before was with bombs that were less than two ounces, and they handled these bombs as if they were like the smaller bombs they had experience with."

Again it was quiet. Ginsky stared at Axel before saying, "If I had known you knew this much about these kinds of bombs, I would have had you go with them."

"Oh, no, I never had any experience with making these kinds of bombs. I got on the computer the other day, after you talked about using this way to gain the attention of the media and the English assholes. What I just said to you was what I got off a Web site about these kinds of bombs. I always try to use the computer to find out something I don't know anything about. It's amazing what one can learn just by looking it up on the computer. I guess Stanski and Frizel should have looked on the computer before they took this adventure on. They probably were overconfident."

Again it was quiet at the table. Ginsky looked around at the remaining sixteen men and said, "I appreciate what Donner just said. I want you all to use the computer to double-check yourselves, no matter how confident you are of what you will be doing from this day on."

No one spoke, and Ginsky went on. "I wonder how much the police found at these two sites. I wonder if they are now alerted to other attempts of this nature. Everyone watch the Telly tonight and read the papers tomorrow. We will go on from here. I want you all to be here tomorrow at seven as the latest. We will talk about this after we find what the authorities have to say. Remember, this is just the beginning. Don't let this little blunder blind you from our mission. The next one will be a big one."

When Axel got home he decided to call Mark. He wasn't in, and Axel left a message for him to call. About half an hour later his cell phone rang; it was the commissioner. Axel told him about the conversations he'd had that evening with the Russian Mafia.

"They think the two guys screwed up mixing the bomb components and that's what killed them, but I think you had better make the stories throughout the media say something else."

"Do you have a suggestion?" Mark asked.

"Yes," said Axel. "I think the stories should say that two terrorist threats were thwarted by Scotland Yard. All the people know is that there were two explosions and there were people killed. I think you should make it look like the local authorities did something good. It will be good for the morale of the locals and it will piss off the Mafia. They will think it might be true."

"That is a very good idea. You are right that no one knows what happened. What I can do is call the local police captain and tell him to find a way to get the word out that they caught two would-be terrorists trying to explode bombs. I will tell him to leak out that efforts were thwarted by some timely police action and that these men had been under surveillance for months. That will put a chill up the spines of those other assholes. They will be looking around to see if someone is watching them. The media will start broadcasting the story first thing in the morning. This will be a ball. I just know it, and I am mad I didn't think of it before you called. Incidentally, I couldn't say anything when you took the actions you took, but I was impressed. I am going to get off the line and make a few calls now. Thanks, Axel."

After Mark hung up, Axel sat back in his chair and thought about what had happened that day. *So far, it looks like they don't know that I am involved, and they maybe even think I can help in some way. Lucky I thought about telling them that I learned about those bombs from Web sites. Hell, I have been making those bombs in the labs for eight years now. In fact, now that I am protected, I can explore them further without worrying about them exploding. I can't wait to hear what the Mafia has to say tomorrow after they hear these stories.*

The next day Axel couldn't wait to hear the radio and TV stories about the explosions. Just as he and Mark had thought, the stories it spread like wildfire. All throughout the day, he saw news broadcasts lauding the local police for stopping a terrorist attack. It was great. The papers in the late afternoon had headlines like, "Local Police Outsmart Would-Be Terrorists." He read some of the articles and couldn't keep from laughing. He couldn't wait till he got to the pub that evening.

Axel arrived about fifteen minutes before seven, going directly to the back room and the round table where they always sat. About ten other men were already there. They had read the papers and watched the Telly, and they were pissed. Soon Ginsky came in and sat down, and he didn't say a word. He was waiting till it was seven o'clock. One by one, the rest of the Mafia came to the table. When it was seven, Ginsky got up and looked around. The place was as quiet as a morgue. He looked up at the ceiling and then began talking.

"Do any of you sons of bitches believe the stories that have been on the Telly and in the papers today? Do you really believe those assholes actually stopped our guys, or do you think our asshole guys screwed up and the frigging police are taking credit for it?"

He waited for an answer. One of the men got up and started shouting. "There is no way the frigging police have been watching those two men. They have been in this country for years and have their citizenship here. They have worked at good jobs and were liked by many. I believe the police took advantage of their screw-up, and we need to make sure we know what we are doing in the future. We can't act like amateurs. We have to make sure the next event goes off like a charm. We need to make those monkeys look like monkeys."

The man sat down and looked toward Ginsky. He said, "I couldn't agree with Alex any more than if I had said those same words myself. We screwed up, and the locals are taking advantage. Let's get this out of our systems. Forget the screw-up. Let's talk about our next big effort. Alex and several of his crew have come up with a beautiful plan. However, I don't want to talk about it tonight when we are in a bad mood. We will cover this tomorrow. So, everyone drink their beer like a normal night. We can't allow this screw-up to take the energy away from our efforts. So, drink up and we will meet again tomorrow at seven."

One of the guys jumped up, his beer raised high, and shouted, "Here's to the coming events."

All the others got to their feet, shouted "Smutska," and drank down their beer. Axel didn't know what that "smutska" was all about, but he drank his beer.

When he got up in the next morning, Axel listened to the news on the radio and television. As he's expected, the media were still having a ball with the terrorist story. They even went so far as to say that there were had been more than two events initiated by terrorist groups that had been disrupted by local authorities. All of this was so much fun for Axel. He kept smiling all day. He went to dinner early before heading out to the pub. He got there about the same time as the day before, and the same ten men were sitting there. Before long, the whole crew there.

Ginsky arrived at seven. His first comments were, "Now I know they are bull shitting. They talk about many events that were fouled up by the police. Wait till they hear what's coming their way. They will be smiling out of the corners of their mouths. Alex, how about standing up and telling the crew what we have in mind?"

The Follower Crushes Terrorist Plans for Bombs on Thames River

Hans stood up. "We're going to load two boats with ANFO bombs. To give you an idea of what size bombs we are talking about, you remember that Oklahoma City bomb back in 1995? That was a six-hundred-pound bomb, and it took out an entire building. These boats will be carrying one thousand pounds each. We intend to direct them down the Thames late in the afternoon. They will be directed by radio control. One is a thirty-five-foot yacht and the other is a thirty-foot yacht. Both have double engines and double fuel systems. They belong to a couple of rich Russians who live here, and they are going to be away for about a week. We will initiate the program day after tomorrow. Tomorrow we will be loading the explosives. Both yachts are docked at a local marina. We have worked on setting them up for the radio control during the past two days and have tested these out. Now all we have to do is load them up with the ANFO. We have moved the materials to a spot about fifteen kilometers down the Thames on the south side of the river. It is in a shack and is well insulated from moisture. We will take the yachts down to this spot early in the day tomorrow. It should take us a few hours to load them. Then we will take off up the Thames toward London. We will navigate both of the boats manually up the Thames for a certain distance, and then leave the boats and have them under radio control.

"We have two major targets in mind. One is an oil tanker that is scheduled to move up the Thames today to a dock near the one big shopping center. It should be docked by the day after tomorrow. We will guide one of the boats alongside it and blow it up. The combination of the ANFO bomb and the fuel in the tanker will create an unbelievable explosion. They will think hell broke loose.

"The other boat will go about two miles farther down the Thames, to a large shopping plaza where the buildings are placed very close to the river bank. We expect to knock out a few of the shops with this one."

One of the men asked if the boats had licenses. "If they don't have licenses, they will be stopped by police boats patrolling the river."

"Yes the boats are licensed," Hans said.

"This sounds like a great strike," another man said, "and should turn some heads. How do you expect to get the pilots off the boats to run them by radio control?"

"Good question," said Ginsky. "We have another motorboat that is smaller and faster. I will be running that boat. We will use it to take the pilots off the two yachts. We will take the radio control onto that speedboat with us. When we eventually activate the explosives, it will take about four minutes before they explode. So, our intentions are to take the lead boat to the riverbank by the mall and kill the engine. The second boat should be arriving at the side of the oil tanker about that time, and we will kill that engine. Once it gets there, we will activate both of the boat's explosives. That gives us four minutes to take off. At the time we activate, we will be about two miles from the tanker site, and after activation we expect to be an additional one to two miles from the sites before there is an explosion. We will throw away the remote controls we are carrying for the other boats. That way we won't have any evidence with us if we get stopped. But once there is an explosion, there will be a lot of action on the river. Boats will be going every which way on the river. Even the police boats will advance slowly toward the explosion sites. That will give us plenty of time to dock the speedboat at a marina and walk away. Are there any more questions?"

The place was quiet, until one beer-drinking bloke jumped up. Holding his mug high, he shouted, "Here's to the success of our naval adventure! May it turn many heads."

The men all stood up and shouted, in British style, "Hip, hip, hooray. Hip, hip, hooray."

As Axel left the pub, he thought about his options. First he needed to contact Scotland Yard and see if they could find those boats. With the information he had, he figured they could. Once he knew where the boats were berthed, he could follow the two boats tomorrow by swimming behind them down the Thames to the site where the explosives were.

He could do the same thing when they sailed the boats back up the Thames with the explosives loaded on them. He would have no trouble keeping up with the boats. When he saw the pilots getting off the yachts and onto the speedboat, he could swim underwater ahead of the boats and get to the target sites first. Once the boats got there, he would have four minutes to deactivate the explosives.

Axel had recorded the conversation at the pub and sent the recoding to the commissioner's office. Now that he had a plan in mind, he called Mark and asked if he had listened to the recording.

"I just listened to it," Mark said. "This is something we have to stop immediately."

"No, I think you should let me take care of this. You will want to take advantage of this venture just as your people did with the one the other day. Anytime we can thwart an effort with the general public knowing about it, it becomes a morale booster for the public and morale killer for the Mafia. We will take care of the Mafia and get the full benefit from our actions."

"I don't know, Axel. This is a dangerous situation. If you can't handle it, then we could have a terrorist act exploding in our faces."

"Let me tell you what my plans are, and then you can make a decision."

"All right, I will be happy to hear what you have to say. You have done a wonderful job on this so far, so I won't be the one to deny you anything reasonable. Let's hear it."

Axel told the commissioner what he envisioned, how he would follow the boats down the river to wherever the explosives were stored. He would then swim back upriver after them the next day. Once the boats neared their targets, he would swim ahead of them and get there first.

"Before the boat intended for the tanker even gets there, I will punch holes in the underneath part of the boat, letting water in on the explosives. These explosives are hygroscopic and suck up water like a sponge. The wetter they get, the less volatile they become. I will then push it out into the middle of the river. As the second boat approaches, I will do the same thing to it.

"At that point, they will probably have detonated the bombs and I will have about four minutes. I will push the second boat out into the middle of the river, which will take a minute, and then rip a hole in it. It will sink in about a minute. They are using two sticks of dynamite as their detonators. Since both boats will be underwater, the only thing that will go off will be those two sticks of dynamite. Two sticks of dynamite exploding underwater is nothing. It may make a noise, but that's about it.

"I will alert you when the boats first start up the Thames, so that you can make sure the river around these two sites is void of any kind of boats. You'd have about half an hour to get the center of the river free from traffic."

The commissioner left out his breath in a long sigh. "How fast can you swim underwater?"

"I'd say thirty-five miles an hour, but I can actually do a little better."

"And you say you can punch holes in the bottom of these boats, enough to sink them. That's hard to believe."

"I have tremendous power when I am in my third level of power. I can punch a hole in a two-inch thick steel panel without any problem. You can call Dr. Kim at USSA and he will verify this."

Mark was quiet for about ten seconds, and then said with excitement, "This is unreal. It's no wonder you were recommended to help us out. But let me think about your plan. In some ways it makes sense, but in other ways we're taking a chance, and that worries me. We have enough information, including the recording you just sent me, that if we were to grab the boats after they're loaded with explosives, we could put these guys in jail for a long time. I will get back to you later this evening. It may be late."

"No problem with the time. I am used to getting calls at all times of the day or night. Maybe you will come up with a different plan. The one thing I recommend is to let this play out like we did the other day.

Let the Mafia think they've succeeded. Then when they find out they failed again, it will destroy their morale and confidence. Keep in mind that I will be with them, and I can take them out anytime you want, or anytime they present an immediate threat."

Mark called back very late that night. "I have thought about it and I believe you are right with your plan. I have talked to several people, and we can keep the center of the river empty for about an hour. That should be enough for you to handle. I called the USSA and talked to Dr. Kim, and he assured me that if you gave me a plan that it will work. He said you are not only physically powerful, but you have great brain power too. That was enough for me.

"Oh, yes, you asked for the boat marina and docking sites. They are in the Ariel Marina and the dock numbers are 787 and 788. The boats are called *Katrina* and *Muriel*."

Axel told the commissioner that he would keep his internal phone on the whole time, so that if anything came up, Mark would know immediately.

Axel got up at five the next morning, wanted to get to the marina as early as possible. He didn't like the idea of possibly missing the boats and having to swim along the river to find them. He ate a good breakfast and then grabbed a handful of candy bars. *Might need this nourishment,* he thought.

Axel was soon at the Ariel Marina and, using his underwater binoculars, spotted the two boats with some men working on them. He recognized Alex and knew he was at the right place. Since it didn't look like they would be leaving anytime soon, Axel walked over to an outdoor hot dog stand. He was soon chomping on the food and watching the two boats. After about an hour, he saw the boats starting to pull out of their docking cribs. He walked toward the end of the dock. When he saw they were clear of the other docks and turning downriver, he pulled off the clothes he'd put on over his swim trunks. He placed his clothes in a plastic bag that he attached to his swimming trunks. He was ready.

Axel followed the two boats as they cruised nicely down the river toward the English Channel. After going about five miles they passed an island and turned south. Axel saw that along the right side of the tributary, the land was like farm land. The boats traveled about half a mile down this tributary, then pulled up to a small dock. Axel swam underwater to go past this point, stopping in some thick water weeds. He watched as they loaded the boats, carrying material from a shed located about fifty feet away from the dock.

In order to conserve his energy, Axel took hold of a few stalks of the weeds, to stay in place, and floated on his back. It was good that he had a great deal of patience at times like this, because he had to lie like that for about two hours. Then he saw the men carry two drums of liquid onto the boats. He knew this was probably the kerosene or diesel fuel they needed.

He told Mark the boats would be heading upriver soon. He estimated they would be in the pickup zone in about two hours. "This will place these boats about eight miles down the Thames from the tanker and shopping center. You will need to start clearing the river then. If something changes, I will let you know."

Axel began to swim, staying about a half mile behind the boats so no one would see him. He would swim underwater for about ten minutes and then come back up to make sure he was on the right trail. One time when he popped up, he could see them pouring the fuel oil into the ammonium nitrate, and he advised Mark of that action.

Traveling at about fifteen knots, they soon came to the place where the third boat was waiting. The two yachts stopped, and the speedboat pulled up beside them to take on the pilots. While this was happening Axel gave the command to his inner self, "Axelvation three," which provided him with maximum energy. Axel could feel the jump in energy, and he dove underwater and began swimming at approximately thirty-five miles an hour up the river toward London. After swimming underwater for about ten minutes, he surfaced. He could swim on top of the water now and watch for the sites the Russian Mafia had picked out. He saw the tanker and swam past it, proceeding on to the shopping center. He could see why they picked this place. The buildings were close to the river, and he could just imagine the damage a bomb could inflict on them.

These bombs are about fifty percent more powerful than the Oklahoma City bomb, he thought. *Even If I don't get the boats to the middle of the river before the bombs are detonated, the amount of water I will have let in on the explosive packages should make them almost passive; and only the two sticks of dynamite would provide the noise.*

The more the thought about it, though, the more he realized he might have underestimated the situation. There would probably be viable explosive material, so that when the dynamite exploded, some percentage of the ANFO bomb would go off. He really had to capture that first boat quickly and get it moved to the center of the river, so he can get back to that second boat.

Looking around, he could see the lead boat coming toward him. It had a high mast with a flag flying from it. He figured they'd run up the flag so they could keep watch on the boat from a distance.

He dove below the rather slow-moving boat and punched a hole in its bottom so he could grab hold of the thing. Then he began to punch holes all along the hull until the boat was taking on water at a terrific rate. Grabbing the rudder, which was being controlled by radio, he gave it a jerk toward the middle of the river. This broke the radio control. He grabbed the back end of the boat and started kicking, propelling the boat toward the center of the river. The boat was sinking rapidly, and by the time he got to the middle of the river, it sank like a rock. Turning, he swam swiftly toward the tanker, reaching it just as the other boat did. He dove beneath the boat and ripped a hole in it. As he had done with the other boat, he grabbed the rudder and twisted it toward the center of the river. As they moved along, Axel stayed beneath it, plunging his fist into the bottom of the boat. It took on water as if it were dying of thirst. Within a minute, he was in the middle of the river and the boat was sinking fast. Axel let go and swam back toward the tanker as rapidly as he could. He had just reached it when he heard an explosion from the first boat. A few seconds later he heard an even louder explosion from the second boat. Both explosions sent huge gushes of water flying in the air.

ANFO bombs are interesting bombs, he thought. *Most bombs give off great amounts of heat when they explode. ANFO bombs are just the opposite. They get their explosive power from the expansion of gases at a terrific speed and pressure. The pressure causes everything within a critical distance to be ripped by gases with a force that makes a tornado look like a baby's balloon exploding. The two bombs going off underwater was like two gigantic farts being expelled by the biggest giant one could imagine. First there was the explosion at the river's bottom, followed by a huge bubble of water and gas rising into the air like a geyser. Boy! That water must have shot up at least one hundred feet; and this after I probably killed 90 percent of its explosive power.*

A voice on his internal phone interrupted his thoughts. "Nice job, Follower. Wait till I give the media the story about this one. It will be like we killed a huge sea monster. I'll talk to you later after the police boats on the river report in. But I'm still working on my statement to the press; any suggestions?"

"I think you play it for all it's worth. Say that you got word that there was going to be a terrorist attack carried out on the river today, and you took steps to prevent it. The less anyone knows about the details, the more advantages you will get from this. It's a winner, as we say back in the States."

"It certainly is a winner. Thanks a million, Axel. Talk to you later."

Axel returned to his apartment, quite content with the day's efforts. He called Tori and spent half an hour on the phone with her. He indicated that he might be coming home soon. He had eliminated a big problem and had some ideas to give the leaders in England to prevent future problems. He went to bed happy and slept well. The next day was a joy to behold, as he read the paper and listened to the news. One article quoted the Commissioner of Scotland Yard, Mark Wilkinson, as saying,

A terrorist threat was thwarted yesterday on the Thames River near the Newton Plaza, as law enforcement was able to detonate bombs on two boats that were part of a terrorist plot. Local authorities had been watching the activities of what they thought were a terrorist group that had been hoping for a "big bang" yesterday. All they got was a little pop, and that pop was underwater as we were able to sink both boats. Further actions will be taken in the next few days to completely eliminate the threat from this terrorist group. The people of England can be well assured that their best interests are being protected.

Axel read this and laughed out loud. As the day proceeded, he heard various reports on the news. Some of them really were exaggerations of what happened. When he went to the pub that evening, the same crew was there, and everyone was in a dour mood. There was no lifting of beers, no congratulations or cheering. It was so silent; it was if the Russian team had just lost their last hockey game in the Olympics. Ginsky made some remarks about the failure of the boats, which he couldn't explain until he got more data. Later, he told Axel he wanted him to go somewhere else with him that night. Ginsky said he had some technical issues he wanted to talk to him about. Axel wondered if they had found out that he had something to do with the failure the day before. *I better arm myself.* He raised his energy level with a silent "Axelvation two, hood down," and then bought some candy bars from a vending machine and quickly consumed them.

A few minutes later, after everyone else had left, Ginsky said he was ready to go. He told Axel he could ride with him. He'd bring Axel back later for his car. They drove in the direction of Axel's apartment in South Surrey, but passed it and headed out toward a wooded area. Soon they came to clearing where there were a lot of cars. Ginsky pulled in and parked. As he got out of the car, Axel recognized the other Russian Mafia members. He immediately turned his internal phone on and called the commissioner's cell phone. He picked up immediately.

Axel quickly explained that he had been taken to some sort of meeting, and he felt the commissioner should listen in. As soon as he had relayed that message, Ginsky got on top of his car and spoke.

"Today was a bad day for us, and I brought you together to tell you why." He turned toward Axel. "I guess you are pretty proud of yourself, Donner."

"Why should I be proud?" Axel asked.

"We saw you yesterday with the two boats on the Thames!" shouted Ginsky. "We had a scout taping the action. We expected him to see the bombs going off and creating a great deal of damage. What he saw was you doing something that the scout has not been able to properly explain to me. You were able to disarm those boats and sink them. How, we don't know. Would you be so kind as to tell us how you accomplished this feat before we give you your just award?"

"I don't know what you are talking about," answered Axel.

"Maybe this will refresh your memory," said Ginsky.

He signaled to one of the men, who was holding a video camera. He turned the camera on, and video suddenly appeared on a large screen. Axel watched as the first boat was disabled and sank, and then the second boat. He was clearly seen, although he had been moving so fast, his actions were jerky and hard to follow, while the images of the boats were clear and in focus. But it was obvious what he'd done.

"What do you say about that Donner?" asked Ginsky.

"I say that the guy on those boats wasn't me," answered Axel. "It looks like you previously took pictures of me doing something, and then superimposed those pictures onto this video of the boats. You can see that the pictures of me are not in sync with everything else. So, I guess you were able to fake these pictures to make me look bad and take the blame for your failure."

Ginsky was beside himself in anger. "That not true! Those pictures have not been tampered with. This is exactly what our man filmed. My question is how did you do this?"

Axel smiled and said, "You can go on with this charade as long as you want, but you aren't going to be able to explain your failure of yesterday. You just want your Russian brothers to believe that I was the one who caused this failure. You are the failure. In fact, all of you are the failures. You live in a country that gives you everything. You live here better than you would if you were back home. The only reason you're here is because the good Russians back in your country wouldn't have you. You were all losers in Russia, and now you are losers here. And I would lift my beer to that if I had a beer."

Ginsky was now red in the face with anger and embarrassment. This had been Axel's intent. Ginsky could no longer contain himself, and he reached behind his back and grabbed his gun; pointing it at Axel he said, "Tell them the truth. Tell them the truth or I will blow your head off."

Axel looked up at Ginsky. "The truth is that you are a loser, and they are losers."

Ginsky began firings at Axel, and so did most of the other Mafia members. A couple of them shot at Ginsky instead, and he fell from the car onto the ground. As the bullets bounced off his body, Axel rushed at the nearest person, grabbing his neck and twisting it as he pulled his gun from him. He began counting as he went from one man to the next chasing them down. He leaped up on the one car and grabbed one of the men who had been firing at him and took his gun and swung it against his head and down he fell. He took the gun and began firing at others; still counting. It didn't take long and there were all fifteen of them scattered about the place. Axel looked and there were no more standing. Axel stood there in silence, looking at the carnage that lay around the lot. *I wonder how these men could get to this level of violence. How could they come to this country and live off it for so long yet not feel some allegiance toward it. All they felt was greediness. I am glad I was able to stop them.*

Finally he said over the phone, "Did you hear that, Mark? Did you hear that?"

"Yes, I heard, Axel. I am sorry you had to do that, but you had no choice. I will send out some squad cars so we can clean up this mess. Someone will give you a ride back to your car."

"You've got a lot of cars to deal with here too. I am going to smash the video camera and destroy the video so no one can see this."

"No, no, Axel. Don't destroy that video. I would like to have it and show it to the prime minister. I also want to send a copy to your president to show what one good American did for England. Will you do that?"

"I will give the video to you tomorrow. But I don't want anyone other than the people you named to ever see it. The big advantage I have. is my anonymity. As long as I am unknown, I am able to move within groups and take actions wherever needed. I can speak their languages and become one of them without their knowing it. This is the only way I can use my enormous capabilities. I am the perfect spy."

"I understand, Axel. It's been a pleasure watching, or rather, listening, to you perform. You have amazed me, and I appreciate having had the chance to work with you. I am very proud that your many talents and strengths are not held by those that would be against the good of people. In this case, the good has vanquished the evil. Take care."

Axel took the video out of the video camera. A zippered leather case lay on the ground. He put the video in the case and then sat down to await the arrival of the English police.

The Follower Frees the U.S. Students from Iranian Jail

The next day, Axel took the leather case to Scotland Yard. Soon he was in the commissioner's office, handing the case to Mark and he said, "I hope you enjoy the film. I did."

"I hope that one day I will be able to show it to the people who work here at Scotland Yard. I will wait till the time is right and you have received your just reward. This has been an experience I will remember all the days of my life. If I can do anything for you, I would be happy to if I am able."

"You might be able to help me do something. It's something that has been digging in my mind for some time now. About six months ago, there were five American college students spending some time in Iraq studying various things, now that the country was fairly stable. One weekend they traveled to the border between Iraq and Iran, and they were sized by Iranian soldiers and taken prisoners. They were considered spies and are going to go on trial soon. When I was in Iraq, I wanted the U.S. Air Force to fly to the border and drop me off, so I could make my way into Iran and free those students. However, at the time there was a significant task that the agency wanted me to pursue in North Korea. Ever since then, I have felt that I let those students down. The gift you could give me and those students would be to help me sneak into Iran. I know you will have to get permission from the United States to accomplish this, but it would be a worthwhile venture."

Mark stared up at the ceiling for a minute, obviously in deep thought. Finally, he said, "I know where you are coming from, and I will do what I can to help you. I must call Prime Minister Benson. He is the only one who could make this happen. If he can do it, he will. Let me make a call."

Mark soon had the prime minister on the phone. He relayed Axel's request, and the two men talked for about fifteen minutes. After he hung up, Mark said to Axel, "The prime minister says he can get you on an RAF flight to Baghdad. Apparently there's an American colonel in Baghdad that knows you, and he said he can get you to the Iranian border. But he can't promise that he can get you back."

Axel's eyes lit up. "Sold; get me there and let me worry about getting back. I will find a way for the six of us to get back. When can you do this?"

"You can fly out tonight and be in Baghdad by morning." "That's fantastic," said Axel. "Where do I pick up the flight?"

"I will drive you to the airfield. It's just outside of London. All you have to do is get together what you want to take with you."

"I have everything I need in my car."

As promised, Axel was in Baghdad by the next morning, and Colonel Rumsey of the American Air Force was there to meet him.

"Axel," Rumsey said, "I never thought you would make it back here so quickly. I know you were disappointed the last time you were here that we couldn't provide you the favor you asked, but today we can. We have a helicopter that is waiting to take you to the general area where those students were captured."

Before long Axel was aboard a copter with Captain Duncan, who had flown him by jet several months back. He dropped Axel in the vicinity of where the military believed the five students had been captured. Axel thanked the captain and said he hoped to see him again in a few days. As Duncan took off, Axel gave his system the command, "Axelvation two, hood down." After eating a couple of candy bars, he began east toward Iran. As he walked, he ate more candy bars. He had just finished one when he heard the sound of voices. He started running in their direction. He didn't go far before he saw about ten soldiers walking along with their automatic guns. He stopped running and walked swiftly in their direction. One of the men shouted and pointed at Axel. The other men turned toward him, all of them pointing their weapons. Axel kept walking toward them. Several of them shouted "Halt" in Farsi. He pretended he didn't understand and kept walking. The soldiers surrounded him, and two of them grabbed him and tossed him to the ground. They frisked him, taking his wallet, and then pulled him to his feet. They kept asking Axel questions, and he kept pretending he didn't understand them. They grabbed his hands and put them behind his back, tying them together with a rope, and then headed toward their main camp.

Axel was happy to be escorted, and hoped that he would end up in the same place as the five students had been taken. After walking for about half a mile, they met up with a troop-carrying truck. He was thrown in the back, and the troops got in with him.

"Now we have six of them," one of the soldiers said. "The commander will be happy. This one is not a student, and he might give us more leverage with the fascist American troops."

Axel was now certain he would be taken to the same jail that the students were in. They drove about ten miles, and when the truck slowed down Axel could tell that they had reached some sort of compound. The truck took several turns and then halted.

The soldiers jumped out, two of them pulling Axel out. They dragged him to a small building. Inside the building, he was taken to an office. An officer sat behind a desk, and Axel could tell by his uniform that he had a high rank. The officer looked at Axel, and then gestured for the two soldiers to release him. They did, moving to the side of the room.

The officer returned his gaze to his paperwork and ignored Axel for at least five minutes. Then he looked up and said in Farsi, "And where did you come from, my friend?"

Axel pretended not to understand, and the officer returned his attention to his paperwork. Another five minutes passed, and then the officer shocked Axel by looking up and saying in perfect English, "And where did you come from, my friend?"

Axel took a few seconds to absorb his shock and finally said, "I was just walking along the route where those five American students had been abducted to see if there was any reason that they should have been taken captive."

"Did you satisfy your curiosity?" questioned the officer.

"Not quite," responded Axel. "I was just walking along like I suppose they were when your soldiers grabbed them. I can see that you had no reason. I can see that you have no basis for declaring them spies. They are just students."

The officer looked back at his paperwork and wrote something. "Your timing is good," he said. "I am just making out the paperwork to have them sent to Tehran early tomorrow. Now I just added that you will be joining them. What is your name?"

Axel laughed and said, "My name is Puddin' Tain. Ask me again and I'll tell you the same.'"

The officer didn't think this was funny, He made a motion with his head, and one of the soldiers came forward and punched Axel in the face. Axel pretended it hurt him and fell to the floor. The soldier lifted him back to his feet.

"Once more, what is your name, idiot?"

"Same answer sir," responded Axel.

"So you think that was funny," the officer said. "You think you are a comedian. I bet by the time you leave here tomorrow, you won't be so funny and so happy. I will put down on the paperwork 'American Comedian' until we have more information about you." He looked at the soldier and said in Farsi, "Take everything he has in his pockets and let's see who he is."

The other soldier stepped forward, holding up Axel's wallet. "I took this from him when we captured him. His name is Donner Poole, and he is British."

"So, you are not an American. You are a citizen of that other fascist country. Now we will have two countries saying that none of you have been spying on Iran. Tomorrow you will be on your way to Tehran and you won't enjoy the rest of your life. I guarantee this. You know, you had me fooled. I could have sworn you were an American. I went to school in the States. You don't have an English accent."

"I was born in Germany," Axel said. "I moved to England about ten years ago. I learned English at school in Germany, and we had an American teacher."

"Very interesting," said the officer. "I learned my English in the States. I spent almost ten years there. I can say I enjoyed most of my time there. We shall see if you enjoy the next thirty or so years here in this country. Between Germany, England, and Iran, you will have quite an education. I would give a few gold coins to see how you talk when you get out of prison. Your accent will be all screwed up." He gestured to Axel to come to the desk, saying he needed to sign something.

"Why should I sign that?" Axel asked.

"Because it will reduce the amount of pain you will go through from this day on," he said.

Axel laughed. "Not today," he said. "I am not interested in your paperwork or making your job easier. It's too bad you didn't stay in the United States and learned how to be human. You still have a chance. Just let me and the five students go home. We would like that, and perhaps you could come with us."

The officer scowled in anger. He shouted to the soldiers, "Take this nut out of here and put him in a cell next to the other nuts."

The soldiers grabbed Axel by the arms and pulled him out of the office.

Axel was taken to a room in the rear of the building. Two cages were at opposite ends of the room from each other. Three students in one "cell" and two were in the other. Axel was placed in the one that had two people in it. The room also held two desks, and a soldier sat at each desk. It looked as the each soldier was responsible for one of the cells. Axel listened as the soldiers talked to each other. They said they were pleased to have taken another prisoner they could use to bargain with the fascist countries.

Axel turned to his cellmates, a man and a woman, and told them he was there to get them out.

"Whatever I do," he said, "I want you to stay in these cells so that you will be safe. When I act, tell the other prisoners to keep their patience and stay in their cell until I come back for them. We have to do this rapidly while it is still light, so we can make it back to Iraq during the daytime."

Axel turned his attention to the nearest guard and waved his hands, calling him over. When the guard came over, Axel pointed at the bars of the cell. As the guard stared at him, Axel grabbed two of the bars and pulled them apart. Stunned, the man turned to the other guard and called him over. When the second guard came over, he stared in astonishment as well. Axel pulled the bars farther apart, and then he grabbed the two astonished guards and smacked their heads together. As the men fell to the floor, he pushed his way out of the cell.

The five students were also staring in amazement at him. He reminded them to stay in the cells, saying he would be back in less than half an hour. Crossing the room to the door, he said internally, "Axelvation three, hood down" and pulled the door open. As he ran down the hall, he smacked the head of every soldier he came upon, knocking them out. At the end of the hall, he opened the door to the officer's room. He was still sitting at the desk. He looked up, and his eyes widened in fear. Axel grabbed him with one hand and lifted him, holding him in the air above his head.

"Call in your soldiers from outside," he told the man.

The officer didn't need that direction; he was already hollering for help. In seconds, Axel heard men running into the building. He threw the officer against the wall and grabbed the first man who entered the room, knocking him out and taking his AK-47. As the rest of the troops poured into the room, Axel started shooting. He was suddenly reminded of the one time he had gone duck hunting. It had been foggy, and as the ducks answered his duck call, they flew below the fog. He couldn't miss them. He stopped firing, since it felt wrong to kill an animal that had no defense. But now he was taking down soldiers who would be glad to kill him and the five students.

Soon, no more soldiers came into the room. Axel ran to the open door and outside. There were still a few dozen soldiers out there, but when they realized their guns had no effect on him, they took off. All of a sudden it was quiet. Axel stood there and surveyed the total area. The soldiers were gone, but there were several trucks. He returned to the office, just as the officer retrieved a gun. He fired at Axel, emptied the gun with no results. His face showed confusion.

Axel grabbed him by the throat with his right hand and took the gun from him with his left hand. "You were right. I am an American, and I came to take home my fellow Americans. Those are the last words you are going to hear. You should have stayed in the States."

He squeezed the man's throat, and the officer dropped as dead as the gun beside him.

Axel ran back to the cells. He took the keys off one of the guards and opened the cells. The students were cheering, even though they couldn't believe their eyes.

"I believe all of the soldiers are gone," Axel said, "but you should be aware and watch for anything. If you see anything at all, I want you to shout. Follow me."

The five of them followed him like hound dogs after prey. As they ran toward the front of the building, they stared in shock at all of the dead soldiers. Once outside they stopped and looked around. Axel told them to get into the nearest truck. One man got in the passenger seat, while the other students got in the back. Axel reached under the steering wheel, exposed the ignition wires, and hot-wired the truck. Once he started the truck, he turned it in the direction he thought they had come from. As he drove, he internally phoned Commander Rumsey.

"This is Axel," he said when the commander answered. "I am in a truck with the five students and heading toward the border. It is about ten miles, as best I can figure. Can you have a helicopter that is big enough to carry six people near the location where you dropped me off this morning?"

"Yes, we will do that," said the commander, "but I don't know how fast I can get there."

"We will keep heading toward the border. I keep this line open and keep you advised of where we are. When you find the copter to pick us up, just let us know."

"You got it," Commander Rumsey said. . "I just can't believe you got those people out of there so quickly. This is unbelievable. Are you sure?"

"Yes, I am as sure as I am talking to you. These students don't know I am talking to you, so they will be surprised when a copter picks us up. But please hurry."

Axel pressed on the accelerator, driving as fast as the truck and the road would allow him. In less than half an hour, he was at the place where the troops had loaded him onto the truck. He parked, told the students to get out, and they started walking to west. They had walked for about twenty minutes when one of the students said, "I think we are in Iraq now."

"You are probably right," said Axel. "However, I want you all to keep close to me and keep walking."

He had just got the words out of his mouth when he heard a rifle shot. He shouted to the students to get down.

"Lie flat on the ground," he said. "I will go and take care of the problem."

As he ran in the direction of the shot, other shots rang out. *More border control,* he thought. *I don't know how many of them there are, but it is probably about the size of the group that picked me up this morning.* Meanwhile, Commander Rumsey was asking him what was going on. Axel told him they'd run into a border patrol and he was going to take them out. He added that the students had crossed over into Iraq.

Axel was now close enough to see the soldiers shooting at him. Bullets kept hitting him, and his shirt and pants were almost gone from all the holes that were in them. He reached the first soldier he saw and grabbed his gun, turning it on him and pulling the trigger. He shot the other soldiers until he ran out of bullets, and then used the other soldiers' guns to crack their heads open. When he'd taken care of all of the soldiers, he began running back toward the students.

"How are we doing on getting a copter here?" he asked the commander.

"One is on its way," Rumsey said. "ETA ten minutes."

"I will get the students to keep walking," said Axel. "The farther they get from the border, the better."

Axel and the students continued walking west, until they reached a flat area that would be a good place for a copter to set down. Soon, they heard the familiar sound of one of a large helicopter approaching. Within a few minutes, the pilot set the copter down, and the students and Axel ran to it.

"That was great heading," Axel said to the pilot.

"We were homing in on your phone signal, and the satellite was sending us information. How could we miss?"

It wasn't long before they were at the airfield and being met by the commander. As the students were taken into a hangar, Axel told Rumsey he wanted to return to England.

"I haven't finished my assignment there. Besides, I don't want to be around when the media show up and begin asking how I was able to get these people out of there. And I could use a new pair of pants and a shirt. These have been torn up with bullet holes."

The Commander stepped back and looked at Axel. "I can't believe what you can do," he said. "You must have been shot twenty-five times. I don't understand this." He paused and then said, "Come with me and I will get you some clothes, and then we'll see what I can do to get you back to England. I think you need some rest."

Rumsey took Axel to his office, where he got him some clothes and then talked to his counterpart in England on the phone. They talked for about fifteen minutes, and then Rumsey told Axel he'd arranged a trip back to England for him on another RAF jet. "It will be here by tomorrow morning, so you can get a good night's sleep. You earned it."

Axel did have a good night's sleep for about six hours, and then thoughts about going back to England woke him. He needed to reconnect with those two guys, Arnie and Maxie, who had showed some interest in violent protests about British soldiers fighting in the Middle East. He needed to find out if they were still serious.

When the digital clock by his bed read. 6:17 am, he decided to get up and take a shower. As he was showering, he thought about Tori. *I surely miss the showers with Tori. If I don't find any major problems in the UK, I am going to push for returning to my teaching and my woman.*

Axel felt quite rested as he ate breakfast with one of the officers, Captain Hill, whom he had met months ago. He knew that the plane taking him back to England would be arriving in less than an hour. He had become anxious, ever since he'd thought about those two guys back in England and about Tori. He missed his teaching, especially since it gave him positive interactions with young students and their bright minds and their openness about their problems and their futures. Most of those interactions were one hundred and eighty degrees different from those he'd had with other people recently. The students were positive, not only about their futures, but also about the world in general. The fighting in the Mideast was sort of secondary to them. They didn't like the war, but it was not on their priority list. They had a fresh outlook. Maybe one would call it naiveté, since they hadn't experienced any of the world's more serious problems. To them, history was something you read about in the books at school. They personally hadn't experienced anything like a war.

Axel's thoughts were interrupted by the officer's cell phone ringing. He spoke briefly into the phone, and then looked at Axel and said, "Your taxi has arrived."

Shortly, Axel was on the RAF fighter jet speeding rapidly across Europe. The flight took about as long as a plane flight from New York to Los Angeles. The pilot was able to talk to Axel on the intercom, and this became an interesting discussion at times. The pilot pointed out various landmarks they passed over. At one point he said to Axel, "I am the pilot that flew you to Iraq the other day. Did you remember that?" Axel said he did. Then the pilot asked Axel how he'd mission had turned out. Axel decided to not answer that and just remained quiet.

The pilot went on, "My CO said you had a successful mission, and the scuttlebutt back at our base in England was that the five students who were being held hostage were freed by an Englishman and they are saying that is you. Is that a fact?"

Axel said he got lucky, but the pilot said that everyone back at the base didn't think it was luck. "They think you have something going for you. Do you?"

Axel smiled. "Yes, I have something going for me. I am an offshoot of an accident my mother was in before I was born. I guess that's where the luck began."

"That's great," remarked the pilot. "I hope you keep your luck going for my country."

"I do too," commented Axel. "You have a great country, and what you are doing for it by flying these fighter jets in Iraq and Afghanistan makes you one of the heroes of your country. Hopefully those wars will soon be over, and your country and my country can go about living peacefully. I hope the fanatics of this world soon learn that they can live in peace and no one is trying to take anything from them."

The rest of the trip was full of conversation about the good and the bad in the world, and before he knew it the plane was starting down for a landing. As Axel got out of the plane, he saluted the pilot and said, "Keep your country safe. You are one of its heroes."

Axel started his days back in England by visiting the pubs again. This time he was interested in finding Arnie and Maxie and seeing if they had made any moves toward the upsetting of the morale of this island nation.

The second night he saw Arnie in a pub and asked him where his buddy Maxie was.

"Oh, he'll be around," said Arnie. "He may be a little late tonight, depending on how long he had to work. He has a job now and it has funny hours. Some days he is off at four o'clock, and some days he works until midnight."

Axel thought it was good that Maxie was working. If he remembered right, Maxie had been out of work before, and that got him kind of pissed off. *Being out of work is a pisser,* thought Axel. *Sometimes I think that is the problem with the people that are bitching. They have too much time on their hands and no money to spend. Being out of work is a real morale killer. It's that way back home also. These highly industrialized countries like the UK and the U.S. are tuned to work. Many people in poorer countries grew up with no jobs; their work is finding enough food to keep them alive. I feel sorry for those countries and their people. There really is a big gap between how the heads of those countries and how the common people live. I think the top people in those countries live at levels that are as good as those in America, but the common people have nothing compared to what we have at home.*

Axel drank his beer, continuing his conversation with Arnie as he waited to see if Maxie was going to show

After a while, Arnie jumped up and said, "Hey Maxie, over here." Axel looked in the direction Arnie was waving, and sure enough, there was Maxie. He waved for him to come over where they were having their beers.

"Come on, Maxie," Axel shouted. "I'm buying tonight."

"That's great, Donner, because I haven't got paid yet," Maxie shouted back.

They all sat down and discussed the world and what was going on. "Are you still angry with your country and want to bomb a few places to stir it up?" asked Axel.

"No, I think I am at peace with myself and with my country," said Maxie.

"What, no more assholes to blow up?" asked Axel with a smile.

"Oh, I am sure there are a lot of assholes to blow up, but I am not going to be the one doing it, right, Arnie?"

"Maxie and I have gained a religion," said Arnie.

"Oh, and what might that be?" asked Axel.

"Well, last week there was this incident on the Thames River, where some real asshole Russian mafia guys wanted to blow up a ship full of oil and a shopping plaza. The police stopped them. Maxie and I talked about that for days and came to the conclusion that we don't want any assholes trying to screw our country. We decided that we live in a great country, and if our leaders want to fight a war in Afghanistan, it must be for a good reason. We decided that they knew more about what was important for our country than we did. They got facts that we don't have. So we decided to support our government and quit bitching. Now when we hear anyone bitching, we tell them to go join the Russian mafia and see where that gets them."

As Axel listened to this, he thought about how last week's antics had paid off more than he'd thought. That meant I didn't have to worry about the real owners of this country. People like Arnie and Maxie were the owners, and now they knew it.

"That's great, guys," he said. "You can't believe how happy that makes me feel. I heard about those Russians last week, and I couldn't stop listening to the radio and watching the Telly. I was so happy for our country. Let's drink to that."

Axel held his beer up high, and so did Maxie and Arnie. The rest of the night was quite nice, and Axel went home half-tanked from all the beer he'd drunk and had to pay for.

When he got back to his apartment, he was so euphoric that he felt he had to call Tori. When she answered her phone, he shouted, "And how are you, sweetie?"

"Axel, have you been drinking?" she asked.

"I certainly have, dearie. And when I am in this good a mood, I felt I should share it with someone I love. So, I called you right away."

That nice answer was enough to allay anymore criticism from her. "And why are you been so happy?" she asked.

"I am happy because I did some good things in the past week, and I am happy because the English people are good people, and I am happy because I am going to tell them I want to go home."

"Oh Axel, are you really coming home? I miss you so much. Life is dead without you around."

"Yes," Axel replied. "Tomorrow I am going to talk to the prime minister and the Commissioner of Scotland Yard, and tell them they have good people here and that I should go home."

He and Tori talked for about half an hour about what was going on in California. After the phone call Axel was happy to go to bed. He slept well that night.

The next day Axel called Prime Minister Benson's office as soon as he could. Benson's secretary said the prime minister was in a meeting, but she would have him call as soon as he could. That satisfied Axel, and he called Commissioner Wilkinson. Mark was available, and Axel began the conversation by telling the commissioner that, in Axel's opinion, he didn't have to worry about the general public.

"I believe that the general public in your country is like the general public in my country. They like to talk and bitch. They have grown up with this kind of background and culture. They know they won't get shot for talking freely. They feel that this is their right, but they also love their country. It's their way of letting off steam. Their bitching is their way of living and enjoying life. Some of their bitching relates to England sending troops to the Midwest. This festers with them, and it comes out in their evening beer-drinking sessions. There are not many places in the world where you can speak your piece without getting into trouble. I have talked to a variety of English citizens. They sometimes have negative opinions about their country, but as soon as anyone else attacks their country, they change their stance and stick up for the UK. There is a problem here that you probably know more about than I do. You have many foreign nationals, people who have come from other countries. They are torn between the culture they were born into and the culture they now have to learn to live with. They may not always know that sometimes people bitching just to let off steam. They might take the remarks seriously and think that there are really people here who want to overthrow the government. Remember, they came from countries where that is the standard MO. 'Overthrow the tyrants that are running our country.' This is what they are used to."

"The Russians we just handled is not an example of this. They were here for a purpose. They wanted to be able to have access to the opium fields of Afghanistan. They wanted the British and Americans out of Afghanistan so they could do get back into the drug trade. This was not a cultural thing, this was a greed thing. However, this is a close example of what I mean. I believe there are pubs that cater to certain cultures. Not because of their own choosing, but because a few of those people started to drink in a given pub and kept bringing their friends in. After a couple of years, the culture of that pub is the culture of the people living, drinking, and complaining in it. These can be dangerous, festering nests of people with the same outlook on life. For example, let's assume that one of the pubs is primarily patronized by people from Iran who became English citizens. These people have great pressures put on them by their religion and by the fact that they are surrounded every evening with people from this same culture. They hear local citizens bitching about the war in Afghanistan and the fact that they believe that Iran is helping the Taliban or Al-Qaeda. These people gathering in the pubs are the ones that should be monitored. There only has to be a couple out of hundreds that take the evening bullshitting and talking seriously to result in a problem. You have a tough job to carry out here.

"Much of the talk of these foreign nationals is no different from that of the standard native British citizens, but there is pressure on them due to their culture. They begin to take their talks seriously, and something can come of this. All you can do is have undercover agents participating in the evening drinking sessions. One agent in each of the main pubs for a length of time will find maybe one out of every thirty pubs with dangerous people. This is the place to catch dangerous seeds being sown. It's a tough job, because the agent really has to differentiate between 'just talk' and real talk. That's about as good as I can sum it up. Besides that, I would like to go back home."

Mark was impressed with this summation from Axel. "I am happy to hear that you think the general public is in tune with what our government has been doing. You have been working the grassroots of our society, and I am happy to hear they are generally happy with their government. Of course, I am not really part of the government per se. The duties of Scotland Yard do cross over international lines, but we have nothing to do with formulating laws or foreign policy. We enforce the laws and protect people's rights. We do have a strong hand in providing information to our government about potential international problems, and sometimes in helping to solve them. Your comments today fit in the category of information about our citizens relative to their feelings about the stableness of our fundamental way of life. For that I am thankful to you. Your comments will be just as meaningful to Prime Minister Benson, of course, and I would expect you will be giving him your impressions."

"Yes sir. I already have a call in to Mr. Benson."

Mark felt Axel should actually see the prime minister, and not just talk to him. He put Axel on hold and called the prime minister's office. When he got back on with Axel, he said the prime minister very much wanted to see Axel, and had set time aside that day at 4:00 pm.

"Thank you very much, sir," said Axel. "That will make my trip here complete."

"Before you leave, I want to tell you that, besides the work you did here, which was very well received by all those concerned, those of us who knew of your trip to Iran were very impressed with the expediency with which you handled that matter. That was marvelous, and I wish I could tell more people here at Scotland Yard about it. Your country owes you a large debt of gratitude; besides the debt those students must owe you. I was very proud that our country had a part in getting you there and getting you back."

Axel thanked him for those compliments, adding that he had been greatly relieved to have the opportunity to handle the situation.

When Axel met with the prime minister, their discussion was similar to the one Axel had had with Commissioner Wilkinson. Benson told Axel he was going to give President Hargrove a thank you call for Axel's services.

"Your services for our country were extraordinary. I don't see how we would have accomplished this without your assistance. I will be telling President Hargrove that he is lucky to have someone like you who can infiltrate dangerous groups like this. They don't know you are there until it's too late for them. And 'too late' means that you snuff out the problem quickly and quietly. That's a rare talent. Thank you."

Axel Returns to the States and Teaching

It seemed like only a few hours ago that Axel was wondering when he would see Tori, since she was about six thousand miles away from London. Now he was halfway home to her, since he was at the agency in Washington D C. As he'd flown over on a British jet, he'd called her on his internal phone.

"Hi there, sweetie. I'm on my way to the States. I won't make it to California today, but at least we'll be in the same country."

"Why won't they let you come home?" she asked.

"They want me to stop at the Agency so I can give them a report. But I should be out of there by tomorrow and heading home."

"That gives me chills, just knowing you will be home," she said. "I can't stand these long trips away. We are too young to miss the early parts of our life."

"I know, honey, but you and I knew it might be this way. I actually see the light at the end of the tunnel. I think these things go in spurts. I know I am going to be in our country for the foreseeable future. Anyhow, I am going to get some sleep. I am halfway across the Atlantic Ocean and am quite tired."

Kim met him at Dulles and whisked him through customs. As they walked out to the parking lot and approached Kim's car, Axel could see someone was sitting in the car. It was his brother Adam.

"Hi there, brother," Adam greeted him. "Have a nice trip?"

"Yeah, I had a great trip. I could learn to love England and their pubs."

As they drove to the agency building, both Adam and Kim said they were proud of what he had done in Iran to free those students.

"Also," said Kim, "the British prime minister sent an e-mail to me thanking me and the agency for the valuable service you provided his country. A copy was sent to President Hargrove, so I would expect you will be hearing from him soon. The prime minister said that what you accomplished probably saved many lives. He detailed some of your actions, and was especially emphatic about the damage that would have occurred if that oil tanker had been destroyed. He commented that we are fortunate to have a 'weapon' like you in these days of possible terrorist threats."

Axel felt a little embarrassed by those comments, but was happy to hear that his actions had been appreciated. As they got close to the agency, Kim explained why he'd wanted Axel to come there first.

"I wanted to talk to you about some plans we have that may involve you in the future. I just wanted to review them with you and see what comments you have. Also, I wanted to go over some problems we have been seeing here, and sort of set you up for some of your next possible actions."

"Oh no," said Axel. "I need to go home and see my woman and get to the school and teach some young people about what makes the world go around."

"I know," said Kim. "I want you to have some time off from all this excitement. All I want to do is provide you with some information and have you mull it around in your head, because we have great confidence in your recommendations."

Once they were in Kim's office, refreshing themselves with coffee and donuts, Kim began to talk. "We have reviewed the various options that we feel terrorists have and sort of classified them. There are four obvious ones."

He walked over to a board hanging on a wall and wrote them down:

1. Hydrogen peroxide/acetone bombs
2. Ammonium nitrate/fuel bombs
3. Grenades or other explosives in gas tanks
4. Poison gas of different types
5. Biological weapons
6. Airplane disasters like the 9/11 incident

    7. Dirty bomb—radioactive material

    8. Atomic Bomb

    9. Human bombs—IED and a person

Kim discussed each of these and pointed out how each was covered by federal or military programs. He related, as an example, that threats like atomic bombs were not an agency matter, but handled by the nation's nuclear programs. After detailing where the main responsibilities lay for each of these, he focused on the ones he felt were of prime interest to the agency. The two major ones the agency could effectively handle were those that related to poisonous substances or biological weapons.

"These could lead to horrific number of deaths and they don't require a huge number of terrorists to be involved. In addition, companies and universities involved in cutting-edge research of new biological material could fall into these categories. The methodologies we have used in the past relate to the elements of search, discover, analyze, and take action.

"Search involves just what it says. The agency monitors activities concerning poisons and biological weapons. The reason the agency is heavily involved is due to the expertise we have in these areas. Our previous experiences with the terrorist groups working out of Baltimore, the Silicon Valley, and Boston are examples of how the agency has handled these types of issues. It is believed that the agency's expertise provided a tangible capability for reviewing what universities and companies in this country are working on. We should continue this surveillance, looking for evidence of poison or biological work being carried out by research organizations. From this information, it will be the agency's responsibility to categorize that work with respect to their capabilities and potential of being dangerous. The laboratories of the universities provide an excellent work area for the development of new and advanced technologies that could provide reason for concern. The agency is responsible for searching for evidence of any outside work being done in the universities. Universities contain our best and brightest young people, and it is possible that others outside of the university might attempt to use these idealistic young people to work in areas that they might not consider dangerous to the country. There are two possible areas that should receive the agency's initial attention. These are in the medical, chemical, biological, and physics departments of these schools. This is not to say it won't happen in other departments of these schools, but it would seem that any advanced work on poisons or biological threats would occur in the above disciplines.

"The second phase is to recognize what you have found as being a threat to the nation. If there is any question, the information must be forwarded to the agency, so we can make any further determinations. If the finding is verified as a danger, the next step is the action required. It may not be obvious what action is to be taken, since some actions could result in undesirable results. Remember, we are talking about subtle things, such as biological threats. Improper action can result in the biological hazard spreading. To prevent mistakes, all actions will be reviewed by our agency and possibly by other federal agencies to determine what actions are to be taken."

After Dr. Kim has reviewed the areas that the agency felt had the prime responsibilities, he asked Axel if he had any questions or concerns. Axel said he understood the situation and intended to go back to teaching. "I feel that I will be in the area of the country where these things might fester. Northern California is full of technical people, technical schools, and technical companies that are at the leading edge of work on these sorts of things. We have already seen where two companies, one in Silicon Valley and one in Boston, that were started by people coming out of the universities and were prone to these kinds of issues. We need to be more sensitive to these issues than we have been in the past.

"Right now I am tired and can't think sharply," Axel remarked. "Maybe after I get back home and relax my mind and get in a groove with my teaching, I will be more inclined to notice little subtleties. The areas you are discussing are not obvious and will require close scrutiny to ascertain whether their work is what they claim it to be."

Kim agreed and after the meeting was over, Adam took Axel to the airport for his flight to California. When Axel was ready to enter the terminal, Adam told him that he really was glad that Axel had found a place in the agency while being able to carry on his work with the university.

"You are the one responsible for that," Axel said. "If it hadn't been for your actions a couple of years ago, I would have enjoyed the normal life of a teacher. Since then, I have enjoyed many experiences I would never have confronted in the university. They have been wonderful experiences."

Axel looked at Adam as he spoke, and it was like looking in a mirror. *What a wonderful gift,* he thought. *I forget with all these things happening and how I have been blessed, but one of the greatest gifts was having a twin* brother like Adam. We have grown up loving each other and understanding each other. Not many people have this gift. I never had to look for someone to play with or discuss kid things with. I was lucky enough to have been born a twin, a built-in person to do these things with. I am so happy for him and Laura and their child. He has found a niche in his work with the agency, and he found me a niche with the agency; how lucky I am, and how fortunate for Adam.

Adam helped Axel get his bags, which included some gifts Axel had found to take back to Tori. "See you soon," Adam said. "Give Tori a hug for us."

When the plane was landing in the San Francisco International Airport, Axel could hardly remain seated. Once off the plane, he ran toward the baggage area, hoping to see his Tori. His luggage was secondary; he only wanted to see that lovely woman of his dreams. When he got to the baggage area, he couldn't see Tori. *She's probably parking,* he thought. *It was too bad no one could wait right outside the terminal for arriving passengers anymore.* Just then he saw this gorgeous woman coming through the door. He thought, *she's more beautiful than I remember. How could that be? I have only been gone for a few weeks.* He ran toward her, calling her name. As he had always down before, he grabbed her by the waist and lifted her above his head, and then slowly let her down till her lips met his lips. He held her that way for almost a minute. When he released her, he said, "God, you taste better than you have ever before. Did you change your lipstick, or is it me that has changed?"

"No, Axel," she said. "I have been using the same lipstick for years. It's just the amount of time since you tasted it that makes the difference."

"Whatever, it's a wonderful taste and I sure missed it."

He grabbed his bags, and soon they were on their way home. Axel could hardly wait to hold her in his arms with no clothes on either of them; just skin to skin. Sure enough, when they entered the house, they held each other in an embrace of love, even as they stripped the clothes off each other. Then they were in bed and taking advantage of all the things they remembered that the other one enjoyed. Axel had his head down between her lovely thighs, his tongue making love to her "little man in the house" situated in that lovely clit.

Soon she said, "Axel, put it in me. I can't stand this anymore. I want you in me."

He shifted his lips to her nipples, which stood tightly up in the air as if waiting for him. He took her nipples in his mouth and she took his tool into her body.

"God," he moaned. "It's like I was made to fit in you."

There was no feeling like this as he slowly rocked his body back and forth. Tori came almost immediately and told him not to stop.

"The second climax is always better than the first," she whispered in his ear.

They continued their lovemaking until they both were overcome by the energy being released with each thrust. Axel lay back and looked up at the ceiling. *Why did we have to wait a year to get married?* he wondered. *I want to be married with her now and have a child we can love together. I guess she is right that I am away much of the time and she could tire of this. But you would think* that she enjoys my returns so much that this makes up for the time I am gone.

"How can we wait so long to get married?" he asked.

Tori didn't speak. After a few moments of silence, she said, "Axel, you know that we agreed on that for a reason. You have been taking off on adventures and helping this country. That's a noble calling, and I didn't want to be the one that stops it. We made each other a promise that we have to endure it for a year to see if we were made for each other. It has been a little over two years, mainly because of the duties you had to perform for this country. I understand that and I still love you and you me. We have to see if we both can take it and then let nature take its place. We are both strong people and we can last out our anxieties. I love you, Axel, and that won't change."

"I love you, Tori, and that won't change either, but it has put a lot of pressure on us. I miss you so much, and when I get back I can't get enough of you. Maybe not being married does put pressure on us and makes these days we have together very special. I just hope it never changes after we are married."

"Amen," said Tori.

With the start of the new school year, Axel returned to his teaching of various subjects related to biology, stem cells, and microbiology. It almost seemed new to him. *It's almost like going backward,* he thought. *What I am teaching is new to the students, but isn't new to me. It seems like this subject matter happened a long time ago, and when I am on my assignments it is like they are in the right time zone. I like to teach, but I wish I could be teaching what I learned lately in my experiences. I guess I will settle down after a week or so. The subjects I teach are really in the highlight of the news now. There are many new companies that have started up on the peninsula, especially in the bay area. Some of the companies have gone public after a couple of years of developing their products. This area is like a spawning ground. It has the great schools like Stanford; the University of California schools at Berkeley, San Francisco, and Davis; San Jose State University; and many junior colleges. In addition, they get the best students from all over the world. If there are any developments in biological weapons or poisons, it probably will come from here. I have to be sensitive to what goes on at UC and Stanford. I have to visit the other universities around here, and see what they are working on. Not the major research, but the side products that bright students are working on their own.*

One of the subjects Axel taught dealt with viruses. This he had found to be interesting, since he kept up with all the new findings on viruses including the one called "swine flu." or H1N1. This particular virus attached the lungs, and many of the people who got the flu died. They hadn't really died from the flu, but from the collateral damage brought on by the flu. Some of the patients succumbed to pneumonia or some bacterial disease brought on by their weakness caused by the flu.

The subject matter one day moved to the pandemic that occurred in 1918 and 1919, killed as many as fifty million people in the world. "The odd thing about that flu was that the majority of people who died from it were young adults. For whatever reason, many of the deaths occurred in people who were considered the healthiest; those in their twenties and thirties. In other illnesses, the very young and the very old were the ones with the most casualties." Axel explained that this had been a mystery until recently. "A biologist went to a town in Alaska where everyone in the town had died from this flu. She brought back one of the bodies and studied the corpse. After some time, she learned that the reason that the healthiest people died was, ironically, because they had the strongest immune system. Their immune systems attacked the virus so ferociously; they ended up killing the victims. It was described as a "cytokine storm." The immune system overwhelmed the virus, but also damaged internal organs. In essence the victims were drowned by their own immune system."

"Keep in mind students," Axel said, "that also this occurred in the 1918 pandemic, doctors and biologists didn't realize that influenza was caused by a virus until 1930. Other more recent analyses have shown that the flu pathogen of 1918 was a H1N1 influenza. There are three basic types of influenza: type C, which is like having a mild cold; type B, which is local, doesn't spread easily, and is found in places like nursing homes, where the patients are old and not very mobile; and type A, which is the one responsible for the annual standard flu. Type A can be carried by pigs and chickens, as well as human beings.

"The type A virus is responsible for the H1N1 'swine flu' that began in Mexico in 2008. It has since spread over the whole world and is considered a pandemic. A vaccine was developed in January 2009 and was expected to be ready with over one hundred million doses by October 2009, but only about a third were available due to a slower than normal growth of a certain part of the pathogen called the epitopes. The epitopes are little hair like extensions on the outer part of the virus. These structures are fundamental in creating contact in the body's cells, where the virus begins to spread. It is important to realize that the body's immune system provides antigens, which normally attack an infection or a virus. Once this antigen has been generated, the body remembers it. Any later invasion by a bacteria or virus will not be successful, since the antigen is available immediately and attacks the invader before it has a chance to establish itself. The latest information on the numbers and ages of those that have been infected by the H1N1 virus in the United States, is that those being infected at the highest rate are children and young adults. This goes against the normal flu pattern which attacks very young children and the elderly. Further studies resulted in a hypothesis that people born before 1957 probably had already experienced a virus that contained the H1N1 strain. Therefore, those born before 1957 probably had the antibodies from that attack. and their immune system prevented today's H1N1 flu from being able to take hold in these people. The advice to the population is that if you were born after 1957, you should get an H1N1 flu vaccination."

In order for the students to have a better feel of the type A flu virus, Axel referred them to a Web site that gave a detailed description of the influenza A virus.

Axel and Iran's Nuclear Program

As had always been the case, Axel read the newspaper from beginning to end each day. He was interested in what was going on in sports, the local government, and the international community, especially the countries that seemed to have a grudge against the U.S. He became very interested in reading about Iran's stance and work on nuclear energy, and about the new site that was found near their religious city, Qom. There had been plenty of information over the years about their nuclear work at Natanz. The Iranians were always coy about what was going on in Natanz, but international inspectors had visited Natanz and came away feeling that as big as Iran's activities had been over the years, they probably were only generating uranium at the level that was allowed for nuclear power systems to provide electricity. This had always bothered Axel since he believed the Iranians were bluffing. They didn't need nuclear power. They were the fourth biggest producer of oil, producing some four million barrels a day. Besides that, they were sitting on probably the biggest natural gas field in the world. Why would they devote so much time pursuing nuclear energy?

Axel had learned several years ago that there was considerable uranium in the world. It was as common as tungsten and many of the other metals of the world. The key was that it was made up of several isotopes, with U-235 and U-238 being the most important.

The U-238 couldn't sustain a chain reaction and it made up about 98 percent of the Uranium in the world. The U-235 made up less than 1 percent. U-235 could sustain a chain reaction and could be used for an atomic bomb. The key was that U-235 couldn't be used in an atomic bomb unless it was at least 90 percent pure. At that point, it was called highly enriched uranium (HEU), since it was enriched over and over to rid of any contaminants. The world's powers had signed an agreement years earlier, prohibited any further of nuclear weapons. Since countries wanted to pursue nuclear energy, the countries agreed to allow the use of U-235 if it was not enriched above 20 percent of purity. This was designated as low-enriched uranium (LER). Iran's Natanz facility was supposedly running well below that 20 percent.

Uranium could be enriched in several ways, but most countries had been using centrifuges to provide the enrichment. The centrifuges separated the U-238 from the U-235 by spinning the material. Centrifugal force threw the heavier material away from the center of the rotor, toward the outside walls. Being the heavier of the two isotopes, U-238 was found close to the outer walls; U-235 remained near the center. After a certain amount of centrifuging, the heavier U-238 was removed, although the centrifuge continued spinning, getting rid of other impurities. Eventually, the U-235 was between 4 and 20 percent pure. But much of the raw material is lost. For every pound of material, less than a tenth of an ounce of U-235 might be left. It can also take years to separate out any significant amount of U-235 from the raw material. The president of Iran had previously announced that Iran had over four thousand centrifuges in Natanz and was increasing the number to over five thousand. He has said these were for the production of more LER for the use in nuclear reactors.

Since he was following news about Iran, Axel was surprised—as were many countries and people—when the Iranian president of Iran announced that Iran was also building another nuclear enrichment plant beneath a mountain near Qom. This was named the Fordo uranium enrichment plant. He said this plant was being built under the mountain to prevent other countries (mainly the U.S.) from bombing the site. He stated that they were installing three thousand centrifuges in this plant. One thing was clear to Axel. Three thousand centrifuges were not enough to supply a nuclear energy plant for the production of electricity. It was, however, enough to supply the amount of enriched fuel needed for one atomic bomb each year, if they took the uranium from Natanz that had been enriched to the20 percent level. Other information bothered Axel.

It was well known that the centrifuges in Natanz were of a design called P-1. Those centrifuges had a central core about six feet tall and two feet in diameter. The energy of a centrifuge was determined by its length and its spin speed of its core. The cores rested on a bearing, and this was the area of the centrifuge that took the most wear and tear, and was the most likely to break down. They did not have a bearing at the top, and were kept in their position at the top by a magnetic force field.

The president of Iran indicated that the new facility at Qom was using a newly designed centrifuge called the IR-2. Its core was half the length of the P-1, but it spun at twice the speed. It was lighter in weight, and therefore was less of a load on the bottom bearing.

Axel's active mind began working overtime when he read this. *The Fordo plant at Qom is not ready to take on the total load of three thousand of these centrifuges. What if Iran, without informing other countries, installed then at Natanz, which is a bigger facility, and these extra centrifuges were used to produce highly enriched uranium? Iran would then be in position to arm their medium range missiles and use that as leverage over Israel. This would be like holding a hostage. If Iran ever got in that position it would, or might, be reason for war.*

As these thoughts went through Axel's mind, he decided to call Kim and tell him of his concerns. He mentioned to Kim the various scenarios he had considered, and how Iran could be fooling the world about its Fordo plant and its actual function. Kim agreed that the scenarios were a high possibility, and maybe a probability.

"But what do you think I can do about it?" asked Kim.

"I think," Axel almost shouted, "that you should talk to someone in the upper level of the administration about these possibilities and see what reaction you can get."

"No use getting upset about this," said Kim. "I am sure there are many people in the CIA and the Pentagon and the State Department that have spent time on these possibilities. The problem is that Iran hasn't allowed us to see anything more than they want us to see, and we can't just come out and accuse them of these things. It's one of those possibilities where we try to negotiate things on peaceful terms and see where we get. It's not a good strategy to continually pound away at another country without any basis. What if we are wrong?"

"What if we are right and they continue saying we are imagining things?" Axel said.

"Without our going to those facilities and seeing what is going on, we are sort of stuck," replied Kim. "What if we accuse them of what you're suggesting, and Iran finally allows us to go there and we find nothing. The world would look at us as a paranoid nation. These are not easy things to accomplish. We can only hope that countries like Iran are sane enough to stop before it goes too far. I even agree with you on the fact that it's sort of out of character for Iran to be building nuclear reactors with all the oil and natural gas they have in their possession. They are one of the countries that probably don't have to worry about energy for a couple hundred years."

"I wouldn't say that," replied Axel. "I believe they will be out of oil by 2037, and they will need energy supplied by renewable sources. I have considered nuclear energy as renewable energy, since there are enough nuclear sources to last over a thousand years. Iran would still have natural gas. Natural gas is better than oil energy and its derivatives, and a lot better than coal, but it is still a fossil fuel. When we reach peak oil, there will be pressure around the world for everyone to use energy from the sun, not from the earth. It's a crazy world at times. But I am playing the devil's advocate on that one. Natural gas will probably be quite acceptable for this century."

Kim told Axel he would contact the right people and see what they had to say.

The more Axel read about what Iran was doing, the more he was interested in doing something about it. *It seems to me that if we could eliminate some or most of their centrifuges, it would provide us many years of sanity in the world. At times I feel like calling Kim and telling him that I would like to go over there and take some action. I know I can't do that, since he wouldn't approve it, and neither would anyone at the Pentagon or White House. I know I could do something about their centrifuges. If I could eliminate the ones they have begun to install in Fordo, it would delay any nuclear weapons program they might have. It would be a sort of peaceful move, and hopefully could be done in secret so no one could blame it on the U.S. The other alternative would be to find out where the new centrifuges are being produced and stop them from supplying them to Iran. That's something I haven't thought about. I wonder if Kim knows where the centrifuges are being produced. I will call him tomorrow and ask him. Then again, that might not fly either. I have to think of a plan of my own and follow it through.*

Each day Axel grew more determined that he had to do something about Iran. It burned in his mind, and he began to think out a plan to follow on his own. After a few days, he talked to Tori and told her he had to go out of the country for a few days. He told her he couldn't tell her any details, and she knew by the tone of his voice and his general demeanor that she shouldn't press the issue. They had a few good days, and celebrated in the evenings like he was going on a vacation. Their lovemaking was as good as it could be, and knowing Axel was going to be gone for a while, Tori was unusually aggressive. He told her he would call her every day and let her know he was all right.

Finally, Axel had a plan and decided to call Kim. When he got him on the phone, Kim told him two more bodies had shown up of men who had died of unknown causes, like the ones who had died the previous years from manipulated nanoparticles. They thought that maybe some of that material was still out there and was being used. They discussed this for a while, until Kim said, "Okay, Axel, what did you call about? I know it wasn't to discuss the weather. What's up?"

"I can't tell you what's up. I want you to tell me if you know of a flight going to Baghdad or someplace in northwestern Afghanistan."

"Why do you need to know that?" questioned Kim.

"I can't tell you the reason. Just understand that it is important to me, and I want you to do it as a favor," stated Axel.

It was quiet on the phone for a few seconds, and then Kim asked, "Is this something to do with anything I know about?"

"It's nothing that you know about," Axel said, "and I want to leave it at that. Is there a flight going to either of those places?" he asked again.

Kim said he didn't know, but he would check and get back to him. That ended the conversation. Not knowing if he could get a flight kept Axel's nerves tight. Every time a phone rang, at the school or at home or on his internal phone, he would jump, hoping it was Kim calling him back. But all of that day and the next morning went by without a call. Meanwhile, Axel called his department head at the school and told him he would be going out of the country in a few days. Then he called his substitute and set it up for him to take his classes. All Axel needed now was a call from Kim. Late that afternoon, he got the call.

"Axel, I have three flights, with two going to Baghdad and one going to Afghanistan by way of Baghdad."

"That's great," said Axel.

"The one flight out of Travis Air Force Base in California leaves for Baghdad tomorrow. Another flight from Dallas also goes to Baghdad tomorrow. The third flight is a military flight going out of the airbase here in Washington. It leaves day after tomorrow, and it will fly to Baghdad and then to an airbase in northwestern Afghanistan. Do you have a preference?"

"I really am happy that you found those flights. Would you have any problem getting me on any of them?"

"No. You are considered a privileged person, and I can get you on any of these flights."

"Travis is about a two hour drive from here," said Axel. "I could get Tori to drive me up there. What time is the flight leaving?"

"Ten thirty tomorrow morning, but you would have to be there about nine."

"No problem," said Axel. "How about calling them up and telling them I will be on that flight?"

Kim said he would call them as soon as they got off the phone. Then he asked Axel if he wanted to tell him anything more about what he was going to be doing. Axel said that it was a confidential thing, and he wanted it to stay that way.

"Is there anything you need from me?" asked Kim.

Axel said no, and added that he would be gone for only a few days. "I might be calling you up to get a flight back to the States. See if there's a flight from either Baghdad or Afghanistan coming this way in three days. I will get back to you by day after tomorrow to let you know how sure I am about the time."

Kim was quiet for a while. "Axel, I am glad you are only going to be gone for three days or so. You can't possibly do too much in that amount of time. I am happy to look for flights leaving Iraq and Afghanistan for three, four, or five days from now. When you get back to me on when you want to leave, I will have a complete picture of what will be available. Meanwhile, you have a great flight out of Travis tomorrow."

Axel hurried home and called Tori at work to tell her he needed a ride to Travis Air Base the next morning at seven. Then he started to pack. *I want to take a plastic bag that can hold one set of clothes, some dried food, and a bunch of candy bars. If I can get them to fly me out over the Caspian Sea and* drop me in the water, then I will need this bag to be able to hold up to the impact with the water and to keep my things dry. I have the perfect bag for that. I got it when I thought I would need it the last time I went to Iran, about a year ago. I will check the temperature of the water of the Caspian Sea this time of the year.

He went to the computer and checked the statistics for the Caspian Sea. The water temperature varied quite a bit from the northern part to the southern part. He intended to enter the water near the southern part, and the temperature there was twenty degrees centigrade, which was sixty-eight degrees Fahrenheit. *That's ideal,* he thought; *just a little cooler than a bath. They do get a lot of rain in the southern part of the sea each year. Looks like it might be raining when I get there. Tehran is near the southern edge of the sea, and also near the Elburz Mountains. The highest point of the mountains is Mt. Damavand, about 19,000 feet high. So there is a big change going from the sea to Tehran. The mountains would have some snow cover at this time of the year. The temperature in Tehran is almost like it is in Northern California. It never gets real cold. During December it ranges from thirty-three to fifty-one degrees Fahrenheit, so I should be warm if I am keeping busy. It is a little warmer in Qom and Natanz, since they are south of Tehran. Qom is about seventy-five miles south of Tehran, where the one nuclear facility is in a cave. Natanz is located in the center of the country, about another seventy-five miles or so southeast from Qom. I might need a blanket at night, especially if I sleep in the woods. It is colder in the mountains, but I don't expect to be in the mountains for more than half an hour or so before reaching the northern limits of Tehran. There is a valley going from the Caspian Sea through the mountains toward Tehran, and that's the way I will go. I should be able to run that in about an hour. I don't want to go into Tehran and should skirt it to get to Natanz and Qom. I need to borrow a vehicle when I get through the mountain pass. With a vehicle I can get to Qom in about an hour and a half, and then would need another hour and a half to two hours to get to Natanz.*

With these thoughts in his mind, Axel decided to go to the grocery store and buy some "vitals." *No telling where I will be getting any food over there. I probably could get hold of some acquaintances in Tehran, but that wouldn't be smart. I need to keep this as secretive as possible.* After picking up the food and candy that he needed, Axel returned home. He packed the food and the other things he needed into the large heavy plastic bag, and then he sat down to think out the itinerary he should follow.

Whatever I do will cause an uproar around both sites If I go to Qom first and then Natanz, it would leave me trapped in the center of Iran. That would be a bad strategy. I need to travel south to Natanz first, which is farther away, do my thing there, and then travel north to Qom. This would leave me about seventy-five miles from Tehran, and then on from there to the Caspian Sea. Whatever I do at Natanz will draw the troops to that site, and while that is happening, I should be heading north to Qom and Fordo. After Fordo, which is about ten miles north of Qom, I need to head out of the country. If I could make it to the Damavand Laboratory, which is on the other side of Tehran and next to the Caspian Sea, I should be able to steal a plane like I did the last time I was in Iran and use that to get out of the country. This provided a good plan. He kept thinking it out, knowing that all plans change once the action begins. He rested his head back on the sofa and went over the details so as not to miss anything.

He was awakened by someone shaking his arm and saying, "Axel, wake up." Then he felt "the love of his life" kiss him on the cheek. "Hey, sleepyhead, are you bored?" Tori asked with a smile.

"No, I was just here thinking about the trip and I fell asleep," Axel replied.

"You mean you were bored by your trip. Doesn't sound like you," she quipped.

Axel grabbed her and pulled her down next to him, kissing her and rubbing her legs and butt. Axel thought, *I better make this a long and good one, because I don't know when I will get back.* Then he stopped thinking as she unbuttoned his shirt and began kissing his bare chest. Soon they were taking off each other's clothes, and then Axel picked her up when she was in her naked best and carried her to the shower. In they went, and what a sexy time it was, rubbing soap on her breasts, which got his tool harder and her breast nipples harder, and then everything was in good harmony as he lifted her by her butt and pulled her to him, with her legs spread to give him a target. Slowly he entered her body.

"God that feels good," he said as he began a rhythm with her that had her moaning, and then him moaning as he came in her body. That was the one thing that took the energy out of him. He always felt like a rag doll when he came in her. They stay clutched like that for a minute, and then she whispered in his ear, "Can we do that again?"

He was instantly hard again, and they began their rhythm again. This time when she climaxed she shouted, "Oh, Axel, I love you and I love doing this with you."

After they got out of the shower and dried off, Tori said, "I hope you aren't going to be away long."

"No honey. I hope to be back in three or four days if everything goes right. For this country's sake, I hope everything goes right."

The next day they were at Travis Air Base in time, and before long he was on a flight to Baghdad. He spent some time talking to the pilot, asking him what he was going over there for.

"I have to deliver some classified information to a certain person over there. Seems we do this every couple of weeks," he responded.

They talked about other things, and then Axel told him he wanted to sit back and think. Axel's thoughts were on the mission. He wanted to make sure his plan made sense.

I know yesterday I decided to go to Natanz first, since it was the greater distance from the Caspian Sea. There's something bothering me about that plan. I do want to go to Natanz to begin my action, but I probably should go to Qom and the Fordo plant first to see the status of that place. That way when I come back, I'll know where everything is located. I will want to use equipment they have there to help me do my thing. This is important, because I will essentially be on the run from Natanz and won't want to spend a lot of time at the Fordo plant. I am glad I thought about this some more.

I guess the other thing I have to think about is what I do when I see those centrifuges. How do I damage them? I must do it with very little loss of life at the facility, and also with little harm to me. After all, this is dangerous stuff I may be working with. The gas that is used to feed into the reactors is uranium hexafluoride. This is whirled in these systems to separate the U-235 from the U-238. The way these systems work is they spin the centrifuge at high speed and the heavier (and more plentiful) U-238 is thrown against the outside wall of the rotor and the lighter U-235 is closer to the center. The bottom of the rotor is heated, and this causes the lighter U-235 to diffuse upward toward the top, where it is scooped out. This is the valuable material, but it is not very pure at this point. The centrifuges are made up of about one hundred and forty of them to a cascade system. The output from the top of the first centrifuge is then fed into the next centrifuge if the cascade to be further enriched. This continues day in and day out, as the U-235 works its way through the 146 centrifuges of the cascade. When it comes out of that final stage it is considered as low-enriched uranium. When the raw material is first started through this cascade, it is 0.0072 parts U-235. When it comes out of the cascade months later, it is 3.5 percent U-235.

I have to think about what part of the centrifuges to put out of order to obtain my objective, and at the same time not causing any deaths. This may not be possible, since if they catch me, they definitely will try to kill me. I think the most sensitive part of the centrifuge is the bearing of the rotor. The full weight of the rotor is concentrated on one small area of the bearing. The bearing not only spins the rotor, but holds it in its perfect vertical position. They would like to have a bearing on the top of the rotor, but found that this doesn't work well. They replaced the upper bearing with an electromagnetic coil that doesn't touch the top of the rotor, but holds it in position with its magnetic field. The other electrical connections include the motor and a heater at the bottom of the rotor.

If I can cut the electrical wires to the electromagnetic core and to the heater at the bottom, the core will continue to spin. But since the electromagnetic field is eliminated from the top of the rotor, it won't stay in position. It will start to wobble, and in a short time the bottom will not be able to be held in position. The rotor will bang against the outer casing, and the centrifuge will destroy itself. That should be a great way to handle this. The thing I must do first at Qom and at Natanz is find the emergency alarm that goes off when the electricity is discontinued. I must disconnect the alarms first, and then the electric wires. I am glad I brought the machete with me. If things go right, the rotors will begin wobbling in ten to twenty minutes, and the system should destroy itself in about an hour. If I think I can't do them all, since there are about five thousand centrifuges in Natanz and I don't know how many at Fordo, I should start at the end of a cascade, which has the highest level of enrichment. There are about thirty-five cascades. So if I cut the wires on the last systems of those thirty-five, it will do more damage than any of the other centrifuges in the cascade. Hopefully I can get to at least three hundred and fifty of them. This would tear up the last ten of each cascade. This cutting of the wires is a quiet approach. If I get the alarms disconnected beforehand and get rid of any guards inside the facility, then I can be out of there before anyone knows there's a problem. Sounds like a plan to me.

Axel leaned back in his seat and relaxed. Then he suddenly remembered, *I have to get out of the country. If I can drive around the western side of Tehran and up to Damavand, where the laboratory used to be, I can steal one of the small planes and fly out of there. But I have to do that without involving or endangering my country. The Iranians must not know that it was done by an American. I think I might have to crash the plane in the Caspian Sea and swim to Turkey or someplace and make my way back to Iraq. I think I can do that. Maybe I can think of a better plan as I go along, but at this point I think this is my best bet. If there is any way I can be caught, I must destroy any information I carry that would incriminate my country. I can do that.*

The pilot told Axel he was beginning the approach to Baghdad and should be down in about fifteen minutes.

"Great," Axel said.

He knew Baghdad was ten hours ahead of San Francisco, and Tehran was eleven and a half hours ahead. When it was 8:30 pm at home, it was 8:00 am of the next day in Tehran. He had left San Francisco in the morning, flown for about twelve hours, but now it was the morning of the next day. He had lost about half a day, but he would gain it back when I went back home.

A short time later Axel was sitting in Commander Rumsey's office. "I unofficially knew you were going to be here," the commander said, "and it has to stay that way. So, what can I do for you?"

"You have to dump me in the Caspian Sea." "I have to do what?" Rumsey asked.

"I need to be dumped in the Caspian Sea about twenty-five miles north of the Iranian shore," Axel said. "Don't ask me why, and the fewer people who know about this, the better. Also, don't ask me what I am going to do. I can't tell you. I want to keep our government out of this. I hope you can think of a way to do that."

Rumsey looked at Axel for a long time. "I'll tell you what, Axel. You let me think about it for about an hour, and I will come up with something. Why don't you go and get something to eat, and I will see you back here in an hour or so."

After eating and picking up some candy bars, Axel walked back to the colonel's office. Rumsey told him to come in and close the door.

"I have given this some thought," Rumsey said, "and I want to know if you can handle this. We have some planes here that are what's left of the Iraqi air force. I know you have a pilot's license. What if you were a disillusioned Iraqi and you stole in one of those planes, heading toward some country north of the Caspian Sea, or flew over Turkey and headed out over the Caspian and crashed. We would put out an emergency alarm that a rogue plane was stolen from Iraq and headed north. Later we would acknowledge that the plane crashed in the Caspian and it looked like the pilot did not survive. In this way, no airplane from the U.S. air base in Baghdad would be involved. Of course, you would have to find a way to crash the plane and swim to shore. Do you think you could handle this?"

"Handle it? Why, I think it is marvelous," Axel said. "I wish I had thought of that. Don't worry, I will find a way to crash and make it to shore."

"How about taking this on this evening?" Rumsey asked.

Axel was shocked. "That would be wonderful," he said. "Don't put a lot of gasoline in the plane; maybe enough to make it about fifty miles past where I will crash it. That way, you can say that the plane may have crashed because it ran out of fuel. If they find the wreckage, it would verify your story. What do you think?"

"I think you just wrote the last chapter of this story. Good thinking, Axel. It has always been a pleasure working with you. Oh, one more thing. You will be having a passenger on your flight."

"What?" Axel shouted.

"We thought this should really look like the real thing," said Rumsey. "We had a 'walking bomb' two days ago. The man went into a food market and blew himself up. He killed 118 civilians. One of the victims is in a coma. I'm told he won't live more than another day or two. No one ever claimed him, so you will take him with you. Before you crash, buckle him into the pilot's seat. If the Iranians find his body, they will see that he is Iraqi, and it will appear that the crash killed him. I hope you can handle that."

"That's a great ploy," remarked Axel. "That really should make this story hold together."

Rumsey walked Axel out to the plane to make sure everything was set up. "That's it, Axel. You have a good flight. We will wait about two hours and then put out an alert. That should give you time to do your thing."

Axel climbed into the cockpit and looked at his passenger. He thought, *he looks like he is sleeping. At least this won't hurt him, and since he was never claimed by anyone after the explosion the other day, no one will miss him. I feel like a sort of undertaker.*

As he took off and headed north, Axel was a little concerned that he would be met by aircraft from other countries that bordered Iran or from Iran itself. His plan was to fly just over the corner of Turkey and take an Eastern turn which would get him above the Caspian. He made the flight as planned and soon reached the Caspian Sea. He took the plane down to only a thousand feet and checked that the wheels were up. He ate a couple of candy bars and then said the magic words: "Axelvation two, hood down." The energy levels rose in his body. Soon the plane was flying at its slowest speed and was only about one hundred feet above the water. Axel set the autopilot, rapidly got out of his seat, and moved the passenger into it. Turning the autopilot off, he grabbed his plastic bag, pushed open the door, and leaped out. As he descended, he formed his body into a ball, with his arms around the plastic bag and his legs bent at the knees, pushing up against the bag. He hoped the protective covering of his body over the plastic bag would take care of the shock of hitting the water.

He hit the water, but then bounced back up, like a stone being skipped across the water. As he flew up in the air, he realized he was about sixty feet up. As he descended at an angle, he opened up his body and said "Up." His feet just hit the water and responded as if he had landed on solid ground. His legs kicked, and it was almost like putting on a brake. He flew up in the air again, but only about six feet, and landed softly in the sea.

He had dropped the plastic bag. As he swam back to it, he saw the plane hitting the water about two miles away. The loud crash came a few seconds later. He got to his bag, which was floating because it had trapped air in it. He let the air out and flipped the rope over his head, wearing the bag like a backpack. Then he started swimming toward the Iranian shore, some twenty-five miles away. Every once in a while he would see a fishing vessel, and he would go underwater for ten minutes or so. He could swim about five miles in ten minutes underwater, and that was plenty of distance from any fishing vessels.

When Axel reached shore, he knew he wasn't that far from the mountain range and where the Damavand Laboratory used to be, before he blew it up a year ago. Axel could run about as fast as he could swim, and he soon reached the base of the mountain range. The mountains dropped off into a valley, and that was where he needed to be. There was a good road in the valley, and it led to the former laboratory and the small airfield located about a mile away. He was hoping to find some cars and trucks at the airfield, and preferably a military vehicle that he could appropriate for his drive to Qom.

The small airfield was only about twenty miles from the shore, and Axel began to run along the highway. About halfway to where he was headed, he saw an army vehicle coming down the road toward him. He wondered if they were responding to the plane crash. He stepped out into the road and held his hands high to flag down the truck. It pulled up, and two soldiers jumped out, guns in their hands.

Still holding his hands up in the air, he shouted in Farsi, "No problem. I just saw a plane crash in the sea."

The two soldiers walked up to him. "Where did you see a plane crash?" one asked.

Axel pointed toward the sea, which was still visible from that vantage point. As they turned to look, he grabbed their heads and rammed them together. He hurriedly carried their bodies to the bushes on the side of the road. One soldier was about his size, and he stripped him off his uniform and put it on. Walking back to the small truck, he put his wet clothes and the plastic bag into the back and jumped into the driver's seat. He turned the vehicle around and was on his way.

As he drove west along the highway, he was relieved that no one seemed to have noticed the missing soldiers yet. Lying on the front seat were two cellular telephones, and they hadn't rung yet. He continued west until he reached the highway that led south to Tehran. He took than, skirted the city, and after about two hours saw signs that said, Qom 10 km.

Qom was in a hilly section of the country, and the road had many curves in it. Under normal conditions he would call Kim on his internal phone, but he didn't want Kim to know that he was in Iran. This had to be a private matter and not related to the agency or the United States. He slowed down and proceeded cautiously along the road. Other military vehicles were on the road, and he suspected they were buzzing in and out of the Fordo Plant. When he was close to Qom, he saw a small dirt road and pulled onto it. The road led into a wooded area. It was now getting dark, which was good. They would have lights on at the Fordo plant, and this would give him the correct direction to head. He pulled the truck into some bushes along the side of the road, got out, and pushed it farther in. Reaching into his plastic bag, he pulled out his binoculars with the infrared lens. They allowed him to see fairly well at night, and had good clarity for about half a mile to a mile. He also pulled out a pair of goggles, in case he needed them.

He trotted along the main road, and when he saw the lights of a vehicle coming from either direction, he hid. At one point, a vehicle that had passed him slowed and turned on its blinker. *This is what I have been looking for,* he thought. *They must be turning in to Fordo.* Axel started to climb through the brush that lined the road, up the side of a hill. After about one hundred yards, he came to a clearing. At the far edge of the clearing, he could see there was a fence that was about fifteen feet high. *That fence probably surrounds the whole facility, and I bet it is wired to shock the life out of any person or animal that tries to climb it. I bet it also sends a signal to the guards stationed at the entrance to the tunnel. But they didn't know I can jump over a fifteen-foot fence like it was a one-foot-high piece of cardboard.* He leaped over the fence, using his "up" command before he hit the ground. Turning to his left, he headed toward what he thought would be the front of the facility. He'd gone about a half mile when he saw lights out in the distance. As he continued in that direction, he realized the lights were for the road that led to the tunnel cut into this mountain. Within one hundred yards, he had reached the edge of the tunnel and was standing right above the entrance. Looking down, he gauged the entrance to the tunnel to be quite wide, maybe fifty yards. He could see a guard post below him on the right-hand entrance to the tunnel.

Axel felt his best bet to get into the facility was to walk up to the guard in his Iranian uniform as if he belonged there. However, he got a surprise, because when he entered the small building, the guard had a different uniform, not a military one. He hardly had time to move before Axel grabbed the back of his neck and pushed the nerve that knocked him out. Axel quickly put on the guard's uniform, and then looked at the display panel at the guard's desk. He could see the buttons that opened the gates and side doors. He didn't want to open the gates, and he pushed the lock release for the door next to the gate entering the tunnel.

Axel hurriedly went in the tunnel and looked around. Many crates were stacked near the entrance, and he wondered if they contained centrifuges of the newest type. He went over to the crates and saw they had been shipped from Uram in Pakistan, confirming his guess. They were huge crates, and they must hold the three thousand centrifuges that the Iranian president had talked about. Hearing noises, he continued to walk slowly toward the back of the tunnel. Soon he could see workers moving framework around and screwing bolts into some of the framework. They were facility workers putting together the mainframes that the centrifuge cascades would go into in the near future. They were making a lot of noise, and they didn't react when they saw Axel. Axel hurriedly walked around the inside of the facility, viewing the conduits that contained the electrical wiring that led to the alarm systems, as well as the conduits that would probably supply power to the centrifuges when they were installed.

When Axel felt that no one was observing him, he leaped to the top of the framework, about fifty feet up. He saw the power hookups, including the alarm hookups.

It looks to me like they are about six months away from having this place running centrifuges, and a year and a half away from supplying enriched uranium that could be made into a bomb, if they started with low-enriched uranium. Maybe that is what this place is being provided for; enriching material that is LEU up to HEU, which is bomb material. If they were provided low-enriched uranium from the Natanz facility, it probably would take less than a year to produce enough HEU for one bomb. If they started with normal UF6, it would take them many years to make 90 percent enriched uranium, which is what is needed for a bomb.

Now that Axel had fixed in his mind where the various power and alarm systems were located, he jumped back down to the floor level and looked around for their munitions storage. He was sure it would be in here under lock and key. His search proved a success, as he found a large shed inside the tunnel. He assumed an alarm would go off if he tried to break the locks on the door. He walked around to the side that was next to the wall and out of plain view, and thrust his fist through the thin metal wall. The light inside the tunnel was enough for him to look inside and to see various munitions. The ones he was interested were the hand grenades. He intended on using them when he came back. He had only intended to see where they were and not take any. However, he changed his mind and reached in, grabbing two of them. He stuck them in the side pockets of his shirt uniform.

In about half an hour, Axel had seen enough and headed back toward the entrance. He went back into the guard's post, removed the uniform, and put it back on the unconscious guard. After putting his first uniform on, he sat the guard in his desk chair and tweaked the nerve in the back of the neck to bring him back to consciousness.

As he opened his eyes and looked around in bewilderment, Axel said, "Hey there. I just came in here to ask you something and you were fast asleep. You are lucky I came in or someone would have had your ass for falling asleep. I am leaving now and I won't tell anyone you were sleeping. But maybe you better get a cup of coffee and keep walking around to stay alert."

The guard didn't say a word, and Axel left. Once outside, he leaped about thirty feet up the side of the hill and began making his way back to the fence.

Back in his truck, Axel drove toward Natanz, which was about seventy-five miles away. The roads were decent, and when he came to a nicely paved highway, he knew from aerial photographs he had reviewed back in the States that he was close to the facility. In about fifteen miles, he saw a dirt road that exited from the highway. His mental picture of the aerial Natanz photos told him this was the road to turn onto. Soon he could see the lights in the distance, indicating that he was on the right road. Even though it was nighttime, he saw several trucks parked outside the high gate, and there were workers digging dirt and loading things on the trucks. He drove past them, deciding to park his truck alongside the road next to the fence. It would fit in with the other trucks. Axel took out his binoculars and looked out at the facility. It was all underground, but he could see a guard shack above what looked like the main entrance to the facility. He would wait till there was a guard change, which would probably be around midnight. It was about eight o'clock now.

He reached into his plastic bag and pulled out a can of baked beans and a soda. He cut the lid open on the beans and scooped them out with the metal spoon he had packed. They were cold, but they still tasted good since he was very hungry. After he finished the beans, he ate an apple and a package of cookies.

The same guards were still on duty when he was done with his dinner. *Time goes slow when you are waiting for something, and it seems to go fast when you find what you were waiting for,* he thought. It was 9:30 now. Using his binoculars with the infrared lens, he kept watching the guard stations. It was quiet, since all the workers he'd seen when he pulled up had left. He reached in his jacket and pulled out an almond chocolate bar to bring up his energy level. Soon he would need his full energy.

At about eleven, a bus arrived carrying about forty women and one man. The gate guard checked the driver's pass and then got out of his shed and got on the bus. He checked that each woman had her badge on, and he checked some sort of paperwork that the man had. Satisfied, the guard returned to his post and pushed a button that opened the gate. Then the bus driver drove to the entrance of the plant. As Axel watched, the people on the bus got off, and then a group of people who had been waiting at the entrance—all women and one man, the previous shift— got on the bus. The bus driver brought them to the gate, and the gate guard let them out.

Sure enough, there was a guard change at the gate as Axel continued his watching. It was a little after 11:30, and he saw a car pulling up to the gate with a driver and a male passenger. The guard checked their passes and opened the gate. The car drove through the gate and proceeded to the guard post that was near the entrance to the building. Axel watched with the binoculars and saw the driver and the other man jump out of the car and enter the guard shack. A few minutes later the driver returned with a different man, and the two of them got in the car. The driver then drove back to the gate and parked his car next to another car. The two men got out, and one walked into the guard's post. Axel could see the new guard talking inside with the guard he was relieving. The guard who was leaving finally walked over to the other car where the other guard whose shift was over was waiting. They got in and drove to the gate; the new guard sent the signal to open the gate. Now Axel knew what was happening. Two new guards arrived together; the guards who were being relieved left together. This was their way of car pooling, and it always left the new guard's car on the inside of the gate.

Happy that he understood what was going on, Axel felt relieved that the two guards would be on duty for the next eight hours. If he could avoid having the guards set off alarms, he just got himself a car to drive to and from the gate to the plant entrance. With that in his mind, he gave the instructions: Axelvation three, hood down. He reached in his plastic bag and pulled out the machete with its long and sharp blade. When he got out of the truck, he took three large leaps forward, each leap about fifty feet in length. The last one got him over the gate. He set the machete on the ground. The guard wasn't looking for anyone inside the gate, and therefore was not aware of Axel's presence. Axel entered the door and grabbed the man by the neck, rendering him unconscious. *I could kill him*, Axel thought, *because they will probably execute him anyway when they find that an intruder got inside their building. But I will let him live, and maybe he will not be killed.*

Reaching under the desk, Axel found the wire that was used to activate an alarm. He disabled it. Taking the keys for the car, he got in the car and headed toward the plant entrance. It was now going on one o'clock in the morning. He still had his Iranian soldier uniform on, so the guard at the plant entrance thought he had just entered and was permitted to be in the plant.

Axel walked in the guard's shack and said in Farsi, "How's the night going?"

"I just got here," the guard said.

"What are you doing back here?" Axel asked,, as he grabbed him by the back of the neck and knocked him out. He took the guard's badge, which contained his picture and an employee number, then reached under the desk and broke the wires that led to the alarm system. *There are probably alarms all over this place. If this were the United States, both guard stations would be monitored by video. They probably have video monitoring of the remote areas of this plant, such as the space between the plant and the fence. This place is a lot bigger than Fordo. Of course, it has been here many years, and the plant at Fordo has only been around for a couple of years.*

Axel opened a door, revealing a set of stairs that led to the floor below. He was inside the plant. He walked down a hallway and saw that it was going to lead him to a man who checked all the people entering the plant. This included all the workers and any visitors. Axel hoped that the badge on his shirt would be enough to at least confuse the guard until he could make a move on him. Axel kept his head down, his cap partly hiding his face as he approached the security desk. The guard first glanced at the badge on Axel's chest and then at a sheet of paper that Axel guessed listed the numbers of the employees who were allowed in the plant. He looked up to say something, and Axel put him to sleep. He picked the man up and put him in a small nearby closet.

Machete in hand, Axel looked around for his first priority—the alarm system wiring. His eyesight was sharp enough to follow the wiring, and he immediately leaped high in the air toward one wall. From this crow's nest view, he could see no operators in the main cascades, which contained five thousand or so centrifuges. He guessed they were in the back of the plant, working on preparing material for going into the first stage of a 146-stage cascade. There were thirty-five to forty of these cascades in operation, as far as Axel could make out. The ones being worked on in the rear of the building were, he thought, to be placed in front as a new cascade. Each of these sequential cascades meant that those further along would take a shorter time to obtain low-enriched uranium that was at the 6 to 10 percent enrichment range.

In addition to material being prepared for the cascades, there were operators taking new centrifuges out of large shipping boxes and cleaning them. These operators were in clean rooms. They wore clean room garments, including hoods over their heads and masks over their noses and mouths. In this operation, cleanliness was next to godliness, since any contamination could ruin a centrifuge. Any dirt or foreign material near the bottom bearing would be sure death for that particular centrifuge. The dirt would grind into the bearing, throwing the rotor off, and eventually the rotor would spin itself to death.

I am sure they not only clean these things well, but have sensors that tell when the bottom bearing is not acting right and they stop the machine. Other cleaning issues relate to the rotor, which spins at very high speed to separate the heavy from the light uranium. If some contaminant gets in the rotor, they could end up with some material other than U-235 in the center of the rotor. This is because almost all material is lighter than U-235, since uranium is one of the heaviest elements in the world.

Axel wanted to find the power lines that led to the electromagnetic equipment at the tops of each of the centrifuges; and the lines that fed the heaters that heated the bottom of the centrifuges. After finding those, he would check for the plumbing that fed water to cool the sides of the centrifuges. Once he found all of those, he would cut the power lines to the heaters first, and then he would cut the power lines that powered the magnetic bearings. While Axel was looking for these lines he heard a shout.

"Hey there! What are you doing up there?" Someone shouted.

Axel looked down and saw two men looking up at him. "I am checking the wiring," he said. "I was told there was a problem with the wiring."

"Come down here and let's check out your story. By the way, how did you get up there?" the one man asked.

"Oh, I found a way."

"Well, let's see if you can find a way down without a ladder," the man said.

"I don't believe you want me to come down there," replied Axel. "It would mean bad news for you and your friend."

The man pointed a gun at him. "Come down, and I mean immediately."

Axel ignored him, continuing his searching. He found the wires he wanted, took the machete, and whacked them. He already could hear the difference in the sound of the swirling centrifuges. Just then there was a rifle shot, and Axel felt a nip at this body. He slashed at more wires; more shots were fired. After finishing with the wires, he leaped down to the floor and ran toward the two men. They realized they couldn't shoot at him when he was in front of the cascades of running centrifuges. If they missed him, they would hit one of the centrifuges. Axel looked at the two men and told them to run. They ran. He walked over to the water pumps that had been supplying cooling water to the centrifuges before he had cut their electrical power line. Even though the power was cut off, he wanted to destroy them so they couldn't be repaired rapidly. He smashed the water pump motors with his fist. He then began running alongside the cascades, taking high arcing swings with the machete and cutting the wires that lead to the top and bottom bearings of the centrifuges. The cutting didn't make any difference in the sound of the swirling machines, but it was insurance that it would take longer for someone to rewire them. Axel was happy that he had cut the right wires.

By now there were alarms going off, and he knew he soon would have a lot of soldiers on his hands. He went back to the water pump and threw it into the center of the cascades. The two men realized they couldn't do anymore damage to the cascades than he was doing, so they began to fire their rifles at him again. Nothing stopped The Follower, though, since he had made it his destiny to destroy the working elements of this nuclear system. When he had finished with the cascades in this room, he headed toward the adjoining room of cascades. He would have to pass the guys shooting at him, and he had gotten tired of that loud noise anyhow. As he ran toward them, two other men came out of another room, and they also began shooting. Axel made short work of the first two men, and then headed toward the other two. By now the women operators were screaming, since they felt their lives were in danger. Axel picked up one of the two men and smashed him against the other one. Then he turned toward the women and put his index finger to his mouth, signaling for them to be quiet.

"I won't harm you," he shouted several times in a couple of languages. "Just keep quiet."

He did his machete act on some of the other cascades, thinking that if he got nothing else done, he had delayed their nuclear weapons program by a few years.

As he continued, he noticed that the first centrifuges were already starting to wobble. This was what he had been hoping for. He knew that as the wobbling got worse, the bearing at the bottom would collapse and the rotor would smash against the outer frame of each system. His goal was to destroy at least half of the centrifuges.

Satisfied that he had reached that goal, Axel turned and began to leave the facility. As he opened the door, a hail of bullets flew at him. All the guards in the facility had gathered and were firing away at him. He knew he didn't have the energy to fight them all. He can only handle so much before he started to lose the nourishment his body needed.

His best bet was to find a way to get back through the gate and into a vehicle. Running toward the gate, which was a couple hundred yards away, He ignored the bullets as they sprayed off his body. He had to smash a couple of the guards on his way, but about fifty others just kept shooting.

He leaped over the fence just as military trucks arrived with reinforcements. These new soldiers began shooting at him, and one of them fired a grenade at him. He didn't have time to jump away, and the grenade hit him in the chest, throwing him back against the guard shack. Axel shook his head. This was a blow to his inner body also, and he felt something had happened. He couldn't run as fast as normal, but he still had enough going for him to rapidly make his way toward the military vehicle that was parked closest to the road. As he passed the truck he had been using, he reached in and grabbed the plastic bag. *I am going to need some food energy after all that back there.*

He jumped into the vehicle, grateful to see the key was still in the ignition. He started the engine and backed up, aiming the vehicle toward the road. Pausing, he took one of the two grenades he had been carrying and lobbed it over the truck nearest him, hitting the one on its far side. Then he pulled the pin on the second grenade, and just as he was pulling away, he threw it at the last vehicle in line. It blew up.

Axel headed down the dirt road toward the highway. As he was leaving, he looked in the rearview mirror and saw that the two trucks he had blown up were blocking the road. Anyone who wanted to follow would need to move one or both of the vehicles. He sped on toward the highway as fast as the vehicle would take him.

The Follower is Hurt

As he drove along, Axel decided to check something that had been bothering him since he got hit with that grenade. He said, "Axelvation zero," and felt his energy to back down. Then he said "Axelvation one," and felt a small upload of energy. He said "Axelvation two," and didn't feel an additional energy surge. He also got no response with "Axelvation three."

Uh oh, he said to himself. *I am in trouble. This means I only have Axelvation one. As he thought that, he got a strange sensation. He realized it was because he had thought "Axelvation One," and that was the energy level he was still in. That's what had made that funny feeling.*

"Hood down," he said, and felt the hood drop down. *Well, I have the energy of ten men instead of the higher levels, and I still have the protective suit and hood. Maybe I need additional nourishment to feed my mitochondria.*

He reached for the plastic bag and took out a couple of candy bars. He munched on them, and then gave the "Axelvation two" command. Nothing happened. He continued his rapid drive up the highway, and as he went along, he saw military vehicles heading south toward Natanz. He kept looking in his rearview mirror, but never saw any traffic coming up behind him.

When he was about halfway to Fordo, he decided to try the different levels of his energy again. He figured he had given the food he'd eaten enough time to provide energy his system. He nervously tried to call up the advanced levels of energy, but got no response. *I am in trouble on this and I'd better call Kim. I think the grenade caused an internal shock that loosened two of the connections to my internal control points inside me. I wonder if my internal phone is even still working. I have to call Kim. It's about a ten hour difference between here and the West Coast so it must be about seven hours difference* between here and Virginia where Kim lives. I will call him at home.

He called Kim, and was relieved when the other man answered.

"Axel, how are you doing?" he asked. "I am so-so," said Axel.

"Actually, I believe I am in a little bit of trouble."

"How's that?" asked Kim.

"I was hit with a rifle grenade about an hour ago and I can't call up my second and third levels of energy. I am able to call up my first level and I can get my hood down and I can use the phone."

"Sounds like a connection problem," replied Kim. "I can remember when we took the spiderweb and nanowires threads and hooked them to the control points in your body. They shouldn't have been any weaker than any of the other connections, but it's possible that the grenade hit you at just the right angle to cause those two wires to disconnect."

Axel thought a second and then said to Kim, "I believe the one level might allow me to complete my next mission. It will be tough, though. I know I have to leap over a fence that is about fifteen feet high. I have already done more than that when I had three levels and only used the first, but it was before I lost those two levels. If I don't clear the fifteen feet, I will hit the top of the fence and set off an alarm, I'll probably also get shocked. Do you believe that could pose a problem with the condition I am in?"

"I don't believe it will physically hurt you, but I am not sure," said Kim. "The shock may cause you to lose the wiring that provides you your first high energy level. It depends on what voltage they use on the fence. Most of those systems use low enough voltage that it will give you a jolt, but not cause any other problems. I think your biggest problem relates to whether you are going to need those higher energy levels later on."

"That's my major concern," Axel said. "I guess I have to make sure I eat enough candy bars to at least achieve my goal. But in the past, I have had to use my second energy level more than any other level. I have only used the third level for extremely hard challenges that required all the strength I could muster. I will miss that second level. My main concern is if I can't reach that level, I won't make it home. My plan was to make it back out to the Caspian Sea and escape, but I don't believe I can make it without my energy levels."

Axel paused as he heard a helicopter overhead. They were now looking for him from above. He told Kim that and added, "Fortunately, I am coming up on the turn-off to Fordo. They won't be looking for me here. They probably think I am headed toward Tehran. I guess that with you hearing those names, you now know I am in Iran. I have just disabled the Natanz facility and am headed toward Fordo. I couldn't stand leaving those Iranian nuclear centrifuges active and putting pressure on the free world. I am sorry, but that is my concern."

Kim was silent for a while, and then he said, "I understand that is why you didn't tell anyone where you were going. I am worried about your physical shape and the possibility that some other connections may be weak and will go. You are going to need someone to open you up and take care of any of those problems. Plus, it's time to add a new and better power supply to your body. These are not tough operations to perform. If I had you here I could do the upgrades you need in about an hour. But I don't know of anyone in that part of the world whom I can contact that would be able to handle your problem. Let me think about this and I will get back to you in a short time. To tell you the truth, Axel, I am concerned that if any other level connections fail, you will have no energy and will die. I don't want you to be frightened, but this is a concern, and I will do whatever I can to fix you. Meanwhile, I don't want you to exert yourself too much."

Axel responded, "I thank you for the concern, but I must do this next thing I came here to do. If I get through that, I will do whatever I can to remain dormant. I promise. Get back to me when you think of something."

That ended their conversation, and Axel concentrated on finding his way along the winding road that led to Fordo.

As Axel drove along, he thought about his situation. *I feel good, but I am concerned I will be able to leap over that fence. I normally could stretch my strength and leap about twenty feet on the first level of energy. I believe I can make that happen and get over. The rest of the trip is along the side of that mountain until I slip down by the guard's shack as I previously did. Inside the mountain, I don't intend to do much except get into their munitions supply and blow up some of those crates carrying the new centrifuges. So, the big deal is getting over the fence.*

He reached the point in the road where he had hid the truck earlier. He took from his plastic bag some fruit and a couple of candy bars and ate them. He now felt his nourishment level was as good as it was going to get for that first level of energy.. He said the magic words, "Axelvation one, hood down," and felt the energy surge. He hiked up the side of the mountain till he came to the fence. He didn't want to spend a lot of time thinking. There was nothing to do but to give it the best shot, and with that he gave it the best shot of leg energy he had. He cleared the fence by a foot. Feeling more confident, he continued on. He finally came to the side of the mountain that was about thirty feet above the guard shack sitting below. As he had done before, he slid down the side of the mountain till he was behind the guard shack. Axel held his breath as he walked around and entered the door of the guard shack. He still had the uniform on with the badge from Natanz. The guard looked up and saw the badge. He was obviously confused. He was about to ask Axel what he was doing there, when Axel grabbed him by the back of his neck and sent him into unconsciousness. Reaching below the desk, he ripped the wires for the alarm system. Leaving the guard shack, he walked into the tunnel as he had done previously. He didn't pause one minute and he didn't try to be quiet. He walked to the munitions storage shed, ripped the lock off the door, and grabbed as many hand grenades as he could carry. When he left, he looked up at where the alarms were. He didn't want to try his luck leaping up to that level. Instead, he pulled the pin on one of the grenades and threw it up at the wiring. The explosion blew the alarm system and some other wiring, but there still was light in the cave.

Thank goodness, he thought. *I probably need that light in here.* Running to the first crate he saw, he rammed his fist through the wood, pulled the pin on a grenade, and dropped the grenade in. He ran to the next and did the same, and by the time he got to the third crate, the first grenade had exploded. He followed this procedure for eight of the crates, until he had only one grenade left.

By this time there were guards shooting pistols and rifles at him. He pulled the pin in the last grenade and threw it in their direction. At the same time, he ran toward the munitions shed again. He grabbed ten more of the grenades and ran toward additional crates. After using those grenades and throwing the last one at the shooters, he ran back toward the munitions shed again. By this time, additional troops had arrived, some at the front gate and others at the door Axel had used. The ones outside the gate couldn't get in, since the guard was still unconscious. Axel threw a grenade at the doorway, and a few of the troops were taken care of. He made what he thought would be his last run up the crate row and blew off another set of grenades. Then he ran back to the munitions shed and grabbed about ten more grenades. When he stepped out of the shed, the tunnel was dark. Apparently, one of the grenade explosions had damaged the wiring for the lights. He still had his infrared goggles, and he put them on. He headed for the entrance, taking large jumping leaps into the air. Each jump took him about fifty feet. He raced into the guard shack and grabbed off the desk a set of keys and a bag that probably held the unconscious guard's lunch. *One of these keys should run his car*, he thought.

As he left the shack, he threw a grenade into it. He ran to the nearest car and tried the first of two keys that looked like car keys. The ignition turned on, and he backed out of the parking place and headed toward the road. He soon got to the military vehicle he had driven from Natanz. He took out the plastic bag and threw the bag into the car. Then he got into the military vehicle and drove it across the main road to the edge of a cliff. He jumped out at the last second and watched it go over the cliff.

They will be looking for that vehicle, he thought. *No one knows this car except the guard from the gate shack at Fordo, and he is dead.* He ran back to the car, jumped in, and headed north, toward Tehran, and away from the danger around him.

Kim to the Rescue

Axel drove for about fifteen minutes and his internal phone rang. It was Kim.

"Axel, I want you to go toward a town I know. You will have to head directly west. This town's name is Kermanshah and it is about the size of San Jose. It is about two hundred miles west of Tehran. As you approach Kermanshah, you will first come to a town named Kardanal, which is about twenty miles outside of Kermanshah. I will send you a fax when I am done talking to you that will show you exactly where to go. I think it will take you about five hours to get there. When you come to this small town of Kardanal, I want you to go to a friend of mine's house. You can stay there without worry. It's a sort of country town with dairy farms around. Do you think you have enough energy to carry you that far?"

"I think so," answered Axel. "I feel pretty good and I have some food in the car. But what am I going to do in that small town?"

"You aren't going to be doing anything. You are going to be resting."

"But, how does that get me home?"

"I am going to come and get you," Kim announced.

"You are kidding, right?" asked Axel.

"No, I am not kidding. It turns out the Kermanshah is only seventy miles from the border with Iraq. In the war between Iraq and Iran, a terrible lot of fighting occurred there and they are still building the city back to where it was. The key is the University of Medical Sciences. It is located in Kermanshah, and I have been there to lecture several times over the last twenty years. I have talked to them and asked if I could come and visit the university, and I got an okay immediately. I still have papers for entering Iran. I am already booked to fly into Baghdad on a military flight. Getting a commercial flight from Baghdad to Kermanshah is okay for someone like me who gives lectures at the University. We are not at war with Iran, and these kinds of visits occur all the time. Their professors and some students visit the U.S. every year. Once I am in Baghdad and schedule a flight to Kermanshah I will call you. I can rent a car and drive to Kardanal. I will bring my diamond scalpel, and needle and threads, fix what's wrong, and sew you back together again. How does that sound?"

"That sounded terrific! I can't believe it. My own private sewing master. That's the best news I have heard for a while. Do you think you are physically up to this and have you talked to your wife about it yet?"

"Believe it or not, Axel, I am in good physical shape for a man of sixty, and my wife approved. She knows how much you mean to me and to this country. I will pick up something for her from Iran.

"Since you are not legally in Iran, we will have to figure out how to get you back into Iraq. You are not going to go up through the Caspian Sea again. Your trip west should be fairly safe, since not much traffic goes from where you are to Kermanshah. It is not a very good highway to this town."

"Incidentally," said Axel. "I was able to make it over that fence I told you about, and that business is taken care of." "I can't discuss it with you, but maybe later I will. How about sending me the fax? I believe my system is working at that level. Also, you didn't give me the name of the man I am supposed to see in Kardanal."

"Yes, I almost forgot that. His name is Albert Chang. He lives out in the country there, but he teaches at the university. It is not a long drive from his house to the university. He doesn't know why you are going to be there, so you keep that to yourself. You can tell him you were a student of mine and you are having some physical problems that only I could fix. He didn't ask me too much about the details, and I am glad of that. I don't want to involve him in any way. When I get there, we may have to go somewhere else to do the operation. But we will get it done. Okay, I am sending you the fax."

Axel closed his eyes and went through his procedure for receiving faxes. Sure enough, there was the image of the way to Kardanal.

"It's almost a direct line west from where I am to there. It is about one hundred and sixty miles," Axel said as he reviewed the image with his eyes closed. "That looks like a good way to go. I don't think they will be looking for the person who disrupted their nuclear plans to be heading that way. They probably already know I took a military vehicle from some soldiers on the road from the Caspian Sea. They don't know that I am driving a car from a soldier who is dead at Fordo. So, they will probably be checking all the roads going north, the airport outside of Tehran, and the road to the Caspian Sea. This looks like a safe route, and I will meet you at Kardanal. Have a safe trip."

Dr. Edward Kim felt like Axel Tressler was his one big success in life. He had developed the special nanowires inside Axel and had determined the routing so that Axel could call up three levels of energy. He also had developed the means by which Axel could send and receive text and pictures. But he was just as proud of the fact that he had worked for five years to develop the special undetectable and indestructible covering for Axel's body, as well as the hood that covered his face and head. Kim had previously used a three-dimensional screen that he had developed to study how he was going to incorporate some of the special talents that Axel had been born with. He had used this technology to determine how to wire the computer chip into Axel's body, so that he could call up his body's different energy levels. After talking to Axel, Kim used this screen to try to determine what had been disconnected and had caused Axel's present problems. The screen showed the various organs within Axel's body, and how the wiring was routed to provide the three energy levels that incorporated his three kidneys, his multiple adrenal glands, and activated his ATP (adenosine tri phosphate) within the mitochondria that supplied Axel's body its energy.

With Axel in a foreign country, Kim knew he was really the only one who could handle the reworking needed inside Axel's body. Kim sat before this special three-dimensional screen and studied it carefully. He wouldn't be able to take it with him to Iran, and he wanted to make sure he really knew where Axel's problems originated. As he had told Axel on the phone, it might be the connection for the second and third levels of energy. It could be the control section that picked up Axel's words or thoughts and converted them to these energy levels.

Kim worked for several hours. He simulated Axel's problems by making changes to the wiring and watched for the outcome. He took away the two connections and from the results, thought this could be Axel's problem. He took the signal line that connected Axel's thoughts and words to these energy levels. They went through logic decode steps to end up selecting the proper activation. Perhaps these decode logic elements had been screwed up. He made various changes to the decoders and observed the results. Cause and effect were the things he checked, and he tried as many as he could technically determine to see if he made the cause on the screen happen, and what was its effect.

Finally, he determined several scenarios that could have caused the effect Axel was experiencing. He also was able to eliminate several possible causes, since they didn't result in Axel's particular problems. He was then satisfied that when he opened up Axel, he would be able to determine which of these could be the culprit. He was being so thorough for another important reason. He knew if he did anything wrong, Axel could die. All of the wiring connected to organs that were essential for the body to work. If he accidentally caused one of these to go out, it could kill Axel. He knew he could handle anything that went wrong if he was here with the agency's facilities to work with, but when he is in Iran, he would be working in much more primitive conditions. He would have limited equipment; only his scalpel, a special light that attached on his head and allowed him to focus it on his work, the special thread and needle for making attachments, and special magnification lenses that went over his glasses. Other ordinary items, such as iodine and gauze bandages, he could probably get from the university.

He decided to go through the causes and effects again to make sure they repeated themselves. They did. He was ready to go.

Dr. Edward Kim knew his business and felt confident about his ability to correct Axel's problem. His big worry was if he was going to get to Kardana in time. When he had called his friend at the University of Kermanshah, he had told him he would have to leave right away, since a good friend who lived not far from Kermanshah had a serious medical problem. Then Kim would have to drive to a place he had never been to, to the home of a friend, who knew he was coming but not why. Kim knew he had to do this as rapidly as possible, since every hour that went by was an hour that Axel might be caught. Or he might begin to suffer other effects in his body as a result of that rifle grenade that hit him. Kim had already decided that if he found the trouble, he was going to double the number of connections to the area, if there was room. He knew from his simulations that there were several possible problems, some of which could take extra wiring and some that couldn't.

Kim had also told his university friend that he would be bringing with him a scalpel and some other small metal instruments. He needed to get them through security at the airport. He suggested that his friend tell security ahead of time that a professor from the United States was coming to give a demonstration of a special operation on stem cell insertion and was bringing some tools with him. Kim realized this might put the professor in a compromised position, but after the successful operation on Axel, he would go to the university and perform this demonstration. So, he wasn't evading the truth. He just wasn't telling the Iranian police when he was going to do the demonstration.

While on the flight to Baghdad, Kim called Axel on his internal phone. He was happy to hear Axel answer the phone.

"Axel, I am on my flight to Baghdad and will arrive there in about an hour. From there, the Commander is getting me a commercial flight to Kermanshah. It will take some time for me to get through security there and obtain a car, but if things go well, I should be at Kardanal in roughly three to four hours. How are you feeling?"

"I am feeling fine," answered Axel. "Your friend and his wife have been nice to me, and I have been resting and eating and talking. Your friend evidently doesn't have many chances to talk casually to anyone, so I have been like a fountain of information for him. I hope you don't have any problems getting through security."

"I hope not," commented Kim." My colleague at the university is supposed to warn them ahead of time that I will be carrying some medical instruments for a demonstration at his university. Of course, my passport shows I have been to Iran before. I am confident about getting through, but you never know. So, with everything going right, I will see you soon."

When Kim arrived at Kermanshah, he was ushered to customs. Professor Kiachian from the university was waiting there. A customs agent nodded for Kim to come over. He gave a quick glance at Kim's passport and his tools and waved him on. Kim had brought no other luggage, and was hoping he could buy something to wear. Professor Kiachian drove Kim to Kermanshah, and the drive gave them plenty of time to catch up. When they got to the university, Kiachian told Kim to take his car and directed him on where he could buy some clothes. Kim couldn't thank him enough. He told Kiachian where he was going and that he hoped to be back in a few days. After a stop at a clothing store, Kim headed toward Kardanal. It was not too bad a road, since it was on the main road from Kermanshah to Tehran. It only took Kim a little over an hour to find the home of his friend, Albert Chang. Albert was elated, since he hadn't seen Kim for many years and Kim had never met his wife. They talked for a couple of hours over dinner. Albert was excited to hear about things in the United States and about Kim's work. No mention was made of the work he had done on Axel, and this satisfied Kim. Finally, Kim said he needed to talk privately with Axel. Albert nodded and took him to the room where Axel had been staying.

Alone with Axel, Kim asked him many questions about his physical being. He told Axel that he had used the three-dimensional model to try to figure out all the possible reasons for the effects he had been experiencing.

"I have it narrowed down to three possibilities," said Kim. "I am too tired now to do anything with you today. Tonight, you and I need to get a good night's sleep and be fresh in the morning for the operation. I don't want you eating anything more tonight. Even though it should be a straightforward operation, one can never tell. Some people have problems if they eat before an operation. Their system gets screwed up and they have stomach problems and other problems."

The next morning, Kim awakened early and was surprised to see that both Axel and Albert were already up. Albert was eating some fruit, and Axel was just watching him, looking hungry. Kim hustled Axel into the next room, where there was a large table. They covered it with the spread from Axel's bed, but that would do little to soften the hard table. Lucky for his special body covering, Axel didn't feel the hard table on his body. Kim got his equipment ready and soon was ready to do his thing. He had Axel get up on the table and lie face down.

"I am going to go in from the back to do this exploratory search. Turns out it is easier to get to the places I might have to get to when coming in from the back," said Kim. "I am going to apply some anesthetic that

Professor Kiachian gave me when he understood that I would need to cut into to someone for an operation. I have the diamond-blade scalpel so I can cut through the outer covering over your body."

Kim swabbed the area with an antiseptic to cleanse it. He couldn't give Axel the shot for the anesthetic through the outer covering of his body. He told Axel he was going to cut through the outer material, and then put the shot into his skin to kill the pain. He made the incision and gave Axel the shot. While they waited for the anesthetic to take effect, Axel told him about his escapades in Natanz and Fordo. Kim couldn't make any comments about those things he had done, because they were a personal secret of Axel's and he swore that he would not talk to anyone about it from that day on.

When Axel's back was numb, Kim was able to use a regular scalpel to make a cut about four inches long on the right side of Axel's back. He used an instrument to pull the skin back and hold it out of the way. With his special telescopic eyepiece and the light attached to his head, Kim was now able to review the situation. As he did he talked out loud to Axel.

"Here is the computer and here is its output, which looks like it should be functional. That is one of the three places I figured might be the problem. But it doesn't appear to be. I will now look at the input, which comes to decoders that determine where the signal is to go. When you say 'Axelvation one,' the decoder is supposed to take that as the input for decoding, and this signal goes through the computer. Its output goes to the cell control that selects the mitochondria locations, and an energy level is provided. This decode function appears to be fine."

Kim then looked at the decoder that determined the signal level for Axelvation two and he could see that it had been disrupted. He checked if the decoder for Axelvation three was likewise disrupted; and he found that it was.

"This appears to be the trouble, Axel, and it should be an easy one to fix."

Axel breathed out a sigh of relief. "That's good news," he said. "I hope that is all there is in the way of problems."

"We will soon find out. I am now taking my special spiderweb nanotitanium thread and will reattach those two signal wires to the decode locations. I am sewing the one right now." After a minute, he said, "I am now sewing the thread to the decoder three section. There, I have completed that. If I am right about this, you should be able to call up your second and third level energy levels now."

It was quiet for about a minute, and then Kim asked, "Axel, did you call up your signal levels for the second and third levels of energy?"

"No," replied Axel. "I didn't know you wanted me to do that. I will call them up now." He paused and then said, "Axelvation two." Immediately he felt the energy level in his body rise. In fact, his body lifted off the table about an inch and then fell back down.

"That's great!" yelled Kim. "Now try the third level."

Axel did, and again his body jumped up off the table and fell back to its original position..

"Fantastic!" Kim said. "I flew more than six thousand miles to see that happen. That really makes me feel good, and I feel that the trip was well worth it. Now I have to stop the bleeding from your back and sew the cut I made in your skin. I did check the power level in your computer and it is fine."

After he sewed the skin, Kim said, "I have a problem."

"What's that?" asked Axel.

"The problem is that I can't sew the protective covering that I had to cut through. I won't be able to do that until you get back in the lab at the agency. This takes a special method which I don't have at my disposal here. What I am going to do is to tape it together with a special tape made for this. However, it is not bulletproof. It probably could stop a twenty-two, but nothing bigger. It will protect you from a knife wound, as long as you're not stabbed with great force. You just have to make sure you don't get shot in that spot by a higher caliber gun, or it will penetrate, and it could destroy your computer and all the other things that make you work. Do you understand what I am saying?"

"No problem, doctor. I will be a good boy and make sure that if anyone wants to shoot me, that I am facing them." He laughed, but Kim told him this was not funny and that he had to be careful.

Axel felt good after getting up from the hard table. He had been thinking while he was lying there, and he said to Kim, "I have been concerned about how I would get back to the States. If I have to get out on my own, I'll probably get shot at. However, if you could arrange for me to be your assistant at the University of Kermanshah when you give your stem cell presentation, I wouldn't have to fight my way out of this country. I would fly back with you if the university visit could be arranged some way."

Kim listened intently to Axel's suggestion, and spoke right away. "That would be a great way to handle your exit from Iran. I believe we could arrange that. My contacts at the university should be able to handle this. They would need your passport, and they would find a way to show that you came in to the country the same time as I did. If they could do that, it would be a piece of cake to get you on a plane with me. That is especially a good idea since you have excellent credential with your doctorate in biology and the stem cell lab you set up at the university."

"I can take this one step further," said Axel. "I have recently begun a course called Adult Stem Cell Recognition. This course provides students the instructions for recognizing adult stem cells. I may be able to answer some questions that the students at this university might ask that you might not have the answer to. I think this is a good way to go. Normally, I wouldn't want to tell the people of Iran anything until I knew our countries were on a friendly basis. But this is different. We want all countries, friends or enemies, to know about stem cell research. This is something for all of humanity."

The two of them were in complete agreement, and Kim decided to call Professor Kiachian and tell him about their approach to the lecture at the university and Axel's needs. After talking for about ten minutes, Kim winked at Axel and gave him a thumbs-up signal. The two of them were pleased they would do some good on this trip. Kim spent some time with Albert and his wife reminiscing about things in the past, while Axel prepared to leave. Axel didn't have much to do, but he felt Kim wanted some more time with Albert and his wife. Soon they were ready to go and wished Albert and his wife a fond farewell and thanks.

While driving to the university, Axel said, "I wish I could have given Albert something for the time I spent there and the food I ate."

Kim looked over at him and said, "Don't worry. I gave him a couple hundred dollars. That's a lot of money here. He will find a way to convert it into Iranian money."

"That's great," said Axel." That makes me feel a lot better."

Professor Kiachian had made arrangements for Drs. Kim and Tressler to give their presentation the next day at one in the afternoon. Kiachian asked Axel for his passport so the proper official entries could be made on it, and so he could return to the United States when Kim left. The presentation was an open session that would last as long as the students wanted to ask questions. Kim provided the introductory remarks and then gave his lecture. After this, Axel gave them a presentation about the type of equipment needed to set up a laboratory that was functional for studying stem cells and for working on methods of providing adult stem cells. Both of these talks were well received, and the questions and answers lasted till after four.

Professor Kiachian had made arrangements for a nighttime flight to Baghdad, so there was no problem with them making that flight. Professor Kiachian gave Axel his papers and said, "That was worth doing for you. I enjoyed your presentation, since it outlined the various tools and proper working conditions for a stem cell laboratory. I am quite interested in your work on adult stem cells. We are just collecting papers on this subject. It is so new, and it was great that you were up to date on the techniques. Perhaps we can have you two come again next year, and hopefully you will be able to see what your lectures created."

Axel Returns Home from Iran to Tori

Once Kim and Axel arrived at Baghdad they felt like they were home to some extent. They were met by Commander Rumsey, as well as several American soldiers. Except for the random suicide bomber, who killed a dozen people every couple of days, the area seemed quite calm. People were going about their business, visiting the food markers and the like as though there was peace in the country. People were hustling around and working as though nothing was an issue. Kim and Axel talked with the American soldiers about life there, and they were happy to hear that things seemed to have settled down recently. One soldier said, "There are still people walking around with bombs strapped to their bodies, exploding them to show their resistance to the government or for religious reasons. They will probably be doing that for years to come, since they have been doing it for a long time now and nothing has changed their religious beliefs."

Axel and Kim had a day to wait for the next plane that was going to the States. As things would have it, the plane was flying into Travis in California, so Kim would have to stay a day and catch a plane to Washington DC. Axel was happy about that. He called Tori and told her when they would be arriving at Travis and asked her to meet them there.

The next day Kim and Axel met the pilot who would be flying to Travis and prepared for the flight. Axel told Kim, "You will be surprised at how different it is to fly in a military plane that only holds the pilot and three others, including the copilot. You don't hear anything but you can see the earth below, when there is no cloud cover, and it seems to be moving fast, especially where flying from East to West. You are chasing the sun."

Kim said that he probably would be scared at first until he got used to it. Axel brushed off that comment, saying, "No problem. You have worse problems when you are sewing people's backs up than flying in one of these fighter jets."

Kim said, "Remember, when I am cutting you, it is your life at stake. When we are flying in a fighter jet, it is both of our lives at stake. That's the part I don't like. I guess I am just a born worrier."

Their conversation was interrupted by the pilot telling them to get aboard. They already had their flight gear on and soon they were in the plane and ready for flight. They no sooner were in the air than Axel began to think about Tori. He sure had missed her these past few days, especially when he was staying at Kardanal. At Kardanal, he had had nothing to do but wait for Kim, and during that time he had sat around thinking how lucky he was to have found such a wonderful and beautiful woman. Now on the plane, those thoughts popped back in his head. He also thought about how lucky he had been to have only a couple of connections faulty after being hit with that grenade. There had been times in the past week when he had fallen asleep and dreamed about the grenade blowing him against the wall. He could see that grenade coming at him, and he usually woke up just as he was hitting the wall. He would awaken and there would be sweat on his brow. Then he would think, *Thank goodness my body covering allows me to sweat like normal.*

While thinking about that, Axel dozed off into a deep sleep. He was awakened by the pilot's voice saying they were about a half hour from landing. *Time goes fast when you are sleeping and dreaming,* Axel thought.

Tori was waiting for the two of them, and she ran and hugged Axel as soon as she saw him. Axel introduced her to Dr. Kim.

"I met Dr. Kim when we were out in DC at Christmas time."

"Oh, yes, I forgot," said Axel.

Kim nodded. "Your man has a little loss of memory, I guess, after the ordeal he has gone through. He has been a good man for this country. When I call on Axel, it is usually an emergency, and no one can help cure the emergency but Axel. His anonymity relates to his looking and acting like a normal person. He is able to do his extraordinary actions without being witnessed. Or if he is witnessed, the witnesses are eliminated. This is a wonderful capability he has."

"This was the first problem we have had with him and his body structure," Kim went on. "It turned out to be a minor problem, but expressed itself as a major problem. Thank goodness it didn't take long to fix him up. The good news is that when you do fix him, he is immediately up to par. Except for his memory, it seems."

Tori didn't know what Kim was talking about, since Axel had never seemed to have this memory problem before and she didn't know about any structural problems. "What are you talking about?" she asked.

Axel answered. "Oh, he is talking about a minor problem with my wiring that he had to fix. It was no biggy."

Tori felt she was missing something, and she turned to Dr. Kim. "Did he have a little or big problem that he didn't tell me about?"

Looking uncomfortable at being caught in the middle, Kim tried to brush it off by saying, "It's a bigger problem now that you know about it."

"Now, Dr. Kim," Tori said, "I know that Axel always comes back from his assignments without you. You are normally in Washington and he is off somewhere else in the world. How come you both were at the same place this time?"

Kim confessed. "Axel had a problem with some wiring inside his body. He probably could have come home and had it taken care of, but I wouldn't let him. I went to where he was and fixed the problem. It took less than an hour."

Tori kept looking at the two men, thinking they were keeping something from her. She decided to drop it and talk to Axel when she was home alone with him. No use upsetting Dr. Kim. Kim changed the subject anyway, asking Tori if she minded his coming along with them to San Francisco. "I have a flight from San Francisco to DC."

Tori replied that this would not be a problem, and soon they were on their way to the San Francisco airport. Kim had to wait a couple of hours for his flight so Tori and Axel kept him company by talking about things going on in the world and with his family. Axel said, "You have a son that graduated with a Doctor's degree in medicine. Looks like he is going to be following his father." "Yes," replied Kim. He is making good moves so far." And so the conversation continued among the three of them till Kim's flight was in and he left to board it.

Once Kim had gone on his way and Axel had spent some time catching up with his substitute teacher's progress, life returned to normal—if one could call this part of their life normal. Axel was pleased to get back to his teaching and learning. He always found this exciting, as well as his trips as The Follower. They were exciting for completely different reasons. When he was teaching, Axel felt that he learned as much as he taught. Questions from the students sometimes brought up subjects he had no experience or knowledge of, and he would have to do some research. Of course, he had the advantage that he could direct questions to the agency's scientists. About 80 percent of the time, he was able to get answers from the computer or from the agency. Sometimes he couldn't get the answers from either place, but he would keep digging. At those times he would think that maybe there weren't any answers available yet. Maybe he would be the one to find the answer for the first time. This excited him more than the questions he could answer or find the answers to. This was the unknown, and almost every scientist worth his or her salt wanted to find the answer to something that was unknown.

Whenever he searched for an answer, Axel was reminded of the years when scientists struggled to figure out why children had some features or behaviors that were similar to their parents'. The scientists felt the answer was in the body's proteins. This went on for years, until eventually an hypothesis focused on the liquid in the humans cells and its two acids. The genetic code for all life was found in that liquid, and inside the chromosomes, and finally in the nucleus of the chromosomes. It took till 1953, when an American and three British scientists found the double helix inside the nucleus. It took several more years to determine that the DNA that made up the double helix was the secret to the genetic code. He thought, *Not all things are obvious. The ones that are obvious are not exciting. The ones that stand on a hypothesis rather than an answer are the ones worth tackling. When you move closer to an answer, it brings one's emotions to a peak. I guess that's why I like teaching. You never know who is going to ask you a question that is difficult to answer. I file those in my memory and am always looking for the answer.*

Tori had driven Axel to school that day, and they planned for her to pick him up and go to dinner somewhere after his classes. When she picked him up, they decided to go to a restaurant in Palo Alto. While driving there, Tori said, "I'll say one thing about you, Axel. You lead an exciting life as Dr. Axel Tressler and The Follower. I don't know how you slow down and teach school after being on the exciting adventures you go on as The Follower; but you seem to be able to handle it. It's like making a fine landing in a slow airplane after you have flown through a windstorm at one thousand miles an hour."

"Well, I'll tell you what allows me to do that," Axel replied. "It's you. You are like a buffer between these things and school. I never go straight from these events to teaching school. I go through you first, and you and my love for you cleanse my mind of everything. With you in my eyesight or in my arms, it is like heaven on earth. When I am with you, there is nothing else on my mind. If I get to spend two days with you before going back to the teaching, it is like I had never been away from school. My body and mind are at rest. I am at peace with the world. I don't know how you do it, Tori, but you meet me like I haven't been away and there hasn't been a break in our togetherness."

"Well, Mr. Tressler that is some compliment. I would think you love me as much as I love you."

"You bettcha," Axel said. "I have been thinking about this past couple of years and our lives together. I know they have been somewhat hectic for you, with me jerking your life around by my traveling all over the world. But I think we have taken our years together pretty well. Do you think you could stand it forever?"

Tori almost drove the car off the road. "Why, Mr. Tressler. Or is it Mr. Follower? I think you just proposed to me. Did you?"

"I certainly did," replied Axel. "Would you marry me and be my wife for life?"

"You bettcha, baby," she responded. "I would love to be Mrs. Axel Tressler for life."

"Then pull over to the side of the road so I can give you a big hug and kiss to seal this moment."

Tori didn't have to be told twice. She pulled the car over to a safe spot on the right side of the road and put on the brake. Axel grabbed and kissed her and said, "I love you like life itself. Would you make me happy and be my bride?"

She hugged him and said, "I already answered that question. Now, let's go home and put some plans together on how and when."

"Oh, I thought we would just drive up to Reno and get married without bothering anyone."

Tori looked at him and said, "I think we have some people on your side of the family and my side of the family that would like to attend this event. You are getting to be an old man you know. Thirty-one years, and your twin brother has a family and is far ahead of you." She laughed. "I guess you really are 'The Follower.'"

And that was how it went. They called Axel's mother and brother and Dr. Kim, and Tori's parents and a few of their close friends. They told them that they were going to get married in Reno in one month, and they would love to have all of them come and enjoy the wedding and gamble away their money. Life was great for Tori and Axel, as well as for The Follower.

By John Durbin Husher 4/13/2010